THE WORLD'S CLASSICS

MARRIAGE

SUSAN EDMONSTONE FERRIER (1782–1854) was born in Edinburgh, where she spent her entire, outwardly uneventful life. Growing up in a large family as the youngest child of a busy lawyer, she gained her full share of human experience all the same. Through her father, who assisted the nobility in legal affairs, she was introduced to the fashionable world. Charlotte Clavering, a niece of the Duke of Argyll, became a close friend and to some extent her collaborator when she began to exercise her narrative talent, which turned out to be best suited to realistic descriptions. *Marriage* (1818), her first novel, took several years to complete, but became an immediate success when it appeared. Two more works of fiction, *The Inheritance* (1824) and *Destiny* (1831), followed after long intervals. All were highly regarded for their accurate presentation of 'ordinary details' and keen satire, yet despite the entreaties of publishers she decided that, after *Destiny*, her literary career had run its course.

Susan Ferrier never married. After the death of her father, for whom she had kept house, her life became very quiet. Failing eyesight forced her to withdraw into darkened rooms. The revisions she imposed upon *Marriage*, when the novel was reissued in 1841, reflect a growing piousness. But the occasional visitor was always struck by her down-to-earth humour and unaffected kindness.

HERBERT FOLTINEK is Professor of English at the University of Vienna. He has published works mainly on eighteenth-century drama and on the English and American eighteenth- and nineteenth-century novel.

THE WORLD'S CLASSICS

SUSAN FERRIER

Marriage

Edited with an Introduction by
HERBERT FOLTINEK

Oxford   New York

OXFORD UNIVERSITY PRESS

1986

Oxford University Press, Walton Street, Oxford OX2 6DP

Oxford New York Toronto
Delhi Bombay Calcutta Madras Karachi
Kuala Lumpur Singapore Hong Kong Tokyo
Nairobi Dar es Salaam Cape Town
Melbourne Auckland

and associated companies in
Beirut Berlin Ibadan Nicosia

Oxford is a trade mark of Oxford University Press

Introduction, Notes, Select Bibliography, and Chronology
© Herbert Foltinek 1971
Select Bibliography updated 1986

First published by Oxford University Press 1971
First published as a World's Classics paperback 1986

British Library Cataloguing in Publication Data

Ferrier, Susan
Marriage.—(The World's classics)
I. Title II. Foltinek, Herbert
823'.7 PR4699.F4

ISBN 0-19-281743-4

Library of Congress Cataloging in Publication Data

Ferrier, Susan, 1782–1854.
Marriage.
(The World's classics)
Bibliography: p.
I. Foltinek, Herbert. II. Title.
[PR4699.F4M3 1986] 823'.7 85-26002

ISBN 0-19-281743-4 (pbk.)

Printed in Great Britain by
Hazell Watson & Viney Ltd.
Aylesbury, Bucks

CONTENTS

CONTENTS

INTRODUCTION

A WRITER's first emergence into print is ever accompanied by a certain element of chance. Had *Marriage* been written twenty or perhaps only fifteen years earlier, had it been composed in a different environment, the novel would in all likelihood never have seen publication. There was nothing professional about Susan Ferrier's literary endeavours. Long after the constant popularity and general prestige of the book could have assured her of unreserved recognition, she still clung to her anonymity, candidly informing a younger generation of readers how the composition had 'afforded occupation and amusement for idle and solitary hours, and was published in the belief that the author's name never would be guessed at or the work heard of beyond a very limited sphere'.[1]

The sceptical attitude towards her own creation rings genuine enough, but it would be wrong to assume from this statement that the author had led a secluded life. Only at an advanced age, when growing blindness and infirmity forced her into retirement, did Susan Ferrier withdraw from company. In her earlier years she had played an active part in the confined and comprehensive world that made up the spirited society of her native Edinburgh, maintaining an intellectual interchange on

[1] Susan Ferrier, *The Inheritance*, Standard Novels (1841), Preface.

equal terms with its literary figures, connoisseurs, and men of learning. Among so perceptive a circle of friends it must have cost considerable pains to keep the authorship a secret. Her natural reticence will not suffice to explain Susan Ferrier's persistent reluctance to acknowledge the publication as her own. We can account for it only within a larger context, understanding it as the symptom of a critical period when the novel was gradually coming into its own as a direct record of human experience. There are in fact a number of contemporary parallels to Susan Ferrier's preference for anonymity. Her wish to avoid publication may have been rooted in an awareness that she had entered upon a new field of writing and that the immediacy and concreteness of her approach might appeal to a much wider and broader number of readers than had hitherto been attracted by prose fiction.

The book had been started as a kind of private competition between two gifted and imaginative young people who enjoyed the exchange of ideas and took delight in comparing their observations of the social scene of the time. In or shortly before 1810 Susan Ferrier and her friend Charlotte Clavering, eight years younger than herself and the niece of the Duke of Argyll, hit upon the idea of writing a joint novel that was to combine romance, moral sentiment, and accounts from real life. Soon it turned out that the talents as well as the temperaments of the two writers were too radically different to permit such an undertaking. All that remains of Charlotte's romantic flights is the 'History of Mrs. Douglas', an inadequate though by no means expendable insertion in the first volume, and an occasional line of verse. Her advice on the composition, however, which was submitted to her judgement step by step as it took shape, seems to have amounted to an actual contribution. Fortunately, the two friends were separated over long periods and some of Charlotte's criticism survives in her letters, showing her keen perception of Susan's narrative faculties.

Though the correspondence is mostly undated, it seems quite evident that large parts of the book were finished several years before publication; a considerable amount, however, must have been written when the author was already under publisher's contract. While the vivid descriptions of the first volume clearly stem from an unaffected and uninhibited imagination, the thinner and more conventional chapters towards the end of the work may have been spun out in anticipation of a more orthodox reaction towards the tale. But whatever Susan Ferrier may at that stage have thought or feared of the literary taste of the time, her narrative talent had responded with great perception to a new tendency in English novel-writing which was to determine its character for a long time to come.

A very low rank was still accorded to the novel in the early years of the nineteenth century; prose was little esteemed except in books of learning and in devout literature, and those who could appreciate the achievement of the masters of English narrative were nevertheless likely to disregard contemporary fiction as so much trivia. The second decade, however, saw a change that was to raise the prestige of the novel beyond all expectation: the tales of Maria Edgeworth, with their representations of ordinary Irish life, are commonly thought to have been its first indication. The searching of the soul and the cultivation of the mind, sentiment, fear, and doctrine, were now beginning to be replaced by a circumstantial documentation of everyday events as they might occur in various spheres of human experience. The unprecedented success of Sir Walter Scott's *Waverley* in 1814, the first of a series of anonymously published narratives which presented in great detail Scottish manners and customs of a more recent past, firmly

entrenched the new mode of writing. Scott himself was
not slow to recognize that the novel had gained ground
on a changed course and was about to touch a different
taste. Reviewing Jane Austen's *Emma* for the *Quarterly
Review* in 1815, he observed that novel-writing had ceased
to paint the idealized figures of romance and would from
now on resort to 'the art of copying from nature as she
really exists in the common walks of life, and presenting
to the reader, instead of splendid scenes of an imaginary
world, a correct and striking representation of that which
is daily taking place around him'.[1]

There is one element still missing from Scott's analysis
of the novel to come, that was to be highly characteristic
of the first stage of nineteenth-century realistic fiction.
Though the reading public might from now on be drawn
by accounts of commonplace events rather than by fanciful stories, they still preferred to inform themselves about
spheres of life which roused their curiosity or appealed
to their emotions. Acting upon the national consciousness
of his countrymen through their setting, Scott's novels
conversely succeeded in exciting the English reader's
interest in that unknown country north of the Border.
Gradually a vogue for 'Scotch' novels built up, favouring
narratives that featured sections of Scottish society and
concentrated on aspects of its culture. John Galt's *Annals
of the Parish*, which recorded the daily engagements of a
lowland parish minister in the most detailed way, was
hailed as yet another piece of Scottish realism upon its
appearance in 1821, whereas its author had failed to
interest a publisher eight years previously. It is easy to
see what acceptance Susan Ferrier's work would have
met with had she attempted to bring it out at an earlier
date. The few years that intervened between the writing
of the first chapters and the actual printing may have
helped to mature and expand her tale; they certainly

[1] *The Quarterly Review*, xiv (1815), 193.

served to establish a market for it which even the most self-conscious of writers could not have failed to respond to. When the 'Waverley-author' at the end of his *Legend of Montrose* (1819) announced the hasty decision to refrain henceforth from portrayals of Scottish life, he was able to assure the reader that his work would be continued by a number of younger writers among whom the author of *Marriage* seemed most promising.[1]

While *Marriage* is quite patently devoted to a documentation of social and cultural conditions, the author's indebtedness to the late eighteenth-century school of novel-writing cannot be overlooked. Its didactic lesson, involving a suitable punishment for the 'victims of self-indulgence' and rich rewards for the well-tutored child, is in accordance with the convention of the educational novel. Conversely, the numerous and extensive character sketches, often featuring figures whose bearing on the plot is slight, would place the author firmly among the followers of the character-painting of Fielding and Smollett. But such traditional elements are always observed rather than imitated by Ferrier and never mar the narrative texture of which they form a part. While the organization and tone of the character drawings would seem to derive from earlier examples there is little doubt that their material was assembled from personal impressions,[2] and as the action progresses the well-rounded figures and vividly conceived scenes assume more weight than the educational point they serve to illustrate. The great eighteenth-century writers had taken human nature as their subject; it was left to the early nineteenth century to prove that the novel might present the fullness of actual life as it appeared to a perceptive author.

Various layers and sections of society are described in *Marriage*. The first and second volumes are largely taken

---

[1] Sir Walter Scott, *A Legend of Montrose*, Postscript.
[2] *The Edinburgh Review*, lxxiv (1841–42), 500.

up by the description of the mode of living among the minor Highland aristocracy but we also get a glimpse of late eighteenth-century Edinburgh, although the author has chosen two very idiosyncratic figures to animate her account. The rest of the work deals exclusively with the domains of the English nobility: the fashionable town residence and the remote country seat. It has been argued that Susan Ferrier's knowledge of the English upper classes was too limited for such an undertaking.[1] But while it is true that the Scottish scenes carry greater conviction, her various journeys to the South of England, involving one or the other season in London and a longer stay at a small spa, should not be overlooked. She was also well acquainted with the affairs of at least one noble household, that of the Duke of Argyll, whom her father assisted as a legal adviser. Miss Clavering did indeed rebuke her for some lapses in reproducing the polite conversation of the day.[2] But this would not necessarily imply that the record was at fault, and we have no evidence that she did not gain from such well-intended corrections.

While most assessments of Susan Ferrier's narrative art assign her to the regional school of Maria Edgeworth, Scott, and Galt, her importance for the less reputable 'fashionable novels' is usually overlooked. The 'fashionable' tale, which attained such prominence in the twenties and thirties, hardly ever introduces a main figure who is as immune to the follies of high life as the heroine of *Marriage*; but the cold-hearted beauty and her passionate paramour who enact the sub-plot in the third volume of the novel might well be regarded as prototypes of the amorous entanglements so typical of the genre, and Lady Juliana's craving for refined amuse-

[1] *The Edinburgh Review*, lxxiv (1841–42), 502.
[2] *Memoir and Correspondence of Susan Ferrier*, ed. John A. Doyle (1898), pp. 115–6.

ments and exclusive luxury in fact anticipates one of its main themes. Susan Ferrier herself would probably have taken little account of such convenient pigeonholes. She endeavoured to portray 'every gradation of social life'[1] whether her object was the Scottish peasantry, of whom there appear unfortunately far too few in her works, or the family of an English lord. And though the social scene is by no means complete, its characters and situations are so arranged as to assume the significance of a survey of human conduct in general.

The contemporary opinion, that she drew from the life, may raise objections among those who are only acquainted with the modified 'Standard' version of her first novel. The original text has certainly all the 'minute accuracy' of 'ordinary details'[2] which the contemporary critics claimed for it. Jane Austen differentiated her characters by nuances in their diction and very speech rhythm; Susan Ferrier took a wider perspective, drawing in the broad dialect of a post-driver as well as the genteel address of a London tradesman. Her heroine, it is true, will seem as 'uninteresting'[3] to the modern reader as she appeared to her contemporaries, and her 'missy-ish' comments may strike even the more discerning as mere ramifications of the general educational lesson. But we should then overlook instances where the author has made sure that a certain distance is kept between the omniscient narrator and his avowed favourite. Though we are meant to regard Lady Emily as the less improved character, many of her 'piquant' observations on Mary's conduct prick the bubble of her 'well-regulated mind' and unworldly saintliness. Seen from this angle, the brisk Emily serves not only as the confidante of the heroine but also as a healthy corrective to her moralizing prig-

[1] *Blackwood's Edinburgh Magazine*, iii (1818), 286.
[2] *Blackwood's Edinburgh Magazine*, iii (1818), 286.
[3] *Blackwood's Edinburgh Magazine*, iii (1818), 287.

gishness.[1] Mary's character is actually neither completely faultless nor quite uncomplicated, as the sight-
seeing incident at Holyroodhouse shows, when the girl
unexpectedly takes 'an undescribable pleasure' in the
sight of blood while her down-to-earth companion can
only wonder at such excitement. A twentieth-century
observer, well-versed in the theories of psychiatry, is less
likely to be baffled by this perverse interest expressed by
a person otherwise so timid and self-restrained.

We should fail to do justice to the author, therefore,
if we saw Mary as a pale allegorical figure only. Nevertheless it will still be Lady Emily to whom the reader's
heart warms, and her waspish reactions to Mary's predicament will always command better attention than the
heroine's own stock responses. Susan Ferrier's letters
clearly show that Emily's lively commentary expressed
very much her own temperament;[2] and the very style
of the narrative indicates that those passages flowed
more easily from her pen than the trite phrases and
colourless summaries that make up the 'lesson' of the
book. Such aberrations from her true forte must be seen
to originate in Susan Ferrier's firm conviction that a
novel ought to serve a moral purpose. 'I don't think,
like all penny-book manufacturers,' she writes in one of
her letters to Charlotte Clavering,

that 'tis absolutely necessary that the good boys and girls
should be rewarded, and the naughty ones punished. Yet, I
think, where there is much tribulation, 'tis fitter it should be the
consequence, rather than the *cause* of misconduct or frailty.

[1] Commenting on the 'juxtaposition of the complementary Lady Emily
and Mary' Nelson S. Bushnell conjectures 'that together they approximate a
projection of the author's own contradictory nature' ('Susan Ferrier's *Marriage*
as Novel of Manners', *Studies in Scottish Literature*, v [1968], 226).

[2] Cf. Scott's comment on her vivid talk: 'Miss Ferrier . . . besides having
great talents has conversation the least *exigeante* of any author, female at least,
whom I have ever seen among the long list I have encountered,—simple, full
of humour, and exceedingly ready at repartee; and all this without the least
affectation of the bluestocking' (*Journal*, 1890, ii. 406).

You'll say that rule is absurd, inasmuch as it is not observed in human life; that I allow, but we know the inflictions of Providence are for wise purposes, therefore our reason willingly submits to them. But as the only good purpose of a book is to inculcate morality, and convey some lesson of instruction as well as delight, I do not see that what is called a *good moral* can be dispensed with in a work of fiction.[1]

Though the book sets out to represent the ordinary course of human events, the element of chance and coincidence is largely replaced by the abstract principle of moral retribution in the account. The ideal of a happy marriage, of which the novel offers so singularly few examples, comes as an ultimate reward to the long-suffering heroine who has proved her good sense, fine sentiment, and strength of character. While the reproduction of her own observations on society seems to have been a major concern of Susan Ferrier, she was equally committed to Samuel Johnson's view that the novelist ought to exalt virtue and is bound to draw human follies in the blackest colours if his work is to be of any 'use'.[2] As she progressed in age she became increasingly disposed to consider a palpable morality as the highest distinction of a narrative. Whatever credit may be attached to the text of the 'Standard' edition (1841), the changes demonstrate a wish to augment the weight of instruction at the expense of accurate description. Old Miss Ferrier may have gained comfort from this increasing attention to the ethical aspects of authorship; as a writer she was far more truthful to herself in her younger and creative years.

We shall be better able to comprehend her standpoint if we bear in mind that the early nineteenth-century novelist could never, as a rule, quite escape the role of a moral preceptor. Even Sir Walter Scott, despite his

[1] *Memoir and Correspondence of Susan Ferrier*, ed. John A. Doyle (1898), p. 75.
[2] *The Rambler*, no. 4, 31 March 1750.

frequent assertions to the contrary, is always guided, if not controlled, by a moral aim in his narratives. The conflicting loyalties and confused notions of right and wrong exhibited by the hero of *Waverley* correspond to that mingling of 'good and bad qualities' which Johnson so strongly condemns in the principal figure of a novel.[1] The gradual maturing of Edward Waverley's character, however, and his final awakening to the duties of life, largely conform to the pattern of moral improvement in the didactic tale proper. The growth of the heroine in *Marriage* is differently conceived. Mary enters the world as a fully-fledged personality whom the careful teachings of her foster-mother have armoured against all possible tribulations. The various afflictions to which she is exposed in exile are borne patiently by her, and the crowning triumph is a reward for her steadfast virtue. But the once ingenuous Mary has gained in maturity in the process: she has learnt to discern and to forgive the narrow complacency of her aunts as well as the egoism of the cold-hearted Lady Juliana and of the simple-minded Mrs. Lennox; her saint-like bearing has been subjected to the wholesome influence of Lady Emily's worldly cynicism; and her childish forwardness has ripened into a firm determination to assert herself against the overbearing guidance of her elders.

Jane Austen, with whom Susan Ferrier has often been uncritically compared,[2] never expresses the eventual compensation of her equally harassed heroines in such obvious terms. Firmly confident of the artistic merits

---

[1] loc. cit.

[2] Originally such comparisons were appreciative rather than censuring. Today few would still subscribe to Blackwood's claim to have been reminded of 'Miss Austen's very best things' when reading *Marriage* (*Memoir and Correspondence of Susan Ferrier*, ed. Doyle, p. 174), but references to the author as the 'Scottish Jane Austen' are far from obsolete. It would be more appropriate to see both writers as committed to the same literary tradition and a similar mode of writing but entirely distinct in their artistic abilities.

of her medium, she may have felt less self-conscious of her role as an educator than did the author of *Marriage*, who informs the reader that her heroine had 'scarcely ever read a novel in her life'. But while Jane Austen's psychology is far superior and the structural devices in her narratives infinitely more complex, the didactic element in her work cannot be disputed. Like Susan Ferrier she uses contrast to make her point: genuine and tried love is shown to excel sentimental infatuation; moral growth can be advanced through self-abnegation only, while self-indulgence must necessarily obstruct it; prudence in itself is a poor guide, but will result in personal harmony and contentment when joined by that emotional warmth which all of Austen's or Ferrier's heroines have. Though we may fail to be persuaded by the moral lesson of *Marriage*, its important function within the narrative structure can hardly be denied. The plot of the novel is largely directed by didactic impulses. Slight as it may seem, it serves to combine the various character portrayals, dialogue passages, and descriptions, which Susan Ferrier's lively imagination suggested to her, into an organized narrative account.

Susan Ferrier's contemporaries were inclined to set her second novel, *The Inheritance*, above her first work; some even gave preference to *Destiny*, her third attempt, in which a growing tendency to comprehend human behaviour in black and white colours becomes apparent. These, after all, were novels with a 'compact and well ordered'[1] framework that could not fail to hold the ordinary reader's interest during its perusal. A more detached view of the works will reveal that the author had sought to control her material by freely employing the devices of melodrama: the beautiful young countess in *The Inheritance* is discovered to be a nurse's offspring, but recovers the lost inheritance when her plain yet

[1] *The Edinburgh Review*, lxxiv (1841–42), 504.

noble-hearted lover eventually gains the estate. Her character is more natural than that of Mary; hence she is prone to errors which the heroine of *Marriage* would have evaded as a matter of course. Yet the dangers and temptations that beset her, the demonic stranger by whom she is harassed, the prodigal fortune-hunter who jilts her, the scheming foster-mother whose true relationship to the heroine is only gradually discovered, are never animated into full reality as they would have been in the hands of a Dickens. Though the character of the main figure obviously does not require a Lady Emily as a complement, one cannot help feeling that the mysterious complications surrounding the inheritance of Rossville Castle would never have burgeoned to such rankness had the penetrating eye of that critical lady been included among the agents of the novel. The chief merit of *The Inheritance* is undoubtedly found in a series of lively scenes involving Scottish middle-class characters that have hardly a function in the artful plot as such. *Destiny* is decidedly weaker than that. Here the uneasy machinations of the story are ill combined with an increasing amount of moralizing, and the paleness that infects very nearly all the figures and incidents of the book betrays them as second impressions of her earlier and more vigorous inventions. Though an occasional telling scene, a quick exchange of dialogue, still show her mastery, the overall flagging of energy is unmistakable. Susan Ferrier showed more judgement than her amicable critics, many of whom held that she had only now reached the summit of her creative ability, when she withdrew from the literary scene after the success of her third publication.

Early nineteenth-century critical opinion was too much determined by the current literary taste to give a valid verdict on the respective merits of Susan Ferrier's individual novels. Her reputation today, in spite of some dissenting voices,[1] rests mainly on her first book, which in the course of the last 150 years has appealed to a much wider number of readers than her other works. It is easy to dispense with the contemporary objections to its lack of plot, which in fact amounted to a desire for more suspense and mystification. Although her later efforts point to the contrary, Susan Ferrier seems to have been quite aware that, artistically, her first narrative did not require additional action. 'There is no story whatever,' she maintained of Jane Austen's *Emma*, 'but the characters are all so true to life, and the style so piquant, that it does not require the adventitious aids of mystery and adventure.'[2] Though her characters, situations, and episodes never grow into a tissue of manifold relationships and variously conceived connections as they do in the hands of greater artists, she was well able to compound them into an organic whole. *Marriage* needed the element of moral fable to become a tale, but the didactic scheme is in fact only the most tangible aspect of the structural unity of the novel.

There is hardly a figure that could be omitted without leaving a noticeable gap in the progress of the plot. Few readers will wish to miss the epicurean Dr. Redgill, whose unabashed adherence to his master passion provides much of the amusement. Of equal importance, however, is his function in the narrative proper; upon Mary's arrival at Beech Park he soon takes sides with the ingenuous visitor from the land of vigorous appetites, only to oppose the heroine at a later instance when this will help to throw her now well-established personality into better relief. In a similar way, the episode of Bob Gawffaw and his affected wife, the first of a series of

[1] E.g. '*The Inheritance* shows the powers of Miss Ferrier at their fullest, but *Destiny*, except for a certain failure in spirits, is a worthy successor' (O. Elton, *A Survey of English Literature, 1780–1830*, 1912, i. 368).

[2] *Memoir and Correspondence of Susan Ferrier*, ed. Doyle, p. 128.

parallels to the infelicitous union of Mary's parents,
exceeds by far the function of a mere diversion; it moti-
vates the heroine's firm determination to avoid a
miserable match for herself. Whatever intrinsic defects
the 'History of Mrs. Douglas' may have, its inclusion is
warranted technically since it helps to raise the strong-
minded yet patient Alicia Douglas into a figure of contrast to the perversely wilful Juliana. The following
sections further develop this polarity, and the juxtaposition is renewed with additional emphasis in Mary
and her sister Adelaide as the experience of either the
mother, or the foster-mother, has contributed to form
the respective characters of the two sisters. In attempting
to avoid the misery of her mother the self-willed Adelaide
gets involved in a worse error while Mary quietly bears
the disappointment of an unhappy love-affair until her
steadfastness prevails over the interference of meddling
elders. A critical situation arises towards the end of the
tale when the virtuous heroine is confronted with the
dilemma of either braving Juliana's maternal prohibition
or losing the lover to whom a pledge 'of a sacred nature'
ties her for ever. But at this point the narrator lets the
rules of true life intervene. Lady Juliana tires of her
obstinacy and makes a convincing exit by her departure
for a more congenial climate. Mary has deserved her
final triumph; that she has not completely gained it
for herself is in accord with her role as the suffering rather
than the active heroine, and corresponds well with early
nineteenth-century manners and opinions.

A definite weakness arises from the author's neglect
to take account of the passing of time between volumes
I and II. More than fifteen years have intervened when
the narrative is fully resumed, and Lady Juliana's twins
have ripened into young ladies; but no visible change
appears among the members of the Glenfern circle. They
all recover their former station as if awakened from a

charmed sleep, and it is only then that Glenfern is allowed to die, that the sisters may enter into the married state, and that the decrepit Sir Sampson can approach his demise. In this respect Susan Ferrier stands convicted of a flagrant offence against the intended truthfulness of her account. But this lapse cannot be held too severely against her; it closely approximates to a traditional practice, of keeping the minor figures static while the main characters are allowed to develop.

Susan Ferrier may have lacked the all-comprehending energy of the great authors, but she was well able to employ the structural principles of contrast and analogy and could make the novel a meaningful system of attitude, incident, and comment. Her use of setting offers a final and striking example of her artistic perception and skill: one of the most pervasive structural antitheses in the narrative is the emphasized contrast between the harsh North and the pleasant but variable South; a fundamental polarity which even the extensive sphere of conduct and observation cannot entirely contain. The Scottish Highlands appear bleak and forbidding as a background to the 'unfortunate association of manners and characters' described in the introductory chapters, and the shallow Juliana is indeed unable to reconcile contrary modes of life and thought. To Mary, who becomes the heroine in the second part of the novel, the Highlands seem a sheltering refuge and source of strength to help her bear her predicament in the alien atmosphere of Beech Park. *Marriage* contains seminally much that is developed and brought to perfection in the great Victorian novel.

NOTE ON THE TEXT

Marriage was first published by William Blackwood in 1818. A second edition in the following year has the same make-up (12°, 3 vols., 2b, B1r–P4r, pp. 319; b, B1r–P1v, pp. 314; b, B1r–Q4r, pp. 343) but introduces a considerable number of alterations. A third edition (8°, 2 vols., 1826) breaks the novel up into two parts while keeping closely to its copy-text of 1819: apart from the corrected spelling and punctuation the number of actual changes is small. In 1841 the novel was newly edited as no. 83 of Richard Bentley's 'Standard Novels' in a completely revised form which extends the text, modifies the Scottish vernacular, and in general deprives the style of much of its individual idiomatic character. A fair number of the minor alterations may have been due to the compositors as the setting had been hasty and the proof-reading was hurried through without the assistance of the author, who disapproved of the result. Notwithstanding the publisher's offer to emend the stereotyped copy wherever the author might consider it necessary, we may take it for granted that later issues still fell short of Susan Ferrier's intentions. Nothing is known about the negotiations that led to a severely curtailed edition in the 'Parlour Library' shortly after her death. Bentley himself reverted to the text of the first edition, without, however, restoring its three-volume division, when

Marriage was republished in 1881 in a collected edition of the works of the author.

The present edition is printed from the British Museum copy of the first edition of 1818, collated with 1819, and incorporating a few substantive alterations from 1826 which may with reasonable certainty be ascribed to the author; some of these clarify inconsistencies of a more far-reaching nature, one or the other adds a new and pertinent touch to the text. A number of obvious errors have been corrected and the spelling of possessives has been normalized. The original division into three units of approximately equal length and consequence has been preserved.

SELECT BIBLIOGRAPHY

Marriage was variously reprinted in the nineteenth century. Mention must be made of Goodrich-Freer's edition of 1902, which adds an introduction and some brief notes to the newly arranged text of 1818. 'Everyman's Library', no. 816 (1928), follows the version of the 'Standard' edition. A more recent edition for Thomas Nelson & Sons (1953) is based on the text of 1819.

COLLECTED EDITIONS. *Miss Ferrier's Novels* (including a biographical memoir, reprinted from *Temple Bar*, liv, and the author's 'Recollections of Visits to Ashestiel and Abbotsford'), 6 vols. (1881–83); *The Novels of Susan Edmonstone Ferrier*, with an introduction by R. Brimley Johnson, 6 vols. (1894); *The Works of Susan Ferrier*, with an introduction by Lady Margaret Sackville, 4 vols. (1928, repr. 1970).

BIOGRAPHY AND CRITICISM. The only primary source is *Memoir and Correspondence of Susan Ferrier, 1782–1854, based on her private correspondence . . . collected by her grandnephew John Ferrier*, ed. John A. Doyle (1898). The earliest appreciations appeared in *Blackwood's Edinburgh Magazine*, iii (1818), 286–94, and xxx (1831), 531 ff.; and in *The Edinburgh Review*, lxxiv (1841–42), 498–505. Further criticism in *Temple Bar*, liv (1878), 308–28; Sir G. B. S. Douglas, *The Blackwood Group* (1897); George Saintsbury, *Collected Essays and Papers*, i (1923). The most recent publications are a biography by Aline Grant (Denver, Col., 1957), W. M. Parker's short introductory study on Susan Ferrier and John Galt (1965), and the following articles: Nelson S. Bushnell, 'Susan Ferrier's *Marriage* as Novel of Manners', in *Studies in Scottish Literature*, V (1968), 216–28; Wendy Craik, 'Susan Ferrier', in *Scott Bicentenary Essays: Selected Papers Read at the Sir Walter Scott Bicentenary Conference*, ed. Alan Bell (1973), 322–31; Nancy L. Paxton, 'Subversive Feminism: A Reassessment of Susan Ferrier's *Marriage*', in *Women and Literature*, IV (1976), 18–29; Barbara Hardy, 'The Fruits of Separation', in *Times Literary Supplement* (1985), 641–2; Herbert Foltinek, 'Susan Ferrier Reconsidered', in *Scottish Studies*, Vol. III: *Studies in Scottish Fiction: Nineteenth Century*, ed. Horst W. Drescher (Frankfurt/M, 1985), 131–45. The sections on Susan Ferrier in O. Elton, *A Survey of English Literature, 1780–1830*, I (1912); E. A. Baker, *The History of the English Novel*, IV (1935); Ian Jack, *English Literature, 1815–1832* (1963); and in Francis Russel Hart's *The Scottish Novel: From Smollett to Spark* (Cambridge, Mass., 1978) should also be noted.

A CHRONOLOGY OF
SUSAN EDMONSTONE FERRIER

Life consists not of a series of illustrious actions; the greater part of our time passes in compliance with necessities—in the performance of daily duties—in the removal of small inconveniencies—in the procurement of petty pleasures; and we are well or ill at ease, as the main stream of life glides on smoothly, or is ruffled by small and frequent interruption.

Johnson.

VOLUME I

Cato did well reprove Alus Albinus for writing the
Roman story in the Greek tongue, of which he had
but imperfect knowledge; and himself was put to
make his apology for so doing: Cato told him that
he was mightily in love with a fault that he had
rather beg a pardon than be innocent. Who forced
him to need the pardon?

Jeremy Taylor.[1]

CHAPTER I

[Love!]—'A word by superstition thought a God; by use
turned to an humour; by self-will made a flattering madness.'
Alexander & Campaspe.[2]

COME HITHER, CHILD,' said the old Earl of Courtland to
his daughter, as, in obedience to his summons, she
entered his study; 'come hither, I say; I wish to have
some serious conversation with you: so dismiss your dogs,
shut the door, and sit down here.'

Lady Juliana rang for the footman to take Venus; bade
Pluto be quiet, like a darling, under the sofa; and, taking
Cupid in her arms, assured his Lordship he need fear no
disturbance from the sweet creatures, and that she would
be all attention to his commands—kissing her cherished
pug as she spoke.

'You are now, I think, seventeen, Juliana,' said his
Lordship, in a solemn important tone.

'And a half, papa.'

'It is therefore time you should be thinking of estab-
lishing yourself in the world. Have you ever turned your
thoughts that way?'

Lady Juliana cast down her beautiful eyes, and was
silent.

'As I can give you no fortune,' continued the Earl, swelling with ill suppressed importance, as he proceeded, 'you have perhaps no great pretensions to a very brilliant establishment.'

'Oh! none in the world, papa,' eagerly interrupted Lady Juliana; 'a mere competence with the man of my heart'—

'The man of a fiddlestick!' exclaimed Lord Courtland in a fury; 'what the devil have you to do with a heart, I should like to know! There's no talking to a young woman now about marriage, but she is all in a blaze about hearts, and darts, and—and—But heark ye, child, I'll suffer no daughter of mine to play the fool with her heart, indeed! She shall marry for the purpose for which matrimony was ordained amongst people of birth—that is, for the aggrandisement of her family, the extending of their political influence—for becoming, in short, the depository of their mutual interest. These are the only purposes for which persons of rank ever think of marriage. And pray what has your heart to say to that?'

'Nothing, papa,' replied Lady Juliana, in a faint dejected tone of voice. 'Have done, Cupid!' addressing her favourite, who was amusing himself in pulling and tearing the beautiful lace veil that partly shaded the head of his fair mistress.

'I thought not,' resumed the Earl, in a triumphant tone—'I thought not indeed.' And as this victory over his daughter put him in unusual good humour, he condescended to sport a little with her curiosity.

'And pray, can this wonderful wise heart of yours inform you, who it is you are going to obtain for a husband?'

Had Lady Juliana dared to utter the wishes of that heart, she would have been at no loss for a reply; but she saw the necessity of dissimulation; and after naming such of her admirers as were most indifferent to her, she

declared herself quite at a loss, and begged her father to
put an end to her suspense.

'Now, what would you think of the Duke of L——?'
asked the Earl, in a voice of half smothered exultation
and delight.

'The Duke of L——!' repeated Lady Juliana, with a
scream of horror and surprise; 'surely, papa, you cannot
be serious: why, he's red haired and squints, and he's as
old as you.'

'If he were as old as the devil, and as ugly too,'
interrupted the enraged Earl, 'he should be your husband;
and may I perish if you shall have any other!'

The youthful beauty burst into tears, while her father
traversed the apartment with an inflamed and wrathful
visage.

'If it had been any body but that odious Duke—'
sobbed the lovely Juliana.

'If it had been any body but that odious Duke!'
repeated the Earl, mimicking her, 'they should not have
had you. It has been my sole study, ever since I saw your
brother settled, to bring about this alliance; and, when
this is accomplished, my utmost ambition will be satisfied. So no more whining—the affair is settled; and all
that remains for you to do, is to study to make yourself
agreeable to his Grace, and to sign the settlements. No
such mighty sacrifice, methinks, when repaid with a
ducal coronet, the most splendid jewels, the finest
equipages, and the largest jointure of any woman in
England.'

Lady Juliana raised her head, and wiped her eyes.
Lord Courtland perceived the effect his eloquence had
produced upon the childish fancy of his daughter, and
continued to expatiate upon the splendid joys that awaited
her, in an union with a nobleman of the Duke's rank and
fortune; till at length, dazzled, if not convinced, she
declared herself 'satisfied that it was her duty to marry

whoever papa pleased; but—' and a sigh escaped her,
as she contrasted her noble suitor with her handsome
lover—'but if I should marry him, papa, I am sure I
shall never be able to love him.'

The Earl smiled at her childish simplicity, as he
assured her that was not at all necessary; that love was
now entirely confined to the *canaille*; that it was very well
for ploughmen and dairy-maids to marry for love; but
for a young woman of rank to think of such a thing, was
plebeian in the extreme!

Lady Juliana did not entirely subscribe to the arguments of her father; but the gay and glorious vision that
floated in her brain, stifled for a while the pleadings of
her heart; and with a sparkling eye, and an elastic step,
she hastened to prepare for the reception of the Duke.

For a few weeks the delusion lasted. Lady Juliana was
flattered with the homage she received as a future
Duchess; she was delighted with the eclat that attended
her, and charmed with the daily presents showered upon
her by her noble suitor.

'Well, really, Favolle,' said she to her maid, one day,
as she clasped on her beautiful arm a resplendent brace-
let, 'it must be owned the Duke has a most exquisite
taste in trinkets; don't you think so? And, do you know,
I don't think him so very—very ugly. When we are
married, I mean to make him get a Brutus,[1] cork his
eye-brows, and have a set of teeth.' But just then, the
smiling eyes, curling hair, and fine formed person of a
certain captivating Scotsman, rose to view in her mind's
eye; and, with a peevish 'pshaw!' she threw the bauble
aside.

Educated for the sole purpose of forming a brilliant
establishment, of catching the eye, and captivating the
senses, the cultivation of her mind, or the correction of
her temper, had formed no part of the system by which
that aim was to be accomplished. Under the auspices

of a fashionable mother, and an obsequious governess, the froward petulance of childhood, fostered and strengthened by indulgence and submission, had gradually ripened into that selfishness and caprice, which now, in youth, formed the prominent features of her character. The Earl was too much engrossed by affairs of importance, to pay much attention to any thing so perfectly insignificant as the mind of his daughter. Her *person* he had predetermined should be entirely at his disposal, and therefore he contemplated with delight the uncommon beauty which already distinguished it; not with the fond partiality of parental love, but with the heartless satisfaction of a crafty politician.

The mind of Lady Juliana was consequently the sport of every passion that by turns assailed it. Now swayed by ambition, and now softened by love: the struggle was violent, but it was short. A few days before the one which was to seal her fate, she granted an interview to her lover, who, young, thoughtless, and enamoured as herself, easily succeeded in persuading her to elope with him to Scotland. There, at the altar of Vulcan,[1] the beautiful daughter of the Earl of Courtland gave her hand to her handsome but pennyless lover; and there vowed to immolate every ambitious desire, every sentiment of vanity and high-born pride. Yet a sigh arose as she looked on the filthy hut, sooty priest, and ragged witnesses; and thought of the special license,[2] splendid saloon,[3] and bridal pomp, that would have attended her union with the Duke. But the rapturous expressions, which burst from the impassioned Douglas, made her forget the gaudy pleasures of pomp and fashion. Amid the sylvan scenes of the neighbouring lakes, the lovers sought a shelter; and, mutually charmed with each other, time flew for a while on downy pinions.

At the end of two months, however, the enamoured husband began to suspect, that the lips of his 'angel

Julia' could utter very silly things; while the fond bride, on her part, discovered, that though her 'adored Henry's' figure was symmetry itself, yet it certainly was deficient in a certain air—a *je ne sçais quoi*—that marks the man of fashion.

'How I wish I had my pretty Cupid here,' said her Ladyship with a sigh one day as she lolled on a sofa: 'he had so many pretty tricks, he would have helped to amuse us, and make the time pass; for really this place grows very stupid and tiresome; don't you think so, love?'

'Most confoundedly so, my darling,' replied her husband, yawning sympathetically as he spoke.

'Then suppose I make one more attempt to soften papa, and be received into favour again?'

'With all my heart.'

'Shall I say, I'm very sorry for what I have done?' asked her Ladyship with a sigh: 'You know I did not say that in my first letter.'

'Aye, do; and, if it will serve any purpose, you may say that I am no less so.'

In a few days the letter was returned, in a blank cover; and, by the same post, Douglas saw himself superseded in the Gazette,[1] being absent without leave!

There now remained but one course to pursue; and that was to seek refuge at his father's, in the Highlands of Scotland. At the first mention of it, Lady Juliana was transported with joy; and begged that a letter might be instantly dispatched, containing the offer of a visit: she had heard the Duchess of M. declare nothing could be so delightful as the style of living in Scotland: the people were so frank and gay, and the manners so easy and engaging: Oh! it was delightful! And then Lady Jane G. and Lady Mary L. and a thousand other Lords and Ladies she knew, were all so charmed with the country, and all so sorry to leave it. Then dear Henry's family must be so charming: an old castle, too, was her delight: she would feel quite at home while wandering through its long galleries; and she quite loved old pictures, and armour, and tapestry; and then her thoughts reverted to her father's magnificent mansion in D——shire.

At length an answer arrived, containing a cordial invitation from the old Laird, to spend the winter with them at Glenfern Castle.

All impatience to quit the scenes of their short-lived felicity, they bade a hasty adieu to the now fading beauties of Windermere; and full of hope and expectation, eagerly turned towards the bleak hills of Scotland. They stopped for a short time at Edinburgh, to provide themselves with a carriage, and some other necessaries. There, too, she fortunately met with an English Abigail[1] and footman, who, for double wages, were prevailed upon to attend her to the Highlands; which, with the addition of two dogs, a tame squirrel, and mackaw, completed the establishment.

CHAPTER II

'What transport to retrace our early plays,
    Our easy bliss, when each thing joy supplied;
    The woods, the mountains, and the warbling maze
    Of the wild brooks.'

Thomson.[2]

MANY WERE THE dreary muirs,[3] and rugged mountains, her Ladyship had to encounter, in her progress to Glenfern castle; and, but for the hope of the new world that awaited her beyond those formidable barriers, her delicate frame, and still more sensitive feelings, must have sunk beneath the horrors of such a journey. But she remembered the Duchess had said, the inns and roads were execrable; and the face of the country, as well as the lower orders of people, frightful; but what signified those things? There were balls, and sailing parties, and rowing matches, and shooting parties, and fishing parties, and parties of every description; and the certainty of being recompensed by the festivities of Glenfern Castle, reconciled her to the ruggedness of the approach.

Douglas had left his paternal home, and native hills, when only eight years of age. A rich relation of his mother's, happening to visit them at that time, took a fancy to the boy; and, under promise of making him his heir, had prevailed on his parents to part with him. At a proper age, he was placed in the guards, and had continued to maintain himself in the favour of his benefactor until his imprudent marriage, which had irritated the old bachelor so much, that he instantly disinherited him, and refused to listen to any terms of reconciliation. The impressions, which the scenes of his infancy had left upon the mind of the young Scotsman, it may easily be supposed, were of a pleasing description. He expatiated to his Juliana, on the wild but august scenery that surrounded his father's castle, and associated with the idea, the boyish exploits, which, though faintly remembered, still served to endear them to his heart. He spoke of the time when he used to make one of a numerous party on the lake, and, when tired of sailing on its glassy surface, to the sound of soft music, they would land at some lovely spot; and, after partaking of their banquet beneath a spreading tree, conclude the day by a dance on the grass.

Lady Juliana would exclaim, 'How delightful! I doat upon pic-nics and dancing!—apropos, Henry, there will surely be a ball to welcome our arrival?'

The conversation was interrupted; for just at that moment they had gained the summit of a very high hill, and the post-boy stopping to give his horses breath, turned round to the carriage, pointing at the same time, with a significant gesture, to a tall thin grey house, something resembling a tower, that stood in the vale beneath. A small sullen looking lake was in front, on whose banks grew neither tree nor shrub. Behind, rose a chain of rugged cloud-capped hills, on the declivities of which, were some faint attempts at young plantations; and the only level ground, consisted of a few dingy turnip fields, enclosed with rude stone walls, or dykes,[1] as the post-boy called them. It was now November; the day was raw and cold; and a thick drizzling rain was beginning to fall. A dreary stillness reigned all around, broken only at intervals by the screams of the sea-fowl that hovered over the lake; on whose dark and troubled waters, was dimly descried a little boat, plied by one solitary being.

'What a scene!' at length Lady Juliana exclaimed, shuddering as she spoke; 'Good God, what a scene! how I pity the unhappy wretches who are doomed to dwell in such a place! and yonder hideous grim house; it makes me sick to look at it. For heaven's sake, bid him drive on.' Another significant look from the driver, made the colour mount to Douglas' cheek, as he stammered out, 'Surely it can't be; yet somehow I don't know— pray, my lad,' letting down one of the glasses, and addressing the post-boy, 'what is the name of that house?'

Hooss!' repeated the driver; 'ca' ye thon a hoose?[2] thon's gude Glenfern Castle.'

Lady Juliana not understanding a word he said, sat silently, wondering at her husband's curiosity respecting such a wretched looking place.

'Impossible! you must be mistaken, my lad: why, what's become of all the fine wood that used to surround it?'

'Gin[1] you mean a wheen[2] auld firs, there's some o'
them to the fore[3] yet,' pointing to two or three tall, bare,
scathed Scotch firs, that scarcely bent their stubborn
heads to the wind, that now began to howl around them.

'I insist upon it that you are mistaken; you must have
wandered from the right road,' cried the now alarmed
Douglas in a loud voice, which vainly attempted to
conceal his agitation.

'We'll shune[4] see that,' replied the phlegmatic Scot;
who, having rested his horses, and affixed a drag to the
wheel, was about to proceed; when Lady Juliana, who
now began to have some vague suspicion of the truth,
called to him to stop; and, almost breathless with alarm,
inquired of her husband the meaning of what had passed.

He tried to force a smile, as he said, 'It seems our journey is nearly ended; that fellow persists in asserting that
that is Glenfern, though I can scarcely think it. If it is,
it is strangely altered since I left it twelve years ago.'

For a moment Lady Juliana was too much alarmed to
make a reply; pale and speechless she sunk back in the
carriage; but the motion of it, as it began to proceed,
roused her to a sense of her situation, and she burst into
tears and exclamations.

The driver, who attributed it all to fears at descending
the hill, assured her 'she need na[5] be the least feared, for
there were na twa[6] cannier beasts atween that and
Johnny Groat's hooss;[7] and that they wad hae her at the
castle door in a crack,[8] gin they were ance down the
brae.'[9]

Douglas' attempts to sooth his high-born bride were
not more successful than those of the driver: in vain he
made use of every endearing epithet and tender expression, and recalled the time when she used to declare that
she could dwell with him in a desert; her only replies
were bitter reproaches and upbraidings for his treachery
and deceit, mingled with floods of tears, and interrupted

by hysterical sobs. Provoked at her folly, yet softened by her extreme distress, Douglas was in the utmost state of perplexity—now ready to give way to a paroxysm of rage; then yielding to the natural goodness of his heart, he sought to soothe her into composure; and, at length, with much difficulty succeeded in changing her passionate indignation into silent dejection.

That no fresh objects of horror or disgust might appear to disturb this calm, the blinds were pulled down, and in this state they reached Glenfern Castle. But there the friendly veil was necessarily withdrawn, and the first object that presented itself to the high-bred English-woman, was an old man clad in a short tartan coat and striped woollen night-cap, with blear eyes and shaking hands, who vainly strove to open the carriage door.

Douglas soon extricated himself, and assisted his lady to alight; then accosting the venerable domestic as 'Old Donald,' asked him, if he recollected him?

'Weel that,[1] weel that, Maister Hairy, and ye're welcome hame; and ye tu,[2] bonny Sir,'* (addressing Lady Juliana, who was calling to her footman to follow her with the mackaw;) then tottering before them, he led the way, while her Ladyship followed, leaning on her husband, her squirrel on her other arm, preceded by her dogs, barking with all their might, and attended by the mackaw, screaming with all his strength; and in this state was the Lady Juliana ushered into the drawing room of Glenfern Castle!

---

* The Highlanders use this term of respect indifferently to both sexes.

CHAPTER III

—————'What can be worse,
Than to dwell here.

Paradise Lost.[1]

IT WAS a long, narrow, low-roofed room, with a number of small windows, that admitted feeble lights in every possible direction. The scanty furniture bore every appearance of having been constructed at the same time as the edifice; and the friendship thus early formed still seemed to subsist, as the high-backed worked chairs adhered most pertinaciously to the grey walls, on which hung, in narrow black frames, some of the venerable ancestors of the Douglas family. A fire, which appeared to have been newly kindled, was beginning to burn, but, previous to shewing itself in flame, had chosen to vent itself in smoke, with which the room was completely filled, and the open windows seemed to produce no other effect than that of admitting the rain and wind.

At the entrance of the strangers, a flock of females rushed forwards to meet them. Douglas good humouredly submitted to be hugged by three long chinned spinsters, whom he recognised as his aunts; and warmly saluted five awkward purple girls he guessed to be his sisters; while Lady Juliana stood the image of despair, and, scarcely conscious, admitted in silence the civilities of her new relations; till, at length, sinking into a chair, she endeavoured to conceal her agitation by calling to the dogs, and caressing her mackaw.

The Laird, who had been hastily summoned from his farming operations, now entered. He was a good looking old man, with something the air of a gentleman, in spite of the inelegance of his dress, his rough manner, and provincial accent. After warmly welcoming his son, he advanced to his beautiful daughter-in-law, and, taking her in his arms, bestowed a loud and hearty kiss on each cheek; then, observing the paleness of her complexion, and the tears that swam in her eyes, 'What! not frightened for[1] our Highland hills, my leddy? Come, cheer up—trust me, ye'll find as warm hearts among them, as ony ye hae left in your fine English *policies*'[2]—shaking her delicate fingers in his hard muscular gripe, as he spoke.

The tears, which had with difficulty been hitherto suppressed, now burst in torrents from the eyes of the high-bred beauty, as she leant her cheek against the back of a chair, and gave way to the anguish which mocked control.

To the loud, anxious inquiries, and oppressive kindness of her homely relatives, she made no reply; but, stretching out her hands to her husband, sobbed, 'Take, oh! take me from this place!'

Mortified, ashamed, and provoked, at a behaviour so childish and absurd, Douglas could only stammer out something about Lady Juliana having been frightened and fatigued; and, requesting to be shewn to their apartment, he supported her almost lifeless to it, while his aunts followed, all three prescribing different remedies in a breath.

'For heaven's sake, take them from me!' faintly articulated Lady Juliana, as she shrank from the many hands that were alternately applied to her pulse and forehead.

After repeated entreaties and plausible excuses from Douglas, his aunts at length consented to withdraw, and he then exerted all the rhetoric he was master of, to reconcile his bride to the situation love and necessity had thrown her into. But in vain he employed reasoning, caresses, and threats; the only answers he could extort were tears and entreaties to be taken from a place, where she declared she felt it impossible to exist.

'If you wish my death, Harry,' said she, in a voice almost inarticulate from excess of weeping, 'oh! kill me quickly, and do not leave me to linger out my days, and perish at last with misery here.'

'For heaven's sake, tell me what you would have me do,' said her husband, softened to pity by her extreme distress, 'and I swear, that, in every thing possible, I will comply with your wishes.'

'O, fly then, stop the horses, and let is return immediately. Do run, dearest Harry, or they will be gone; and we shall never get away from this odious place.'

'Where would you go?' asked he, with affected calmness.

'Oh, any where; no matter where, so as we do but get away from hence: we can be at no loss.'

'None in the world,' interrupted Douglas, with a bitter smile, 'as long as there is a prison to receive us. See,' continued he, throwing a few shillings down on the table, 'there is every sixpence I possess in the world, so help me heaven!'

Lady Juliana stood aghast.

At that instant, the English Abigail burst into the room; and in a voice, choaking with passion, she requested her discharge, that she might return with the driver who had brought them there.

'A pretty way of travelling, to be sure, it will be,' continued she, 'to go bumping behind a dirty chaise-driver; but better to be shook to a jelly altogether, than stay amongst such a set of *Oaten-toads*.'*

'What do you mean?' inquired Douglas, as soon as the voluble Abigail allowed him an opportunity of asking.

'Why, my meaning, Sir, is to leave this here place immediately; not that I have any objections, either to my Lady, or you, Sir; but, to be sure, it was a sad day for me, that I engaged myself to her Ladyship. Little did I think, that a Lady of distinction would be coming to such a poor pitiful place as this. I am sure, I thought I should

---

* Hottentots.

ha' swooned, when I was shewed the hole where I was to sleep.'

At the bare idea of this indignity to her person, the fury of the incensed fair one blazed forth with such strength, as to choke her utterance.

Amazement had hitherto kept Lady Juliana silent; for to such scenes she was a stranger. Born in an elevated rank; reared in state; accustomed to the most obsequious attention; and never approached, but with the respect due rather to a *divinity* than to a mortal, the strain of vulgar insolence that now assailed her, was no less new to her ears than shocking to her feelings. With a voice and look, that awed the woman into obedience, she commanded her to quit her presence for ever; and then, no longer able to suppress the emotions of insulted pride, wounded vanity, and indignant disappointment, she gave way to a violent fit of hysterics.

In the utmost perplexity, the unfortunate husband, by turns, cursed the hour that had given him such a wife; now tried to soothe her into composure; but at length, seriously alarmed at the increasing attack, he called loudly for assistance.

In a moment, the three aunts, and the five sisters, all rushed together into the room, full of wonder, exclamation, and enquiry. Many were the remedies that were tried, and the experiments that were suggested; till, at length, the violence of passion exhausted itself, and a faint sob, or deep sigh, succeeded the hysteric scream.

Douglas now attempted to account for the behaviour of his noble spouse, by ascribing it to the fatigue she had lately undergone, joined to distress of mind at her father's unrelenting severity towards her.

'Oh, the amiable creature!' interrupted the unsuspecting spinsters, almost stifling her with their caresses as they spoke. 'Welcome, a thousand times welcome, to Glenfern Castle,' said Miss Jacky, who was esteemed by

much the most sensible woman, as well as the greatest
orator in the whole parish; 'nothing shall be wanting,
dearest Lady Juliana, to compensate for a parent's rigour,
and make you happy and comfortable. Consider this as
your future home! My sisters and myself will be as
mothers to you; and see these charming young creatures,'
dragging forward two tall frightened girls, with sandy
hair and great purple arms; 'thank Providence, for
having blest you with such sisters!'

'Don't speak too much, Jacky, to our dear niece at
present,' said Miss Grizzy; 'I think one of Lady Maclaughlan's composing draughts would be the best thing
for her.'

'Composing draughts at this time of day!' cried Miss
Nicky; 'I should think a little good broth a much wiser
thing. There are some excellent family broth making
below, and I'll desire Tibby to bring a few.'

'Will you take a little soup, love?' asked Douglas. His
Lady assented; and Miss Nicky vanished, but quickly
re-entered, followed by Tibby, carrying a huge bowl of
coarse Scotch broth, swimming with leeks, greens, and
grease. Lady Juliana attempted to taste it; but her
delicate palate revolted at the homely fare; and she gave
up the attempt, in spite of Miss Nicky's earnest entreaties
to take a few more of these excellent family broth.

'I should think,' said Henry, as he vainly attempted to
stir it round, 'that a little wine would be more to the
purpose than this stuff.'

The aunts looked at each other; and, withdrawing to a
corner, a whispering consultation took place, in which
'Lady Maclaughlan's opinion, birch, balm, currant,
heating, cooling, running risks,' &c. &c. transpired. At
length the question was carried; and some tolerable
sherry, and a piece of very substantial *short-bread* were
produced.

It was now voted by Miss Jacky, and carried *nem.*

con.[1] that her Ladyship ought to take a little repose till the hour of dinner.

'And don't trouble to dress,' continued the considerate aunt, 'for we are not very dressy here; and we are to be quite a charming family party, nobody but ourselves; and,' turning to her nephew, 'your brother and his wife. She is a most superior woman, though she has rather too many of her English prejudices yet to be all we could wish; but I have no doubt, when she has lived a little longer amongst us, she will just become one of ourselves.'

'I forget who she was?' said Douglas.

'A grand-daughter of Sir Duncan Malcolm's, a very old family of the ——— blood, and nearly allied to the present Earl. And here they come,' exclaimed she, on hearing the sound of a carriage; and all rushed out to receive them.

'Let us have a glimpse of this scion from a noble stock,' said Lady Juliana, mimicking the accent of the poor spinsters, as she rose and ran to the window.

'Good heavens, Henry! do come and behold this equipage;' and she laughed with childish glee, as she pointed to a plain, old fashioned whisky,[2] with a large top. A tall handsome young man now alighted, and lifted out a female figure, so enveloped in a cloak, that eyes less penetrating than Lady Juliana's could not, at a single glance, have discovered her to be a 'frightful quiz.'[3]

'Only conceive the effect of this dashing equipage in Bond-street!' continued she, redoubling her mirth at the bright idea; then suddenly stopping, and sighing—'Ah, my pretty vis-a-vis!'[4] I remember the first time I saw you, Henry, I was in it at a review;' and she sighed still deeper.

'True; I was then aid-de-camp to your handsome lover, the Duke of L———.'

'Perhaps I might think him handsome now. People's taste alter according to circumstances.'

'Yours must have undergone a wonderful revolution, if you can find charms in a hunchback of fifty-three.'

'He is not a hunchback,' returned her Ladyship warmly; 'only a little high shouldered; but, at any rate, he has the most beautiful place, and the finest house in England.'

Douglas saw the storm gathering on the brow of his capricious wife, and clasping her in his arms, 'Are you, indeed, so changed, my Julia, that you have forgot the time when you used to declare, you would prefer a desert with your Henry, to a throne with another.'

'No, certainly, not changed; but—I—I did not very well know then what a desert was; or, at least, I had formed rather a different idea of it.'

'What was your idea of a desert?' said her husband, laughing; 'do tell me love?'

'Oh! I had fancied it a beautiful place, full of roses and myrtles, and smooth green turf, and murmuring rivulets, and, though very retired, not absolutely out of the world; where one could occasionally see one's friends, and give *dejeunés et fêtes champetres.*'[1]

'Well, perhaps the time may come, Juliana, when we may realize your Elysian[2] deserts; but at present, you know, I am wholly dependent on my father. I hope to prevail on him to do something for me; and that our stay here will be short; as, you may be sure, the moment I can, I will take you hence. I am sensible it is not a situation for you; but for my sake, dearest Juliana, bear with it for a while, without betraying your disgust. Will you do this, darling?' and he kissed away the sullen tear that hung on her cheek.

'You know, love, there's nothing in the world I wou'dnt do for you,' replied she, as she played with her squirrel; 'and as you promise our stay shall be short, if I don't die of the horrors, I shall certainly try to make the agreeable. Oh! my cherub!' flying to her pug, who came barking into the room, 'Where have you been, and where's my darling Psyche, and sweet mackaw. Do, Harry, go and see after the darlings?'

'I must go and see my brother and his wife first. Will you come, love?'

'O, not now; I don't feel equal to the encounter; besides, I must dress. But what shall I do; since that vile woman's gone, I can't dress myself. I never did such a thing in my life; and I am sure, it's impossible that I can,' almost weeping at the hardships she was doomed to experience in making her own toilette.

'Shall I be your Abigail?' asked her husband, smiling at the distress; 'methinks it would be no difficult task to deck my Julia.'

'Dear Harry, will you really dress me? Oh! that will be delightful! I shall die with laughing at your awkwardness;' and her beautiful eyes sparkled with childish delight at the idea.

'In the mean time,' said Douglas, 'I'll send some one to unpack your things; and after I have shook hands with Archie, and been introduced to my new sister, I shall enter on my office.'

'Now do, pray, make haste; for I die to see your great hands tying strings, and sticking pins.'

Delighted with her gaiety and good humour, he left her caressing her favourites; and finding rather a scarcity of female attendance, he dispatched two of his sisters, to assist his helpless beauty in her arrangements.

CHAPTER IV

'And ever against eating cares,
Lap me in soft Lydian airs.'

L'Allegro.[1]

WHEN DOUGLAS RETURNED, he found the floor
strewed with dresses of every description, his sisters on
their knees before a great trunk, they were busied in
unpacking, and his Lady in her wrapper, with her hair
about her ears, still amusing herself with her pets.

'See, how good your sisters are,' said she, pointing
to the poor girls, whose inflamed faces bore testimony to
their labours. 'I declare, I am quite sorry to see them
take so much trouble,' yawning as she leant back in her
chair; 'is it not quite shocking, Tommy?' kissing her
squirrel. 'Oh! pray, Henry, do tell me, what I am to put
on; for I protest I don't know. Favolle always used to
choose for me; and so did that odious Martin, for she
had an exquisite taste.'

'Not so exquisite as your own, I am sure; so for once
choose for yourself,' replied the good-humoured husband;
'and pray make haste, for my father waits dinner.'

Betwixt scolding, laughing, and blundering, the dress
was at length completed; and Lady Juliana, in all the
pomp of dress and pride of beauty, descended, leaning on
her husband's arm.

On entering the drawing-room, which was now in a
more comfortable state, Douglas led her to a lady who
was sitting by the fire: and, placing her hand within that
of the stranger, 'Juliana, my love,' said he, 'this is a
sister whom you have not yet seen, and with whom I
am sure you will gladly make acquaintance.'

The stranger received her noble sister with graceful
ease; and, with a sweet smile and pleasing accent,
expressed herself happy in the introduction. Lady
Juliana was surprised, and somewhat disconcerted. She

had arranged her plans, and made up her mind to be *condescending*; she had resolved to enchant by her sweetness, dazzle by her brilliancy, and overpower by her affability. But there was a simple dignity in the air and address of the lady, before which even high-bred affectation sunk abashed. Before she found a reply to the courteous, yet respectful salutation of her sister-in-law, Douglas introduced his brother; and the old gentleman, impatient at any farther delay, taking Lady Juliana by the hand, pulled, rather than led her into the dining-room.

Even Lady Juliana contrived to make a meal of the roast mutton and moorfowl;[1] for the Laird piqued himself on the breed of his sheep, and his son was too good a sportsman to allow his friends to want for game.

'I think my darling Tommy would relish this grouse very much,' observed Lady Juliana, as she secured the last remaining wing for her favourite; 'bring him here!' turning to the tall, dashing lacquey who stood behind her chair, and whose handsome livery, and well dressed hair, formed a striking contrast to old Donald's tartan jacket and bob-wig.[2]

'Come hither, my sweetest cherubs!' extending her arms towards the charming *trio*, as they entered, barking, and chattering, and flying to their mistress. A scene of noise and nonsense ensued.

Douglas remained silent, mortified and provoked at the weakness of his wife, which not even the silver tones of her voice, or the elegance of her manners, could longer conceal from him. But still there was a charm in her very folly, to the eye of love, which had not yet wholly lost its power.

After the table was cleared, observing that he was still silent and abstracted, Lady Juliana turned to her husband; and, laying her hand on his shoulder, 'You are not well, love!' said she, looking up in his face, and shaking back the redundant ringlets that shaded her own.

'Perfectly so,' replied her husband, with a sigh.

'What, dull; then I must sing to enliven you.' And, leaning her head on his shoulder, she warbled a verse of the beautiful little Venetian air, *La Biondina in Gondoletta*.[1] Then suddenly stopping, and fixing her eyes on Mrs. Douglas, 'I beg pardon, perhaps you don't like music; perhaps my singing's a bore.'

'You pay us a bad compliment in saying so,' said her sister-in-law, smiling; 'and the only atonement you can make for such an injurious doubt, is to proceed.'

'Does any body sing here?' asked she, without noticing this request: 'Do, somebody, sing me a song.'

'O! we all sing, and dance too,' said one of the old young ladies; 'and after tea we will shew you some of our Scotch steps; but, in the mean time, Mrs. Douglas will favour us with her song.'

Mrs. Douglas assented good-humouredly, though aware that it would be rather a nice point to please all parties in the choice of a song. The Laird reckoned all foreign music, *i.e.* every thing that was not Scotch, an outrage upon his ears; and Mrs. Douglas had too much taste to murder Scotch songs with her English accent. She therefore compromised the matter as well as she could, by selecting a Highland ditty clothed in her own native tongue; and sung, with much pathos and simplicity, the lamented Leyden's 'Fall of Macgregor.'[2]

'In the vale of Glenorchy the night breeze was sighing
O'er the tomb where the ancient Macgregors are lying;
Green are their graves by their soft murmuring river,
But the name of Macgregor has perished for ever.

'On a red stream of light, by his grey mountains glancing,
Soon I beheld a dim spirit advancing;
Slow o'er the heath of the dead was its motion,
Like the shadow of mist o'er the foam of the ocean.

'Like the sound of a stream through the still evening dying,—
Stranger! who treads where Macgregor is lying?
Darest thou to walk, unappalled and firm-hearted,
'Mid the shadowy steps of the mighty departed?

'See! round thee the caves of the dead are disclosing
The shades that have long been in silence reposing;
Thro' their forms dimly twinkles the moon-beam descending,
As upon thee their red eyes of wrath they are bending.

'Our grey stones of fame though the heath-blossom cover,
Round the fields of our battles our spirits still hover;
Where we oft saw the streams running red from the
      mountains;
But dark are our forms by our blue native fountains.

'For our fame melts away like the foam of the river,
Like the last yellow leaves on the oak-boughs that shiver:
The name is unknown of our fathers so gallant;
And our blood beats no more in the breasts of the valiant.

'The hunter of red deer now ceases to number
The lonely grey stones on the field of our slumber.—
Fly, stranger! and let not thine eye be reverted;
Why should'st thou see that our fame is departed?'

'Pray, do you play on the harp?' asked the volatile
lady, scarcely waiting till the first stanza was ended;
'and, apropos, have you a good harp here?'

'We've neither gude nor bad,' said the old gentleman
gruffly, 'the lasses hae something else to do than to be
strumming upon harps.'

'We've a very sweet spinnet,' said Miss Jacky, 'which,
in my opinion, is a far superior instrument: and Bella
will give us a tune upon it. Bella, my dear, let Lady
Juliana hear how well you can play.'

Bella, blushing like a piony rose, retired to a corner
of the room, where stood the spinnet; and with great,

heavy, trembling hands, began to belabour the unfortunate instrument, while the aunts beat time, and encouraged her to proceed, with exclamations of admiration and applause.

'You have done very well, Bella,' said Mrs. Douglas, seeing her preparing to *execute* another piece, and pitying the poor girl, as well as her auditors. Then whispering Miss Jacky that Lady Juliana looked fatigued, they arose to quit the room.

'Give me your arm, love, to the drawing-room,' said her Ladyship, languidly. 'And now, pray, don't be long away,' continued she, as he placed her on the sofa, and returned to the gentlemen.

CHAPTER V

'You have displaced the mirth, broke the good meeting,
With most admired disorder.'

Macbeth.[1]

THE INTERVAL, WHICH seemed of endless duration to the hapless Lady Juliana, was passed by the aunts in giving sage cousel as to the course of life to be pursued by married ladies. Worsted stockings and quilted petticoats were insisted upon as indispensable articles of dress; while it was plainly insinuated, that it was utterly impossible any child could be healthy, whose mother had not confined her wishes to barley broth and oatmeal porridge.

'Only look at thae[2] young lambs,' said Miss Grizzy, pointing to the five great girls; 'see what pickters[3] of health they are! I'm sure I hope, my dear niece, your children will be just the same—only boys, for we are sadly in want of boys. It's melancholy to think we have not a boy among us, and that a fine auntient race like ours should be dying away for want of male heirs.' And the tears streamed down the cheeks of the good spinster as she spoke.

The entrance of the gentlemen put a stop to the conversation.

Flying to her husband, Lady Juliana began to whisper, in very audible tones, her inquiries, whether he had yet got any money—when they were to go away, &c. &c.

'Does your Ladyship choose any tea?' asked Miss Nicky, as she disseminated the little cups of coarse black liquid.[1]

'Tea! oh no, I never drink tea—I'll' take some coffee though; and Psyche doats on a dish of tea.'—And she tendered the beverage, that had been intended for herself, to her favourite.

'Here's no coffee,' said Douglas, surveying the tea-table; 'but I will ring for some,' as he pulled the bell.

Old Donald answered the summons.

'Where's the coffee?' demanded Miss Nicky.

'The coffee!' repeated the Highlander; 'troth, Miss Nicky, an' it's been clean[2] forgot.'

'Well, but you can get it yet?' said Douglas.

''Deed, Maister Harry, the night's owre far gane for't noo;[3] for the fire's a' ta'en up, ye see,' reckoning with his fingers, as he proceeded; 'there's parritch[4] makin' for oor supper; and there's patatees[5] boiling for the beasts; and—'

'I'll see about it myself,' said Miss Nicky, leaving the room, with old Donald at her back, muttering all the way.

The old Laird, all this while, had been enjoying his evening nap; but, that now ended, and the tea equipage being dismissed, starting up, he asked what they were about, that the dancing was not begun.

'Come, my Leddy, we'll set the example,' snapping his fingers, and singing, in a hoarse voice,

'The mouse is a merry beastie,
And the moudiwort[1] wants the een;[2]
But folk sall ne'er get wit,[3]
Sae merry as we twa ha'e been.'[4]

'But whar's the girlies?,' cried he; 'Ho! Belle, Becky, Betty, Babby, Beenie—to your posts!'

The young ladies, eager for the delights of music and dancing, now entered, followed by Coil, the piper, dressed in the native garb, with cheeks seemingly ready blown for the occasion. After a little strutting and puffing, the pipes were fairly set agoing in Coil's most spirited manner. But vain would be the attempt to describe Lady Juliana's horror and amazement at the hideous sounds that for the first time assailed her ear. Tearing herself from the grasp of the old gentleman, who was just setting off in the reel, she flew shrieking to her husband, and threw herself trembling into his arms, while he called loudly to the self-delighted Coil to stop.

'What's the matter—what's the matter?' cried the whole family, gathering round.

'Matter!' repeated Douglas furiously, 'you have frightened Lady Juliana to death with your infernal music. What did you mean,' turning fiercely to the astonished piper, 'by blowing that confounded bladder?'

Poor Coil gaped with astonishment; for never before had his performance on the bagpipe been heard but with admiration and applause.

'A bonny bargain,[5] indeed, the canna[6] stand the pipes,' said the old gentleman, as he went puffing up and down the room; 'She's no the wife for a Heelandman. Confoonded blather, indeed! By my faith, ye're no blate!'[7]

'I declare it's the most distressing thing I ever met

with,' sighed Miss Grizzy; 'I wonder whether it could be the sight or the sound of the bagpipe that frightened ourour dear niece. I wish to goodness Lady Maclaughlan was here!'

'It's impossible the bagpipe could frighten any body,' said Miss Jacky, in a high key; 'nobody with common sense could be frightened at a bagpipe.'

Mrs. Douglas here mildly interposed, and soothed down the offended pride of the Highlanders, by attributing Lady Juliana's agitation entirely to *surprise*. The word operated like a charm; all were ready to admit, that it was a surprising thing when heard for the first time. Miss Jacky remarked, that we are all liable to be surprised; and the still more sapient Grizzy said, that indeed it was most surprising the effect that surprise had upon some people. For her own part, she could not deny, but that she was very often frightened when she was surprised.

Douglas, meanwhile, was employed in soothing the terrors, real or affected, of his delicate bride; who declared herself so exhausted with the fatigue she had undergone, and the sufferings she had endured, that she must retire for the night. Henry, eager to escape from the questions and remarks of his family, gladly availed himself of the same excuse; and, to the infinite mortification of both aunts and nieces, the ball was broke up.

CHAPTER VI

'What choice to choose for delicacy best.'

Milton.[1]

OF WHAT NATURE were the remarks passed in the parlour upon the new married couple, has not reached the writer of these memoirs with as much exactness as the fore-

going circumstances; but they may in part be imagined
from the sketch already given of the characters which
formed the Glenfern party. The conciliatory indulgence
of Mrs. Douglas, when aided by the good-natured Miss
Grizzy, doubtless had a favourable effect on the irritated
pride, but short-lived acrimony, of the old gentleman.
Certain it is, that before the evening concluded, they
appeared all restored to harmony, and retired to their
respective chambers in hopes of beholding a more
propitious morrow.

Who has not perused sonnets, odes, and speeches, in
praise of that balmy blessing, sleep;[1] from the divine
effusions of Shakespeare, down to the drowsy notes of
newspaper poets?

Yet cannot too much be said in its commendation.
Sweet is its influence on the care-worn eyes, to tears
accustomed! In its arms the statesman forgets his harassed
thoughts; the weary and the poor are blessed with its
charms; and conscience—even conscience—is sometimes soothed into silence, while the sufferer sleeps. But
no where, perhaps, is its influence more happily felt, than
in the heart oppressed by the harassing accumulation
of petty ills: like a troop of locusts, making up by their
number and their stings, what they want in magnitude.

Mortified pride in discovering the fallacy of our own
judgement; to be ashamed of what we love, yet still to
love, are feelings most unpleasant; and, though they
assume not the dignity of deep distress, yet philosophy
has scarce any power to soothe their worrying, incessant
annoyance. Douglas was glad to forget himself in sleep.
He had thought a vast deal that day, and, of unpleasant
subjects, more than the whole of his foregoing life would
have produced. If he did not curse the fair object of his
imprudence, he at least cursed his own folly and himself;
and these were his last waking thoughts.

But Douglas could not repose as long as the seven

sleepers;[1] and, in consequence of having retired sooner to bed than he was accustomed to do, he waked at an early hour in the morning.

The wonderful activity which people sometimes feel when they have little to do with their bodies, and less with their minds, caused him to rise hastily and dress, hoping to pick up a new set of ideas, by virtue of his locomotive powers.

On descending to the dining parlour, he found his father seated at the window, carefully perusing a pamphlet, written to illustrate the principle, *Let nothing be lost*, and containing many sage and erudite directions for the composition and dimensions of that ornament to a gentleman's farm-yard, and a cottager's front door, ycleped,[2] in the language of the country, a *midden*[3]— with the signification of which we would not, for the world, shock the more refined feelings of our southern readers.

Many were the inquiries about dear Lady Juliana: hoped she had rested well: hoped they found the bed comfortable, not too many blankets, nor too few pillows, &c. &c. These inquiries were interrupted by the Laird, who requested his son to take a turn with him, while breakfast was getting ready, that they might talk over past events, and new plans; that he might see the new planting[4] on the hill; the draining of the great moss;[5] with other agricultural concerns which we shall omit, not having the same power of commanding attention from our readers, as the Laird had from his hearers.

After repeated summonses, and many inquiries, from the impatient party already assembled round the breakfast table, Lady Juliana made her appearance, accompanied by her favourites, whom no persuasions of her husband could prevail upon her to leave behind.

As she entered the room, her olfactory nerves were smote with gales, not of 'Araby the blest,'[6] but of old cheese and herrings, with which the hospitable board was amply provided.

The ladies, having severally exchanged the salutations of the morning, Miss Nicky commenced the operation of pouring out tea, while the Laird laid a large piece of herring on her Ladyship's plate.

'Good heavens! what am I to do with this?' exclaimed she: 'do take it away, or I shall faint!'

'Brother, brother!' cried Miss Grizzy, in a tone of alarm, 'I beg you won't place any unpleasant object before the eyes of our dear niece. I declare!—Pray, was it the sight or the smell of the beast* that shocked you so much, my dear Lady Juliana? I'm sure, I wish to goodness Lady Maclaughlan was come!'

Mr. Douglas, or the Major, as he was styled, immediately rose, and pulled the bell.

'Desire my gig¹ to be got ready directly!' said he.

The aunts drew up stiffly, and looked at each other, without speaking; but the old gentleman expressed his surprise, that his son should think of leaving them so soon.

'May we inquire the reason of this sudden resolution?' at length said Miss Jacky, in a tone of stifled indignation.

'Certainly, if you are disposed to hear it: It is because I find there is company expected.'

The three ladies turned up their hands and eyes in speechless horror.

'Is it that virtuous woman, Lady Maclaughlan, you would shun, nephew?' demanded Miss Jacky.

'It is that insufferable pest I would shun,' replied her nephew, with a heightened colour, and a violence very unusual with him.

The good Miss Grizzy drew out her pocket hand-

---

* In Scotland, every thing that flies and swims, ranks in the bestial tribe.

kerchief; while Mrs. Douglas vainly endeavoured to silence her husband, and avert the rising storm.

'Dear Douglas!' whispered she in a tone of reproach.

'O pray, let him go on,' said Miss Jacky, almost choking under the effort she made to appear calm, 'Let him go on. Lady Maclaughlan's character, luckily, is far above the reach of calumny; nothing that Mr. Archibald Douglas can say, will have power to change our opinions, or, I hope, to prejudice his brother and Lady Juliana against this most exemplary, virtuous woman—a woman of family—of fortune—of talents—of accomplishments!—a woman of unblemished reputation! of the strictest morals! sweetest temper! charming heart! delightful spirits! so charitable! every year gives fifty flannel petticoats to the old people of the parish——'

'Then such a wife as she is!' sobbed out Miss Grizzy: 'She has invented, I don't know how many different medicines for Sir Sampson's complaint, and makes a point of his taking some of them every day; but for her, I'm sure he would have been in his grave long ago.'

'She's doing all she can to send him there, as she has done many a poor wretch already, with her infernal compositions.'

Here Miss Grizzy sunk back in her chair, overcome with horror; and Miss Nicky let fall the tea-pot, the scalding contents of which discharged themselves upon the unfortunate Psyche, whose yells, mingling with the screams of its fair mistress, for a while drowned even Miss Jacky's oratory.

'Oh! what shall I do?' cried Lady Juliana, as she bent over her favourite: 'Do send for a surgeon; pray, Henry, fly! Do fetch one directly, or she will die; and it would quite kill me to lose my darling. Do run, dearest Harry!'

'My dear Julia, how can you be so absurd? there's no surgeon within twenty miles of this.'

'No surgeon within twenty miles!' exclaimed she, starting up. 'How could you bring me to such a place! Good God! those dear creatures may die; I may die myself before I can get any assistance!'

'Don't be alarmed, my dearest niece,' said the good Miss Grizzy; 'we are all doctors here. I understand something of physic myself; and our friend Lady Maclaughlan, who, I dare say, will be here presently, is perfect mistress of every disease of the human frame.'

'Clap a cauld potatae to the brute's tae,'[1] cried the old Laird gruffly.

'I've a box of her scald ointment that will cure it in a minute.'

'If it don't cure, it will kill,' said Mr. Douglas, with a smile.

'Brother,' said Miss Jacky, rising with dignity from her chair, and waving her hand as she spoke—'Brother, I appeal to you, to protect the character of this most amiable respectable matron from the insults and calumny your son thinks proper to load it with. Sir Sampson Maclaughlan is your friend; and it therefore becomes your duty to defend his wife.'

'Troth,[2] but I'll hae aneugh to do, if I am to stand up for a' my friends' wives,' said the old gentleman. 'But, however, Archie, you are to blame: Leddy Maclaughlan is a very decent woman; at least, as far as I ken,[3] though she is a little free in the gab; and, out of respect to my auld friend Sir Sampson, it is my desire that you should remain here to receive him, and that you trait[4] baith him and his Leddy discreetly.'[5]

This was said in too serious a tone to be disputed; and his son was obliged to submit.

The ointment meanwhile having been applied to Psyche's paw, peace was restored, and breakfast recommenced.

'I declare our dear niece has not tasted a morsel,'

observed Miss Nicky.

'Bless me, here's charming barley meal scones,' cried one, thrusting a plateful of them before her. 'Here's tempting pease bannocks,'[1] interposed another, 'and oat cakes![2] I'm sure your Ladyship never saw such cakes.'

'I can't eat any of those things,' said their delicate niece, with an air of disgust. 'I should like some muffin and chocolate.'

'You forget you are not in London, my love,' said her husband reproachfully.

'No indeed, I do not forget it. Well then, give me some toast,' with an air of languid condescension.

'Unfortunately, we happen to be quite out of loaf bread[3] at present,' said Miss Nicky; 'but we've sent to Drymsine for some. They bake excellent bread at Drymsine.'

'Is there nothing within the bounds of possibility, you would fancy, Julia?' asked Douglas. 'Do think, love.'

'I think I should like some grouse, or a beef steak, if it was very nicely done,' returned her Ladyship, in a languishing tone.

'Beef steak!' repeated Miss Grizzy.

'Beef steak!' responded Miss Jacky.

'Beef steak!' reverberated Miss Nicky.

After much deliberation and consultation amongst the three spinsters, it was at length unanimously carried, that the Lady's whim should be indulged.

'Only think, sisters,' observed Miss Grizzy, in an under tone, 'what reflections we should have to make upon ourselves, if the child was to resemble a moor-fowl!'

'Or have a face like a raw beef steak!' said Miss Nicky.

These arguments were unanswerable; and a smoking steak and plump moor-fowl were quickly produced, of which Lady Juliana partook, in company with her four-footed favourites.

CHAPTER VII

'When winter soaks the fields, and female feet—
Too weak to struggle with tenacious clay,
Or ford the rivulets—are best at home.'

The Task.[1]

THE MEAL BEING at length concluded, Glenfern desired Henry to attend him on a walk, as he wished to have a little more private conversation with him. Lady Juliana was beginning a remonstrance against the cruelty of taking Harry away from her; when her husband whispering her, that he hoped to make something of the old gentleman,[2] and that he should soon be back, she suffered him to depart in silence.

Old Donald having at length succeeded in clearing the table of its heterogeneous banquet, it was quickly covered with the young ladies' work.

Miss Nicky withdrew to her household affairs. Miss Jacky sat with one eye upon Lady Juliana, the other upon her five nieces. Miss Grizzy seated herself by her Ladyship, holding a spread letter of Lady Maclaughlan's before her as a skreen.

While the young ladies busily plied their needles, the elder ones left no means untried to entertain their listless niece, whose only replies were exclamations of weariness, or expressions of affection bestowed upon her favourites.

At length even Miss Jacky's sense, and Miss Grizzy's good nature, were *at fault*;[3] when a ray of sunshine darting into the room, suggested the idea of a walk. The proposal was made, and assented to by her Ladyship, in the twofold hope of meeting her husband, and pleasing her dogs, whose whining and scratching had for some time testified their desire of a change. The ladies therefore separated to prepare for their *sortie*, after many recommendations from the aunts to be sure to *hap** well;

* Wrap.

but, as if distrusting her powers in that way, they speedily equipped themselves, and repaired to her chamber, arrayed *cap-a-pee*[1] in the walking costume of Glenfern Castle. And, indeed, it must be owned their style of dress was infinitely more judicious than that of their fashionable niece; and it was not surprising, that they, in their shrunk duffle great-coats, vast poke-bonnets,[2] red worsted neckcloths, and pattens,[3] should gaze with horror at her lace cap, lilac satin pelisse, and silk shoes. Ruin to the whole race of Glenfern, present and future, seemed inevitable from such a display of extravagance and imprudence. Having surmounted the first shock, Miss Jacky made a violent effort to subdue her rising wrath; and, with a sort of convulsive smile, addressed Lady Juliana: 'Your Ladyship, I perceive, is not of the opinion of our inimitable bard, who, in his charming poem, the Seasons, says, "Beauty needs not the foreign aid of ornament; but is, when unadorned, adorned the most."[4] That is a truth that ought to be impressed on every young woman's mind.'

Lady Juliana only stared. She was as little accustomed to be advised as she was to hear Thomson's Seasons quoted.

'I declare that's all quite true,' said the more temporizing Grizzy; 'and certainly our girls are not in the least taken up about their dress, poor things! which is a great comfort. At the same time, I'm sure it's no wonder your Ladyship should be taken up about yours, for certainly that pelisse is most beautiful. Nobody can deny that; and I daresay it is the very newest fashion. At the same time, I'm just afraid that it's rather too delicate, and that it might perhaps get a little dirty on our roads;[5] for although, in general, our roads are quite remarkable for being always dry, which is a great comfort in the country, yet, you know, the very best roads of course must be wet sometimes. And there's a very bad step just at the door almost, which Glenfern has been always speaking about getting mended. But, to be sure, he has so many things to think about, that it's no wonder he forgets sometimes; but I daresay he will get it done very soon now.'

The prospect of the road being mended, produced no better effect than the quotation from Thomson's Seasons. It was now Miss Nicky's turn.

'I'm afraid your Ladyship will frighten our stirks and stots[1] with your finery. I assure you they are not accustomed to see such fine figures; and,' putting her hand out at the window, 'I think it's spitting already.'*

All three now joined in the chorus, beseeching Lady Juliana to put on something warmer and more wise-like.[2]

'I positively have nothing,' cried she, wearied with their importunities, 'and I sha'nt get any winter things now till I return to town. My *roquelaire*[3] does very well for the carriage.'

The acknowledgement at the beginning of this speech was enough. All three instantly disappeared, like the genii of Aladin's lamp,[4] and, like that same person, presently returned, loaded with what, in their eyes, were precious as the gold of Arabia. One displayed a hard worsted shawl, with a flower-pot at each corner; another held up a tartan cloak, with a hood; and a third thrust forward a dark cloth Joseph,[5] lined with flannel; while one and all showered down a variety of old bonnets, fur tippets, hair soles, clogs, pattens, and endless *et ceteras*. Lady Juliana shrank with disgust from these 'delightful haps', and resisted all attempts to have them forced upon her, declaring, in a manner which shewed her determined to have her own way, that she would either go out as she was, or not go out at all. The aunts were therefore obliged to submit, and the party proceeded to

---

* A common expression in Scotland to signify slight rain.

what was termed the high road, though a stranger would
have sought in vain for its pretensions to that title. Far
as the eye could reach, and that was far enough, not a
single vehicle could be descried on it, though its deep
ruts shewed that it was well frequented by carts. The
scenery might have had charms for Ossian, but it had
none for Lady Juliana; who would rather have been
entangled in a string of Bond Street equipages, than
traversing 'the lonely heath, with the stream murmuring
hoarsely; the old trees groaning in the wind; the
troubled lake;'[1] and the still more troubled sisters. As
may be supposed, she very soon grew weary of the walk.
The bleak wind pierced her to the soul; her silk slippers
and lace flounces became undistinguishable masses of
mud; her dogs chased the sheep, and were, in their turn,
pursued by the 'nowts',[2] as the ladies termed the steers.
One sister expatiated on the great blessing of having a
peat moss at their door; another was at pains to point
out the purposed site of a set of new offices;[3] and the
third lamented that her Ladyship had not on thicker
shoes, that she might have gone and seen the garden.
More than ever disgusted and wretched, the hapless
Lady Juliana returned to the house, to fret away the time
till her husband's return.

CHAPTER VIII

——'On se rend insupportable dans la société par des défauts
légers, mais qui se font sentir à tout moment.'

Voltaire.[4]

THE FAMILY OF Glenfern have already said so much for
themselves, that it seems as if little remained to be told
by their biographer. Mrs. Douglas was the only member

of the community, who was at all conscious of the unfortunate association of characters and habits that had just taken place. She was a stranger to Lady Juliana; but she was interested by her youth, beauty, and elegance, and felt for the sacrifice she had made; a sacrifice so much greater than it was possible she ever could have conceived or anticipated. She could in some degree enter into the nature of her feelings towards the old ladies; for she, too, had felt how disagreeable people might contrive to render themselves, without being guilty of any particular fault; and how much more difficult it is to bear with the weaknesses than the vices of our neighbours. Had these ladies' failings been greater in a moral point of view, it might not have been so arduous a task to put up with them. But to love such a set of little, trifling, tormenting foibles, all dignified with the name of virtues, required, from her elegant mind, an exertion of its highest principles; a continual remembrance of that difficult Christian precept, 'to bear with one another.'[1] A person of less sense than Mrs. Douglas would have endeavoured to open the eyes of their understandings, on what appeared to be the folly and narrow-mindedness of their ways; but she refrained from the attempt, not from want of benevolent exertion, but from an innate conviction, that their foibles all originated in what was now incurable; viz. the natural weakness of their minds, together with their ignorance of the world, and the illiberality and prejudices of a vulgar education. 'These poor women,' reasoned the charitable Mrs. Douglas, 'are, perhaps, after all, better characters in the sight of God than I am. He who has endowed us all, as his wisdom has seen fit, and has placed me amongst them; Oh! may he teach me to remember, that we are all his children, and enable me to bear with their faults, while I study to correct my own.'

Thus did this amiable woman contrive, not only to live in peace, but, without sacrificing her own liberal ideas, to be actually beloved by those amongst whom her lot had been cast, however dissimilar to herself. But for that Christian spirit, (in which must ever be included a liberal mind and gentle temper,) she must have felt towards her connexions a still stronger repugnance than was even manifested by Lady Juliana; for Lady Juliana's superiority over them was merely that of refined habits and elegant manners; whereas Mrs. Douglas' was the superiority of a noble and highly gifted mind, which could hold no intercourse with theirs, except by stooping to the level of their low capacities. But, that the merit of her conduct may be duly appreciated, I shall endeavour to give a slight sketch of the female *dramatis personae* of Glenfern Castle.

Miss Jacky, the senior of the trio, was what is reckoned a very sensible woman—which generally means, a very disagreeable, obstinate, illiberal director of all men, women, and children—a sort of superintendant of all actions, time, and place—with unquestioned authority to arraign, judge, and condemn, upon the statutes of her own supposed sense. Most country parishes have their sensible woman, who lays down the law on all affairs spiritual and temporal. Miss Jacky stood unrivalled as the sensible woman of Glenfern. She had attained this eminence, partly from having a little more understanding than her sisters, but principally from her dictatorial manner, and the pompous, decisive tone, in which she delivered the most common-place truths. At home, her supremacy in all matters of sense was perfectly established; and thence the infection, like other superstitions, had spread over the whole neighbourhood. As sensible woman, she regulated the family, which she took care to let every body see; she was conductor of her nieces' education, which she took care to let every body hear; she was a sort of post-mistress general—a detector of all abuses and impositions; and deemed it her prerogative to be consulted about all the useful and useless things, which every body else could have done as well. She was liberal of her advice to the poor, always enforcing upon them the iniquity of idleness, but doing nothing for them in the way of employment—strict economy being one of the many points in which she was particularly sensible. The consequence was, while she was lecturing half the poor women in the parish for their idleness, the bread was kept out of their mouths, by the incessant carding of wool and knitting of stockings, and spinning, and reeling, and winding, and pirning,[1] that went on amongst the ladies themselves. And, by the bye, Miss Jacky is not the only sensible woman who thinks she is acting a meritorious part, when she converts what ought to be the portion of the poor into the employment of the affluent.

In short, Miss Jacky was all over sense. A skilful physiognomist would, at a single glance, have detected the sensible woman, in the erect head, the compressed lips, square elbows, and firm judicious step. Even her very garments seemed to partake of the prevailing character of their mistress: her ruff always looked more sensible than any other body's; her shawl sat most sensibly on her shoulders; her walking shoes were acknowledged to be very sensible; and she drew on her gloves with an air of sense, as if the one arm had been Seneca, the other Socrates. From what has been said, it may easily be inferred, that Miss Jacky was in fact any thing but a sensible woman; as indeed no woman can be, who bears such visible outward marks of what is in reality the most quiet and unostentatious of all good qualities. But there is a spurious sense, which passes equally well with the multitude: it is easily assumed, and still easier maintained, common truths and a grave dictatorial air being all that is necessary for its support.

Miss Grizzy's character will not admit of so long a

commentary as that of her sister: she was merely distinguishable from nothing by her simple good nature, the inextricable entanglement of her thoughts, her love of letter writing, and her friendship with Lady Maclaughlan. Miss Nicky had about as much sense as Miss Jacky; but, as no kingdom can maintain two kings, so no family can admit of two sensible women; and Nicky was, therefore, obliged to confine hers to the narrowest possible channels of house-keeping, mantua-making, &c. and to sit down for life (or at least till Miss Jacky should be married) with the dubious character of 'not wanting for sense either'. With all these little peccadilloes, the sisters possessed some good properties: They were well-meaning, kind-hearted, and, upon the whole, good-tempered; they loved one another, revered their brother, doated upon their nephews and nieces, took a lively interest in the poorest of their poor cousins, a hundred degrees removed, and had a firm conviction of the perfectibility of human nature, as exemplified in the persons of all their own friends. 'Even their failings leaned to virtue's side;'[1] for whatever they did was with the intention of doing good, though the means they made use of generally produced an opposite effect. But there are so many Miss Douglas' in the world, that doubtless every one of my readers is as well acquainted with them as I am myself. I shall, therefore, leave them to finish the picture according to their own ideas, while I return to the parlour, where the worthy spinsters are seated in expectation of the arrival of their friend.

CHAPTER IX

—————'Though both
Not equal, as their sex not equal seemed—
For contemplation he, and valour formed;
For softness she, and sweet attractive grace.'

Milton.[1]

'WHAT *can* have come over Lady Maclaughlan?' said Miss Grizzy, as she sat at the window in a dejected attitude.

'I think I hear a carriage at last,' cried Miss Jacky, turning up her ears: 'Wisht! let us listen.'

'It's only the wind,' sighed Miss Grizzy.

'It's the cart with the bread,' said Miss Nicky.

'It's Lady Maclaughlan, I assure you,' pronounced Miss Jacky.

The heavy rumble of a ponderous vehicle now proclaimed the approach of the expected visitor; which pleasing anticipation was soon changed into blissful certainty, by the approach of a high-roofed, square-bottomed, pea-green chariot, drawn by two long-tailed white horses, and followed by a lacquey in the Highland garb. Out of this equipage issued a figure, clothed in a light coloured, large flowered chintz raiment, carefully drawn though the pocket holes, either for its own preservation, or the more disinterested purpose of displaying a dark short stuff petticoat, which, with the same liberality, afforded ample scope for the survey of a pair of worsted stockings and black leather shoes, something resembling buckets. A faded red cloth jacket, which bore evident marks of having been severed from its native skirts, now acted in the capacity of a spencer. On the head rose a stupendous fabric, in the form of a cap, on the summit of which was place a black beaver hat, tied *à la poissarde*.[2] A small black satin muff in one hand, and a gold-headed walking-stick in the other, completed the dress and decoration of this personage.

The lacquey, meanwhile, advanced to the carriage; and, putting in both his hands, as if to catch something, he pulled forth a small bundle, enveloped in a military cloke, the contents of which would have baffled conjecture, but for the large cocked hat, and little booted leg, which protruded at opposite extremities.

A loud, but slow and well modulated voice, now resounded through the narrow stone passage that conducted to the drawing-room.

'Bring him in—bring him in, Philistine! I always call my man Philistine, because he has Sampson in his hands. Set him down there,' pointing to an easy chair, as the group now entered, headed by Lady Maclaughlan.

'Well, girls!' addressing the venerable spinsters, as they severally exchanged a tender salute: 'so you're all alive, I see;—humph!'

'Dear Lady Maclaughlan, allow me to introduce our beloved niece, Lady Juliana Douglas,' said Miss Grizzy, leading her up, and bridling as she spoke, with ill suppressed exultation.

'So—you're very pretty—yes, you are very pretty!' kissing the forehead, cheeks, and chin of the youthful beauty, between every pause. Then, holding her at arm's length, she surveyed her from head to foot, with elevated brows, and a broad fixed stare.

'Pray sit down, Lady Maclaughlan,' cried her three friends all at once, each tendering a chair.

'Sit down!' repeated she; 'why, what should I sit down for? I choose to stand—I don't like to sit—I never sit at home—Do I, Sir Sampson?' turning to the little warrior, who, having been seized with a violent fit of coughing on his entrance, had now sunk back, seemingly quite exhausted, while the *Philistine* was endeavouring to disencumber him of his military accoutrements.

'How very distressing Sir Sampson's cough is!' said the sympathising Miss Grizzy.

'Distressing, child! No—it's not the least distressing. How can a thing be distressing that does no harm? He's much the better of it—it's the only exercise he gets.'

'Oh! well, indeed, if that's the case, it would be a thousand pities to stop it,' replied the accommodating spinster.

'No, it wouldn't be the least pity to stop it!' returned Lady Maclaughlan, in her loud authoritative tone; 'because, though it's not distressing, it's very disagreeable. But it cannot be stopped—you might as well talk of stopping the wind—it is a cradle cough.'

'My dear Lady Maclaughlan!' screamed Sir Sampson, in a shrill pipe, as he made an effort to raise himself, and rescue his cough from this aspersion; 'how can you persist in saying so, when I have told you so often it proceeds entirely from a cold caught a few years ago, when I attended his Majesty at—' Here a violent relapse carried the conclusion of the sentence along with it.

'Let him alone—don't meddle with him,' called his lady to the assiduous nymphs who were bustling around him,—'Leave him to Philistine; he's in very good hands when he is in Philistine's.' Then resting her chin upon the head of her stick, she resumed her scrutiny of Lady Juliana.

'You really are a pretty creature! You've got a very handsome nose, and your mouth's very well, but I don't like your eyes, they're too large and too light; they're saucer eyes, and I don't like saucer eyes. Why ha'nt you black eyes? you're not a bit like your father—I knew him very well. Your mother was an heiress, your father married her for her money, and she married him to be a Countess, and so that's the history of their marriage— humph.'

This well-bred harangue was delivered in an unvarying

tone, and with unmoved muscles; for though the lady seldom failed of calling forth some conspicuous emotion, either of shame, mirth, or anger, on the countenances of her hearers, she had never been known to betray any correspondent feelings on her own; yet her features were finely formed, marked, and expressive; and, in spite of her ridiculous dress and eccentric manners, an air of dignity was diffused over her whole person, that screened her from the ridicule to which she must otherwise have been exposed. Amazement at the uncouth garb and singular address of Lady Maclaughlan, was seldom unmixed with terror at the stern imperious manner that accompanied all her actions. Such were the feelings of Lady Juliana, as she remained subjected to her rude gaze, and impertinent remarks.

'My Lady!' squeaked Sir Sampson from forth his easy chair.

'My love?' interrogated his lady as she leant upon her stick.

'I want to be introduced to my Lady Juliana Douglas; so give me your hand,' attempting, at the same time, to emerge from the huge leathern receptacle into which he had been plunged by the care of the kind sisters.

'O pray sit still, dear Sir Sampson,' cried they as usual all at once; 'our sweet niece will come to you, don't take the trouble to rise; pray don't,' each putting a hand on this man of might, as he was half risen, and pushing him down.

'Aye, come here, my dear,' said Lady Maclaughlan; 'you're abler to walk to Sir Sampson than he to you,' pulling Lady Juliana in front of the easy chair; 'there—that's her; you see she is very pretty.'

'Zounds, what is the meaning of all this!' screamed the enraged baronet: 'My Lady Juliana Douglas, I am shocked beyond expression at this freedom of my Lady's. I beg your Ladyship ten thousand pardons; pray be seated. I'm shocked; I am ready to faint at the impropriety of this introduction, so contrary to all rules of etiquette. How *could* you behave in such a manner, my Lady Maclaughlan?'

'Why, you know, my dear, your legs may be very good legs, but they can't walk,' replied she, with her usual *sang froid*.

'My Lady Maclaughlan, you perfectly confound me,' stuttering with rage. 'My Lady Juliana Douglas, see here,' stretching out a meagre shank, to which not even the military boot and large spur could give a respectable appearance: 'You see that leg strong and straight,' stroking it down; 'now, behold the fate of war!' dragging forward the other, which was shrunk and shrivelled to almost one half its original dimensions. 'These legs were once the same; but I repine not—I sacrificed it in a noble cause: to that leg my sovereign owes his life!'

'Well, I declare,—I had no idea;—I thought always it had been rheumatism,' burst from the lips of the astonished spinsters, as they crowded round the illustrious limb, and regarded it with looks of veneration.

'Humph!' emphatically uttered his lady.

'The story's a simple one, ladies, and soon told: I happened to be attending his Majesty at a review; I was then aid-de-camp to Lord——. His horse took fright, I—I—I,'—here, in spite of all the efforts that could be made to suppress it, the *royal cough* burst forth with a violence that threatened to silence its brave owner for ever.

'It's very strange you will talk, my love,' said his sympathising lady, as she supported him; 'talking never did, nor never will agree with you; it's very strange what pleasure people take in talking—humph!'

'Is there any thing dear Sir Sampson could take?' asked Miss Grizzy.

'*Could* take? I don't know what you mean by *could* take. He couldn't take the moon, if you mean that; but he

must take what I give him; so call Philistine, he knows
where my cough tincture is.'

'Oh, we have plenty of it in this press,' said Miss
Grizzy, flying to a cupboard; and, drawing forth a bottle,
she poured out a bumper, and presented it to Sir
Sampson.

'I'm poisoned!' gasped he, feebly; 'that's not my
Lady's cough-tincture.'

'Not cough-tincture!' repeated the horror-struck
doctress, as for the first time she examined the label;
'O! I declare, neither it is—it's my own stomach lotion.
Bless me, what will be done!' and she wrung her hands
in despair. 'Oh Murdoch,' flying to the *Philistine*, as he
entered with the real cough-tincture, 'I've given Sir
Sampson a dose of my own stomach lotion by mistake,
and I am terrified for the consequences!'

'Oo, but hur need na be feared,[1] hur will no be a hair
the war o't;[2] for hurs wad na tak' the feesick that the
leddie ordered hur yestreen.'[3]

'Well, I declare things are wisely ordered,' observed
Miss Grizzy; 'in that case, it may do dear Sir Sampson a
great deal of good.'

Just as this pleasing idea was suggested, Douglas and
his father entered, and the ceremony of presenting her
nephew to her friend, was performed by Miss Grizzy in
her most conciliating manner.

'Dear Lady Maclaughlan, this is our nephew Henry,
who, I know, has the highest veneration for Sir Sampson
and you. Henry, I assure you, Lady Maclaughlan takes
the greatest interest in every thing that concerns Lady
Juliana and you.'

'Humph!' rejoined her Ladyship, as she surveyed
him from head to foot: 'So your wife fell in love with
you, it seems; well, the more fool she, I never knew any
good come of love marriages.'

Douglas coloured, while he affected to laugh at this

extraordinary address, and withdrawing himself from her scrutiny, resumed his station by the side of his Juliana.

'Now, girls, I must go to my toilette; which of you am I to have for my handmaid?'

'O! we'll all go,' eagerly exclaimed the three nymphs; 'our dear niece will excuse us for a little; young people are never at a loss to amuse one another.'

'Venus and the Graces, by Jove!' exclaimed Sir Sampson, bowing with an air of gallantry; 'and now I must go and adonise[1] a little myself.'

The company then separated to perform the important offices of the toilette.

CHAPTER X

> '————Nature here
> Wanton'd as in her prime, and played at will
> Her virgin fancies.'
>
> *Milton*[2]

THE GENTLEMEN WERE already assembled round the drawing-room fire, impatiently waiting the hour of dinner,[3] when Lady Maclaughlan and her three friends entered. The masculine habiliments of the morning had been exchanged for a more feminine costume. She was now arrayed in a pompadour[4] satin négligée, and petti-coat trimmed with Brussels lace. A high starched hand-kerchief formed a complete breastwork, on which, amid a large bouquet of truly artificial roses, reposed a minia-ture of Sir Sampson, *a la militaire*.[5] A small fly cap[6] of antique lace was scarcely perceptible on the summit of a stupendous frizzled toupee,[7] hemmed in on each side by large curls. The muff and stick had been relinquished for a large fan, something resembling an Indian skreen, which she waved to and fro in one hand, while a vast brocaded work-bag was suspended from the other.

'So, Major Douglas, your servant,' said she, in answer to the constrained formal bow with which he saluted her on her entrance—'Why, it's so long since I've seen you, that you may be a grandfather for ought I know.'

The poor awkward Misses at that moment came sneaking into the room: 'As for you, girls, you'll never be grandmothers, you'll never be married, unless to wild men of the woods. I suppose you'd like that; it would save you the trouble of combing your hair, and tying your shoes, for then you could go without clothes altogether—humph! you'd be much better without clothes than to put them on as you do,' seizing upon the luckless Miss Babby, as she endeavoured to steal behind backs.

And, here, in justice to the lady, it must be owned, that, for once, she had some grounds for animadversion in the dress and appearance of the Misses Douglas.

They had staid out, running races, and riding on a poney, until near the dinner hour; and, dreading their father's displeasure should they be too late, they had, with the utmost haste, exchanged their thick morning dresses for thin muslin gowns, made, by a mantua-maker of the neighbourhood, in the extreme of a two-year old fashion, when waists *were not*.[1]

But as dame nature had been particularly lavish in the length of theirs, and the stay-maker had, according to their aunt's direction, given them *full measure* of their new dark stays,[2] there existed a visible breach between the waists of their gowns and the bands of their petticoats,[3] which they had vainly sought to adjust by a meeting. Their hair had been curled, but not combed, and dark gloves had been hastily drawn on to hide red arms.

'I suppose,' continued the stern Lady Maclaughlan,

as she twirled her victim round and round; 'I suppose
you think yourself vastly smart and well dressed. Yes,
you are very neat, very neat indeed; one would suppose
Ben Jonson had you in his eye when he composed that
song:' Then in a voice like thunder, she chanted forth—

> 'Give me a look, give me a face
> That makes simplicity a grace;
> Robes loosely flowing, hair as free,
> Such sweet neglect more taketh me.'[1]

Miss Grizzy was in the utmost perplexity, between her
inclination to urge something in extenuation for the poor
girls, and her fear of dissenting from Lady Maclaughlan,
or rather of not immediately agreeing with her; she,
therefore, steered, as usual, the middle course, and kept
saying, 'Well, children, really what Lady Maclaughlan
says, is all very true; at the same time,' turning to her
friend,—'I declare it's not much to be wondered at;
young people are so thoughtless, poor lambs!'

'Thoughtless!' in a tone that struck a panic into poor
Miss Grizzy's gentle breast. 'Thoughtless! why, what
have these girls to think about but lacing their stays, and
curling their hair? It don't signify what you wear,'
continued she, addressing the culprits, as they sat in a
corner, in all the various postures which awkwardness
suggests—'I say, it don't signify what you wear, so as it's
clean and well put on—you would be more respectable
figures in your father's night caps than with these mops.'

'What's aw this wark aboot,'[2] said the old gentleman,
angrily; 'the girlies are weel eneugh;[3] I see naething the
matter wi' them—they're no dressed like auld queens, or
stage-actresses;' and he glanced his eye from Lady
Maclaughlan to his elegant daughter-in-law, who just
then entered, hanging, according to custom, on her
husband, and preceded by Cupid; Mrs. Douglas followed,

and the sound of the dinner bell put a stop to the dispute.

'Come, my Leddie, we'll see how the dinner's dressed,' said the Laird, as he seized Lady Maclaughlan by the tip of the finger, and holding it up aloft, they marched into the dining-room.

'Permit me, my Lady Juliana Douglas,' said the little Baronet, with much difficulty hobbling towards her, and attempting to take her hand[1]—'Come, Harry, love; here, Cupid,' cried she; and without noticing the enraged Sir Sampson, she passed on, humming a tune, and leaning upon her husband.

'Astonishing! perfectly astonishing!' exclaimed the Baronet; 'how a young woman of Lady Juliana's rank and fashion, should be guilty of such a solecism in good breeding.'

'She is very young,' said Mrs. Douglas, smiling, as he limped along with her, 'and you must make allowances for her; but, indeed, I think her beauty must ever be a sufficient excuse for any little errors she may commit, with a person of such taste and gallantry as Sir Sampson Maclaughlan.'

The little Baronet smiled, pressed the hand he held; and, soothed by the well-timed compliment, he seated himself next to Lady Juliana with some complacency. As she insisted on having her husband on the other side of her, Mr. Douglas was condemned to take his station by the hated Lady Maclaughlan, who, for the first time, observing Mrs. Douglas, called to her.

'Come here, my love; I hav'nt seen you these hundred years;' then seizing her face between her hands, she saluted her in the usual style: 'There,' at length releasing Mrs. Douglas from her gripe—'there's for you; I love you very much; you're neither a fool, nor a hoyden; you're a fine intelligent being.'

Having carefully rolled up, and deposited her gloves in her pocket, she pulled out a pin-cushion, and calling

Miss Bella, desired her to pin her napkin over her
shoulders; which done, she began to devour her soup
in silence.

Peace was, however, of short duration. Old Donald,
in removing a dish of whipt-cream, unfortunately over-
turned one upon Lady Maclaughlan's pompadour satin
petticoat; the only part of her dress that was unprotected.

'Do you see what you have done, you old Donald
you!' cried she, seizing the culprit by the sleeve; 'why,
you've got St. Vitus' dance—a fit hand to carry whipt-
cream to be sure! why, I could as well carry a custard on
point of a bayonet—humph!'

'Dear me, Donald, how could you be so senseless!'
cried Miss Jacky.

'Preserve me, Donald, I thought you had more sense!'
squeaked Miss Nicky.

'I am sure, Donald, that was na' like you!' said Miss
Grizzy, as the friends all flocked around the petticoat,
each suggesting a different remedy.

'It's all of you, girls, that this has happened; why
can't you have a larger table-cloth upon your table?
and that old man has the palsy; why don't you electrify
him?' in a tone admirably calculated to have that effect.

'I declare, it's all very true,' observed Miss Grizzy;
'the table-cloth *is* very small, and Donald certainly *does*
shake, that cannot be denied;' but, lowering her voice,
'he is so obstinate, we really don't know what to do with
him; my sisters, and I, attempted to use the flesh-brush
with him.'

'Oh, and an excellent thing it is; I make Philistine
rub Sir Sampson every morning and night. If it was not
for that, and his cough, nobody would know whether
he were dead or alive; I don't believe he would know
himself—humph!'

Sir Sampson's lemon-face assumed an orange hue, as
he overheard this domestic detail; but not daring to

contradict the facts, he prudently turned a deaf ear to them, and attempted to carry on a flirtation with Lady Juliana, through the medium of Cupid, whom he had coaxed upon his knee.

Dinner being at length ended, toasts succeeded;[1] and each of the ladies having given her favourite laird, the signal of retreat was given, and a general movement took place.

Lady Juliana throwing herself upon a sofa, with her pugs, called Mrs. Douglas to her: 'Do, sit down here, and talk with me,' yawned she.

Her sister-in-law, with great good humour, fetched her work, and seated herself by the spoilt child.

'What strange thing is that you are making?' asked she, as Mrs. Douglas pulled out her knitting.

'It's a child's stocking,' replied her sister-in-law.

'A child's stocking! Oh, by the bye, have you a great many children?'

'I have none,' answered Mrs. Douglas, with a half-stifled sigh.

'None at all!' repeated Lady Juliana, with surprise; 'then, why do you make children's stockings?'

'I make them for those whose parents cannot afford to purchase them.'

'La! what poor wretches they must be, that can't afford to buy stockings,' rejoined Lady Juliana, with a yawn; 'it's monstrous good of you to make them, to be sure; but it must be a shocking bore! and such a trouble!' and another long yawn succeeded.

'Not half such a bore to me, as to sit idle,' returned Mrs. Douglas, with a smile, 'nor near so much trouble as you undergo with your favourites.'

Lady Juliana made no reply, but turning from her sister-in-law, soon was, or affected to be, sound asleep, from which she was only roused by the entrance of the gentlemen. 'A rubber or a reel, my Leddie?' asked the laird, going up to his daughter-in-law.

'Julia, love,' said her husband, 'my father asks you if you choose cards or dancing.'

'There's nobody to dance with,'[1] said she, casting a languid glance around; 'I'll play at cards.'

'Not whist, surely!' said Henry.

'Whist! oh heavens, no.'

'Weel, weel, you youngsters will get a round game; come, my Leddy Maclaughlan, Grizzy, Mrs. Douglas, hey for the odd trick and the honours!'[2]

'What would your Ladyship choose to play at?' asked Miss Jacky, advancing with a pack of cards in one hand, and a box of counters in the other.

'O, any thing; I like loo[3] very well, or quadrille,[4] or —I really don't care what.'

The Misses, who had gathered round, and were standing gaping in joyful expectation of Pope Joan,[5] or a pool at commerce,[6] here exchanged sorrowful glances.

'I am afraid the young people don't play these games,' replied Miss Jacky; 'but we've counters enough,' shaking her little box, 'for Pope Joan, and we all know that.'

'Pope Joan! I never heard of such a game,' replied Lady Juliana.

'O, we can soon learn you,' said Miss Nicky, who having spread the green cloth on the tea-table, now advanced to join the consultation.

'I hate to be taught,' said Lady Juliana, with a yawn; 'besides, I am sure it must be something very stupid.'

'Ask if she plays commerce,' whispered Miss Bella to Miss Babby.

The question was put, but with no better success, and the young ladies' faces again bespoke their disappointment; which their brother observing, he good-naturedly declared his perfect knowledge of commerce; 'and I must insist upon teaching you, Juliana,' gently dragging her to the table.

'What's the pool to be?' asked one of the young ladies.

'I'm sure I don't know,' said the aunts, looking to each other.

'I suppose we must make it sixpence,' said Miss Jacky, after a whispering consultation with her sister.

'In that case we can afford nothing to the best hand,' observed Miss Nicky. 'And we ought to have five lives and grace,'[1] added one of the nieces.

These points having been conceded, the preliminaries were at length settled. The cards were slowly *doled* out by Miss Jacky; and Lady Juliana was carefully instructed in the rules of the game, and strongly recommended always to try for a sequence,[2] or pairs, &c. 'And if you win,' rejoined Miss Nicky, shaking the snuffer-stand in which was deposited the sixpences, 'you get all this.'

As may be conjectured, Lady Juliana's patience could not survive more than one life;[3] she had no notion of playing for sixpences, and could not be at the trouble to attend to any instructions; she therefore quickly retired in disgust, leaving the aunts and nieces to struggle for the glorious prize.

CHAPTER XI

'O thoughtless mortals, ever blind to fate,
Too soon dejected, and too soon elate,
Sudden these honours shall be snatched away!'

Pope[4]

'MY DEAR CHILD, you played that last stroke like a perfect natural,' cried Lady Maclaughlan to Miss Grizzy, as, the rubber ended, they arose from the table.

'Indeed, I declare, I daresay I did,' replied her friend, in a deprecating tone.

'Daresay you did! I know you did—humph! I knew

the ace lay with you; I knew that as well as if I had seen it. I suppose you have eyes—but I don't know; if you have, did'nt you see Glenfern turn up the king, and yet you returned his lead—returned your adversary's lead[1] in the face of his king. I've been telling you these twenty years, not to return your adversary's lead; nothing can be more despicable; nothing can be a greater proof of imbecility of mind—humph!' Then, seating herself, she began to exercise her fan with considerable activity. 'This has been the most disagreeable day I ever spent in this house, girls. I don't know what's come over you, but you are all wrong; my petticoat's ruined; my pocket's picked at cards: It won't do, girls; it won't do—humph!'

'I am sure, I can't understand it,' said Miss Grizzy, in a rueful accent; 'there really appears to have been some fatality.'

'Fatality!—humph! I wish you would give every thing its right name. What do you mean by fatality?'

'I declare—I am sure—I—I really don't know,' stammered the unfortunate Grizzy.

'Do you mean that the spilling of the custard was the work of an angel?' demanded her unrelenting friend.

'O, certainly not.'

'Or that it was the devil tempted you to throw away your ace there? I suppose there's a fatality in our going to supper just now,' continued she, as her deep-toned voice resounded through the passage that conducted to the dining room; 'and I suppose it will be called a fatality, if that old Fate,' pointing to Donald, 'scalds me to death with that mess of porridge he's going to put on the table—humph!'

No such fatality, however, occurred; and the rest of the evening passed off in as much harmony as could be expected from the very heterogeneous parts of which the society was formed.

The family group had already assembled round the breakfast table, with the exception of Lady Juliana, who chose to take that meal in bed; but, contrary to her usual custom, no Lady Maclaughlan had yet made her appearance.

'The scones will be like leather,' said Miss Grizzy, as she wrapped another napkin round them.

'The eggs will be like snow balls,' cried Miss Jacky, popping them into the slop-bason.[1]

'The tea will be like brandy,' observed Miss Nicky, as she poured more water to the three tea spoonfuls she had infused.

'I wish we saw our breakfast,' said the Laird, as he finished the newspapers, and deposited his spectacles in his pocket.

'It's very hard to be kept starving all day for that ——,' said Mr. Douglas, as he swallowed a slice of cold beef, that carried the conclusion of the sentence along with it.

At that moment the door opened, and the person in question entered in her travelling dress, followed by Sir Sampson, Philistine bringing up the rear with a large green bag and a little band-box.

'I hope your bed was warm and comfortable? I hope you rested well? I hope Sir Sampson's quite well?' immediately burst, as if from a thousand voices, while the sisters officiously fluttered round their friend.

'I rested very ill; my bed was very uncomfortable; and Sir Sampson's as sick as a cat—humph!'

Three disconsolate 'Bless me's!' here burst forth.

'Perhaps your bed was too hard?' said Miss Grizzy.

'Or too soft?' suggested Miss Jacky.

'Or too hot?' added Miss Nicky.

'It was neither too hard, nor too soft, nor too hot, nor too cold,' thundered the Lady, as she seated herself at the table; 'but it was all of them.'

'I declare, that's most distressing,' said Miss Grizzy, in

a tone of sorrowful amazement. 'Was your head high enough, dear Lady Maclaughlan?'

'Perhaps it was too high,' said Miss Jacky.

'I know nothing more disagreeable than a high head,' remarked Miss Nicky.

'Except a fool's head—humph!'

The sound of a carriage here set all ears on full stretch, and presently the well-known pea-green drew up.

'Dear me! Bless me! Goodness me!' shrieked the three ladies at once. 'Surely, Lady Maclaughlan, you can't—you don't—you won't; this must be a mistake.'

'There's no mistake in the matter, girls,' replied their friend, with her accustomed *sang froid*. 'I'm going home; so I ordered the carriage; that's all—humph!'

'Going home!' faintly murmured the disconsolate spinsters.

'What! I suppose you think I ought to stay here and have another petticoat spoiled; or lose another half-crown at cards; or have the finishing stroke put to Sir Sampson—humph!'

'Oh! Lady Maclaughlan!' was three times uttered in reproachful accents.

'I don't know what else I should stay for; you are not yourselves, girls; you've all turned topsy-turvy. I've visited here these twenty years, and I never saw things in the state they are now—humph!'

'I declare it's very true,' sighed Miss Grizzy; 'we certainly are a little in confusion, that can't be denied.'

'Denied! Why, can you deny that my petticoat's ruined? Can you deny that my pocket was picked of half-a-crown for nothing? Can you deny that Sir Sampson has been half-poisoned? and—'

'My Lady Maclaughlan,' interrupted the enraged husband, 'I—I—I am surprised—I am shocked! Zounds, my Lady, I won't suffer this! I cannot stand it;' and pushing his tea-cup away, he arose, and limped to the window. Philistine here entered to inform his mistress, that 'aw thing was ready.'—'Steady, boys steady! I always am ready,'[1] responded the Lady in a tone adapted to the song. 'Now I am ready—say nothing, girls—you know my rules—Here, Philistine, wrap up Sir Sampson, and put him in—Get along, my love—Good bye, girls; and I hope you will all be restored to your right senses soon.'

'O, Lady Maclaughlan!' whined the weeping Grizzy, as she embraced her friend, who somewhat melted at the signs of her distress, bawled out from the carriage, as the door was shut, 'Well, God bless you, girls, and make you what you have been; and come to Lochmarlie Castle soon, and bring your wits along with you.'

The carriage then drove off, and the three disconsolate sisters returned to the parlour, to hold a cabinet council as to the causes of the late disasters.

CHAPTER XII

'————If there be cure or charm
To respite or relieve, or slack the pain
Of this ill mansion.'

                                          Milton.[2]

TIME, WHICH GENERALLY alleviates ordinary distresses, served only to augment the severity of Lady Juliana's; as day after day rolled heavily on, and found her still an inmate of Glenfern Castle. Destitute of every resource in herself, she yet turned with contempt from the scanty sources of occupation or amusement that were suggested by others; and Mrs. Douglas' attempts to teach her to play at chess and read Shakespeare, were as unsuccessful as the endeavours of the good aunts to persuade her to study Fordyce's Sermons,[1] and make baby linen.

In languid dejection, or fretful repinings, did the unhappy beauty therefore consume the tedious hours, while her husband sought alternately to soothe with fondness he no longer felt, or flatter with hopes which he knew to be groundless. To his father alone could he now look for any assistance, and from him he was not likely to obtain it in the form he desired; as the old gentleman repeatedly declared his utter inability to advance him any ready money, or to allow him more than a hundred a year,[2] moreover to be paid quarterly; a sum which could not defray their expenses to London.

Such was the state of affairs, when the Laird one morning entered the dining room, with a face of much importance, and addressed his son with 'Weel, Harry, you're a lucky man; and it's an ill wind that blaws naebody gude:[3] here's puir[4] Macglashan gane like snaw aff a dyke.'

'Macglashan gone!' exclaimed Miss Grizzy. 'Impossible, brother; it was only yesterday I sent him a large blister for his back?'

'And I,' said Miss Jacky, 'talked to him for upwards of two hours last night, on the impropriety of his allowing his daughter to wear white gowns on Sunday.'

'By my troth, an' that was eneugh to kill ony man,' muttered the Laird.

'How I am to derive any benefit from this important demise, is more than I can perceive,' said Henry, in a somewhat contemptuous tone.

'You see,' replied his father, 'that by our agreement, his farm falls vacant in consequence.'

'And I hope I am to succeed to it?' replied the son, with a smile of derision.

'Exactly—By my faith, but you have a bein downset.[5] There's three thousand and seventy-five acres of as good sheep-walk as any in the whole country-side; and I shall advance you stocking and stedding,[1] and every thing complete to your very peat-stacks. What think ye of that?' slapping his son's shoulder, and rubbing his own hands with delight as he spoke.

Horror-struck at a scheme which appeared to him a thousand times worse than any thing his imagination had ever painted, poor Henry stood in speechless consternation; while 'charming! excellent! delightful!' was echoed by the aunts, as they crowded round, wishing him joy, and applauding their brother's generosity.

'What will our sweet niece say to this, I wonder?' said the innocent Grizzy, who in truth wondered none. 'I would like to see her face when she hears it;' and her own was puckered into various shapes of delight.

'I have no doubt but her good sense will teach her to appreciate properly the blessings of her lot,' observed the more reflecting Jacky.

'She has had her own good luck,' quoth the sententious Nicky, 'to find such a down-set all cut and dry.'

At that instant the door opened, and the favoured individual in question entered. In vain Douglas strove to impose silence on his father and aunts. The latter sat, bursting with impatience to break out into exclamation, while the former, advancing to his fair daughter-in-law, saluted her as 'Lady Clackandow!' Then the torrent burst forth; and, stupified with surprise, Lady Juliana suffered herself to be kissed and hugged by the whole host of aunts and nieces; while the very walls seemed to reverberate the shouts; and the pugs and mackaw, who never failed to take part in every commotion, began to bark and scream in chorus.

The old gentleman, clapping his hands to his ears, rushed out of the room. His son, cursing his aunts, and every thing around him, kicked Cupid, and gave the

mackaw a box on the ear, as he also quitted the apartment, with more appearance of anger than he had ever
yet betrayed.

The tumult at length began to subside. The mackaw's
screams gave place to a low quivering croak; and the
insulted pug's yells yielded to a gentle whine. The aunts'
obstreperous joy began to be chastened with fear for the
consequences that might follow an abrupt disclosure;
and, while Lady Juliana condoled with her favourites,
it was concerted between the prudent aunts, that the
joyful news should be broke to their niece in the most
cautious manner possible. For that purpose, Misses
Grizzy and Jacky seated themselves on each side of her;
and, after duly preparing their voices, by sundry small
hems, Miss Grizzy thus began:

'I'm sure—I declare—I dare say, my dear Lady
Juliana, you must think we are all distracted.'

Her auditor made no attempt to contradict the
supposition.

'We certainly ought, to be sure, to have been more
cautious, considering your delicate situation; but the
joy—though, indeed, it seems cruel to say so. And I am
sure you will sympathise, my dear niece, in the cause,
when you hear that it is occasioned by our poor neighbour Macglashan's death, which, I'm sure, was quite
unexpected. Indeed, I declare I can't conceive how it
came about; for Lady Maclaughlan, who is an excellent
judge of these things, thought he was really a remarkable
stout-looking man for his time of life; and indeed, except
occasional colds, which you know we are all subject to, I
really never knew him complain. At the same time—'

'I don't think, sister, you are taking the right method
of communicating the intelligence to our niece,' said
Miss Jacky.

'You cannot communicate any thing that would give
me the least pleasure, unless you could tell me that I was

going to leave this place,' cried Lady Juliana, in a voice of deep despondency.

'Indeed! if it can afford your Ladyship so much pleasure to be at liberty to quit the hospitable mansion of your amiable husband's respectable father,' said Miss Jacky, with an inflamed visage and outspread hands, 'you are at perfect liberty to depart when you think proper. The generosity, I may say the munificence, of my excellent brother, has now put it in your power to do as you please, and to form your own plans.'

'O delightful!' exclaimed Lady Juliana, starting up; 'now I shall be quite happy. Where's Harry? Does he know—is he gone to order the carriage—can we get away to-day?' And she was flying out of the room, when Miss Jacky caught her by one hand, while Miss Grizzy secured the other.

'Oh! pray don't detain me! I must find Harry; and I have all my things to put up,' struggling to release herself from the gripe of the sisters; when the door opened, and Harry entered, eager, yet dreading, to know the effects of the *eclaircissement*.[1] His surprise was extreme at beholding his wife, with her eyes sparkling, her cheeks glowing, and her whole countenance expressing extreme pleasure. Darting from her keepers, she bounded towards him with the wildest ejaculations of delight; while he stood alternately gazing at her and his aunts, seeking, by his eyes, the explanation he feared to demand.

'My dearest Juliana, what is the meaning of all this?' he at length articulated.

'O, you cunning thing! So you think I don't know that your father has given you a great—great quantity of money, and that we may go away whenever we please, and do just as we like, and live in London, and—and— Oh delightful!' And she bounded and skipped before the eyes of the petrified spinsters.

'In the name of heaven, what does all this mean?'

asked Henry, addressing his aunts, who, for the first time in their lives, were struck dumb by astonishment. But Miss Jacky, at length recollecting herself, turned to Lady Juliana, who was still testifying her delight by a variety of childish but graceful movements, and thus addressed her:

'Permit me to put a few questions to your Ladyship, in presence of those who were witnesses of what has already passed.'

'O, I can't endure to be asked questions; besides I have no time to answer them.'

'Your Ladyship must excuse me; but I can't permit you to leave this room under the influence of an error. Have the goodness to answer me the following questions, and you will then be at liberty to depart: Did I inform your Ladyship, that my brother had given my nephew a great quantity of money?'

'O yes—a great, great deal—I don't know how much, though—'

'Did I?' returned her interrogator.

'Come, come, have done with all this confounded nonsense!' exclaimed Henry passionately: 'Do you imagine I will allow Lady Juliana to stand here all day, to answer all the absurd questions that come into the heads of three old women? You stupify and bewilder her with your eternal tattling and round-about harangues.' And he paced the room in a paroxysm of rage, while his wife suspended her dancing, and stood in breathless amazement.

'I declare—I'm sure—it's a thousand pities that there should have been any mistake made,' whined poor Miss Grizzy.

'The only remedy is to explain the matter quickly,' observed Miss Nicky; 'better late than never.'[1]

'I have done,' said Miss Jacky, seating herself with much dignity.

'The short and the long of it is this,' said Miss Nicky: 'My brother has not made Henry a present of money. I assure you money is not so rife; but he has done what is much better for you both,—he has made over to him that fine thriving farm of poor Macglashan's.'

'No money!' repeated Lady Juliana, in a disconsolate tone: then quickly brightening up, 'It would have been better, to be sure, to have had the money directly; but you know we can easily sell the estate. How long will it take?—a week?'

'Sell Clackandow!' exclaimed the three horror-struck daughters of the house of Douglas: 'Sell Clackandow! Oh! oh! oh!'

'What else could we do with it?' inquired her Ladyship.

'Live at it, to be sure,' cried all three.

'Live at it!' repeated she, with a shriek of horror that vied with that of the spinsters—'Live at it! Live on a thriving farm! Live all my life in such a place as this! Oh! the very thought is enough to kill me!'

'There is no occasion to think or say any more about it,' interrupted Henry, in a calmer tone; and, glancing round on his aunts, 'I therefore desire no more may be said on the subject.'

'And is this really all! And have you got no money? And are we not going away?' gasped the disappointed Lady Juliana, as she gave way to a violent burst of tears, that terminated in a fit of hysterics; at sight of which, the good spinsters entirely forgot their wrath; and, while one burnt feathers under her nose, and another held her hands, a third drenched her in floods of Lady Maclaughlan's hysteric water. After going through the regular routine, the lady's paroxysm subsided; and, being carried to bed, she soon sobbed herself into a feverish slumber; in which state the harassed husband left her, to attend a summons from his father.

CHAPTER XIII

—————'Haply this life is best,
Sweetest to you, well corresponding
With your stiff age; but unto us it is
A cell of ignorance, a prison for a debtor.'

Cymbeline.[1]

HE FOUND THE old gentleman in no very complaisant humour, from the disturbances that had taken place, but the chief cause of which he was still in ignorance of. He therefore accosted his son with—

'What was the meaning o' a' that skirling[2] and squeeling I heard a while ago? By my faith, there's nae bearing this din! Thae beasts o' your wife's are aneugh to drive a body oot o' their judgment. But she maun gie up thae maggots[3] when she becomes a farmer's wife. She maun get stirks and stots[4] to make pets o', if she maun hae *four-fitted* favourites; but, to my mind, it wad set her better[5] to be carrying a wise-like wean[6] in her arms, than trailing aboot wi' thae confoonded dougs an' paurits.'[7]

Henry coloured, bit his lips, but made no reply to this elegant address of his father's; who continued, 'I sent for you, Sir, to have some conversation about this farm of Macglashan's; so sit down there, till[8] I shew you the plans.'

Hardly conscious of what he was doing, poor Henry gazed in silent confusion, as his father pointed out the various properties of this his future possession. Wholly occupied in debating within himself how he was to decline the offer, without a down-right quarrel, he heard, without understanding a word, all the old gentleman's plans and proposals for building dikes, draining moss, &c.; and, perfectly unconscious of what he was doing, yielded a ready assent to all the improvements that were suggested.

'Then as for the hooss and offices[9]—let me see,'

continued the Laird, as he rolled up the plans of the
farm, and pulled forth that of the dwelling-house, from
a bundle of papers: 'Aye, here it is. By my troth, ye'll be
weel lodged here. The hooss is in a manner quite new,
for it has never had a brush upon it yet. And there's a
byre—fient a bit, if I would mean the best man i' the
country to sleep there himself.'[1]

A pause followed, during which Glenfern was busily
employed in poring over his parchment; then taking off
his spectacles, and surveying his son, 'And now, Sir,
that you've heard a' the oots an' ins[2] o' the business,
what think you your farm should bring you at the year's
end?'

'I—I—I'm sure—I—I don't know,' stammered poor
Henry, awakening from his reverie.

'Come, come, gie a guess.'

'I really—I cannot—I haven't the least idea.'

'I desire, Sir, ye'll say something directly, that I may
judge whether or no ye hae common sense,' cried the
old gentleman angrily.

'I should suppose—I imagine—I don't suppose it
will exceed seven or eight hundred a year,' said his son,
in the greatest trepidation at this trial of his intellect.

'Seven or eight hunder deevils!' cried the incensed
Laird, starting up and pushing his papers from him;
'by my faith, I believe ye're a born idiot! Seven or eight
hunder pounds!' repeated he, at least a dozen times, as
he whisked up and down the little apartment with
extraordinary velocity, while poor Henry affected to be
busily employed in gathering up the parchments with
which the floor was strewed.

'I'll tell you what, Sir,' continued he, stopping; 'you're
no fit to manage a farm; you're as ignorant as yon coo,[3]
an' as senseless as its cauf.[4] Wi' gude management,
Clackandow should produce you twa hunder and odd
pounds yearly; but, in your guiding, I doot[5] if it will

yield the half. However, tak it or want it, mind me, Sir,
that it's a' ye hae to trust to in my lifetime; so ye may
mak the maist o't.'[1]

Various and painful were the emotions that struggled
in Henry's breast at this declaration. Shame, regret,
indignation, all burned within him; but the fear he
entertained of his father, and the consciousness of his
absolute dependence, chained his tongue, while the
bitter emotions that agitated him, painted themselves
legibly in his countenance. His father observed his
agitation; and, mistaking the cause, felt somewhat
softened at what he conceived his son's shame and
penitence for his folly: he therefore extended his hand
towards him, saying 'Weel, weel, nae mair aboot it;[2]
Clackandow's yours, as soon as I can put you in possession: in the mean time, stay still here, and welcome.'

'I—am much obliged to you for the offer, Sir; I—feel
very grateful for your kindness,' at length articulated his
son; 'but—I—am, as you observe, so perfectly ignorant
of country matters, that I—I—In short, I am afraid I
should make a bad hand of the business.'

'Nae doot, nae doot ye would, if ye was left to your ain[3]
discretion; but ye'll get mair sense, and I shall put ye
upon a method, and provide ye wi' a grieve;[4] an' if
you are active, and your wife managing, there's nae fear
o' you.'[5]

'But Lady Juliana, Sir, has never been accustomed—'

'Let her serve an apprenticeship to your aunts; she
cou'dna be in a better school.'

'But her education, Sir, has been so different from what
would be required in that station,' resumed her husband,
choking with vexation, at the idea of his beauteous high-
born bride being doomed to the drudgery of household
cares.

'Edication![6] what has her edication been, to mak her
different frae other women? If a woman can nurse her

bairns,[1] mak their claes,[2] and manage her hooss, what mair need she do? If she can play a tune on the spinnet, and dance a reel, and play a rubber at whist—nae doot these are accomplishments, but they're soon learnt. Edication! pooh!—I'll be bound Leddy Jully Anie wull mak as gude a figure by and bye as the best edicated woman in the country.'

'But she dislikes the country, and—'

She'll soon come to like it. Wait a wee[3] till she has a wheen bairns,[4] an' a hooss o' her ain, an' I'll be bound she'll be happy as the day's lang.'

'But the climate does not agree with her,' continued the tender husband, almost driven to extremities by the persevering simplicity of his father.

'Stay a wee till she gets to Clackandow! there's no a finer, freer-aired situation in a' Scotland: the air's sharpish, to be sure, but fine and bracing; and you have a braw[5] peat moss at your back to keep you warm.'

Finding it in vain to attempt *insinuating* his objections to a pastoral life, poor Henry was at length reduced to the necessity of coming to the point with the old gentleman, and telling him plainly, that it was not at all suited to his inclinations, or Lady Juliana's rank and beauty.

Vain would be the attempt to paint the fiery wrath and indignation of the ancient Highlander, as the naked truth stood revealed before him: that his son despised the occupation of his fathers, even the feeding of sheep, and the breeding of black cattle; and that his high-born spouse was above fulfilling those duties, which he had ever considered the chief end for which woman was created. He swore, stamped, screamed, and even skipped with rage, and, in short, went through all the evolutions, as usually performed by testy old gentlemen, on first discovering that they have disobedient sons and undutiful daughters. Henry, who, though uncommonly good tempered, inherited a portion of his father's warmth, became at length irritated at the invectives that were so liberally bestowed on him, and replied in language less respectful than the old Laird was accustomed to hear; and the altercation became so violent, that they parted in mutual anger; Henry returning to his wife's apartment in a state of the greatest disquietude he had ever known. To her childish questions, and tiresome complaints, he no longer vouchsafed to reply, but paced the chamber with a disordered mien, in sullen silence; till at length, distracted by her reproaches, and disgusted with her selfishness, he rushed from the apartment, and quitted the house.

CHAPTER XIV

'Never talk to me; I will weep.'
As You Like It.[1]

TWICE HAD THE dinner bell been loudly sounded by old Donald, and the family of Glenfern were all assembled, yet their fashionable guests had not appeared. Impatient of delay, Miss Jacky hastened to ascertain the cause. Presently she returned in the utmost perturbation, and announced, that Lady Juliana was in bed in a high fever, and Henry nowhere to be found. The whole eight rushed up stairs to ascertain the fact, leaving the old gentleman much discomposed at this unseasonable delay.

Some time elapsed ere they again returned, which they did with lengthened faces, and in extreme perturbation. They had found their noble niece, according to Miss Jacky's report, in bed—according to Miss Grizzy's opinion, in a brain fever; as she no sooner perceived them enter, than she covered her head with the bed-clothes, and continued screaming for them to be gone, till they had actually quitted the apartment.

'And what proves beyond a doubt, that our sweet niece is not herself,' continued poor Miss Grizzy, in a lamentable tone, 'is, that we appeared to her in every form but our own! She sometimes took us for cats; then thought we were ghosts haunting her; and, in short, it is impossible to tell all the things she called us; and she screams so for Harry to come and take her away, that I am sure—I declare—I don't know what's come over her!'

Mrs. Douglas could scarce suppress a smile at the simplicity of the good spinsters. Her husband and she had gone out, immediately after breakfast, to pay a visit a few miles off, and did not return till near the dinner hour. They were therefore ignorant of all that had been acted during their absence; but, as she suspected something was amiss, she requested the rest of the company would proceed to dinner, and leave her to ascertain the nature of Lady Juliana's disorder.

'Don't come near me!' shrieked her Ladyship, on hearing the door open: 'Send Harry to take me away—I don't want any body but Harry!'—and a torrent of tears, sobs, and exclamations followed.

'My dear Lady Juliana,' said Mrs. Douglas, softly approaching the bed, 'compose yourself; and if my presence is disagreeable to you, I shall immediately withdraw.'

'O, is it you?' cried her sister-in-law, uncovering her face at the sound of her voice: 'I thought it had been these frightful old women come to torment me; and I shall die—I know I shall—if ever I look at them again. But I don't dislike *you*; so you may stay if you choose, though I don't want any body but Harry, to come and take me away.'

A fresh fit of sobbing here impeded her utterance; and

Mrs. Douglas, compassionating her distress, while she despised her folly, seated herself by the bedside, and taking her hand, in the sweetest tone of complacency, attempted to soothe her into composure.

'The only way in which you can be less miserable,' said Mrs. Douglas, in a soothing tone, 'is to support your present situation with patience, which you may do by looking forward to brighter prospects. It is *possible* that your stay here may be short; and it is *certain* that it is in your own power to render your life more agreeable, by endeavouring to accommodate yourself to the peculiarities of your husband's family. No doubt, they are often tiresome and ridiculous; but they are always kind and well meaning.'

'You may say what you please, but I think them all odious creatures; and I won't live here with patience; and I shan't be agreeable to them; and all the talking in the world won't make me less miserable. If you were me, you would be just the same; but you have never been in London—that's the reason.'

'Pardon me,' replied her sister-in-law, 'I spent many years of my life there.'

'You lived in London!' repeated Lady Juliana, in astonishment. 'And how then can you contrive to exist here?'

'I not only contrive to exist, but to be extremely contented with existence,' said Mrs. Douglas, with a smile. Then assuming a more serious air, 'I possess health, peace of mind, and the affections of a worthy husband; and I should be very undeserving of these blessings, were I to give way to useless regrets, or indulge in impious repinings, because my happiness might once have been more perfect, and still admits of improvement.'

'I don't understand you,' said Lady Juliana, with a peevish yawn. 'Who did you live with in London?'

'With my aunt, Lady Audley.'

'With Lady Audley!' repeated her sister-in-law, in accents of astonishment. 'Why, I have heard of her; she lived quite in the world; and gave balls and assemblies; so that's the reason you are not so disagreeable as the rest of them. Why did you not remain with her, or marry an Englishman? but I suppose, like me, you did'nt know what Scotland was!'

Happy to have excited an interest, even through the medium of childish curiosity, in the bosom of her fashionable relative, Mrs. Douglas briefly related such circumstances of her past life, as she judged proper to communicate; but as she sought rather to amuse than instruct by her simple narrative, we shall allow her to pursue her charitable intentions, while we do more justice to her character, by introducing her regularly to the acquaintance of our readers.

HISTORY OF MRS. DOUGLAS

'The selfish heart deserves the pang it feels;
More generous sorrow, while it sinks, exalts,
And conscious virtue mitigates the pang.'

Young.[1]

MRS. DOUGLAS WAS, on the maternal side, related to an English family. Her mother had died in giving birth to her; and her father, shortly after, falling in the service of his country, she had been consigned in infancy to the care of her aunt. Lady Audley had taken charge of her, on condition, that she should never be claimed by her Scottish relations, for whom that lady entertained as much aversion as contempt. A latent feeling of affection for her departed sister, and a large portion of family pride, had prompted her wish of becoming the protectress of her orphan niece; and possessed of a high sense of rectitude and honour, she fulfilled the duty, thus voluntarily imposed, in a manner that secured the unshaken gratitude of the virtuous Alicia.

Lady Audley was a character more esteemed and feared than loved, even by those with whom she was most intimate. Firm, upright, and rigid, she exacted from others, those inflexible virtues, which in herself she found no obstacle to performing. Neglecting the softer attractions which shed their benign influence over the commerce of social life, she was content to enjoy the esteem of her associates; for friends she had none. She sought in the world for objects to fill up the void which her heart could not supply. She loved eclat, and had succeeded in creating herself an existence of importance in the circles of high life, which she considered more as due to her consequence, than essential to her enjoyment. She had early in life been left a widow, with the sole tutelage and management of an only son; whose large estate she regulated with the most admirable prudence and judgment.

Alicia Malcolm was put under the care of her aunt at two years of age. A governess had been procured for her, whose character was such as not to impair the promising dispositions of her pupil. Alicia was gifted by nature with a warm affectionate heart, and a calm imagination attempered its influence. Her governess, a woman of a strong understanding and enlarged mind, early instilled into her a deep and strong sense of religion; and to it she owed the support which had safely guided her through the most trying vicissitudes.

When at the age of seventeen, Alicia Malcolm was produced in the world, she was a rational, cheerful, and sweet tempered girl, with a fine formed person, and a countenance in which was so clearly painted the sunshine of her breast, that it attracted the *beinveillance*,[1] even of those who had not taste or judgment to define the charm. Her open natural manner, blending the frankness of the Scotch with the polished reserve of the English woman, her total exemption from vanity, were calculated alike to please others, and maintain her own cheerfulness undimmed by a single cloud.

Lady Audley felt for her niece a sentiment which she mistook for affection: her self-approbation was gratified at the contemplation of a being who owed every advantage to her, and whom she had rescued from the coarseness and vulgarity which she deemed inseparable from the manners of every Scotch woman.

If Lady Audley really loved any human being, it was her son. In him were centred her dearest interests; on his aggrandisement and future importance hung her most sanguine hopes. She had acted contrary to the advice of her male relations, and followed her own judgment, by giving her son a private education. He was brought up under her own eye, by a tutor of deep erudition, but who was totally unfitted for forming the mind, and compensating for those advantages which may be derived from a public education. The circumstances of his education, therefore, combined rather to stifle the exposure than to destroy the existence of some very dangerous qualities that seemed inherent in Sir Edmund's nature. He was ardent, impetuous, and passionate, though these propensities were cloked by a reserve, partly natural, and partly arising from the repelling manners of his mother and tutor.

His was not the effervescence of character, which bursts forth on every trivial occasion; but when any powerful cause awakened the slumbering inmates of his breast, they blazed with an uncontrouled fury, that defied all opposition, and overleaped all bounds of reason and decorum.

Experience often shews us, that minds formed of the most opposite attributes, more forcibly attract each other, than those which appear cast in the same mould. The source of this fascination is difficult to trace; it possesses not reason for its basis, yet it is perhaps the more tyrannical in its influence from that very cause. The weakness of our natures occasionally makes us feel a potent charm in 'errors of a noble mind.'[1]

Sir Edmund Audley and Alicia Malcolm proved examples of this observation. The affection of childhood had so gradually ripened into a warmer sentiment, that neither were conscious of the nature of that sentiment till after it had attained strength to cast a material influence on their after lives. The familiarity of near relatives associating constantly together, produced a warm sentiment of affection, cemented by similarity of pursuits, and enlivened by diversity of character; while the perfect tranquillity of their lives afforded no event that could withdraw the veil of ignorance from their eyes.

Could a woman of Lady Audley's discernment, it may be asked, place two young persons in such a situation, and doubt the consequences? Those who are no longer young are liable to forget that love is a plant of early growth, and that the individuals that they have but a short time before beheld placing their supreme felicity on a rattle and a go-cart, can so soon be actuated by the strongest passions of the human breast.

Sir Edmund completed his nineteenth year, and Alicia entered her eighteenth, when this happy state of unconscious security was destroyed by a circumstance which rent the veil from her eyes, and disclosed his sentiments in all their energy and warmth. This circumstance was no other than a proposal of marriage to Alicia, from a gentleman of large fortune, and brilliant connexions, who resided in their neighbourhood. His character was

as little calculated as his appearance, to engage the
affections of a young woman of delicacy and good sense.
But he was a man of consequence; heir to an earldom;
member for the county; and Lady Audley, rejoicing at
what she termed Alicia's good fortune, determined that
she should become his wife.

With mild firmness she rejected the honour intended
her; but it was with difficulty that Lady Audley's mind
could adopt or understand the idea of an opposition to
her wishes. She could not seriously embrace the conviction, that Alicia was determined to disobey her; and
in order to bring her to a right understanding, she
underwent a system of persecution, that tended naturally
to increase the antipathy her suitor had inspired. Lady
Audley, with the undiscriminating zeal of prejudiced
and overbearing persons, strove to recommend him to
her niece by all those attributes which were of value in
her own eyes; making allowance for a certain degree of
indecision in her niece, but never admitting a doubt that
in due time her will should be obeyed, as it had always
hitherto been.

At this juncture, Sir Edmund came down to the
country, and was struck by the altered looks and pensive
manners of his once cheerful cousin. About a week after
his arrival, he found Alicia one morning in tears, after a
long conversation with Lady Audley. Sir Edmund
tenderly soothed her, and entreated to be made
acquainted with the cause of her distress. She was so
habituated to impart every thought to her cousin, the
intimacy and sympathy of their souls was so entire, that
she would not have concealed the late occurrence from
him, had she not been withheld by the natural timidity
and delicacy a young woman feels in making her own
conquests the subject of conversation. But now so
pathetically and irresistibly persuaded by Sir Edmund,
and sensible that every distress of hers wounded his

heart, Alicia candidly related to him the pursuit of her disagreeable suitor, and the importunities of Lady Audley in his favour. Every word she had spoken had more and more dispelled the mist that had so long hung over Sir Edmund's inclinations. At the first mention of a suitor, he had felt that to be hers, was a happiness that comprised all others; and that the idea of losing her made the whole of existence appear a frightful blank. These feelings were no sooner known to himself, than spontaneously poured into her delighted ears; while she felt that every sentiment met a kindred one in her breast. Alicia sought not a moment to disguise those feelings, which she now, for the first time, became aware of; they were known to the object of her innocent affection as soon as to herself, and both were convinced, that though not conscious before of the nature of their sentiments, friendship had long been mistaken for love in their hearts.

But this state of blissful serenity did not last long. On the evening of the following day, Lady Audley sent for her to her dressing room. On entering, Alicia was panic struck at her aunt's pale countenance, fiery eyes, and frame convulsed with passion. With difficulty, Lady Audley, struggling for calmness, demanded an instant and decided reply to the proposals of Mr. Compton, the gentleman who had solicited her hand. Alicia entreated her aunt to waive the subject, as she found it impossible ever to consent to such an union.

Scarcely was her answer uttered, when Lady Audley's anger burst forth uncontrolably. She accused her niece of the vilest ingratitude, in having seduced her son from the obedience he owed his mother; of having plotted to ally her base Scotch blood to the noble blood of the Audleys; and, having exhausted every opprobrious epithet, she was forced to stop from want of breath to proceed. As Alicia listened to the cruel unfounded reproaches of her aunt, her spirit rose under the unmerited ill usage, but her conscience absolved her from all intention of injuring or deceiving a human being; and she calmly waited till Lady Audley's anger should have exhausted itself, and then entreated to know what part of her conduct had excited her aunt's displeasure.

Lady Audley's reply was diffuse and intemperate. Alicia gathered from it that her rage had its source in a declaration her son had made to her of his affection for his cousin, and his resolution of marrying her as soon as he was of age. Which open avowal of his sentiments had followed Lady Audley's injunctions to him to forward the suit of Mr. Compton.

That her son, for whom she had in view one of the first matches in the kingdom, should dare to choose for himself; and, above all, to choose one whom she considered as much his inferior in birth, as she was in fortune, was a circumstance quite insupportable to her feelings.

Of the existence of love, Lady Audley had little conception; and she attributed her son's conduct to wilful disobedience and obstinacy. In proportion as she had hitherto found him complying and gentle, her wrath had kindled at his present firmness and inflexibility. So bitter were her reflections on his conduct, so severe her animadversions on the being he loved, that Sir Edmund, fired with resentment, expressed his resolution of acting according to the dictates of his own will; and expressed his contempt for her authority, in terms the most unequivocal. Lady Audley, ignorant of the arts of persuasion, by every word she uttered more and more widened the breach her imperiousness had occasioned, until Sir Edmund, feeling himself no longer master of his temper, announced his intention of leaving the house, to allow his mother time to reconcile herself to the inevitable misfortune of beholding him the husband of Alicia Malcolm.

He instantly ordered his horses and departed, leaving the following letter for his cousin.

'I have been compelled, by motives of prudence, of which you are the sole object, to depart without seeing you. My absence became necessary, from the unexpected conduct of Lady Audley, which has led me so near to forgetting that she was my mother, that I dare not remain, and subject myself to excesses of temper, which I might afterwards repent. Two years must elapse before I can become legally my own master, and should Lady Audley so far depart from the dictates of cool judgment, as still to oppose what she knows to be inevitable, I fear that we cannot meet till then. My heart is well known to you; therefore I need not enlarge on the pain I feel at this unlooked-for separation. At the same time, I am cheered with the prospect of the unspeakable happiness that awaits me—the possession of your hand; and the confidence I feel in your constancy, is in proportion to the certainty I experience in my own; I cannot therefore fear that any of the means which may be put in practice to disunite us, will have more effect on you than on me.

'Looking forward to the moment that shall make you mine for ever, I remain with steady confidence, and unspeakable affection, your

'EDMUND AUDLEY.'

With a trembling frame, Alicia handed the note to Lady Audley, and begged leave to retire for a short time; expressing her willingness to reply at another moment to any question her aunt might choose to put to her with regard to her engagement with Sir Edmund.

In the solitude of her own chamber, Alicia gave way to those feelings of wretchedness, which she had with difficulty stifled in the presence of Lady Audley, and bitterly wept over the extinction of her bright and newly-formed visions of felicity. To yield to unmerited ill usage, or to crouch beneath imperious and self-arrogated power, was not in the nature of Alicia; and, had Lady Audley been a stranger to her, the path of duty would have been less intricate. However much her own pride might have been wounded, by entering into a family which considered her as an intruding beggar, never would she have consented to sacrifice the virtuous inclinations of the man she loved, to the will of an arrogant and imperious mother. But alas! the case was far different. The recent ill treatment she had experienced from Lady Audley, could not efface from her noble mind the recollection of benefits conferred from the earliest period of her life, and of unvarying attention to her welfare. To her aunt she owed all but existence: she had wholly supported her; bestowed on her the most liberal education; and from Lady Audley sprung every pleasure she had hitherto enjoyed.

Had she been brought up by her paternal relations, she would in all probability never have beheld her cousin; and the mother and son might have lived in uninterrupted concord. Could she be the person to inflict on Lady Audley the severest disappointment she could experience? The thought was too dreadful to bear; and, knowing that procrastination could but increase her misery, no sooner had she felt convinced of the true nature of her duty, than she made a steady resolution to perform and to adhere to it. Lady Audley had *vowed, that while she had life, she would never give her consent and approbation to her son's marriage;* and Alicia was too well acquainted with her disposition, to have the faintest expectation that she would relent.

But to remain any longer under her protection was impossible; and she resolved to anticipate any proposal of that sort from her protectress.

When Lady Audley's passion had somewhat cooled, she again sent for Alicia. She began by repeating her *eternal enmity* to the marriage, in a manner impressive to the greatest degree and still more decisive in its form, by the cool collectedness of her manner. She then desired to hear what Alicia had to say in exculpation of her conduct.

The profound sorrow which filled the heart of Alicia, left no room for timidity or indecision. She answered her without hesitation and embarrassment, and asserted her innocence of all deceit, in such a manner as to leave no doubt, at least, of honourable proceeding. In a few impressive words, she proved herself sensible of the benefits her aunt had through life conferred upon her; and, while she openly professed to think herself, in the present instance, deeply wronged, she declared her determination of never uniting herself to her cousin without Lady Audley's permission, which she felt convinced was unattainable.

She then proceeded to ask, where she should deem it most advisable for her to reside in future.

Lady Audley, convinced that moderate measures would be most likely to ensure a continuation of Alicia's obedience, expressed herself grieved at the necessity of parting with her, and pleased that she should have the good sense to perceive the propriety of such a separation.

Sir Duncan Malcolm, the grandfather of Alicia, had, in the few communications that had passed between Lady Audley and him, always expressed a wish to see his granddaughter before he died. Her Ladyship's antipathy to Scotland was such, that she would have deemed it absolute contamination for her niece to have entered the country; and she had, therefore, always eluded the request.

It was now, of all plans, the most eligible; and she graciously offered to convey her niece as far as Edinburgh. The journey was immediately settled; and before Alicia left her aunt's presence, a promise was exacted with unfeeling tenacity, and given with melancholy firmness, never to unite herself to Sir Edmund unsanctioned by his mother.

Alas! how imperfect is human wisdom! even in seeking to do right, how many are the errors we commit! Alicia judged wrong in thus sacrificing the happiness of Sir Edmund to the pride and injustice of his mother;—but her error was that of a noble, self-denying spirit, entitled to respect, even though it cannot claim approbation. The honourable open conduct of her niece had so far gained upon Lady Audley, that she did not object to her writing to Sir Edmund, which she did as follows:

LETTER

'DEAR SIR EDMUND,

'A painful line of conduct is pointed out to me by duty; yet, of all the regrets I feel, not one is so poignant as the consciousness of that which you will feel at learning, that I have for ever resigned the claims you so lately gave me to your heart and hand. It was not weakness— it could not be inconstancy—that produced the painful sacrifice of a distinction, still more gratifying to my heart, than flattering to my pride.

'Need I remind you, that to your mother I owe every benefit in life; nothing can release me from the tribute of gratitude, which would be ill repaid by braving her authority, and despising her will. Should I give her reason to regret the hour she received me under her roof, to repent of every benefit she has hitherto bestowed on me; should I draw down a mother's displeasure, what reasonable hopes could we entertain of solid peace through life? I am not in a situation which entitles me to question the

justice of Lady Audley's will; and that will has pronounced, that I shall never be Sir Edmund's wife.

'Your first impulse may perhaps be, to accuse me of
coldness and ingratitude, in quitting the place and
country you inhabit, and resigning you back to yourself,
without personally taking leave of you; but I trust that
you will, on reflection, absolve me from the charge.

'Could I have had any grounds to suppose that a
personal interview would be productive of comfort to
you, I would have joyfully supported the sufferings it
would have inflicted on myself. But question your own
heart as to the use you would have made of such a
meeting; bear in mind, that Lady Audley has my
solemn promise never to be yours—a promise not lightly
given—then imagine what must have been an interview
between us, under such circumstances.

'In proof of an affection which I can have no reason
to doubt, I conjure you to listen to the last request I
shall ever make to my dear cousin. Give me the heart-felt
satisfaction to know that my departure has put an end
to those disagreements between mother and son, of
which I have been the innocent cause.

'You have no reason to blame Lady Audley for this
last step of mine. I have not been intimidated—threats,
believe me, never would have extorted from me a
promise to renounce you, had not virtue herself dictated
the sacrifice; and my reward will spring from the conviction, that, as far as my judgment could discern, I have
acted right.

'Forget, I entreat you, this inauspicious passion.
Resolve, like me, to resign yourself, without murmuring,
to what is now past recall; and, instead of indulging
melancholy, regain, by a timely exertion of mind and
body, that serenity which is the portion of those who have
obeyed the dictates of rectitude.

'Farewell, Sir Edmund—May every happiness attend

your future life: While I strive to forget my ill-fated
affection, the still stronger feelings of gratitude and
esteem for you can never fade from the heart of

'ALICIA MALCOLM.'

To say that no tears were shed during the composition
of this letter, would be to overstrain fortitude beyond
natural bounds. With difficulty, Alicia checked the
effusions of her pen: she wished to have said much more,
and to have soothed the agony of renunciation, by painting with warmth her tenderness and her regret; but
reason urged, that, in exciting his feelings and displaying
her own, she would defeat the chief purpose of her letter;
she hastily closed and directed it, with a feeling almost
akin to despair.

The necessary arrangements for the journey having
been hastily made, the ladies set out two days after Sir
Edmund had so hastily quitted them. The uncomplaining Alicia buried her woes in her own bosom; and neither
murmurs on the one hand, nor reproaches on the other,
were heard.

At the end of four days, the travellers entered Scotland;
and, when they stopped for the night, Alicia, fatigued
and dispirited, retired immediately to her apartment.

She had been there but a few minutes, when the
chambermaid knocked at the door, and informed her
that she was wanted below.

Supposing that Lady Audley had sent for her, she
followed the girl without observing that she was conducted
in an opposite direction; when, upon entering an
apartment, what was her astonishment at finding herself,
not in the presence of Lady Audley, but in the arms of
Sir Edmund! In the utmost agitation, she sought to
disengage herself from his almost frantic embrace; while
he poured forth a torrent of rapturous exclamations, and

swore that no human power should ever divide them again.

'I have followed your steps, dearest Alicia, from the moment I received your letter. We are now in Scotland —in this blessed land of liberty.[1] Every thing is arranged; the clergyman is now in waiting; and, in five minutes, you shall be my own beyond the power of fate to sever us.'

Too much agitated to reply, Alicia wept in silence; and, in the delight of once more beholding him she had thought never more to behold, forgot, for a moment, the duty she had imposed upon herself. But the native energy of her character returned. She raised her head, and attempted to withdraw from the encircling arms of her cousin.

'Never until you have vowed to be mine! The clergy-man—the carriage—every thing is in readiness. Speak but the word, dearest.' And he knelt at her feet.

At this juncture, the door opened, and, pale with rage, her eyes flashing fire, Lady Audley stood before them. A dreadful scene now ensued. Sir Edmund disdained to enter into any justification of his conduct, or even to reply to the invectives of his mother, but lavished the most tender assiduities on Alicia; who, overcome more by the conflicts of her own heart, than with alarm at Lady Audley's violence, sat the pale and silent image of consternation.

Baffled by her son's indignant disregard, Lady Audley turned all her fury on her niece; and, in the most opprobrious terms that rage could invent, upbraided her with deceit and treachery—accusing her of making her pretended submission instrumental to the more speedy accomplishment of her marriage. Too much incensed to reply, Sir Edmund seized his cousin's hand, and was leading her from the room.

'Go, then—go, marry her; but first hear me swear,

solemnly swear!'—and she raised her hand and eyes to heaven—'that my malediction shall be your portion! Speak but the word, and no power shall make me withhold it!'

'Dear Edmund!' exclaimed Alicia distractedly, 'never ought I to have allowed time for the terrifying words that have fallen from Lady Audley's lips: never for me shall your mother's malediction fall on you. Farewell for ever!' and, with the strength of desperation, she rushed past him, and quitted the room. Sir Edmund madly followed, but in vain. Alicia's feelings were too highly wrought at that moment to be touched even by the man she loved; and, without an additional pang, she saw him throw himself into the carriage which he had destined for so different a purpose, and quit for ever the woman he adored.

It may easily be conceived of how painful a nature must have been the future intercourse betwixt Lady Audley and her niece. The former seemed to regard her victim with that haughty distance which the unrelenting oppressor never fails to entertain towards the object of his tyranny; while even the gentle Alicia, on her part, shrunk, with ill-concealed abhorrence, from the presence of that being whose stern decree had blasted all the fairest blossoms of her happiness.

Alicia was received with affection by her grandfather; and she laboured to drive away the heavy despondency which pressed on her spirits, by studying his taste and humours, and striving to contribute to his comfort and amusement.

Sir Duncan had chosen the time of Alicia's arrival to transact some business; and, instead of returning immediately to the Highlands, he determined to remain some weeks in Edinburgh for her amusement.

But, little attractive as dissipation had ever been, it was now absolutely repugnant to Alicia. She loathed the idea of mixing in scenes of amusement with a heart incapable of joy, a spirit indifferent to every object that surrounded her; and, in solitude alone, she expected gradually to regain her peace of mind.

In the amusements of the gay season of Edinburgh, Alicia expected to find all the vanity, emptiness, and frivolity of London dissipation, without its varied brilliancy, and elegant luxury; yet, so much was it the habit of her mind to look to the fairest side of things, and to extract some advantage from every situation in which she was placed, that, pensive and thoughtful as was her disposition, the discriminating only perceived her deep dejection, while all admired her benevolence of manner, and unaffected desire to please.

By degrees, Alicia found that, in some points, she had been inaccurate in her idea of the style of living of those who form the best society of Edinburgh. The circle is so confined, that its members are almost universally known to each other; and those various gradations of gentility, from the cit's¹ snug party to the duchess' most crowded assembly, all totally distinct and separate, which are to be met with in London, have no prototype in Edinburgh. There, the ranks and fortunes being more on an equality, no one is able greatly to exceed his neighbour in luxury and extravagance. Great magnificence, and the consequent gratification produced by the envy of others being out of the question, the object for which a reunion of individuals was originally invented, becomes less of a secondary consideration. Private parties for the actual purpose of society and conversation are frequent, and answer the destined end; and, in the societies of professed amusement, are to be met the learned, the studious, and the rational; not presented as shows to the company by the host and hostess, but professedly seeking their own gratification.

Still the lack of beauty, fashion, and elegance, disappoint the stranger accustomed to their brilliant combination in a London world. But Alicia had long since sickened in the metropolis at the frivolity of beauty, the heartlessness of fashion, and the insipidity of elegance; and it was a relief to her to turn to the variety of character she found beneath the cloke of simple, eccentric, and sometimes coarse manners.

We are never long so totally abstracted by our own feelings, as to be unconscious of the attempts of others to please us.

Amongst the many who expressed good will towards Alicia, there were a few whose kindness and real affection failed not to meet with a return from her; and others, whose rich and varied powers of mind, for the first time, afforded her a true specimen of the exalting enjoyment produced by a communion of intellect. She felt the powers of her understanding enlarge in proportion; and, with this mental activity, she sought to solace the languor of her heart, and save it from the listlessness of despair.

Alicia had been about six weeks in Edinburgh, when she received a letter from Lady Audley. No allusions were made to the past; she wrote upon general topics, in the cold manner that might be used to a common acquaintance; and slightly named her son as having set out upon a tour to the Continent.

Alicia's heart was heavy, as she read the heartless letter of the woman, whose cruelty had not been able to eradicate wholly from her breast the strong durable affection of early habit.

Sir Duncan and Alicia spent two months in Edinburgh, at the end of which time they went to his country seat in ———shire. The adjacent country was picturesque; and Sir Duncan's residence, though bearing marks of the absence of taste and comfort in its arrangements, possessed much natural beauty.

Two years of tranquil seclusion had passed over her head, when her dormant feelings were all aroused by a letter from Sir Edmund. It informed her, that he was now of age; that his affection remained unalterable; that he was newly arrived from abroad; and that, notwithstanding the death-blow she had given to his hopes, he could not refrain, on returning to his native land, from assuring her, that he was resolved never to pay his addresses to any other woman. He concluded, by declaring his intention of presenting himself at once to Sir Duncan, and soliciting his permission to claim her hand; when all scruples relating to Lady Audley must, from her change of abode, be at an end.

Alicia read the letter with grateful affection, and poignant regret. Again she shed the bitter tears of disappointment, at the hard task of refusing for a second time so noble and affectionate a heart. But conscience whispered, that, to hold a passive line of conduct, would be, in some measure, to deceive Lady Audley's expectations; and she felt, with exquisite anguish, that she had no means to put a final stop to Sir Edmund's pursuits, and to her own trials, but by bestowing her hand on another. The first dawning of this idea was accompanied by the most violent burst of anguish; but, far from driving away the painful subject, she strove to render it less appalling by dwelling upon it, and labouring to reconcile herself to what seemed her only plan of conduct. She acknowledged to herself, that, to remain still single, a prey to Sir Edmund's importunities, and the continual temptations of her own heart, was, for the sake of present indulgence, submitting to a fiery ordeal, from which she could not escape unblameable without the most repeated and agonizing conflicts.

Three months still remained for her of peace and liberty, after which Sir Duncan would go to Edinburgh. There she would be sure of meeting with the loved companion of her youthful days; and the lurking weakness of her own breast, would then be seconded by the passionate eloquence of the being she most loved and admired upon earth.

She wrote to him, repeating her former arguments; declaring that she could never feel herself absolved from the promise she had given Lady Audley, but by that Lady herself, and imploring him to abandon a pursuit which would be productive only of lasting pain to both.

Her arguments, her representations, all failed in their effect on Sir Edmund's impetuous character. His answer was short and decided; the purport of it, that he should see her in Edinburgh the moment she arrived there.

'My fate then is fixed,' thought Alicia, as she read this letter; 'I must finish the sacrifice.'

The more severe had been the struggle between love and victorious duty, the more firmly was she determined to maintain this dear-bought victory.

Alicia's resolution of marrying was now decided, and the opportunity was not wanting. She had become acquainted, during the preceding winter in Edinburgh, with Major Douglas, eldest son of Mr. Douglas of Glenfern. He had then paid her the most marked attention; and, since her return to the country, had been a frequent visitor at Sir Duncan's. At length he avowed his partiality, which was heard by Sir Duncan with pleasure; by Alicia with dread and submission. Yet she felt less repugnance towards him than to any other of her suitors. He was pleasing in his person; quiet and simple in his manners; and his character stood high for integrity, good temper, and plain sense. The sequel requires little farther detail. Alicia Malcolm became the wife of Archibald Douglas.

An eternal constancy is a thing so rare to be met with, that persons who desire that sort of reputation, strive to obtain it by nourishing the ideas that recall the passion, even though guilt and sorrow should go hand in hand with it. But Alicia, far from piqueing herself in the lovelorn pensiveness she might have assumed, had she yielded to the impulse of her feelings, diligently strove, not only to make up her mind to the lot which had devolved to her, but to bring it to such a frame of cheerfulness, as should enable her to contribute to her husband's happiness.

When the soul is no longer buffeted by the storms of hope or fear, when all is fixed unchangeably for life, sorrow for the past will never long prey on a pious and well regulated mind. If Alicia lost the buoyant spirit of youth, the bright and quick play of fancy, yet a placid contentment crowned her days; and, at the end of two years, she would have been astonished had any one marked her as an object of compassion.

She scarcely ever heard from Lady Audley; and, in the few letters her aunt had favoured her with, she gave favourable, though vague, accounts of her son. Alicia did not court a more unreserved communication, and had long since taught herself to hope that he was now happy. Soon after their marriage, Major Douglas quitted the army, upon succeeding to a small estate on the banks of Lochmarlie by the death of an uncle; and there, in the calm seclusion of domestic life, Mrs. Douglas found that peace which might have been denied her amid gayer scenes.

CHAPTER XV

'And joyous was the scene in early summer.'

Madoc.[1]

On Henry's return from his solitary ramble, Mrs. Douglas learnt from him the cause of the misunderstanding that had taken place; and judging that, in the present state of affairs, a temporary separation might be of use to both parties, as they were now about to return home, she proposed to her husband to invite his brother and Lady Juliana to follow and spend a few weeks with them at Lochmarlie Cottage.

The invitation was eagerly accepted; for though Lady Juliana did not anticipate any positive pleasure from the change, still she thought that every place must be more agreeable than her present abode, especially as she stipulated for the utter exclusion of the aunts from the party. To atone for this mortification, Miss Becky was invited to fill the vacant seat in the carriage; and, accordingly, with a cargo of strong shoes, great coats, and a large work-bag well stuffed with white-seam,[2] she took her place at the appointed hour.

The day they had chosen for their expedition was one that 'sent a summer feeling to the heart.'[3]

The air was soft and genial; not a cloud stained the bright azure of the heavens; and the sun shone out in all his splendour, shedding life and beauty even over the desolate heath-clad hills of Glenfern. But, after they had journied a few miles, suddenly emerging from the valley, a scene of matchless beauty burst at once upon the eye. Before them lay the dark blue waters of Lochmarlie, reflecting, as in a mirror, every surrounding object, and bearing on its placid transparent bosom a fleet of herring boats, the drapery of whose black suspended nets, contrasted with picturesque effect the white sails of the larger vessels, which were vainly spread to catch a breeze. All around, rocks, meadows, woods, and hills, mingled in wild and lovely irregularity.

On a projecting point of land stood a little fishing village; its white cottages reflected in the glassy waters that almost surrounded it. On the opposite side of the lake, or rather estuary, embosomed in wood, rose the lofty turrets of Lochmarlie Castle; while here and there, perched on some mountain's brow, were to be seen the shepherd's lonely hut, and the heath-covered summer shealing.[1]

Not a breath was stirring, not a sound was heard save the rushing of a waterfall, the tinkling of some silver rivulet, or the calm rippling of the tranquil lake; now and then, at intervals, the fisherman's Gaelic ditty chanted, as he lay stretched on the sand in some sunny nook; or the shrill distant sound of childish glee. How delicious to the feeling heart to behold so fair a scene of unsophisticated nature, and to listen to her voice alone, breathing the accents of innocence and joy!

But none of the party who now gazed on it, had minds capable of being touched with the emotions it was calculated to inspire.

Henry, indeed, was rapturous in his expressions of admiration; but he concluded his panegyrics by wondering his brother did not keep a cutter, and resolving to pass a night on board one of the herring boats, that he might eat the fish in perfection.

Lady Juliana thought it might be very pretty, if, instead of those frightful rocks and shabby cottages, there could be villas, and gardens, and lawns, and conservatories, and summer-houses, and statues.

Miss Becky observed, if it was hers, she would cut down the woods, and level the hills, and have races.

The road wound along the sides of the lake, sometimes overhung with banks of natural wood, which, though scarcely budding, grew so thick as to exclude the prospect;

in other places surmounted by large masses of rock, festooned with ivy, and embroidered by mosses of a thousand hues that glittered under the little mountain streamlets. Two miles further on stood the simple mansion of Mr. Douglas. It was situated in a wild sequestered nook, formed by a little bay at the farther end of the lake. On three sides, it was surrounded by wooded hills, that offered a complete shelter from every nipping blast. To the south, the lawn, sprinkled with trees and shrubs, sloped gradually down to the water.

At the door, they were met by Mrs. Douglas, who welcomed them with the most affectionate cordiality, and conducted them into the house through a little circular hall, filled with flowering shrubs and foreign plants.

'How delightful!' exclaimed Lady Juliana, as she stopped to inhale the rich fragrance: 'Moss roses! I do delight in them,' twisting off a rich cluster of flowers and buds in token of her affection: 'and I quite doat upon Heliotrope,' gathering a handful of flowers as she spoke. Then extending her hand towards a most luxuriant Cape jessamine[1]—

'I must really petition you to spare this, my favourite child,' said her sister-in-law, as she gently withheld her arm; 'and, to tell you the truth, dear Lady Juliana, you have already infringed the rules of my little conservatory, which admit only of the gratification of two senses— seeing and smelling.'

'What! don't you like your flowers to be gathered?' exclaimed Lady Juliana, in a tone of surprise and disappointment: 'I don't know any other use they're of. What quantities I used to have from Papa's hot-houses!'

Mrs. Doulgas made no reply; but conducted her to the drawing-room, where her chagrin was dispelled by the appearance of comfort and even elegance that it bore. 'Now, this is really what I like,' cried she, throwing herself on one of the couches; 'a large fire, open windows, quantities of roses, comfortable Ottomans,[1] and pictures; only what a pity you haven't a large mirror.'

Mrs. Douglas now rang for refreshments, and apologized for the absence of her husband, who, she said, was so much interested in his ploughing, that he seldom made his appearance till sent for.

Henry then proposed that they should all go out and surprise his brother; and though walking in the country formed no part of Lady Juliana's amusements, yet, as Mrs. Douglas assured her the walks were perfectly dry, and her husband was so pressing, she consented. The way lay through a shrubbery, by the side of a brawling brook, whose banks retained all the wildness of unadorned nature. Moss, and ivy, and fern, clothed the ground; and, under the banks, the young primroses and violets began to raise their heads; while the red wintry berry still hung thick on the hollies.

'This is really very pleasant,' said Henry, stopping to contemplate a view of the lake through the branches of a weeping birch, 'the sound of the stream, and the singing of the birds, and all those wild flowers, make it appear as if it was summer in this spot; and only look, Julia, how pretty that wherry looks lying at anchor.' Then whispering to her, 'What would you think of such a desert as this, with the man of your heart?'

Lady Juliana made no reply, but by complaining of the heat of the sun, the hardness of the gravel, and the damp from the water.

Henry, who now began to look upon the condition of a Highland farmer with more complacency than formerly, was confirmed in his favourable sentiments at sight of his brother, following the primitive occupation of the plough, his fine face glowing with health, and lighted up with good humour and happiness. He hastily advanced towards the party, and shaking his brother and sister-in-law most warmly by the hand, expressed, with all the warmth of a good heart, the pleasure he had in receiving them at his house:—then observing Lady Juliana's languid air, and imputing to fatigue of body what, in fact, was the consequence of mental vacuity, he proposed returning home by a shorter road than that by which they had come. Henry was again in raptures, at the new beauties this walk presented, and at the high order and neatness in which the grounds were kept.

'This must be a very expensive place of yours, though,' said he, addressing his sister-in-law; 'there is so much garden and shrubbery, and such a number of rustic bridges, bowers, and so forth: it must require half a dozen men to keep it in any order.'

'Such an establishment would very ill accord with our moderate means,' replied she; 'we do not pretend to one regular gardener; and had our little embellishments been productive of much expense, or tending solely to my gratification, I should never have suggested them. When we first took possession of this spot, it was a perfect wilderness, with a dirty farm-house on it: nothing but mud about the doors, nothing but wood, and briers, and brambles beyond it; and the village presented a still more melancholy scene of rank luxuriance, in its swarms of dirty idle girls, and mischievous boys. I have generally found, that wherever an evil exists, the remedy is not far off; and in this case, it was strikingly obvious. It was only engaging these ill-directed children, by trifling rewards, to apply their lively energies in improving in- stead of destroying the works of nature, as had formerly been their zealous practice. In a short time, the change on the moral as well as the vegetable part of creation became very perceptible: the children grew industrious and peaceable; and, instead of destroying trees, robbing nests, and worrying cats, the bigger boys, under Douglas' direction, constructed these wooden bridges and seats, or cut out and gravelled the little winding paths that we had previously marked out. The task of keeping every thing in order is now easy, as you may believe, when I tell you the whole of our pleasure-grounds, as you are pleased to term them, receive no other attention than what is bestowed by children under twelve years of age. And now having, I hope, acquitted myself of the charge of extravagance, I ought to beg Lady Juliana's pardon for this long, and, I fear, tiresome detail.'

Having now reached the house, Mrs. Douglas conducted her guest to the apartment prepared for her; while the brothers pursued their walk.

As long as novelty retained its power, and the comparison between Glenfern and Lochmarlie was fresh in remembrance, Lady Juliana, charmed with every thing, was in high good humour. But as the horrors of the one were forgotten, and the comforts of the other became familiar, the demon of *ennui* again took possession of her vacant mind; and she relapsed into all her capricious humours and childish impertinences. The harpsichord, which, on her first arrival, she had pronounced to be excellent, was now declared quite shocking; so much out of tune, that there was no possibility of playing upon it. The small collection of well-chosen novels she soon exhausted, and then they became 'the stupidest books she had ever read;' the smell of the Heliotrope now gave her the head-ache; the sight of the lake made her sea-sick.

Mrs. Douglas heard all these civilities in silence; and much more 'in sorrow than in anger.'[1] In the wayward inclinations, variable temper, and wretched inanity of this poor victim of indulgence, she beheld the sad fruits of a fashionable education; and thought, with humility, that, under similar circumstances, such might have been her own character.

'Oh, what an awful responsibility do those parents incur,' she would mentally exclaim, 'who thus neglect or corrupt the noble deposit of an immortal soul! And who, alas! can tell where the mischief may end. This unfortunate will herself become a mother; yet wholly ignorant of the duties, incapable of the self-denial of that sacred office, she will bring into the world creatures to whom she can only transmit her errors and her weaknesses!'

These reflections at times deeply affected the generous heart and truly Christian spirit of Mrs. Douglas; and she sought, by every means in her power, to restrain those faults, which she knew it would be vain to attempt eradicating.

To diversify the routine of days which grew more and more tedious to Lady Juliana, the weather being remarkably fine, many little excursions were made to the nearest country seats; which, though they did not afford her any actual pleasure, answered the purpose of consuming a considerable portion of her time.

Several weeks passed away, during which little inclination was shewn on the part of the guests, to quit their present residence; when Mr. and Mrs. Douglas were summoned to attend the sick bed of Sir Duncan Malcolm; and though they pressed their guests to remain during their absence, yet Henry felt that it would be highly offensive to his father were they to do so, and therefore resolved immediately to return to Glenfern.

CHAPTER XVI

'They steeked doors, they steeked yetts,
   Close to the cheek and chin;
They steeked them a' but a little wicket,
   And Lammikin crap in.

Now quhere's the Lady of this castle?'
                              Old Ballad.[1]

THE PARTY WERE received with the loudest acclamations of joy by the good old ladies; and even the Laird seemed to have forgotten that his son had refused to breed black cattle, and that his daughter-in-law was above the management of her household.

The usual salutations were scarcely over, when Miss Grizzy, flying to her little writing-box, pulled out a letter, and, with an air of importance, having enjoined silence, she read as follows:

LETTER

'*Lochmarlie Castle,
March* 27, 17—.

'DEAR CHILD,

'Sir Sampson's stomach has been as bad as it could well be, but not so bad as your roads—He was shook to a jelly. My petticoat will never do. Mrs. M'Hall has had a girl. I wonder what makes people have girls; they never come to good—Boys may go to the mischief, and be good for something—if girls go, they're good for nothing I know of. I never saw such roads—I suppose Glenfern means to bury you all in the high-way—there are holes enough to make you graves, and stones big enough for coffins. You must all come, and spend Tuesday here—not all, but some of you—you, dear child, and your brother, and a sister, and your pretty

niece, and handsome nephew—I love handsome people.
—Miss M'Kraken has bounced away with her father's
footman—I hope he will clean his knives on her. Come
early, and come dressed, to your loving friend,

'ISABELLA MACLAUGHLAN.'

The letter ended, a volley of applause ensued, which
at length gave place to consultation. 'Of course, we all
go—at least as many as the carriage will hold: we have
no engagements, and there can be no objections.'

Lady Juliana had already frowned a contemptuous
refusal, but in due time it was changed to a sullen assent,
at the pressing entreaties of her husband, to whom any
place was now preferable to home. In truth, the mention
of a party had more weight with her than either her husband's wishes or her aunts' remonstrances; and they had
assured her, that she should meet with a large assemblage
of the very first company at Lochmarlie Castle.

The day appointed for the important visit arrived;
and it was arranged that two of the elder ladies, and one
of the young ones, should accompany Lady Juliana in
her barouche,[1] which Henry was to drive.

At peep of dawn, the ladies were a-stir, and at eight
o'clock breakfast was hurried over, that they might begin
the preparations necessary for appearing with dignity
at the shrine of this their patron saint. At eleven they
re-appeared in all the majesty of sweeping silk-trains,
and well powdered toupees.[2] In outward show, Miss
Becky was not less elaborate; the united strength and
skill of her three aunts and four sisters, had evidently
been exerted in forcing her hair into every position, but
that for which nature had intended it; curls stood on end
around her forehead, and tresses were dragged up from
the roots, and formed into a club on the crown;[3] her arms
had been strapped back till her elbows met, and her

respiration seemed suspended, by means of a pink ribbon of no ordinary strength or doubtful hue.

Three hours were passed in all the anguish of full dressed impatience; an anguish in which every female breast must be ready to sympathise. But Lady Juliana sympathised in no one's distresses but her own, and the difference of waiting in high dress or in *dishabille*,[1] was a distinction to her inconceivable. But those to whom *to be dressed* is an event, will readily enter into the feelings of the ladies in question, as they sat, walked, wondered, exclaimed, opened windows, wrung their hands, adjusted their dress, &c. &c. during the three tedious hours they were doomed to wait the appearance of their niece.

Two o'clock came, and with it Lady Juliana, as if purposely to testify her contempt, in a loose morning dress and mob cap.[2] The sisters looked blank with disappointment; for having made themselves mistresses of the contents of her Ladyship's wardrobe, they had settled amongst themselves that the most suitable dress for the occasion would be black velvet, and accordingly many hints had been given the preceding evening on the virtues of black velvet gowns; they were warm, and not too warm; they were dressy, and not too dressy; Lady Maclaughlan was a great admirer of black velvet gowns; she had one herself with long sleeves, and that buttoned behind; black velvet gowns were very much wore; they knew several ladies who had them; and they were certain, there would be nothing else wore amongst the matrons at Lady Maclaughlan's, &c. &c.

Time was however too precious to be given either to remonstrance or lamentation. Miss Jacky could only give an angry look, and Miss Grizzy a sorrowful one, as they hurried away to the carriage, uttering exclamations of despair at the lateness of the hour, and the impossibility that any body could have time to dress, after getting to Lochmarlie Castle.

The consequence of the delay was, that it was dark by the time they reached the place of destination. The carriage drove up to the grand entrance; but neither lights nor servants greeted their arrival; and no answer was returned to the ringing of the bell.

'This is most alarming, I declare!' cried Miss Grizzy.

'It is quite incomprehensible!' observed Miss Jacky. 'We had best get out, and try the back door.'

The party alighted, and another attack being made upon the rear, it met with better success; for a little boy now presented himself at a narrow opening of the door, and in a strong Highland accent, demanded 'wha ta war seekin'.'[1]

'Lady Maclaughlan, to be sure, Colin,' was the reply.

'Weel, weel,' still refusing admittance; 'but te leddie's no to be spoken wi' tonight.'

'Not to be spoken with!' exclaimed Miss Grizzy, almost sinking to the ground with apprehension. 'Good gracious! —I hope!—I declare!—Sir Sampson!——'

'Oo aye, hur may see Lochmarlie hursel.[2] Then opening the door, he led the way to a small sitting-room, and ushered them into the presence of Sir Sampson, who was reclining in an easy chair, arrayed in a *robe-de-chambre*, and night cap. The opening of the door seemed to have broken his slumber; for, gazing around with a look of stupefaction, he demanded, in a sleepy peevish tone, 'Who was there?'

'Bless me, Sir Sampson!' exclaimed both spinsters at once, darting forward and seizing a hand; 'Bless me, don't you know us? and here is our niece, Lady Juliana.'

'My Lady Juliana Douglas!' cried he with a shriek of horror, sinking again upon his cushions—'I am betrayed—I—Where is my Lady Maclaughlan?— Where is Philistine?—Where is—the devil! This is not to be borne! My Lady Juliana Douglas, the Earl of Courtland's daughter, to be introduced to Lochmarlie

Castle in so vile a manner, and myself surprised in so indecorous a situation!' And, his lips quivering with passion, he rang the bell.

The summons was answered by the same attendant that had acted as gentleman usher.

'Where are all my people?' demanded his incensed master.

'Hurs aw awa tull ta Sandy Mor's.'[1]

'Where is my Lady?'

'Hurs i' ta teach tap.'*[2]

'Where is Murdoch?'

'Hur's helpin' ta leddie i' ta teach tap.'

'O, we'll all go up stairs, and see what Lady Maclaughlan and Philistine are about in the laboratory,' said Miss Grizzy. 'So pray, just go on with your nap, Sir Sampson; we shall find the way—don't stir;' and taking Lady Juliana by the hand, away tripped the spinsters in search of their friend. 'I cannot conceive the meaning of all this,' whispered Miss Grizzy to her sister as they went along. 'Something must be wrong; but I said nothing to dear Sir Sampson, his nerves are so easily agitated. But what can be the meaning of all this? I declare it's quite a mystery.'

After ascending several long dark stairs, and following divers windings and turnings, the party at length reached the door of the *sanctum sanctorum*,[3] and having gently tapped, the voice of the priestess was heard in no very encouraging accents, demanding 'Who was there?'

'It's only us,' replied her trembling friend.

'Only us! humph! I wonder what fool is called *only us!* Open the door, Philistine, and see what *only us* wants.'

The door was opened and the party entered. The day was closing in, but by the faint twilight that mingled with the gleams from a smoky smouldering fire, Lady

---

* House top.

Maclaughlan was dimly discernible, as she stood upon the hearth,[1] watching the contents of an enormous kettle, that emitted both steam and odour. She regarded the invaders with her usual marble aspect, and without moving either joint or muscle as they drew near.

'I declare—I don't think you know us, Lady Maclaughlan,' said Miss Grizzy, in a tone of affected vivacity, with which she strove to conceal her agitation.

'Know you!' repeated her friend—'humph! Who you are, I know very well; but what brings you here, I do *not* know. Do you know yourselves?'

'I declare—I can't conceive—' began Miss Grizzy; but her trepidation arrested her speech, and her sister therefore proceeded—

'Your Ladyship's declaration is no less astonishing than incomprehensible. We have waited upon you by your own express invitation on the day appointed by yourself; and we have been received in a manner, I must say, we did not expect, considering this is the first visit of our niece, Lady Juliana Douglas.'

'I'll tell you what, girls,' replied their friend, as she still stood with her back to the fire, and her hands behind her; 'I'll tell you what,—you are not yourselves—you are all lost—quite mad—that's all—humph!'

'If that's the case, we cannot be fit company for your Ladyship,' retorted Miss Jacky warmly; 'and therefore the best thing we can do, is to return the way we came: Come, Lady Juliana—come, sister.'

'I declare, Jacky, the impetuosity of your temper is— I really cannot stand it—' and the gentle Grizzy gave way to a flood of tears.

'You used to be rational, intelligent creatures,' resumed her Ladyship; 'but what has come over you, I don't know. You come tumbling in here at the middle of the night—and the top of the house—nobody knows how —when I never was thinking of you; and because I don't tell a parcel of lies, and pretend I expected you, you are for flying off again—humph! Is this the behaviour of women in their senses? But, since you are here, you may as well sit down, and say what brought you. Get down, Gil Blas—go along, Tom Jones,' addressing two huge cats, who occupied a three-cornered leather chair by the fire side, and who relinquished it with much reluctance.

'How do you do, pretty creature?' kissing Lady Juliana, as she seated her in this cat's cradle. 'Now, girls, sit down, and tell what brought you here to-day—humph!'

'Can your Ladyship ask such a question, after having formally invited us?' demanded the wrathful Jacky.

'I'll tell you what, girls; you were just as much invited by me to dine here to day, as you were appointed to sup with the Grand Seignior[1]—humph!'

'What day of the week does your Ladyship call this?'

'I call it Tuesday; but I suppose the Glenfern calendar calls it Thursday: Thursday was the day I invited you to come.'

'I'm sure—thankful we're got to the bottom of it at last,' cried Miss Grizzy; 'I read it, because I'm sure you wrote it, Tuesday.'

'How could you be such a fool, my love, as to read it any such thing? Even if it had been written Tuesday, you might have had the sense to know it meant Thursday. When did you know me invite any body for a Tuesday?'

'I declare it's very true; I certainly ought to have known better. I am quite confounded at my own stupidity; for, as you observe, even though you had said Tuesday, I might have known that you must have meant Thursday.'

'Well, well, no more about it: Since you are here, you must stay here, and you must have something to eat, I suppose. Sir Sampson and I have dined two hours ago;

but you shall have your dinner for all that. I must shut shop for this day, it seems, and leave my resuscitating tincture all in the dead-thraw[1]—Methusalem pills quite in their infancy. But there's no help for it: Since you are here, you must stay here, and you must be fed and lodged: so get along, girls, get along. Here, Gil Blas—come, Tom Jones.' And, preceded by her cats, and followed by her guests, she led the way to the parlour.

CHAPTER XVII

> 'Point de milieu: l'hymen et ses liens
> Sont les plus grands ou des maux ou des biens.'
> *L'Enfant Prodigue.*[2]

ON RETURNING TO the parlour, they found Sir Sampson had, by means of the indefatigable Philistine, been transported into a suit of regimentals, and well powdered peruke, which had, in some measure, restored him to his usual complacency. Henry, who had gone in quest of some person to take charge of the horses, now entered; and shortly after a tray of provisions was brought, which the half-famished party eagerly attacked, regardless of their hostess' admonitions to eat sparingly, as nothing was so dangerous as eating heartily when people were hungry.

The repast being at length concluded, Lady Maclaughlan led her guests into the saloon.[3] They passed through an anti-chamber, which seemed, by the faint light of the lamp, to contain nothing but piles on piles of china, and entered the room of state.

The eye at first wandered in uncertain obscurity; and the guests cautiously proceeded over a bare oaken floor, whose dark polished surface seemed to emulate a mirror, through an apartment of formidable extent. The walls were hung with rich, but grotesque, tapestry. The ceiling, by its height and massy carving, bespoke the age of the apartment; but the beauty of the design was lost in the gloom.

A Turkey carpet was placed in the middle of the floor; and, on the middle of the carpet, stood the card table, at which two footmen, hastily summoned from the revels at Sandy Mor's, were placing chairs and cards; seemingly eager to display themselves, as if to prove that they were always at their posts.

Cards were a matter of course with Sir Sampson and his lady; but, as whist was the only game they ever played, a difficulty arose as to the means of providing amusement for the younger part of the company.

'I have plenty of books for you, my loves,' said Lady Maclaughlan; and, taking one of the candles, she made a journey to the other end of the room, and entered a small turret, from which her voice was heard issuing most audibly, 'All the books that should ever have been published are here. Read these, and you need read no more: all the world's in these books[1]—humph! Here's the Bible, great and small,[2] with apocrypha and concordance! Here's Floyer's Medicina Gerocomica, or, the Galenic Art of preserving Old Men's Health;—Love's Art of Surveying and Measuring Land;—Transactions of the Highland Society;—Glass' Cookery;—Flavel's Fountain of Life Opened;—Fencing Familiarized;— Observations on the use of Bath Waters;—Cure for Soul Sores;—De Blondt's Military Memoirs;—Mac-Ghie's Book-keeping;—Mead on Pestilence;—Asten-thology, or the Art of preserving Feeble Life!'

As she enumerated the contents of her library, she paused at the end of each title, in hopes of hearing the book called for; but she was allowed to proceed without interruption to the end of her catalogue.

'Why! what would you have, children?' cried she in one of her sternest accents. 'I don't know! Do you know yourselves? Here are two novels, the only ones worth any Christian's reading.'

Henry gladly accepted the first volumes of Gil Blas,[1] and Clarissa Harlowe;[2] and, giving the latter to Lady Juliana, began the other himself. Miss Becky was settled with her hands across; and, the whist party being arranged, a solemn silence ensued.

Lady Juliana turned over a few pages of her own book, then begged Henry would exchange with her; but both were in so different a style from the French and German school[3] she had been accustomed to, that they were soon relinquished in disappointment and disgust.

On the table, which had been placed by the fire for her accommodation, lay an English Newspaper; and to that she had recourse, as a last effort at amusement. But, alas! even the dulness of Clarissa Harlowe was delight, compared to the anguish with which this fatal paper was fraught, in the shape of the following paragraph, which presented itself to the unfortunate fair one's eye.

'Yesterday was married, by special license, at the house of Mrs. D——, his Grace the Duke of L——, to the beautiful and accomplished Miss D——. His Royal Highness the Duke of —— was gracious enough to act as father to the bride upon this occasion, and was present in person, as were their Royal Highnesses the Dukes of ——, and of ——. The bride looked most bewitchingly lovely, in a simple robe of the finest Mechlin[4] lace, with a superb veil of the same costly material, which hung down to her feet. She wore a set of pearls estimated at thirty thousand pounds, whose chaste elegance corresponded with the rest of the dress. Immediately after the ceremony, they partook of a sumptuous collation; and the happy pair set off in a chariot and four, attended by six out-riders, and two coaches and four.

'After spending the honey-moon at his Grace's unique villa on the Thames, their Graces will receive company at their splendid mansion in Portman Square. The wedding paraphernalia is said to have cost ten thousand pounds; and her Grace's jewel-box is estimated at little less than half a million.'

Wretched as Lady Juliana had long felt herself to be, her former state of mind was positive happiness compared to what she now endured. Envy, regret, self-reproach, and resentment, all struggled in the breast of the self-devoted beauty, while the paper dropped from her hand, and she cast a fearful glance around, as if to ascertain the reality of her fate. The dreadful certainty smote her with a sense of wretchedness too acute to be suppressed; and, darting a look of horror at her unconscious husband, she threw herself back in her chair, while the scalding tears of envy, anger, and repentance, fell from her eyes.

Accustomed as Henry now was to these ebullitions of *feeling* from his beauteous partner, he was not yet so indifferent as to behold them unmoved; and he sought to sooth her by the kindest expressions, and most tender epithets. These, indeed, had long since ceased to charm away the Lady's ill-humour, but they sometimes succeeded in mollifying it. But now, their only effect seemed to be increasing the irritation, as she turned from all her husband's inquiries, and impatiently withdrew her hands from his.

Astonished at a conduct so incomprehensible, Douglas earnestly besought an explanation.

'There!' cried she, at length, pushing the paper towards him: 'see there what I might have been but for you; and then compare it with what you have made me!'

Confounded by this reproach, Henry eagerly snatched up the paper, and his eye instantly fell on the fatal paragraph; the poisoned dart that struck the death-blow to all that now remained to him of happiness—the fond idea that, even amidst childish folly, and capricious estrangement, still, in the main, he was beloved! With a quivering lip, and cheek blanched with mortification, and indignant contempt, he laid down the paper; and, without casting a look upon, uttering a word to, his once *adored and adoring Juliana*, quitted the apartment in all that bitterness of spirit, which a generous nature must feel, when it first discovers the fallacy of a cherished affection. Henry had, indeed, ceased to regard his wife with the ardour of romantic passion; nor had the solid feelings of affectionate esteem supplied its place: but he loved her still, because he believed himself the engrossing object of her tenderness; and, in that blest delusion, he had hitherto found palliatives for her folly, and consolation for all his own distresses.

To indifference he might for a time have remained insensible; because, though his feelings were strong, his perceptions were not acute. But the veil of illusion was now rudely withdrawn. He beheld himself detested where he imagined himself adored; and the anguish of disappointed affection was heightened by the stings of wounded pride, and deluded self-love.

CHAPTER XVIII

'What's done, cannot be undone; to bed, to bed, to bed!'
Exit Lady Macbeth.[1]

THE DISTANCE AT which the whist party had placed themselves, and the deep interest in which their senses were involved, while the fate of the odd trick was pending, had rendered them insensible to the scene that

was acting at the other extremity of the apartment. The
task of administering succour to the afflicted fair one
therefore devolved upon Miss Becky, whose sympathetic
powers never had been called into action before. Slowly
approaching the wretched Lady Juliana as she lay back
in her chair, the tears coursing each other down her
cheeks, she tendered her a smelling bottle, to which her
own nose, and the noses of her sisters, were wont to be
applied, whenever, as they choicely expressed it, they
wanted a 'fine smell'. But, upon this trying occasion,
she went still further: She unscrewed the stopper;
unfolded a cotton handkerchief, upon which she poured
a few drops of lavender water, and offered it to her
Ladyship, deeming that the most elegant and efficient
manner in which she could afford relief. But the well-
meant offering was silently waved off; and poor Miss
Becky, having done all that the light of reason suggested
to her, retreated to her seat, wondering what it was her
fine sister-in-law would be at.

By the time the rubber was ended, her Ladyship's
fears of Lady Maclaughlan had enabled her to conquer
her feelings so far, that they had now sunk into a state of
sullen dejection, which the good aunts eagerly inter-
preted into the fatigue of the journey; Miss Grizzy
declaring, that although the drive was most delightful—
nobody could deny that—and they all enjoyed it excessively, as indeed every body must who had eyes in their
head; yet she must own, at the same time, that she really
felt as if all her bones were broke.

A general rising therefore took place at an early hour,
and Lady Juliana, attended by all the females of the
party, was ushered into the chamber of state, which was
fitted up in a style acknowledged to be truly magnificent,
by all who had ever enjoyed the honour of being permitted to gaze on its white velvet bed curtains, surmounted by the family arms, and gracefully tucked up

by hands *sinister-couped*[1] at the wrists, &c. But least[2] my fashionable readers should be of a different opinion, I shall refrain from giving an inventory of the various articles with which this favoured chamber was furnished. Misses Grizzy and Jacky occupied the green room which had been fitted up at Sir Sampson's birth. The curtains hung at a respectful distance from the ground; the chimney-piece was far beyond the reach even of the majestic Jacky's arm; and the painted tiffany toilette[3] was covered with a shoal of little tortoise-shell boxes of all shapes and sizes. A grim visage, scowling from under a Highland bonnet, graced by a single black feather, hung on high. Miss Grizzy placed herself before it, and, holding up the candle, contemplated it for about the nine hundredth time, with an awe bordering almost on adoration.

'Certainly Sir Eneas must have been a most wonderful man—nobody can deny that; and there can be no question but he had the second-sight to the greatest degree—indeed, I never heard it disputed; many of his prophecies, indeed, seem to have been quite incomprehensible; but that is so much the more extraordinary, you know—for instance, the one with regard to our family,' lowering her voice—'for my part I declare I never could comprehend it: and yet there must be something in it, too; but how any branch from the Glenfern tree—of course, you know, that can only mean the family tree—should help to prop Lochmarlie's walls, is what I can't conceive. If Sir Sampson had a son, to be sure, some of the girls—for you know it can't be any of us; at least I declare for my own part—I'm sure even if any thing—which I trust, in goodness, there is not the least chance of, should ever happen to dear Lady Maclaughlan, and Sir Sampson should take it into his head—which, of course, is a thing not to be thought about—and indeed I'm quite convinced it would be very much out of respect to dear Lady Maclaughlan, as well as friendship for us, if such a thing was ever to come into his head—'

Here the tender Grizzy got so involved in her own ideas, as to the possibility of Lady Maclaughlan's death, and the propriety of Sir Sampson's proposals, together with the fulfilling of Sir Eneas the seer's prophecy, that there is no saying how far she strayed in her self-created labyrinth. Such as choose to follow her may. For our part, we prefer accompanying the youthful Becky to her chamber, whither she was also attended by the Lady of the mansion. Becky's destiny for the night lay at the top of one of those little straggling wooden stairs common in old houses, which creaked in all directions. The bed was placed in a recess dark as Erebus,[1] and betwixt the bed and the wall was a depth profound, which Becky's eye dared not attempt to penetrate.

'You will find every thing right here, child,' said Lady Maclaughlan; 'and if any thing should be wrong, you must think it right. I never suffer any thing to be wrong here—humph!' Becky, emboldened by despair, cast a look towards the recess; and, in a faint voice, ventured to inquire, 'Is there no fear that Tom Jones, or Gil Blas, may be in that place behind the bed?'

'And if they should,' answered her hostess, in her most appalling tone, 'what is that to you? Are you a mouse, that you are afraid they will eat you? Yes, I suppose you are. You are perhaps the princess in the fairy tale, who was a woman by day, and a mouse by night.[2] I believe you are bewitched! So I wish your mouseship a good night.' And she descended the creaking stair, singing, 'Mrs. Mouse, are you within,[3] till even her stentorian voice was lost in distance. Poor Becky's heart died with the retreating sounds, and only revived to beat time with the worm in the wood. Long and eerie was the night, as she gave herself up to all the horrors of a superstitious mind—ghosts, grey, black, and white,[1] flitted around her couch—cats, half human, held her throat—the death-watch ticked in her ears. At length, the light of morning shed its brightening influence on the dim opaque of her understanding; and when all things stood disclosed in light, she shut her eyes, and ope'd her mouth, in all the blissfulness of security.

The light of day was indeed favourable for displaying to advantage the beauties of Lochmarlie Castle, which owed more to nature than art. It was beautifully situated on a smooth green bank, that rose somewhat abruptly from the lake, and commanded a view, which, if not extensive, was yet full of variety and grandeur.

Its venerable turrets reared themselves above the trees, which seemed coeval with them; and the vast magnificence of its wide spreading lawns and extensive forests, seemed to appertain to some feudal prince's lofty domain. But in vain were creation's charms spread before Lady Juliana's eyes. Woods, and mountains, and lakes, and rivers, were odious things; and her heart panted for dusty squares, and suffocating drawing-rooms.

Something was said of departing, by the sisters, when the party met at breakfast; but this was immediately negatived, in the most decided manner, by their hostess. 'Since you have taken your own time to come, my dears, you must take mine to go. Thursday was the day I invited you for, or at least wanted you for, so you must stay Thursday, and go away on Friday, and my blessing go with you—humph!'

The sisters, charmed with what they termed the hospitality and friendship of this invitation, delightedly agreed to remain; and as things were at least conducted in better style there than at Glenfern, uncomfortable as it was, Lady Juliana found herself somewhat nearer home there than at the family chateau. Lady Maclaughlan, who *could* be commonly civil in her own house, was at some pains to amuse her guest, by shewing her collection of china, and cabinet of gems, both of which were remarkably fine. There was also a library, and a gallery, containing some good pictures, and, what Lady Juliana prized still more, a billiard-table. Thursday, the destined day, at length arrived, and a large party assembled to dinner. Lady Juliana, as she half reclined on a sofa, surveyed the company with a supercilious stare, and without deigning to take any part in the general conversation that went on. It was enough that they spoke with a peculiar accent—every thing they said must be barbarous; but she was pleased once more to eat off plate, and to find herself in rooms which, though grotesque and comfortless, yet wore an air of state, and whose vastness enabled her to keep aloof from those with whom she never willingly came in contact. It was therefore with regret she saw the day of her departure arrive, and found herself once more an unwilling inmate of her only asylum, particularly as her situation now required comforts and indulgences which it was there impossible to procure.

CHAPTER XIX

> ———— 'No mother's care
> Shielded my infant innocence with prayer:
> . . . .
> Mother, miscall'd, farewell!'
>
> *Savage.*[1]

THE HAPPY PERIOD, so long and anxiously anticipated by the ladies of Glenfern, at length arrived, and Lady Juliana presented to the house of Douglas—not, alas! the ardently desired heir to its ancient consequence, but twin-daughters, who could only be regarded as additional burdens on its poverty.

The old gentleman's disappointment was excessive; and, as he paced up and down the parlour, with his hands in his pockets, he muttered, 'Twa lasses! I ne'er heard tell o' the like o't. I wonder whar their tochers¹ are to come frae?'

Miss Grizzy, in great perturbation, declared, it certainly was a great pity it had so happened, but these things couldn't be helped; she was sure Lady Maclaughlan would be greatly surprised.

Miss Jacky saw no cause for regret, and promised herself an endless source of delight in forming the minds and training the ideas of her infant nieces.

Miss Nicky wondered how they were to be nursed. She was afraid Lady Juliana would not be able for both, and wet-nurses had such stomachs!

Henry, meanwhile, whose love had all revived in anxiety for the safety, and anguish for the sufferings of his youthful partner, had hastened to her apartment, and, kneeling by her side, he pressed her hands to his lips with feelings of the deepest emotion.

'Dearer—a thousand times dearer to me than ever,' whispered he, as he fondly embraced her, 'and those sweet pledges of our love!'

'Ah, don't mention them,' interrupted his lady, in a languid tone: 'How very provoking! I hate girls so— and two of them—oh!' and she sighed deeply. Her husband sighed too; but from a different cause. The nurse now appeared, and approached with her helpless charges; and both parents, for the first time, looked on their own offspring.

'What nice little creatures!' said the delighted father, as, taking them in his arms, he imprinted the first kiss on the innocent faces of his daughters, and then held them to their mother; who, turning from them with disgust, exclaimed, 'How can you kiss them, Harry! They are so ugly, and they squall so! Oh do, for heaven's sake, take them away! And see, there is poor Psyche, quite wretched at being so long away from me—Pray, put her on the bed.'

'She will grow fond of her babies by and by,' said poor Henry to himself, as he quitted the apartment, with feelings very different from those with which he entered it.

At the pressing solicitations of her husband, the fashionable mother was prevailed upon to attempt nursing one of her poor starving infants; but the first trial proved also the last, as she declared nothing upon earth should ever induce her to perform so odious an office; and as Henry's entreaties, and her aunt's[1] remonstrances, served alike to irritate and agitate her, the contest was, by the advice of her medical attendant, completely given up. A wet-nurse was therefore procured; but as she refused to undertake both children, and the old gentleman would not hear of having two such incumbrances in his family, it was settled, to the unspeakable delight of the maiden sisters, that the youngest should be entrusted entirely to their management, and brought up by hand.

The consequence was such as might have been foreseen. The child, who was naturally weak and delicate at its birth, daily lost a portion of its little strength, while its continued cries declared the intensity of its sufferings, though they produced no other effect on its unfeeling mother, than her having it removed to a more distant apartment, as she could not endure to hear the cross little thing scream so for nothing. On the other hand, the more favoured twin, who was from its birth a remarkably strong lively infant, and met with all justice from its nurse, throve apace, and was pronounced by her to be the very picture of the *bonnie leddie, its mamma*; and then, with all the low cunning of her kind, she would launch forth into panegyrics of its beauty, and prophecies of the great dignities and honours that would one day be showered upon it; until, by her fawning and flattery, she succeeded in exciting a degree of interest, which nature had not secured for it in the mother's breast.

Things were in this situation, when, at the end of three weeks, Mr. and Mrs. Douglas arrived to offer their congratulations on the birth of the twins. Lady Juliana received her sister-in-law in her apartment, which she had not yet quitted, and replied to her congratulations, only by querulous complaints, and childish murmurs.

'I am sure you are very happy in not having children,' continued she, as the cries of the little sufferer reached her ear; 'I hope to goodness I shall never have any more. —I wonder if any body ever had twin daughters before! and I, too, who hate girls so!'

Mrs. Douglas, disgusted with her unfeeling folly, knew not what to reply, and a pause ensued; but a fresh burst of cries from the unfortunate baby, again called forth its mother's indignation.

'I wish to goodness that child was gagged,' cried she, holding her hands to her ears. 'It has done nothing but scream since the hour it was born, and it makes me quite sick to hear it.'

'Poor little dear!' said Mrs. Douglas, compassionately, 'it appears to suffer a great deal.'

'Suffer!' repeated her sister-in-law: 'What can it suffer? I am sure it meets with a great deal more attention than any person in the house. These three old women do nothing but feed it from morning to night, with every thing they can think of, and make such a fuss about it!'

'I suspect, my dear sister, you would be very sorry for yourself,' said Mrs. Douglas with a smile, 'were you to endure the same treatment as your poor baby; stuffed with improper food, and loathsome drugs, and bandied about from one person to another.'

'You may say what you please,' retorted Lady Juliana, pettishly; 'but I know it's nothing but ill temper: nurse says so too; and it is so ugly with constantly crying, that I cannot bear to look at it;' and she turned away her head, as Miss Jacky entered with the little culprit in her arms, which she was vainly endeavouring to *talk* into silence, while she dandled it in the most awkward *maiden-like* manner imaginable.

'Good heavens! what a fright!' exclaimed the tender parent, as her child was held up to her. 'Why, it is much less than when it was born, and its skin is as yellow as saffron, and it squints! Only look what a difference,' as the nurse advanced and ostentatiously displayed her charge, who had just waked out of a long sleep; its cheeks flushed with heat; its skin completely filled up; and its large eyes rolling under its already dark eyelashes.

'The bonny wean's[1] just her mamma's pickter,' drawled out the nurse, 'but the wee[2] missy's unco[3] like her aunties.'

'Take her away,' cried Lady Juliana, in a tone of despair—'I wish I could send her out of my hearing altogether, for her noise will be the death of me.'

'Alas! what would I give to hear the blessed sound of a living child!' exclaimed Mrs. Douglas, taking the infant in her arms. 'And how great would be my happiness, could I call the poor rejected one mine!'

'I'm sure you are welcome to my share of the little plague,' said her sister-in-law, with a laugh, 'if you can prevail upon Harry to give up his.'

'I would give up a great deal, could my poor child find a mother,' replied her husband, who just then entered.

'My dear brother!' cried Mrs. Douglas, her eyes beaming with delight, 'do you then confirm Lady Juliana's kind promise? Indeed I will be a mother to your dear baby, and love her as if she were my own; and in a month—Oh! in much less time—you shall see her as stout as her sister.'

Henry sighed, as he thought, why has not my poor babe such a mother of its own! Then thanking his sister-in-law for her generous intentions, he reminded her that she must consult her husband, as few men liked to be troubled with any children but their own.

'You are in the right,' said Mrs. Douglas, blushing at the impetuosity of feeling, which had made her forget for an instant the deference due to her husband; 'I shall instantly ask his permission, and he is so indulgent to all my wishes, that I have little doubt of obtaining his consent;' and, with the child in her arms, she hastened to her husband, and made known her request.

Mr. Douglas received the proposal with considerable coolness; wondering what his wife could see in such an ugly squalling thing, to plague herself about it. If it had been a boy, old enough to speak and run about, there might be some amusement in it; but he could not see the use of a squalling sickly infant—and a girl too!

His wife sighed deeply, and the tears stole down her cheeks, as she looked on the wan visage and closed eyes of the little sufferer. 'God help thee, poor baby!' said she mournfully; 'you are rejected on all hands, but your misery will soon be at an end;' and she was slowly leaving the room with her helpless charge, when her husband, touched at the sight of her distress, though the feeling that caused it he did not comprehend, called to her, 'I am sure, Alicia, if you really wish to take charge of the infant, I have no objections; only I think you will find it a great plague, and the mother is such a fool.'

'Worse than a fool,' said Mrs. Douglas indignantly, 'for she hates and abjures this her poor unoffending babe.'

'Does she so?' cried Mr. Douglas, every kindling feel-

ing roused within him at the idea of his blood being
hated and abjured; 'then, hang me! if she shall have
any child of Harry's to hate, as long as I have a house
to shelter it, and a sixpence to bestow upon it,' taking
the infant in his arms, and kindly kissing it.

Mrs. Douglas smiled through her tears, as she embraced
her husband, and praised his goodness and generosity;
then, full of exultation and delight, she flew to impart
the success of her mission to the parents of her *protégé*.

Great was the surprise of the maiden-nurses, at finding
they were to be bereft of their little charge.

'I declare, I think the child is doing as well as possible,'
said Miss Grizzy. 'To be sure, it does yammer[1] constantly
—that can't be denied; and it is uncommonly small—
nobody can dispute that. At the same time, I am sure,
I can't tell what makes it cry, for I've given it two
cholic powders every day, and a tea-spoonful of Lady
Maclaughlan's carminative every three hours.'

'And I've done nothing but make water-gruel, and
chop rusks for it,' quoth Miss Nicky, 'and yet it is never
satisfied. I wonder what it would be at.'

'I know perfectly well what it would be at,' said Miss
Jacky, with an air of importance. 'All this crying and
screaming, is for nothing else but a nurse; but it ought
not to be indulged: there is no end of indulging the
desires, and 'tis amazing how cunning children are, and
how soon they know how to take advantage of people's
weakness,' glancing an eye of fire at Mrs. Douglas. 'Were
that my child, I would feed her on bread and water,
before I would humour her fancies. A pretty lesson indeed!
If she's to have her own way before she's a month old.'

Mrs. Douglas knew that it was in vain to attempt
arguing with her aunts. She therefore allowed them to
wonder, and declaim over their sucking pots,[2] cholic
powders, and other instruments of torture, while she sent
to the wife of one of her tenants who had lately lain in,

and who wished for the situation of nurse, appointing her to be at Lochmarlie the following day. Having made her arrangements, and collected the scanty portion of clothing Mrs. Nurse chose to allow, Mrs. Douglas repaired to her sister-in-law's apartment, with her little charge in her arms. She found her still in bed, and surrounded with her favourites.

'So you really are going to torment yourself with that little screech-owl,' said she. 'Well, I must say it's very good of you; but I am afraid you will soon tire of her. Children are such plagues! Are they not, my darling?' added she, kissing her pug.

'You will not say so, when you have seen my little girl a month hence,' said Mrs. Douglas, trying to conceal her disgust for Henry's sake, who had just then entered the room. 'She has promised me never to cry any more; so give her a kiss, and let us be gone.'

The high-bred mother slightly touched the cheek of her sleeping babe, extended her finger to her sister-in-law, and carelessly bidding them good-bye, returned to her pillow and her pugs.

Henry accompanied Mrs. Douglas to the carriage, and, before they parted, he promised his brother to ride over to Lochmarlie in a few days. He said nothing of his child, but his glistening eye, and the warm pressure of his hand, spoke volumes to the kind heart of his brother; who assured him that Alice would be very good to his little girl, and that he was sure she would get quite well when she got a nurse. The carriage drove off, and Henry, with a heavy spirit, returned to the house to listen to his father's lectures, his aunts' ejaculations, and his wife's murmurs.

CHAPTER XX

'We may boldly spend upon the hope of what
Is to come in.'

Henry IV.[1]

THE BIRTH OF twin daughters awakened the young father to a still stronger sense of the total dependence and extreme helplessness of his condition. Yet how to remedy it he knew not: to accept of his father's proposal was out of the question, and it was equally impossible for him, were he ever so inclined, to remain much longer a burden on the narrow income of the Laird of Glenfern. One alternative only remained, which was to address the friend and patron of his youth, General Cameron; and to him he therefore wrote, describing all the misery of his situation, and imploring his forgiveness and assistance. 'The old General's passion must have cooled by this time,' thought he to himself, as he sealed the letter, 'and, as he has often overlooked former scrapes, I think, after all, he will help me out of this greatest one of all.'

For once Henry was not mistaken. He received an answer to his letter, in which the General, after execrating his folly in marrying a lady of quality; swearing at the birth of his twin daughters; and giving him some wholesome counsel as to his future mode of life; concluded by informing that he had got him reinstated in his former rank in the army; that he should settle seven hundred per annum on him, till he saw how matters were conducted, and, in the mean time, enclosed a draught for four hundred pounds, to open the campaign.

Though this was not, according to Henry's notions, 'coming down handsomely,' still it was better than not coming down at all, and with a mixture of delight and disappointment, he flew to communicate the tidings to Lady Juliana.

'Seven hundred pounds a year!' exclaimed she, in raptures: 'Heavens! what a quantity of money! why, we shall be quite rich, and I shall have such a beautiful house, and such pretty carriages, and give such parties, and buy so many fine things—Oh dear, how happy I shall be!'

'You know little of money, Julia, if you think seven hundred pounds will do all that,' replied her husband gravely. 'I hardly think we can afford a house in town; but we may have a pretty cottage at Richmond or Twickenham, and I can keep a curricle,[1] and drive you about, you know; and we may give famous good family dinners.'

A dispute here ensued; her Ladyship hated cottages, and curricles, and good family dinners, as much as her husband despised fancy balls,[2] opera boxes, and chariots.

The fact was, that the one knew very nearly as much of the real value of money as the other, and Henry's *sober* scheme was just about as practicable as his wife's extravagant one.

Brought up in the luxurious profusion of a great house; accustomed to issue her orders, and have them obeyed, Lady Juliana, at the time she married, was in the most blissful state of ignorance, respecting the value of pounds, shillings, and pence. Her maid took care to have her wardrobe supplied with all things needful; and when she wanted a new dress or a fashionable jewel, it was only driving to Madame D.'s, or Mr. Y.'s, and desiring the article to be sent to herself, while the bill went to her papa.

From never seeing money in its own vulgar form, Lady Juliana had learned to consider it as a mere nominal thing; while, on the other hand, her husband, from seeing too much of it, had formed almost equally erroneous ideas of its powers. By the mistaken kindness of General Cameron, he had been indulged in all the fashionable follies of the day, and allowed to use his patron's ample fortune as if it had already been his own; nor was it until he found himself a prisoner at Glenfern from want of money, that he had ever attached the smallest import-ance to it. In short, both the husband and wife, had been accustomed to look upon it in the same light as the air they breathed. They knew it essential to life, and concluded that it would come some way or other; either from the east or west, north or south. As for the vulgar concerns of meat and drink, servants' wages, taxes,[1] and so forth, they never found a place in the calculations of either. Birth-day dresses, fêtes, operas, equipages, and state liveries,[2] whirled in rapid succession through Lady Juliana's brain, while clubs, curricles, horses, and claret, took possession of her husband's mind.

However much they differed in the proposed modes of shewing off in London, both agreed perfectly in the necessity of going there, and Henry therefore hastened to inform his father of the change in his circumstances, and apprize him of his intention of immediately joining his regiment, the ——— Guards.

'Seven hunder pound a year!' exclaimed the old gentle-man; 'Seven hunder pound! Oo what can ye mak o' a' that siller?[3] Ye'll surely lay by the half o't to tocher[4] your bairns—Seven hunder pound a year for doing naething!'

Miss Jacky was afraid, unless they got some person of sense, (which would not be an easy matter,) to take the management of it, it would perhaps be found little enough in the long run.

Miss Grizzy declared it was a very handsome income, nobody could dispute that; at the same time, every body must allow, that the money could not have been better bestowed.

Miss Nicky observed, 'there was a great deal of good eating and drinking in seven hundred a year, if people knew how to manage it.'

All was bustle and preparation throughout Glenfern Castle, and the young ladies' good natured activity and muscular powers were again in requisition to collect the wardrobe, and pack the trunks, imperial,[1] &c. of their noble sister.

Glenfern remarked, 'that fules war fond o' flitting,[2] for they seemed glad to leave the good quarters they were in.'

Miss Grizzy declared, there was a great excuse for their being glad, poor things! young people were always so fond of a change; at the same time, nobody could deny but that it would have been quite natural for them to feel sorry too.

Miss Jacky was astonished how any person's mind could be so callous as to think of leaving Glenfern without emotion.

Miss Nicky wondered what was to become of the christening cake she had ordered from Perth; it might be as old as the hills before there would be another child born amongst them.

The Misses were ready to weep at the disappointment of the dreaming bread.[3]

In the midst of all this agitation, mental and bodily, the long-looked-for moment arrived. The carriage drove round ready packed and loaded, and, absolutely screaming with delight, Lady Juliana sprung into it; as she nodded, and kissed her hand to the assembled group, she impatiently called to Henry to follow. His adieus were, however, not quite so tonish as those of his high-bred lady, for he went duly and severally through all the evolutions of kissing, embracing, shaking of hands, and promises to write; then taking his station by the side of the nurse and child, the rest of the carriage being completely filled by the favourites, he bade a long farewell to his paternal halls and the land of his birth.

CHAPTER XXI

———'For trifles, why should I displease
The man I love? For trifles such as these
To serious mischiefs lead the man I love.'

Horace.[1]

BRIGHT PROSPECTS OF future happiness, and endless plans of expense, floated through Lady Juliana's
brain, and kept her temper in some degree of serenity
during the journey.

Arrived in London, she expressed herself enraptured
at being once more in a civilized country, and restored
to the society of human creatures. An elegant house,
and suitable establishment, were immediately provided;
and a thousand dear friends, who had completely forgotten her existence, were now eager to welcome her
to her former haunts, and lead her thoughtless and willing
steps in the paths of dissipation and extravagance.

Soon after their arrival, they were visited by General
Cameron. It was two o'clock, yet Lady Juliana had not
appeared; and Henry, half-stretched upon a sopha, was
dawdling over his breakfast, with half-a-dozen newspapers scattered round.

The first salutations over, the General demanded—
'Am I not to be favoured with a sight of your lady? Is
she afraid that I am one of your country relations, and
taken her flight from the breakfast table in consequence?'

'She has not yet made her appearance,' replied
Douglas; 'but I will let her know you are here. I am
sure she will be happy to make acquaintance with one to
whom I am so much indebted.'

A message was dispatched to Lady Juliana, who
returned for answer, that she would be down immediately. Three-quarters of an hour, however, elapsed; and
the General, provoked with this inattention and affec-

tation, was preparing to depart, when the Lady made her appearance.

'Juliana, my love,' said her husband, 'let me present you to General Cameron—the generous friend who has acted the part of a father towards me, and to whom you owe all the comforts you enjoy.'

Lady Juliana slightly bowed with careless ease, and half uttered a 'How d'ye do—very happy indeed—' as she glided on to pull the bell for breakfast. 'Cupid, Cupid!' cried she to the dog, who had flown upon the General, and was barking most vehemently; 'poor darling Cupid! are you almost starved to death? Harry, do give him that muffin on your plate.'

'You are very late to day, my love,' cried the mortified husband.

'I have been pestered for the last hour with Duval and the court dresses, and I could not fix on what I should like.'

'I think you might have deferred the ceremony of choosing to another opportunity. General Cameron has been here above an hour.'

'Dear! I hope you did not wait for me—I shall be quite shocked!' drawled out her Ladyship in a tone denoting how very indifferent the answer would be to her.

'I beg your Ladyship would be under no uneasiness on that account,' replied the General, in an ironical tone, which, though lost upon her, was obvious enough to Henry.

'Have you breakfasted?' asked Lady Juliana, exerting herself to be polite.

'Absurd, my love!' cried her husband. 'Do you suppose I should have allowed the General to wait for that too all this time, if he had not breakfasted many hours ago?'

'How cross you are this morning, my Harry! I protest

my Cupidon is quite ashamed of your *grossièreté!*'[1]

A servant now entered to say Mr. Shagg was come to know her Ladyship's final decision about the hammer-cloths;[2] and the new footman was come to be engaged; and the china merchant was below.

'Send up one of them at a time; and, as to the footman, you may say, I'll have him at once,' said Lady Juliana.

'I thought you had engaged Mrs. D.'s footman last week. She gave him the best character, did she not?' asked her husband.

'O yes! his character was good enough; but he was a horrid cheat for all that. He called himself five feet nine, and when he was measured, he turned out to be only five feet seven and a half.'

'Pshaw!' exclaimed Henry angrily. 'What the devil did that signify, if the man had a good character?'

'How absurdly you talk, Harry, as if a man's character signified, who has nothing to do but to stand behind my carriage!—A pretty figure he'd made there beside Thomas, who is at least five feet ten!'

The entrance of Mr. Shagg, bowing and scraping, and laden with cloths, lace, and fringes, interrupted the conversation.

'Well, Mr. Shagg,' cried Lady Juliana, 'what's to be done with that odious leopard's skin? you must positively take it off my hands. I would rather never go in a carriage again as shew myself in the Park with that frightful thing.'

'Certainly, my Lady,' replied the obsequious Mr. Shagg, 'any thing your Ladyship pleases; your Ladyship can have any hammer-cloth you like; and I have accordingly brought patterns of the very newest fashions for your Ladyship to make choice. Here are some uncommon elegant articles. At the same time, my Lady, your Ladyship must be sensible, that it is impossible that we can take back the leopard's skin. It was not only cut out to fit your Ladyship's coach-box—and consequently your Ladyship understands it would not fit any other— but the silver feet and crests have also been affixed quite ready for use, so that the article is quite lost to us. I am confident, therefore, that your Ladyship will consider of this, and allow it to be put down in your bill.'

'Put it any where but on my coach-box, and don't bore me!' answered Lady Juliana, tossing over the patterns, and humming a tune.

'What,' said her husband, 'is that the leopard's skin you were raving about last week, and are you tired of it before it has been used?'

'And no wonder. Who do you think I saw in the Park yesterday, but that old quiz, Lady Denham, just come from the country, with her frightful old coach set off with a hammer-cloth precisely like the one I had ordered. Only fancy people saying, Lady Denham sets the fashion for Lady Juliana Douglas! O, there's confusion and despair in the thought!'

Confusion, at least, if not despair, was painted in Henry's face, as he saw the General's glance directed alternately with contempt at Lady Juliana, and at himself, mingled with pity. He continued to fidget about in all directions, while Lady Juliana talked nonsense to Mr. Shagg, and wondered if the General never meant to go away. But he calmly kept his ground till the man was dismissed, and another introduced, loaded with china jars, monsters, and distorted tea-pots, for the capricious fair one's choice and approbation.

'Beg ten thousand pardons, my Lady, for not calling yesterday, according to appointment—quite an unforeseen impediment. The Countess of Godolphin had somehow got private intelligence that I had a set of fresh commodities just cleared from the custom-house, and well knowing such things are not long in hand; her La'ship came up from the country on purpose—the

Countess has so much taste!—she drove straight to my
warehouse, and kept me a close prisoner till after your
La'ship's hour; but I hope it may not be taken amiss,
seeing that it is not a customary thing with us to be
calling on customers, not to mention, that this line of
goods is not easily transported about. However, I flatter
myself the articles now brought for your Ladyship's
inspection will not be found beneath your notice. Please
to observe this choice piece—it represents a Chinese
cripple, squat on the ground, with his legs crossed. Your
Ladyship may observe the head and chin advanced forwards, as in the act of begging. The tea pours from the
open mouth; and, till your Ladyship tries, you can have
no idea of the elegant effect it produces.'

'That is really droll,' cried Lady Juliana, with a laugh
of delight; 'and I must have the dear sick beggar, he is
so deliciously hideous.'

'And here,' continued Mr. Brittle, 'is an amazing
delicate article, in the way of a jewel: a frog of Turkish
agate for burning pastiles in, my Lady; just such as
they use in the seraglio; and indeed this one I may call
invaluable, for it was the favourite toy of one of the
widowed Sultanas, till she grew devout and gave up
perfumes. One of her slaves disposed of it to my foreign
partner. Here it opens at the tail, where you put in the
pastiles, and closing it up, the vapour issues beautifully
through the nostrils, eyes, ears, and mouth, all at once.
Here, Sir,' turning to Douglas, 'if you are curious in new
workmanship, I would have you examine this. I defy
any jeweller in London to come up to the fineness of
these hinges, and delicacy of the carving—'

'Pshaw, damn it!' said Douglas, turning away, and
addressing some remark to the General, who was
provokingly attentive to every thing that went on.

'Here,' continued Mr. Brittle, 'are a set of jars, tea-
pots, mandarins, sea-monsters, and pug-dogs, all of

superior beauty, but such as your Ladyship may have seen before.'

'Oh, the dear, dear little puggies! I must have them to amuse my own darlings. I protest here is one the image of Psyche; positively I must kiss it!'

'O dear! I am sure,' cried Mr. Brittle, simpering, and making a conceited bow, 'your Ladyship does it and me too much honour. But here, as I was going to say, is the phœnix of all porcelain ware—the *ne plus ultra* of perfection—what I have kept in my back room, concealed from all eyes, until your Ladyship shall pronounce upon it. Somehow one of my shopmen got word of it, and told her Grace of L———[1] (who has a pretty taste in these things for a young lady,) that I had some particular choice article, that I was keeping for a lady that was a favourite of mine. Her Grace was in the shop the matter of a full hour and a half, trying to wheedle me out of a sight of this rare piece; and I, pretending not to know what her Grace would be after, but shewing her thing after thing, to put it out of her head. But she was not so easily bubbled,[2] and at last went away ill enough pleased. Now, my Lady, prepare all your eyes:' He then went to the door, and returned, carrying with difficulty a large basket, which till then had been kept by one of his satellites. After removing coverings of all descriptions, an uncouth group of monstrous size was displayed; which, on investigation, appeared to be a serpent coiled in regular folds round the body of a tiger placed on end; and the whole structure, which was intended for a vessel of some kind, was formed of the celebrated green mottled china,[3] invaluable to connoisseurs.

'View that well,' exclaimed Mr. Brittle, in a transport of enthusiasm, 'for such a specimen not one of half the size has ever been imported to Europe. There is a long story about this my phœnix, as I call it; but, to be brief, it was secretly procured from one of the temples, where, gigantic as it may seem, and uncouth for the purpose, it was the idol's principal tea-pot!'

'O delicious!' cried Lady Juliana, clasping her hands in extasy; 'I will give a party, for the sole purpose of drinking tea out of this machine; and I will have the whole room fitted up like an Indian temple. Oh! it will be so new! I die to send out my cards. The Duchess of B—— told me the other day, with such a triumphant air, when I was looking at her two little green jars, not a quarter the size of this, that there was not a bit more of that china to be had for love or money. Oh, she will be so provoked!' And she absolutely skipped for joy.

A loud rap at the door now announcing a visitor, Lady Juliana ran to the balcony, crying, 'Oh, it must be Lady Gerard, for she promised to call early in the morning, that we might go together to a wonderful sale in some far off place in the city—at Wapping, for aught I know. Mr. Brittle, Mr. Brittle, for the love of heaven, carry the dragon into the back drawing-room—I purchase it, remember!—make haste!—Lady Gerard is not to get a glimpse of it for the world.'

The servant now entered with a message from Lady Gerard, who would not alight, begging that Lady Juliana would make haste down to her, as they had not a moment to lose. She was flying away, without further ceremony than a 'Pray, excuse me,' to the General, when her husband called after her to know whether the child was gone out, as he wished to shew her to the General.

'I don't know, indeed,' replied the fashionable mother; 'I haven't had time to see her to-day;' and, before Douglas could reply, she was down stairs.

A pause ensued—the General whistled a quick step,[1] and Douglas walked up and down the room, in a pitiable state of mind, guessing pretty much what was passing in the mind of his friend, and fully sensible that it must be of a severer nature than any thing he could yet allow himself to think of his Juliana.

'Douglas,' said the General, 'have you made any step towards a reconciliation with your father-in-law? I believe it will become shortly necessary for your support.'

'Juliana wrote twice after her marriage,' replied he; 'but the reception which her letters met with was not such as to encourage perseverance on our part. With regard to myself, it is not an affair in which delicacy will permit me to be very active, as I might be accused of mercenary motives, which I am far from having.'

'Oh, of that I acquit you; but surely it ought to be a matter of moment, even to a —— Lady Juliana. The case is now altered. Time must have accustomed him to the idea of this imaginary affront; and, on my honour, if he thought like a gentleman, and a man of sense, I know where he would think the misfortune lay. Nay, don't interrupt me. The old Earl must now, I say, have cooled in his resentment; perhaps, too, his grand-children may soften his heart; this must have occurred to you. Has her Ladyship taken any farther steps, since her arrival in town?'

'I—I believe she has not; but I will put her in mind.'

'A daughter who requires to have her memory refreshed on such a subject, is likely to make a valuable wife!' said the General drily.

Douglas felt as if it was incumbent on him to be angry, but remained silent.

'Hark ye, Douglas,' continued the General, 'I speak this for your interest. You cannot go on without the Earl's help. You know, I am not on ceremony with you; and, if I refrain from saying what you see I think, about your present ruinous mode of life, it is not to spare your feelings, but from a sense of the uselessness of any such remonstrance. What I do give you is with good will; but all my fortune would not suffice to furnish pug-dogs, and

deformed tea-pots, for such a vitiated taste; and if it
would, hang me if it should. But enough on this head.
The Earl has been in bad health, and is lately come to
town. His son, too, and his lady, are to come about the
same time, and are to reside with him during the season.
I have heard Lord Lindore spoken of as a good-natured
easy man, and he would probably enter willingly into
any scheme to reinstate his sister into his father's good
graces. Think of this, and make what you can of it; and
my particular advice to you personally is, try to exchange
into a marching regiment; for a fellow like you, with
such a wife, London is the very devil! and so good
morning to you.' He snatched up his hat, and was off in
a moment.

CHAPTER XXII

> 'To reckon up a thousand of her pranks,
> Her pride, her wasteful spending, her unkindness,
> Her scolding, pouting, ——— ———
> Were to reap an endless catalogue.'

Old Play.[1]

WHEN LADY JULIANA returned from her expedition,
it was so late, that Douglas had not time to speak to her;
and separate engagements carrying them different ways,
he had no opportunity to do so until the following
morning at breakfast. He then resolved no longer to
defer what he had to say, and began by reproaching
her with the cavalier manner in which she had behaved
to his good friend, the General.

'Upon my life, Harry, you are grown perfectly
savage,' cried his Lady. 'I was most particularly civil;
I wonder what you would have me to do? You know
very well, I cannot have any thing to say to old men of
that sort.'

'I think,' returned Henry, 'you might have been gratified by making an acquaintance with my benefactor, and the man to whom you owe the enjoyment of your favourite pleasures. At any rate, you need not have made yourself ridiculous. May I perish, if I did not wish myself under ground, while you were talking nonsense to those sneaking rascals, who wheedle you out of your money! S'death! I had a good mind to throw them and their trumpery out of the window, when I saw you make such a fool of yourself.'

'A fool of myself! how foolishly you talk! and as for that vulgar awkward General, he ought to have been too much flattered. Some of the monsters were so like himself, I am sure he must have thought I took them for the love of his round bare pate.'

'Upon my soul, Julia! I am ashamed of you! Do leave off this excessive folly, and try to be rational. What I particularly wished to say to you, is, that your father is in town, and it will be proper that you should make another effort to be reconciled to him.'

'I dare say it will,' answered Lady Juliana, with a yawn.

'And you must lose no time. When will you write?'

'There's no use in writing, or indeed doing any thing in the matter. I am sure he won't forgive me.'

'And why not?'

'Oh, why should he do it now? He did not forgive me when I asked him before.'

'And do you think then, for a father's forgiveness, it is not worth while to have a little perseverance?'

'I am sure he won't do it; so 'tis in vain to try;' repeated she, going to the glass, and singing, '*Papa non dite di no*,'[1] &c.

'By heavens, Julia!' cried her husband passionately, 'you are past all endurance! Can nothing touch you?—nothing fix your thoughts, and make you serious for a single moment? Can I not make you understand, that you are ruining yourself and me; that we have nothing to depend upon but the bounty of that man whom you disgust by your caprice, extravagance, and impertinence; and that if you don't get reconciled to your father, what is to become of you? You already know what you have to expect from my family, and how you like living with them.'

'Heavens, Harry!' exclaimed her Ladyship, 'what is all this tirade about? Is it because I said, papa would'nt forgive me? I'm sure, I don't mind writing to him; I have no objection, the first leisure moment I have; but really, in town, one's time is so engrossed.'

At this moment her maid entered in triumph, carrying on her arms a satin dress, embroidered with gold and flowers.

'See, my Lady,' cried she, 'your new robe, as Madame has sent home half a day sooner than her word; and she has disobliged several of the quality,[1] by not giving the pattern.'

'Oh, lovely! charming! Spread it out, Gage; hold it to the light; all my own fancy. Only look, Harry; how exquisite! how divine!'

Harry had no time to express his contempt for embroidered robes; for just then one of his knowing friends came, by appointment, to accompany him to Tattersall's,[2] where he was to bid for a famous pair of curricle greys.

Days passed on without Lady Juliana's ever thinking it worth while to follow her husband's advice, about applying to her father; until a week after, Douglas overheard the following conversation between his wife and one of her acquaintance.

'You are going to this grand fête of course,' said Mrs. G. 'I'm told it is to eclipse every thing that has been yet seen or heard of.'

'Of what fête do you speak?' demanded Lady Juliana.

'Lord, my dear creature, how gothic[1] you are! Don't you know any thing about this grand affair, that every body has been talking of for two days? Lady Lindore gives, at your father's house, an entertainment, which is to be a concert, ball, and masquerade at once. All London is asked, of any distinction, *c'a s'entend*.[2] But, bless me, I beg pardon, I totally forgot that you were not on the best terms possible in that quarter—but, never mind, we must have you go; there is not a person of fashion that will stay away; I must get you asked; I shall petition Lady Lindore in your favour.'

'O pray don't trouble yourself,' cried Lady Juliana, in extreme pique. 'I believe I can get this done without your obliging interference; but I don't know whether I shall be in town then.'

From this moment, Lady Juliana resolved to make a vigorous effort to regain a footing in her father's house. Her first action, the next morning, was to write to her brother, who had hitherto kept aloof, because he could not be at the trouble of having a difference with the Earl, entreating him to use his influence in promoting a reconciliation between her father and herself.

No answer was returned for four days, at the end of which time Lady Juliana received the following note from her brother:

'DEAR JULIA,

'I quite agree with you in thinking that you have been kept long enough in the corner, and shall certainly tell Papa that you are ready to become a good girl, whenever he shall please to take you out of it. I shall endeavour to see Douglas and you soon.

'Yours affectionately,

'LINDORE.

'Lady Lindore desires me to say you can have tickets for her ball, if you choose to come *en masque*.'

Lady Juliana was delighted with this billet, which she protested was every thing that was kind and generous; but the postscript was the part on which she dwelt with the greatest delight, as she repeatedly declared it was a great deal more than she expected. 'You see, Harry,' said she, as she tossed the note to him, 'I was in the right. Papa won't forgive me; but Lindore says he will send me a ticket for the fête; it is vastly attentive of him, for I did not ask it. But I must go disguised, which is monstrous provoking, for I'm afraid nobody will know me.'

A dispute here ensued. Henry swore she should not steal into her father's house as long as she was his wife. The Lady insisted that she should go to her brother's fête when she was invited; and the altercation ended as altercations commonly do, leaving both parties more wedded to their own opinion than at first.

In the evening, Lady Juliana went to a large party; and, as she was passing from one room into another, she was startled by a little paper pellet thrown at her. Turning round to look for the offender, she saw her brother standing at a little distance, smiling at her surprise. This was the first time she had seen him for two years, and she went up to him with an extended hand, while he gave her a familiar nod, and a 'How d'ye do, Julia,' and one finger of his hand, while he turned round to speak to one of his companions. Nothing could be more characteristic of both parties than this fraternal meeting; and, from this time, they were the best friends imaginable.

CHAPTER XXIII

'Helas! où donc chercher ou trouver le bonheur
Nulle part tout entier, partout avec mesure!'

Voltaire.[1]

SOME DAYS BEFORE the expected fête, Lady Juliana, at the instigation of her adviser, Lady Gerard, resolved upon taking the field against the Duchess of L———. Her Grace had issued cards for a concert; and, after mature deliberation, it was decided, that her rival should strike out something new, and announce a christening for the same night.

The first intimation Douglas had of the honour intended him by this arrangement, was through the medium of the newspaper, for the husband and wife were now much too fashionable to be at all *au fait* of each other's schemes. His first emotion was to be extremely surprised; the next to be exceedingly displeased; and the last to be highly gratified at the *eclat* with which his child was to be made a Christian. True, he had intended requesting the General to act as godfather upon the occasion; but Lady Juliana protested, she would rather the child never should be christened at all, (which already seemed nearly to have been the case) than have that cross vulgar-looking man to stand sponsor. Her Ladyship, however, so far conceded, that the General was to have the honour of giving his name to the next, if a boy, for she was now near her second confinement; and, with this promise, Henry was satisfied to slight the only being in the world, to whom he looked for support to himself and his children. In the utmost delight, the fond mother drove away to consult her confidants upon the name and decorations[2] of the child, whom she had not even looked at for many days.

Every thing succeeded to admiration. Amid crowds of spectators, in all the pomp of lace and satin, surrounded by princes and peers, and handed from duchesses to countesses, the twin daughter of Henry Douglas, and the heroine of future story, became a Christian by the names of Adelaide Julia.

Some months previous to this event, Lady Juliana had received a letter from Mrs. Douglas, informing her of the rapid improvement that had taken place in her little charge, and requesting to know by what name she should have her christened; at the same time gently insinuating her wish, that, in compliance with the custom of the country, and as a compliment due to the family, it should be named after its paternal grandmother.

Lady Juliana glanced over the first line of the letter, then looked at the signature, resolved to read the rest as soon as she should have time to answer it; and, in the meantime, tossed it into a drawer, amongst old visiting cards and unpaid bills.

After vainly waiting for an answer, much beyond the accustomed time when children are baptised, Mrs. Douglas could no longer refuse to accede to the desires of the venerable inmates of Glenfern; and about a month before her favoured sister received her more elegant appellations, the neglected twin was baptized by the name of Mary.

Mrs. Douglas' letter had been enclosed in the following one from Miss Grizzy, and as it had not the good fortune to be perused by the person to whom it was addressed, we deem it but justice to the writer to insert it here.

> 'Glenfern Castle,
> July 30th, 17—.

'MY DEAREST NIECE, LADY JULIANA,

'I am Certain, as indeed we all are, that it will Afford your Ladyship and our dear Nephew the greatest Pleasure to see this letter Franked by our Worthy and

Respectable Friend Sir Sampson Maclaughlan, Bart. especially as it is the First he has ever franked; out of compliment to you, as I assure you he admires you excessively, as indeed we all do. At the same Time, you will of course, I am sure, Sympathise with us all in the distress Occasioned by the melancholy Death of our late Most Obliging Member, Duncan M'Dunsmuir, Esquire, of Dhunacrag and Auchnagoil, who you never have had the Pleasure of seeing. What renders his death Particularly distressing, is, that Lady Maclaughlan is of opinion it was entirely owing to eating Raw oysters, and damp feet. This ought to be a warning to all Young people to take care of Wet feet, and Especially eating Raw oysters, which are certainly Highly dangerous, particularly where there is any Tendency to Gout. I hope, my dear Niece, you have got a pair of Stout walking shoes, and that both Henry and you remember to Change your feet after Walking. I am told Raw Oysters are much the fashion in London at present; but when this Fatal Event comes to be Known, it will of course Alarm people very much, and put them upon their guard both as to Damp Feet, and Raw oysters. Lady Maclaughlan is in High spirits at Sir Sampson's Success, though, at the Same Time, I assure you, she Felt much for the Distress of poor Mr. M'Dunsmuir, and had sent him a Large Box of Pills, and a Bottle of Gout Tincture, only two days before he died. This will be a great Thing for you, and especially for Henry, my dear niece, as Sir Sampson and Lady Maclaughlan are going to London directly to take his Seat in Parliament; and she will make a point of Paying you every attention, and will Matronize you to the play, and any other Public places you may wish to go; as both my Sisters and I are of opinion you are rather Young to matronize yourself yet, and you could not get a more Respectable Matron than Lady Maclaughlan. I hope Harry wont take it amiss, if Sir Sampson does not pay

him so much Attention as he might expect; but he says
that he will not be master of a moment of his own Time
in London. He will be so much taken up with the King
and the Duke of York, that he is afraid he will Disoblige
a great Number of the Nobility by it, besides injuring his
own health by such Constant application to business.
He is to make a very fine Speech in Parliament, but it is
not yet Fixed what his First Motion is to be upon. He
himself wishes to move for a New Subsidy to the Emperor
of Germany;[1] but Lady Maclaughlan is of opinion, that
it would be better to Bring in a Bill for Building a bridge
over the Water of Dlin; which, to be sure, is very much
wanted, as a Horse and Cart were drowned at the Ford
last Speat.[2] We are All, I am happy to Say, in excellent
Health. Becky is recovering from the Measles as well as
could be Wished, and the Rose* is quite gone out of
Bella's Face. Beenie has been prevented from Finishing
a most Beautiful Pair of bottle Sliders[3] for your Ladyship
by a whitlow,[4] but it is now Mending, and I hope will
be done in Time to go with Babby's Vase Carpet, which
is extremely elegant, by Sir S. and Lady Maclaughlan.
This Place is in great Beauty at present, and the new
Byre is completely finished. My Sisters and I regret
Excessively that Henry and you should have seen
Glenfern to such disadvantage; but when next you
favour us with a visit, I hope it will be in Summer, and
the New Byre you will think a Prodigious Improvement.
Our dear Little Grand-niece is in great health, and much
improved. We reckon her Extremely like our Family,
Particularly Becky; though she has a great Look of
Bella, at the Same Time, when she Laughs. Excuse the
Shortness of this Letter, my dear Niece, as I shall Write a
much Longer one by Lady Maclaughlan.

> 'Meantime, I remain, my
>   'Dear Lady Juliana, yours and
>   'Henry's most affect. aunt,

* Erysipelas.   'GRIZZEL DOUGLAS.'

In spite of her husband's remonstrance, Lady Juliana persisted in her resolution of attending her sister-in-law's masked ball, from which she returned, worn out with amusement, and surfeited with pleasure; protesting all the while she dawdled over her evening breakfast the following day, that there was nobody in the world so much to be envied as Lady Lindore. Such jewels! such dresses! such a house! such a husband! so easy and good-natured, and rich and generous! She was sure Lindore did not care what his wife did. She might give what parties she pleased; go where she liked; spend as much money as she chose; and he would never trouble his head about the matter. She was quite certain Lady Lindore had not a single thing to wish for: *ergo*, she must be the happiest woman in the world! All this was addressed to Henry, who had, however, attained the happy art of not hearing above one word out of a hundred that happened to fall from the 'angel lips of his adored Julia;' and, having finished the newspapers, and made himself acquainted with all the blood-horses, thorough-bred *fillies*, and brood mares therein set forth, with a yawn and whistle sauntered away to G.'s, to look at the last regulation epaulettes.[1]

Not long after, as Lady Juliana was stepping into the carriage, that was to whirl her to Bond Street, she was met by her husband; who, with a solemnity of manner that would have startled any one but his volatile lady, requested she would return with him into the house, as he wished to converse with her upon a subject of some importance. He prevailed on her to return, upon condition that he would not detain her above five minutes. When shutting the drawing-room doors, he said, with earnestness, 'I think, Julia, you were talking of Lady Lindore this morning: oblige me by repeating what you said, as I was reading the papers, and really did not attend much to what passed.'

Her Ladyship, in extreme surprise, wondered how
Harry could be so tiresome and absurd as to stop her
airing for any such purpose. She really did not know
what she said. How could she? It was more than an hour
ago.

'Well, then, say what you think of her now,' cried
Douglas impatiently.

'Think of her! why, what all the world must think—
that she is the happiest woman in it. She looked so
uncommonly well last night, and was in such spirits, in
her fancy dress, before she masked. After that, I quite
lost sight of her.'

'As every one else has done: She has not been seen
since. Her favourite St. Leger is missing too, and there
is hardly a doubt but that they are gone off together.'

Even Lady Juliana was shocked at this intelligence,
though the folly, more than the wickedness, of the thing,
seemed to strike her mind; but Henry was no nice
observer, and was therefore completely satisfied with the
disapprobation she expressed for her sister-in-law's
conduct.

'I am so sorry for poor dear Lindore,' said Lady
Juliana, after having exhausted herself in invectives
against his wife: 'Such a generous creature as he to be
used in such a manner—it is quite shocking to think of
it! If he had been an ill-natured stingy wretch, it would
have been nothing; but Frederick is such a noble-hearted
fellow—I dare say he would give me a thousand pounds
if I were to ask him, for he don't care about money.'

'Lord Lindore takes the matter very coolly, I understand,' replied her husband; 'but—don't be alarmed,
dear Julia—your father has suffered a little from the
violence of his feelings. He has had a sort of apoplectic
fit, but is not considered in immediate danger.'

Lady Juliana burst into tears, desired the carriage
might be put up, as she should not go out, and even

declared her intention of abstaining from Mrs. D.'s assembly that evening. Henry warmly commended the extreme propriety of these measures; and, not to be outdone in greatness of mind, most heroically sent an apology to a grand military dinner at the Duke of Y——'s; observing, at the same time, that, in the present state of the family, one or two friends to a quiet family dinner was as much as they should be up to.

CHAPTER XXIV

——'I but purpose to embark with thee,
On the smooth surface of a summer sea,
While gentle zephyrs play in prosp'rous gales,
And Fortune's favour fills the swelling sails.'——
Henry and Emma.[1]

HOW LONG THESE voluntary sacrifices to duty and propriety might have been made, it would not be difficult to guess; but Lady Juliana's approaching confinement rendered her seclusion more and more a matter of necessity; and shortly after these events took place, she presented her delighted husband with a son. Henry lost no time in announcing the birth of his child to General Cameron; and, at the same time, requesting he would stand godfather, and give his name to the child. The answer was as follows:—

'*Hort Lodge, Berks.*

'DEAR HENRY,

'By this time twelvemonth, I hope it will be my turn to communicate to you a similar event in my family, to that which your letter announces to me. As a preliminary step, I am just about to march into quarters for life,

with a young woman, daughter to my steward. She is
healthy, good humoured, and of course vulgar; since she
is no connoisseur in china, and never spoke to a pug-dog
in her life.

'Your allowance will be remitted regularly from my
banker until the day of my death; you will then succeed
to ten thousand pounds, secured to your children, which
is all you have to expect from me. If, after this, you think
it worth your while, you are very welcome to give your
son the name of yours faithfully,

'WILLIAM CAMERON.'

Henry's consternation at the contents of this epistle
was almost equalled by Juliana's indignation. The
daughter of a steward!—heavens! it made her sick to
think of it. It was too shocking! The man ought to be
shut up. Henry ought to prevent him from disgracing
his connexions in such a manner—There ought to be a
law against old men marrying—

'And young ones too,' groaned Douglas, as he thought
of the debts he had contracted on the faith and credit
of being the General's heir; for with all the sanguine
presumption of thoughtless youth, and buoyant spirits,
Henry had no sooner found his fault forgiven, than he
immediately fancied it forgotten, and himself completely
restored to favour. His friends and the world were of the
same opinion; and, as the future possessor of immense
wealth, he found nothing so easy as to borrow money
and contract debts, which he now saw the impossibility
of ever discharging. Still he flattered himself the General
might only mean to frighten him; or he might relent;
or the marriage might go off; or he might not have any
children; and, with these *mighty* hopes, things went on
as usual for some time longer. Lady Juliana, who, to
do her justice, was not of a more desponding character
than her husband, had also her stock of hopes and

expectations always ready to act upon. She was quite sure, that if papa ever came to his senses, (for he had remained in a state of stupefaction since the apoplectic stroke,) he would forgive her, and take her to live with him, now that that vile Lady Lindore was gone: or, if he should never recover, she was equally sure of benefiting by his death; for though he had said he was not to leave her a shilling, she did not believe it: She was sure papa would never do any thing so cruel; and, at any rate, if he did, Lindore was so generous, he would do something very handsome for her; and so forth.

At length the bubbles burst. The same paper that stated the marriage of General William Cameron, to Judith Broadcast, spinster, announced, in all the dignity of woe, the death of that most revered nobleman, and eminent statesman, Augustus Earl of Courtland.

In weak minds, it has generally been remarked, that no medium can be maintained. Where hope holds her dominion, she is too buoyant to be accompanied by her anchor; and between her and despair there are no gradations. Desperate, indeed, now became the condition of the misjudging pair. Lady Juliana's name was not even mentioned in her father's will, and the General's marriage rendered his settlements no longer a secret. In all the horrors of desperation, Henry now found himself daily beset by creditors of every description. At length the fatal blow came. Horses—carriages—every thing they could call their own, were seized. The term for which they held the house was expired, and they found themselves on the point of being turned into the street; when Lady Juliana, who had been for two days, as her woman expressed it, *out of one fit into another*, suddenly recovered strength to signify her desire of being conveyed to her brother's house. A hackney coach was procured, into which the hapless victim of her own follies was carried. Shuddering with disgust, and accompanied by her children and their attendants, she was set down at the noble mansion from which she had fled two years before.

Her brother, whom she fortunately found at home, lolling upon a sofa with a new novel in his hand, received her without any marks of surprise; said those things happened every day; hoped Captain Douglas would contrive to get himself extricated from this slight embarrassment; and informed his sister that she was welcome to occupy her old apartments, which had been lately fitted up for Lady Lindore. Then ringing the bell, he desired the housekeeper might shew Lady Juliana up stairs, and put the children in the nursery; mentioned that he generally dined at eight o'clock;[1] and, nodding to his sister as she quitted the room, returned to his book, as if nothing had occurred to disturb him from it.

In ten minutes after her entrance into Courtland house, Lady Juliana had made greater advances in *religion* and *philosophy* than she had done in the whole nineteen years of her life; for she not only perceived that 'out of evil cometh good;'[2] but was perfectly ready to admit that 'all is for the best,'[3] and that 'whatever is, is right.'[4]

'How lucky is it for me,' exclaimed she to herself, as she surveyed the splendid suite of apartments that were destined for her accommodation—'how very fortunate that things have turned out as they have done; that Lady Lindore should have run off, and that the General's marriage should have taken place, just at the time of poor papa's death'—and, in short, Lady Juliana set no bounds to her self-gratulations, on the happy turn of affairs which had brought about this change in her situation.

To a heart not wholly devoid of feeling, and a mind capable of any thing like reflection, the desolate appearance of this magnificent mansion would have excited emotions of a very different nature. The apartments of the late Earl, with their wide extended doors and windows, sheeted furniture, and air of dreary order, exhibited that waste and chilling aspect, which marks the chambers of death; and even Lady Juliana shuddered, she knew not why, as she passed through them.

Those of Lady Lindore presented a picture not less striking, could her thoughtless successor have profited by the lesson they offered. Here was all that the most capricious fancy, the most boundless extravagance, the most refined luxury, could wish for or suggest. The bed-chamber, dressing-room, and boudoir, were each fitted up in a style that seemed rather suited for the pleasures of an Eastern sultana, or Grecian courtezan, than for the domestic comfort of a British matron.

'I wonder how Lady Lindore could find in her heart to leave this delicious boudoir,' observed Lady Juliana to the old housekeeper.

'I rather wonder, my Lady, how she could find in her heart to leave these pretty babes,' returned the good woman, as a little boy came running into the room, calling, 'mamma, mamma!' Lady Juliana had nothing to say to children beyond a 'how d'ye do, love;' and the child, after regarding her, for a moment, with a look of disappointment, ran away back to his nursery.

When Lady Juliana had fairly settled herself in her new apartments, and the tumult of delight began to subside, it occurred to her that something must be done for poor Harry, whom she had left in the hands of a brother officer, in a state little short of distraction. She accordingly went in search of her brother, to request his advice and assistance, and found him, it being nearly dark, preparing to set out on his morning's ride. Upon hearing the situation of his brother-in-law, he declared himself ready to assist Mr. Douglas as far as he was able, but he had just learned from his people of business, that

his own affairs were somewhat involved. The late Earl
had expended enormous sums on political purposes—
Lady Lindore had run through a prodigious deal of
money, he believed; and he himself had some debts,
amounting, he was told, to seventy thousand pounds.
Lady Juliana was all aghast at this information, which
was delivered with the most perfect *nonchalance* by the
Earl, while he amused himself with his Newfoundland
dog. Unable to conceal her disappointment at these
effects of her brother's 'liberality and generosity,' Lady
Juliana burst into tears.

The Earl's sensibility was akin to his generosity; he
gave money, (or rather allowed it to be taken,) freely
when he had it, from indolence and easiness of temper;
he hated the sight of distress in any individual, because
it occasioned trouble, and was, in short, a *bore*. He
therefore made haste to relieve his sister's alarm, by
assuring her that these were mere trifles. That, as for
Douglas' affairs, he would order his agent to arrange
every thing in his name—hoped to have the pleasure of
seeing him at dinner—recommended to his sister to have
some pheasant pye for luncheon—and, calling Carlo,
set out upon his ride.

However much Lady Juliana had felt mortified and
disappointed at learning the state of her brother's
finances, she began, by degrees, to extract the greatest
consolation from the comparative insignificance of her
own debts to those of the Earl; and accordingly, in
high spirits at this newly discovered and judicious source
of comfort, she dispatched the following note to her
husband:

'DEAREST HENRY,

'I have been received in the kindest manner imaginable by Frederick, and have been put in possession of my
old apartments, which are so much altered, I should

never have known them. They were furnished by Lady
Lindore, who really has a divine taste. I long to shew you
all the delights of this abode. Frederick desired me to
say, that he expects to see you here at dinner, and that he
will take charge of paying all our bills whenever he gets
money. Only think of his owing a hundred thousand
pounds, besides all papa's and Lady Lindore's debts! I
assure you I was almost ashamed to tell him of ours,
they sounded so trifling; but it is quite a relief to find
other people so much worse. Indeed, I always thought it
quite natural for us to run in debt, considering that we
had no money to pay any thing, while Courtland, who
is as rich as a Jew, is so hampered. I shall expect you at
eight, until when, adieu, *mio caro*,[1]

'Your JULIE.

'I am quite wretched about you.'

This tender and consolatory billet Henry had not the
satisfaction of receiving, having been arrested, shortly
after his wife's departure, at the suit of Mr. Shagg, for
the sum of two thousand some odd hundreds, for carriages jobbed, bought, exchanged, repaired, returned,
&c.

Lady Juliana's horror and dismay at the news of
her husband's arrest was excessive. Her only ideas of
confinement were taken from those pictures of the Bastille
and Inquisition, that she had read so much of in French
and German novels; and the idea of a prison was
indissolubly united in her mind with bread and water,
chains and straw, dungeons and darkness. Callous and
selfish, therefore, as she might be, she was not yet so
wholly void of all natural feeling as to think with indifference of the man she had once fondly loved reduced to
such a pitiable condition.

Almost frantic at the phantom of her own creation,
she flew to her brother's apartment, and, in the wildest

and most incoherent manner, besought him to rescue her
poor Henry from chains and a dungeon.

With some difficulty Lord Courtland at length
apprehended the extent of his brother-in-law's misfortune; and, with his usual *sang froid*, smiled at his sister's
simplicity; assured her the King's Bench[1] was the
pleasantest place in the world; that some of his own most
particular friends were there, who gave capital dinners,
and led most desirable lives imaginable.

'And will he really not be fed on bread and water, and
wear chains, and sleep upon straw?' asked the tender
wife, in the utmost surprise and delight: 'Oh, then, he
is not so much to be pitied, though I daresay he would
rather get out of prison too.'

The Earl promised to obtain his release the following
day, and Lady Juliana returned to her toilette, with a
much higher opinion of prisons than she had ever
entertained before.

Lord Courtland, for once in his life, was punctual to
his promise; and even interested himself so thoroughly
in Douglas' affairs, though without inquiring into any
particulars, as to take upon himself the discharge of his
debts, and to procure leave for him to exchange into a
regiment of the line,[2] then under orders for India.

Upon hearing of this arrangement, Lady Juliana's
grief and despair, as usual, set all reason at defiance.
She would not suffer her dear, dear Harry, to leave her.
She knew she could not live without him—she was sure
she should die; and Harry would be sea-sick, and grow
so yellow, and so ugly, that, when he came back, she
should never have any comfort in him again.

Henry, who had never doubted her readiness to
accompany him, immediately hastened to assuage her
anguish, by assuring her, that it had always been his
intention to take her along with him.

That was worse and worse:—she wondered how he

could be so barbarous and absurd as to think of her leaving all her friends, and going to live amongst savages. She had done a great deal in living so long contentedly with him in Scotland; but she never could, nor would make, such another sacrifice. Besides, she was sure poor Courtland could not do without her; she knew he never would marry again; and who would take care of his dear children, and educate them properly, if she did not. It would be too ungrateful to desert Frederick, after all he had done for them.

The pride of the man, as much as the affection of the husband, was irritated by this resistance to his will; and a violent scene of reproach and recrimination terminated in an eternal farewell.

END OF VOLUME FIRST

VOLUME II

CHAPTER I

'In age, in infancy, from others aid
Is all our hope; to teach us to be kind,
That nature's first, last lesson.'

Young.[1]

THE NEGLECTED DAUGHTER of Lady Juliana Douglas,
experienced all the advantages naturally to be expected
from her change of situation. Her watchful aunt super-
intended the years of her infancy, and all that a tender
and judicious mother *could* do—all that most mothers
think they do—she performed. Mrs. Douglas, though
not a woman either of words or systems, possessed a
reflecting mind, and a heart warm with benevolence
towards every thing that had a being; and all the best
feelings of her nature were excited by the little outcast,
thus abandoned by her unnatural parent. As she pressed
the unconscious babe to her bosom, she thought how
blest she should have been, had a child of her own thus
filled her arms; but the reflection called forth no selfish
murmurs from her chastened spirit. While the tear of soft
regret trembled in her eye, that eye was yet raised in
gratitude to heaven for having called forth those delightful affections which might otherwise have slumbered in
her heart.

Mrs. Douglas had read much, and reflected more; and many faultless theories of education had floated in her mind. But her good sense soon discovered how unavailing all theories were, whose foundations rested upon the inferred wisdom of the teacher; and how intricate and unwieldy must be the machinery for the human mind, where the human hand alone is to guide and uphold it. To engraft into her infant soul the purest principles of religion, was therefore the chief aim of Mary's preceptress. The fear of God was the only restraint imposed upon her dawning intellect; and from the Bible alone was she taught the duties of morality—not in the form of a dry code of laws, to be read with a solemn face on Sundays, or learned with weeping eyes as a weekday task—but adapted to her youthful capacity by judicious illustration, and familiarized to her taste by hearing its stories and precepts from the lips she best loved. Mrs. Douglas was the friend and confidant of her pupil: to her all her hopes and fears, wishes and dreads, were confided; and the first effort of her reason was the discovery, that to please her aunt, she must study to please her Maker.

'L'inutilité de la vie des femmes, est la première source de leurs désordres.'[1]

Mrs. Douglas was fully convinced of the truth of this observation, and that the mere selfish cares and vulgar bustle of life are not sufficient to satisfy the immortal soul, however they may serve to engross it.

A portion of Mary's time was therefore devoted to the daily practice of the great duties of life; in administering, in some shape or other, to the wants and misfortunes of her fellow-creatures, without requiring from them that their virtue should have been immaculate, or expecting that their gratitude should be everlasting.

'It is better,' thought Mrs. Douglas, 'that we should sometimes be deceived by others, than that we should learn to deceive ourselves; and the charity and good will that is suffered to lie dormant, or feed itself on speculative acts of beneficence, for want of proper objects to call it into use, will soon become the corroding rust that will destroy the best feelings of our nature.'

But, although Mary strenuously applied herself to the uses of life, its embellishments were by no means neglected. She was happily endowed by nature; and, under the judicious management of her aunt, made rapid though unostentatious progress in the improvement of the talents committed to her care. Without having been blessed with the advantages of a dancing-master, her step was light, and her motions free and graceful; and if her aunt had not been able to impart to her the favourite graces of the most fashionable singer of the day, neither had she thwarted the efforts of her own natural taste, in forming a style full of simplicity and feeling. In the modern languages she was perfectly skilled; and if her drawings wanted the enlivening touches of the master to give them effect; as an atonement, they displayed a perfect knowledge of the rules of perspective and the study of the bust.

All this was however mere leather and prunella[1] to the ladies of Glenfern; and many were the cogitations and consultations that took place on the subject of Mary's mismanagement. According to their ideas, there could be but one good system of education; and that was the one that had been pursued with them, and through them transmitted to their nieces.

To attend the parish church, and remember the text; to observe who was there, and who was *not* there; and to wind up the evening with a sermon stuttered and stammered through by one of the girls, (the worst reader always piously selected, for the purpose of improving their reading,) and particularly addressed to the Laird, openly and avowedly snoring in his arm

chair, though at every pause starting up with a peevish
'Weel?'[1]—this was the sum total of their religious duties.
Their moral virtues were much upon the same scale;
to knit stockings, scold servants, cement china, trim
bonnets, lecture the poor, and look up to Lady Maclaughlan, comprised nearly their whole code. But these
were the virtues of ripened years and enlarged understandings; what their pupils might hope to arrive at, but
could not presume to meddle with. *Their* merits consisted
in being compelled to sew certain large portions of white
work; learning to read and write in the worst manner;
occasionally *wearing a collar*,[2] and learning the notes on
the spinnet. These acquirements, accompanied with a
great deal of lecturing and fault-finding, sufficed for the
first fifteen years; when the two next, passed at a provincial boarding-school, were supposed to impart every
graceful accomplishment to which women could attain.

Mrs. Douglas' method of conveying instruction, it
may easily be imagined, did not square with their ideas
on that subject. They did nothing themselves without
a bustle, and to do a thing quietly, was to them the same
as not doing it at all—it could not be done, for nobody
had ever heard of it. In short, like many other worthy
people, their ears were their only organs of intelligence—
they believed every thing they were told; but, unless they
were told, they believed nothing. They had never heard
Mrs. Douglas expatiate on the importance of the trust
reposed in her, or enlarge on the difficulties of female
education; *ergo*, Mrs. Douglas could have no idea of the
nature of the duties she had undertaken.

Their visits to Lochmarlie only served to confirm the
fact. Miss Jacky deponed, that during the month she
was there, she never could discover when or how it was,
that Mary got her lessons; luckily the child was quick,
and had contrived, poor thing! to pick up things wonderfully, nobody knew how, for it was really astonishing to

see how little pains were bestowed upon her; and the worst of it was, that she seemed to do just as she liked, for nobody ever heard her reproved, and every body knew that young people never could have enough said to them. All this differed widely from the *eclat* of their system, and could not fail of causing great disquiet to the sisters.

'I declare, I'm quite confounded at all this!' said Miss Grizzy, at the conclusion of Miss Jacky's communication. 'It really appears, as if Mary, poor thing! was getting no education at all; and yet she *can* do things, too. I can't understand it; and it's very odd in Mrs. Douglas to allow her to be so much neglected, for certainly Mary's constantly with herself; which, to be sure, shews that she is very much spoilt; for although our girls are as fond of us as, I am sure, any creatures can be, yet, at the same time, they are always very glad—which is quite natural —to run away from us.'

'I think it's high time Mary had done something fit to be seen,' said Miss Nicky. 'She is now sixteen past.'

'Most girls of Mary's time of life, that ever *I* had any thing to do with,' replied Jacky, with a certain wave of the head, peculiar to sensible women, 'had something to shew before her age. Bella had worked the globe[1] long before she was sixteen; and Babby did her fillagree tea-caddy the first quarter she was at Miss Macgowk's,' glancing with triumph from the one which hung in a gilt frame over the mantle-piece, to the other which stood on the tea table, shrouded in a green bag.

'And, to be sure,' rejoined Grizzy, 'although Betsy's[2] skreen did cost a great deal of money—that can't be denied; and her father certainly grudged it very much at the time—there's no doubt of that; yet certainly it does her the greatest credit, and it is a great satisfaction to us all to have these things to shew. I am sure nobody would ever think that ass was made of crape, and how naturally it seems to be eating the beautiful chenille thistle! I declare, I think the ass is as like an ass as any thing can be! And as to Mary's drawing,' continued the narrator of her deficiencies, 'there is not one of them fit for framing: mere scratches with a chalk pencil—what any child might do.'

'And to think,' said Nicky, with indignation, 'how little Mrs. Douglas seemed to think of the handsome coloured views of Inverary and Dunkeld[1] the girls did at Miss Macgowk's.'

'All our girls have the greatest genius for drawing,' observed Grizzy; 'there can be no doubt of that; but it's a thousand pities, I'm sure, that none of them seem to like it. To be sure, they say—what I daresay is very true —that they can't get such good paper as they got at Miss Macgowk's; but they have shewed that they *can* do, for their drawings are quite astonishing. Somebody lately took them to be Mr. Touchup's own doing; and I'm sure there could'nt be a greater compliment than that! I represented all that to Mrs. Douglas, and urged her very strongly to give Mary the benefit of, at least, a quarter of Miss Macgowk's, were it only for the sake of her carriage; or, at least, to make her wear our collar.'

This was the tenderest of all themes, and bursts of sorrowful exclamations ensued. The collar had long been a galling yoke upon their minds; its iron had entered into their very souls; for it was a collar presented to the family of Glenfern, by the wisest, virtuousest, best of women, and of grandmothers, the good Lady Girnach-gowl; and had been worn in regular rotation by every female of the family, till now, that Mrs. Douglas positively refused to subject Mary's pliant form to its thral-dom. Even the Laird, albeit no connoisseur in any shapes, save those of his kine,[2] was of opinion, that since the thing was in the house, it was a pity it should be lost. Not Venus' girdle[3] even was supposed to confer greater charms than the Girnachgowl collar.

'It's really most distressing!' said Miss Grizzy, to her friend Lady Maclaughlan. 'Mary's back won't be worth a farthing; and we have always been quite famous for our backs.'

'Humph!—that's the reason people are always so glad to see them, child.'

With regard to Mary's looks, opinions were not so decided. Mrs. Douglas thought her, what she was, an elegant interesting looking girl. The Laird, as he peered at her over his spectacles, pronounced her to be but a shilpit[1] thing, though weel aneugh, considering the ne'er-do-weels that were aught her.[2] Miss Jacky opined, that she would have been quite a different creature, had she been brought up like any other girl. Miss Grizzy did not know what to think; she certainly was pretty— nobody could dispute that. At the same time, many people would prefer Bella's looks; and Babby was certainly uncommonly comely. Miss Nicky thought it was no wonder she looked pale sometimes. She never supped her broth in a wise-like way at dinner; and it was a shame to hear of a girl of Mary's age being set up with tea[3] to her breakfast, and wearing white petticoats in winter—and such roads, too!

Lady Maclaughlan pronounced (and that was next to a special revelation) that the girl would be handsome when she was forty, not a day sooner; and she would be clever, for her mother was a fool; and foolish mothers had always wise children, and *vice versa*, 'and your mother was a very clever woman, girls—humph!'

Thus passed the early years of the almost forgotten twin; blest in the warm affection and mild authority of her more than mother. Sometimes Mrs. Douglas half-formed the wish, that her beloved pupil should mix in society, and become known to the world; but when she reflected on the dangers of that world, and on the little solid happiness its pleasures afford, she repressed the wish, and only prayed she might be allowed to rest secure in the simple pleasures she then enjoyed. 'Happiness is not a plant of this earth,' said she to herself with a sigh; 'but God gives peace and tranquillity to the virtuous in all situations, and under every trial. Let me then strive to make Mary virtuous, and leave the rest to Him who alone knoweth what is good for us!'[1]

CHAPTER II

'Th' immortal line in sure succession reigns,
The fortune of the family remains,
And grandsires' grandsons the long list contains.'

Dryden's Virgil.[2]

————————'We are such stuff
As dreams are made on; and our little life
Is rounded with a sleep.'

Tempest.[3]

BUT MARY'S BACK, and Mary's complexion, now ceased to be the first objects of interest at Glenfern; for, to the inexpressible delight and amazement of the sisters, Mrs. Douglas, after due warning, became the mother of a son. How this event had been brought about without the intervention of Lady Maclaughlan, was past the powers of Miss Grizzy's comprehension. To the last moment, they had been sceptical; for Lady Maclaughlan had shook her head, and humphed whenever the subject was mentioned. For several months they had therefore vibrated between their own sanguine hopes, and their oracle's disheartening doubts; and, even when the truth was manifest, a sort of vague tremor took possession of their mind as to what Lady Maclaughlan would think of it.

'I declare I don't very well know how to announce this happy event to Lady Maclaughlan,' said Miss Grizzy, as she sat in a ruminating posture, with her pen in her hand; 'it will give her the greatest pleasure, I know that; she has such a regard for our family, she would go any lengths for us. At the same time, every body must be sensible it is a delicate matter to tell a person of Lady Maclaughlan's skill they have been mistaken. I'm sure I don't know how she may take it; and yet she can't suppose it will make any difference in our sentiments for her. She must be sensible we have all the greatest respect for her opinion.'

'The wisest people are sometimes mistaken,' observed Miss Jacky.

'I'm sure, Jacky, that's very true,' said Grizzy, brightening up at the brilliancy of this remark.

'And it's better she should have been mistaken than Mrs. Douglas,' followed up Miss Nicky.

'I declare, Nicky, you are perfectly right; and I shall just say so at once to Lady Maclaughlan.'

The epistle was forthwith commenced by the enlightened Grizelda. Miss Joan applied herself to the study of 'The Whole Duty of Man,'[1] which she was determined to make herself mistress of for the benefit of her grand-nephew; and Miss Nicholas fell to reckoning all who could, would, or should, be at the christening, that she might calculate upon the quantity of *dreamingbread* that would be required. The younger ladies were busily engaged in divers and sundry disputes regarding the right to succession to a once-white lutestring[2] negligée of their mother's, which three of them had laid their accounts with figuring in at the approaching celebration. The old gentleman was the only one in the family who took the least of the general happiness. He had got into a habit of being fretted about every thing that happened, and he could not entirely divest himself of it even upon this occasion. His parsimonious turns, too, had considerably increased; and his only criterion of judging of any thing was according to what it would bring.

'Sorra tak me,[1] if ane wad nae think, to hear ye, this was the first bairn that e'er was born! What's a' the fraize[2] aboot, ye gowks?[3] (to his daughters)—a whingin get![4] that'll tak mair oot o' fowk's pockets than e'er it'll pit[5] into them! Mony a guid profitable beast's been brought into the warld, and ne'er a word in'ts heed.'[6]

All went on smoothly. Lady Maclaughlan testified no resentment. Miss Jacky had 'The Whole Duty of Man' at her finger-ends; and Miss Nicky was not more serene than could have been expected, considering, as she did, how the servants at Lochmarlie must be living at hack and manger.[7] It had been decided at Glenfern, that the infant heir to its consequence could not, with propriety, be christened any where but at the seat of his forefathers. Mr. and Mrs. Douglas had good-humouredly yielded the point; and, as soon as she was able for the change, the whole family took up their residence for a season under the paternal roof.

Blissful visions floated around the pillows of the happy spinsters the night preceding the christening, which were duly detailed at the breakfast-table the following morning.

'I declare I don't know what to think of my dream,' began Miss Grizzy: 'I dreamt, that Lady Maclaughlan was upon her knees to you, brother, to get you to take an emetic; and, just as she had mixed it up so nicely in some of our black currant jelly, little Norman snatched it out of your hand, and ran away with it.'

'You're aneugh to turn ony body's stamick[8] wi' your nonsense,' returned the Laird gruffly.

'And I,' said Miss Jacky, 'thought I saw you standing in your shirt, brother, as straight as a rash,[9] and good

Lady Girnachgowl buckling her collar upon you with her own hands.'

'I wish ye wad na deive me wi' your havers!'[1] still more indignantly, and turning his shoulder to the fair dreamer, as he continued to con over the newspaper.

'And I,' cried Miss Nicky, eager to get her mystic tale disclosed, 'I thought, brother, I saw you take and throw all the good dreaming-bread into the ash-hole.'

'By my troth, an' ye deserve to be thrown after't!' exclaimed the exasperated Laird, as he quitted the room in high wrath, muttering to himself, 'Hard case—canna get peace—eat my vittals—fules—tawpies[2]—clavers!'[3] &c. &c.

'I declare I can't conceive why Glenfern should be so ill pleased at our dreams,' said Miss Grizzy. 'Every body knows dreams are always contrary; and, even were it otherwise, I'm sure I should think no shame to take an emetic, especially when Lady Maclaughlan was at the trouble of mixing it up so nicely.'

'And we have all worn good Lady Girnachgowl's collar before now,' said Miss Jacky.

'I think I had the worst of it, that had all my good dreaming-bread destroyed,' added Miss Nicky.

'Nothing could be more natural than your dreams,' said Mrs. Douglas, 'considering how all these subjects have engrossed you for some time past. You, aunt Grizzy, may remember how desirous you were of administering one of Lady Maclaughlan's powders to my little boy yesterday; and you, aunt Jacky, made a point of trying Lady Girnachgowl's collar upon Mary, to convince her how pleasant it was; while you, aunt Nicky, had experienced a great alarm in supposing your cake had been burned in the oven. And these being the most vivid impressions you had received during the day, it was perfectly natural that they should have retained their influence during a portion of the night.'

The interpretations were received with high disdain. One and all declared they never dreamed of any thing that *had* occurred; and therefore the visions of the night portended some extraordinary good fortune to the family in general, and to little Norman in particular.

'The best fortune I can wish for him, and all of us for this day, is, that he should remain quiet during the ceremony,' said his mother, who was not so elated as Lady Macbeth at the predictions of the sisters.[1]

The christening party mustered strong; and the rites of baptism were duly performed by the Rev. Duncan M'Drone. The little Christian had been kissed by every lady in company, and pronounced by the matrons to be 'a dainty little *doug!*'[2] and by the misses to be 'the sweetest lamb they had ever seen!' The cake and wine was in its progress round the company; when, upon its being tendered to the old gentleman, who was sitting silent in his arm-chair, he abruptly exclaimed, in a most discordant voice, 'Hey! what's a' this wastery[3] for?'—and, ere an answer could be returned, his jaw dropped, his eyes fixed, and the Laird of Glenfern ceased to breathe!

CHAPTER III

'They say miracles are past; and we have our philosophical persons to make modern and familiar things supernatural and causeless. Hence it is, that we make trifles of terrors; ensconcing ourselves into seeming knowledge, when we should submit ourselves to an unknown fear.'

All's Well that Ends Well.[4]

ALL ATTEMPTS TO reanimate the lifeless form proved unavailing; and the horror and consternation that reigned in the castle of Glenfern may be imagined, but cannot be described. There is perhaps no feeling of our nature so vague, so complicated, so mysterious, as that with which we look upon the cold remains of our fellow-mortals. The dignity with which death invests even the meanest of his victims, inspires us with an awe no living thing can create. The monarch on this throne is less awful than the beggar in his shroud. The marble features—the powerless hand—the stiffened limbs—oh! who can contemplate these with feelings that can be defined? These are the mockery of all our hopes and fears, our fondest love, our fellest hate. Can it be, that we now shrink with horror from the touch of that hand, which but yesterday was fondly clasped in our own? Is that tongue, whose accents even now dwell in our ear, for ever chained in the silence of death? These black and heavy eye-lids, are they for ever to seal up in darkness the eyes whose glance no earthly power could restrain? And the spirit which animated the clay, where is it now? Is it wrapt in bliss, or dissolved in woe? Does it witness our grief, and share our sorrows? or is the mysterious tye that linked it with mortality for ever broken? and the remembrance of earthly scenes, are they indeed to the enfranchised spirit as the morning dream, or the dew upon the early flowers? Reflections such as these naturally arise in every breast. Their influence is felt, though their import cannot always be expressed. The principle is in all the same, however it may differ in its operations.

In the family assembled round the lifeless form, that had so long been the centre of their domestic circle, grief shewed itself under various forms. The calm and manly sorrow of the son; the saint-like feelings of his wife; the youthful agitation of Mary; the weak super-stitious wailings of the sisters; and the loud uncontrolled lamentations of the daughters; all betokened an intensity of suffering that arose from the same source, varied

according to the different channels in which it flowed.
Even the stern Lady Maclaughlan was subdued to
something of kindred feeling; and though no tears
dropped from her eyes, she sat by her friends, and
sought, in her own way, to soften their affliction.

The assembled guests, who had not yet been able to
take their departure,[1] remained in the drawing-room in a
sort of restless solemnity peculiar to seasons of collateral
affliction, where all seek to heighten the effect upon others,
and shift the lesson from themselves. Various were the
surmises and speculations as to the cause of the awful
transition that had just taken place.

'Glenfern was nae like a man that wad hae gaen aff
in this gate,'[2] said one.

'I dinna ken,'[3] said another; 'I've notic'd a chainge
on Glenfern for a gay while[4] noo.'

'I agree wi' you, Sir,' said a third: 'In my mind,
Glenfern's been droopin' very sair[5] ever since the last
tryst.'[6]

'At Glenfern's time o' life, it's no surprisin',' remarked
a fourth, who felt perfectly secure of being fifteen years
his junior.

'Glenfern was na that auld neither,' retorted a fifth,
whose conscience smote him with being several years his
senior.

'But he had a deal o' vexation frae his faemilly,' said
an elderly bachelor.

'Ye offen see a hale stoot man, like our puir freend,
gang like the snuff o' a cannel,' coughed up a phthisicky
gentleman.

'He was ay a tume boss-lookin'[7] man, ever since I
mind him,' wheezed out a swollen asthmatic figure.

'An' he took nae care o' himsel,' said the Laird of
Pettlechass. 'His diet was nae what it should hae been
at his time o' life. An' he was oot an' in, up an' doon, in a'
wathers, wat an' dry.'

'Glenfern's doings had naething to du wi' his death,' said an ancient gentlewoman with solemnity. 'They maun ken[1] little wha ne'er heard the bod-word[2] of the familly.' And she repeated in Gaelic words to the following effect:

'When Lochdow shall turn to a lin,*
In Glenfern ye'll hear the din;
When frae Benenck they shool the sna',[2]
O'er Glenfern the leaves will fa';
When foreign geer grows on Benenck tap,
Then the fir tree will be Glenfern's hap.'

'An' noo, ma'am, will ye be sae gude as point oot the meanin' o' this freet,'[4] said an incredulous looking member of the company; 'for when I passed Lochdow this mornin', I neither saw nor heard o' a lin; an' frae this window we can aw see Benenck wi' his white night-cap on; an' he wad hae little to do that wad try to shool it aff.'

'It's neither o' the still water, nor the stay brae,[5] that the word was spoke,' replied the dame, with a disdainful frown; 'they tak nae part in our doings: but kent ye nae that Lochdow himself had tined[6] his sight in a cataract; an' is nae there dule[7] an' din aneuch in Glenfern the day? An' kent ye nae that Benenck had his auld white pow[8] shaven, an' that he's gettin' a jeezy[9] frae Edinburgh?—an' I'se warran'[10] he'll be in his braw[11] wig the very day that Glenfern'll be laid in his deal coffin.'

The company admitted the application was too close to be resisted; but the same sceptic (who, by the bye, was only a low country merchant, elevated, by purchase, to the dignity of a Highland laird,) was seen to shrug his shoulders, and heard to make some sneering remarks on the days of second sights, and such superstitious non-

* Cataract.

sense, being past. This was instantly laid hold of; and, amongst many others of the same sort, the truth of the following story was attested by one of the party, as having actually occurred in his family within his own remembrance.

'As Duncan M'Crae was one evening descending Benvoilloich, he perceived a funeral procession in the vale beneath. He was greatly surprised, not having heard of any death in the country; and this appeared to be the burial of some person of consequence from the number of the attendants. He made all the haste he could to get down; and, as he drew near, he counted all the lairds of the country except my father, Sir Murdoch. He was astonished at this, till he recollected that he was away to the low country to his cousin's marriage; but he felt curious to know who it was, though some unaccountable feeling prevented him from mixing with the followers. He therefore kept on the ridge of the hill, right over their heads, and near enough to hear them speak; but although he saw them move their lips, no sound reached his ear. He kept along with the procession in this way, till it reached the Castle Dochart burying-ground, and there it stopped. The evening was close and warm, and a thick mist had gathered in the glen, while the tops of the hills shone like gold. Not a breath of air was stirring; but the trees that grew round the burying-ground, waved and soughed, and some withered leaves were swirled round and round, as if by the wind. The company stood a while to rest, and then they proceeded to open the iron gates of the burying-ground; but the lock was rusted, and would not open. Then they began to pull down part of the wall; and Duncan thought how angry his master would be at this, and he raised his voice, and shouted, and hallooed to them, but to no purpose. Nobody seemed to hear him. At last the wall was taken down, and the coffin was lifted over, and just then the sun broke out, and glinted on a new made grave; and as they were laying the coffin in it, it gave way, and disclosed Sir Murdoch himself in his dead clothes; and then the mist grew so thick, Duncan could see no more, and how to get home he knew not; but when he entered his own door, he was bathed in sweat, and white as any corpse; and all that he could say was, that he had seen Castle Dochart's burying.[1]

'The following day,' continued the narrator, 'he was more composed, and gave the account you have now heard; and three days after came the intelligence of my father's death. He had dropt down in a fit that very evening, when entertaining a large company in honour of his cousin's marriage; and that day week his funeral passed through Glenvalloch exactly as described by Duncan M'Crae, with all the particulars: The gates of the burying ground could not be opened; part of the wall was taken down to admit the coffin, which received some injury, and gave way as they were placing it in the grave.'

Even the low-country infidel was silenced by the solemnity of this story; and soon after the company dispersed, every one panting to be the first to circulate the intelligence of Glenfern's death.

But soon!—Oh, how soon!—'dies in human hearts the thought of death!'[2] Even the paltry detail which death creates, serves to detach our minds from the cause itself. So it was with the family of Glenfern. Their light did not 'shine inward;'[3] and after the first burst of sorrow, their ideas fastened with avidity on all the paraphernalia of affliction. Mr. Douglas, indeed, found much to do, and to direct to be done. The elder ladies began to calculate how many yards of broad hemming would be required, and to form a muster-roll of the company; with this improvement, that it was to be ten times as numerous as the one that had assembled at the christening: while the young ones busied their imaginations as to the effect of new mournings—a luxury to them hitherto unknown. Mrs. Douglas and Mary were differently affected. Religion and reflection had taught the former, the enviable lesson of possessing her soul in patience under every trial; and while she inwardly mourned the fate of the poor old man who had been thus suddenly snatched from the only world that ever had engaged his thoughts, her outward aspect was calm and serene. The impression made upon Mary's feelings was of a more powerful nature. She had witnessed suffering, and watched by sick-beds; but death, and death in so terrific a form, was new to her. She had been standing by her grandfather's chair—her head was bent to his—her hand rested upon his, when, by a momentary convulsion, she beheld the last dread change—the living man transformed into the lifeless corpse. The countenance but now fraught with life and human thoughts, in the twinkling of an eye, was covered with the shades of death! It was in vain that Mary prayed, and reasoned, and strove against the feelings that had been thus powerfully excited. One object alone possessed her imagination—the image of her grandfather dying—dead; his grim features—his ghastly visage—his convulsive grasp—were ever present, by day and by night. Her nervous system had received a shock too powerful for all the strength of her understanding to contend with. Mrs. Douglas sought, by every means, to sooth her feelings, and divert her attention; and flattered herself that a short time would allay the perturbation of her youthful emotions.

Five hundred persons, horse and foot, high and low, male and female, graced the obsequies of the Laird of Glenfern. Benenck was there in his new wig, and the autumnal leaves dropped on the coffin as it was borne slowly along the vale!

CHAPTER IV

'It is no diminution, but a recommendation of human nature,
that, in some instances, passion gets the better of reason, and all
that we can think, is impotent against half what we feel.'

Spectator.[1]

'LIFE IS A mingled yarn;'[2] few of its afflictions but
are accompanied with some alleviation—none of its
blessings that do not bring some alloy. Like most other
events, that long have formed the object of yearning and
almost hopeless wishes, and on which have been built
the fairest structure of human felicity, the arrival
of the young heir of Glenfern produced a less extraordinary degree of happiness than had been anticipated. The melancholy event which had marked the
first ceremonial of his life, had cast its gloom alike on all
nearly connected with him; and when time had dispelled
the clouds of recent mourning, and restored the mourners
to their habitual train of thought and action, somewhat
of the novelty, which had given him such lively interest
in the hearts of the sisters, had subsided. The distressing
conviction, too, more and more forced itself upon them,
that their advice and assistance were likely to be wholly
overlooked in the nurture of the infant mind, and
management of the thriving frame of their little nephew.
Their active energies therefore, driven back to the
accustomed channels, after many murmurs and severe
struggles, again revolved in the same sphere as before.
True, they sighed and mourned for a time, but soon found
occupation congenial to their nature in the little depart-
ments of life: dressing crape; reviving black silk; con-
verting narrow hems into broad hems; and, in short,
who so busy, who so important, as the ladies of Glenfern?
As Madame de Stael, or de Something says, 'they fulfilled
their destinies.'[3] Their walk lay amongst tapes and pickles;
their sphere extended from the garret to the pantry; and

often, as they sought to diverge from it, their instinct always led them to return to it, as the tract in which they were destined to move. There are creatures of the same sort in the male part of the creation, but it is foreign to my purpose to describe them at present. Neither are the trifling and insignificant of either sex to be treated with contempt, or looked upon as useless by those whom God has gifted with higher powers. In the arrangements of an all-wise Providence, there is nothing created in vain. Every link of the vast chain[1] that embraces creation helps to hold together the various relations of life; and all is beautiful gradation, from the human vegetable to the glorious archangel.

If patient hope, if unexulting joy, and chastened anticipation, sanctifying a mother's love, could have secured her happiness, Mrs. Douglas would have found, in the smiles of her infant, all the comfort her virtue deserved. But she still had to drink of that cup of sweet and bitter, which must bathe the lips of all who breathe the breath of life.

While the instinct of a parent's love warmed her heart, as she pressed her infant to her bosom, the sadness of affectionate and rational solicitude stifled every sentiment of pleasure, as she gazed on the altered and drooping form of her adopted daughter—of the child who had already repaid the cares that had been lavished on her, and in whom she descried the promise of a plenteous harvest from the good seed she had sown. Though Mary had been healthy in childhood, her constitution was naturally delicate, and she had latterly outgrown her strength. The shock she had sustained by her grandfather's death, thus operating on a weakened frame, had produced an effect apparently most alarming; and the efforts she made to exert herself, only served to exhaust her. She felt all the watchful solicitude, the tender anxieties of her aunt, and bitterly reproached herself with not better repaying these exertions for her happiness. A thousand times she tried to analyse and extirpate the saddening impression that weighed upon her heart.

'It is not sorrow,' reasoned she with herself, 'that thus oppresses me; for though I reverenced my grandfather, yet the loss of his society has scarcely been felt by me. It cannot be fear—the fear of death; for my soul is not so abject as to confine its desires to this sublunary scene. What then is this mysterious dread that has taken possession of me? Why do I suffer my mind to suggest to me images of horror, instead of visions of bliss? Why can I not, as formerly, picture to myself the beauty and the brightness of a soul casting off mortality? Why must the convulsed grasp, the stifled groan, the glaring eye, for ever come betwixt heaven and me?'

Alas! Mary was unskilled to answer. Hers was the season for feeling, not for reasoning. She knew not that hers was the struggle of imagination striving to maintain its ascendancy over reality. She had heard and read, and thought, and talked of death; but it was of death in its fairest form—in its softest transition: and the veil had been abruptly torn from her eyes; the gloomy pass had suddenly disclosed itself before her, not strewed with flowers, but shrouded in horrors. Like all persons of sensibility, Mary had a disposition to view every thing in a *beau-idéal*: whether that is a boon most fraught with good or ill, it were difficult to ascertain. While the delusion lasts, it is productive of pleasure to its possessor; but oh! the thousand aches that heart is destined to endure, which clings to the stability, and relies on the permanency of earthly happiness! But the youthful heart must ever remain a stranger to this saddening truth. Experience only can convince us, that happiness is not a plant of this world; and that, though many an eye hath beheld its blossoms, no mortal hand hath ever gathered its fruits. This, then, was Mary's first lesson in what is called the knowledge of life, as opposed to the *beau-idéal* of a young and ardent imagination, in love with life, and luxuriating in its own happiness. And, upon such a mind, it could not fail of producing a powerful impression.

The anguish Mrs. Douglas experienced, as she witnessed the changing colour, lifeless step, and forced smile of her darling *élève*, was not mitigated by the good sense or sympathy of those around her. While Mary had prospered under her management, in the consciousness that she was fulfilling her duty to the best of her abilities, she could listen, with placid cheerfulness, to the broken hints of disapprobation, or forced good wishes for the success of her new-fangled schemes, that were levelled at her by the sisters. But now, when her cares seemed defeated, it was an additional thorn in her heart to have to endure the common-place wisdom, and self-gratulations of the almost exulting aunts; not that they had the slightest intention of wounding the feelings of their niece, whom they really loved, but the temptation was irresistible of proving, that they had been in the right, and she in the wrong, especially as no such acknowledgment had yet been extorted from her.

'It is nonsense to ascribe Mary's dwining[1] to her grandfather's death,' said Miss Jacky. 'We were all nearer to him in propinquity than she was, and none of our healths have suffered.'

'And there's his own daughters,' added Miss Grizzy, 'who, of course, must have felt a great deal more than any body else—there can be no doubt of that—Such sensible creatures as them must feel a great deal; but yet you see how they have got up their spirits—I'm sure it's wonderful!'

'It shews their sense, and the effects of education,' said Miss Jacky.

'Girls that sup their porridge, will always cut a good figure,' quoth Nicky.

'With their fine feelings, I'm sure, we have all reason to be thankful that they have been blest with such hearty stomachs,' observed Miss Grizzy; 'if they had been delicate, like poor Mary's, I'm sure, I declare I don't know what we would have done; for certainly they were all most dreadfully affected at their excellent father's death; which was quite natural, poor things! I'm sure there was no pacifying poor Babby, and even yet, neither Bella nor Betsy can bear to be left alone in a dark room. Tibby has to sleep with them still every night; and a lighted candle too—which is much to their credit—and yet I'm sure it's not with reading. I'm certain—indeed, I think there's no doubt of it—that reading does young people much harm. It puts things into their heads that never would have been there, but for books. I declare, I think reading's a very dangerous thing. I'm certain all Mary's bad health is entirely owing to reading. You know, we always thought she read a great deal too much for her good.'

'Much depends upon the choice of books,' said Jacky, with an air of the most profound wisdom. 'Fordyce's Sermons,[1] and the History of Scotland,[2] are two of the very few books *I* would put into the hands of a young woman. Our girls have read little else,'—casting a look at Mrs. Douglas, who was calmly pursuing her work in the midst of this shower of darts all levelled at her.

'To be sure,' returned Grizzy, 'it is a thousand pities that Mary has been allowed to go on so long; not, I'm sure, that any of us mean to reflect upon you, my dear Mrs. Douglas; for of course it was all owing to your ignorance and inexperience; and that, you know, you could not help; so it was not your fault; nobody can blame you. I'm certain you would have done what was right, if you had only known better; but, of course, we must all know much better than you; because, you know, we are all a great deal older, and especially Lady

Maclaughlan, who has the greatest experience in the diseases of old men especially, and infants. Indeed it has been the study of her life almost; for, you know, poor Sir Sampson is never well; and, I dare say, if Mary had taken some of her nice worm-lozenges, which certainly cured Duncan M'Nab's wife's daughter's little girl of the jaundice, and used that valuable growing embrocation, which we are all sensible made Babby a great deal fatter, I dare say there would have been nothing the matter with her to-day.'

'Mary has been too much accustomed to spend both her time and money amongst idle vagrants,' said Nicky.

'Economy of both,' subjoined Jacky, with an air of humility, 'I confess *I* have ever been accustomed to consider as virtues. These handsome respectable new bonnets,' looking *from* Mrs. Douglas, 'that our girls got just before their poor father's death, were entirely the fruits of their own saving.'

'And I declare,' said Grizzy, who did not excel in innuendos; 'I declare, for my part—although at the same time, my dear niece, I'm certain you are far from intending it—I really think it's very disrespectful to Sir Sampson and Lady Maclaughlan, in any body, and especially such near neighbours, to give more in charity than they do; for, you may be sure, they give as much as they think proper, and they must be the best judges, and can afford to give what they please; for Sir Sampson could buy and sell all of us a hundred times over, if he liked. It's long since the Lochmarlie estate was called seven thousand a year; and, besides that, there's the Birkendale property, and the Glenmavis estate; and, I'm sure, I can't tell you all what; but there's no doubt he's a man of immense fortune.'

Well it was known, and frequently was it discussed, the iniquity of Mary being allowed to waste her time, and squander her money amongst the poor, instead of being taught the practical virtues of making her own gowns, and of hoarding up her pocket-money for some selfish gratification.

In colloquies such as these, day after day passed on without any visible improvement taking place in her health. Only one remedy suggested itself to Mrs. Douglas, and that was to remove her to the South of England for the winter. Milder air, and change of scene, she had no doubt would prove efficacious; and her opinion was confirmed by that of the celebrated Dr.——, who having been summoned to the Laird of Pettlechass, had paid a visit at Glenfern *en passant*. How so desirable an event was to be accomplished, was the difficulty. By the death of his father, a variety of business, and an extent of farming had devolved upon Mr. Douglas, which obliged him to fix his residence at Glenfern, and rendered it impossible for him to be long absent from it. Mrs. Douglas had engaged in the duties of a nurse to her little boy, and to take him, or leave him, was equally out of the question.

In this dilemma, the only resource that offered, was that of sending Mary for a few months to her mother. True, it was a painful necessity; for Mrs. Douglas seldom heard from her sister-in-law, and when she did, her letters were short and cold. She sometimes desired a 'kiss to her (Mrs. Douglas') little girl,' and once, in an extraordinary fit of good humour, had actually sent a locket with her hair in a letter by post, for which Mrs. Douglas had to pay something more than the value of the present. This was all that Mary knew of her mother, and the rest of her family were still greater strangers to her. Her father remained in a distant station in India, and was seldom heard of. Her brother was gone to sea; and though she had written repeatedly to her sister, her letters remained unnoticed. Under these circumstances, there was something revolting in the idea of obtruding

Mary upon the notice of her relations, and trusting to their kindness even for a few months; yet her health, perhaps her life, was at stake, and Mrs. Douglas felt she had scarcely a right to hesitate.

'Mary has perhaps been too long an alien from her own family,' said she to herself; 'this will be a means of her becoming acquainted with them, and of introducing her to that sphere in which she is probably destined to walk. Under her uncle's roof she will surely be safe, and in the society of her mother and sister she cannot be unhappy. New scenes will give a stimulus to her mind; the necessity of exertion will brace the languid faculties of her soul, and a few short months, I trust, will restore her to me such, and even superior to what she was. Why then should I hesitate to do what my conscience tells me ought to be done? Alas! it is because I selfishly shrink from the pain of separation, and am unwilling to relinquish even for a season, one of the many blessings heaven has bestowed upon me.' And Mrs. Douglas, noble and dis-interested as ever, rose superior to the weakness that she felt was besetting her. Mary listened to her communication with a throbbing heart, and eyes suffused with tears, to part from her aunt was agony; but to behold her mother—she to whom she owed her existence—to embrace a sister too—and one for whom she felt all those mysterious yearnings which twins are said to entertain towards each other—O, there was rapture in the thought, and Mary's buoyant heart fluctuated between the extremes of anguish and delight.

The venerable sisters received the intelligence with much surprise: they did not know very well what to say about it; there was much to be said both for and against it. Lady Maclaughlan had a high opinion of English air; but then they had heard the morals of the people were not so good, and there were a great many dissipated young men in England; though, to be sure, there was no denying but the mineral waters were excellent; and, in short, it ended in Miss Grizzy's sitting down to concoct an epistle to Lady Maclaughlan; in Miss Jacky's beginning to draw up a code of instructions for a young woman upon her entrance into life; and Miss Nicky hoping, that if Mary did go, she would take care not to bring back any extravagant English notions with her. The younger set debated amongst themselves how many of them would be invited to accompany Mary to England, and from thence fell to disputing the possession of a brown hair trunk, with a flourished D, in brass letters, on the top.

Mrs. Douglas, with repressed feelings, set about offering the sacrifice she had planned, and in a letter to Lady Juliana, descriptive of her daughter's situation, she sought to excite her tenderness without creating an alarm. How far she succeeded will be seen hereafter. In the meantime, we must take a retrospective glance at the last seventeen years of her Ladyship's life.

CHAPTER V

Her 'only labour was to still the time;
And labour dire it is, and weary woe.'
                                    Castle of Indolence.[1]

YEARS HAD ROLLED on, amidst heartless pleasures and joyless amusements, but Lady Juliana was made neither the wiser nor the better, by added years and increased experience. Time had in vain turned his glass before eyes still dazzled with the gaudy allurements of the world, for she took 'no note of time,'[2] but as the thing that was to take her to the Opera and the Park, and that sometimes hurried her excessively, and sometimes bored her to death. At length she was compelled to abandon her chace after happiness, in the only sphere where she believed it was to be found. Lord Courtland's declining health unfitted him for the dissipation of a London life; and, by the advice of his physician, he resolved upon retiring to a country seat, which he possessed in the vicinity of Bath. Lady Juliana was in despair at the thoughts of this sudden wrench from what she termed life; but she had no resource; for though her good-natured husband gave her the whole of General Cameron's allowance, that scarcely served to keep her in clothes; and though her brother was perfectly willing, that she and her children should occupy apartments in his house, yet he would have been equally acquiescent, had she proposed to remove from it. Lady Juliana had a sort of instinctive knowledge of this, which prevented her from breaking out into open remonstrance. She therefore contented herself with being more than usually peevish and irascible to her servants and children; and talking to her friends of the prodigious sacrifice she was about to make for her brother and his family, as if it had been the cutting off of a hand, or the plucking out of an eye. To have heard her, any one unaccustomed to the hyperbole of fashionable language, would have deemed Botany Bay[1] the nearest possible point of destination. Parting from her fashionable acquaintances, was tearing herself from all she loved—quitting London was bidding adieu to the world. Of course there could be no society where she was going, but still she would do her duty—she would not desert dear Frederick, and his poor children! In short, no martyr was ever led to the stake, with half the notions of heroism and self devotion, as those with which Lady Juliana stepped into the barouche[2] that was to conduct her to Beech Park.

In the society of piping bulfinches, pink canaries, grey parrots, gold fish, green squirrels, Italian greyhounds,

and French poodles, she sought a refuge from despair.
But even these varied charms, after a while, failed to
please: the bulfinches grew hoarse—the canaries turned
brown—the parrots became stupid—the gold fish would
not eat—the squirrels were cross—the dogs fought; even
a shell grotto that was constructing fell down; and, by
the time the aviary and conservatory were filled, they
had lost their interest. The children were the next subjects for her Ladyship's *ennui* to discharge itself upon.
Lord Courtland had a son, some years older, and a
daughter nearly of the same age as her own. It suddenly
occurred to her, that they must be educated, and that
she would educate the girls herself. As the first step,
she engaged two governesses, French and Italian;—
modern treatises on the subject of education were
ordered from London—looked at, admired and arranged
on gilded shelves, and sofa tables; and could their contents have exhaled with the odours of their Russia
leather[1] bindings, Lady Juliana's dressing-room would
have been, what Sir Joshua Reynolds says every seminary
of learning *is*, 'an atmosphere of floating knowledge.'[2]
But amidst this splendid display of human lore, THE
BOOK found no place. She *had* heard of the Bible, however, and even knew it was a book appointed to be read
in churches, and given to poor people, along with Rumford soup,[3] and flannel shirts; but as the rule of life—
as the book that alone could make wise unto salvation,
this Christian parent was ignorant as the Hottentot or
Hindoo.

Three days beheld the rise, progress, and decline of
Lady Juliana's whole system of education; and it would
have been well for the children, had the trust been
delegated to those better qualified to discharge it. But
neither of the preceptresses were better skilled in the
only true knowledge. Signora Cicianai was a bigotted
Catholic, whose faith hung upon her beads, and Madame

Grignon was an *esprit fort*,[1] who had no faith in any thing but *le plaisir*. But the Signora's singing was heavenly, and Madame's dancing was divine, and what lacked there more?

So passed the first years of beings training for immortality. The children insensibly ceased to be children, and Lady Juliana would have beheld the increasing height and beauty of her daughter, with extreme disapprobation, had not that beauty, by awakening her ambition, also excited her affection, if the term affection could be applied to that heterogeneous mass of feelings and propensities that 'shape had none distinguishable.'[2] Lady Juliana had fallen into an error, very common with wiser heads than hers—that of mistaking the *effect* for the *cause*. She looked no farther than to her union with Henry Douglas, for the foundation of all her unhappiness —it never once occurred to her, that her marriage was only the *consequence* of something previously wrong; she saw not the headstrong passions that had impelled her to please herself—no matter at what price. She thought not of the want of principle—she blushed not at the want of delicacy, that had led her to deceive a parent, and elope with a man to whose character she was a total stranger. She therefore considered herself as having fallen a victim to love; and could she only save her daughter from a similar error, she might yet by her means retrieve her fallen fortune. To implant principles of religion and virtue in her mind, was not within the compass of her own; but she could scoff at every pure and generous affection—she could ridicule every disinterested attachment—and she could expatiate on the never fading joys that attend on wealth and titles, jewels and equipages—and all this she did in the belief that she was acting the part of a most wise and tender parent! The seed, thus carefully sown, promised to bring forth an abundant harvest. At eighteen, Adelaide Douglas was as heartless and ambitious as she was beautiful and accomplished—but the surface was covered with flowers, and who would have thought of analysing the soil?

It sometimes happens, that the very means used, with success, in the formation of one character, produce a totally opposite effect upon another. The mind of Lady Emily Lindore had undergone exactly the same process in its formation as that of her cousin; yet in all things they differed. Whether it were the independence of high birth, or the pride of a mind conscious of its own powers, she had hitherto resisted the sophistry of her governesses, and the solecisms of her aunt. But her notions of right and wrong were too crude to influence the general tenor of her life, or operate as restraints upon a naturally high spirit, and impetuous temper. Not all the united efforts of her preceptresses had been able to form a manner for their pupil; nor could their authority restrain her from saying what she thought, and doing what she pleased; and, in spite of both precept and example, Lady Emily remained, as insupportably natural and sincere, as she was beautiful and *piquante*.[1] At six years old, she had declared her intention of marrying her cousin, Edward Douglas; and, at eighteen, her words were little less equivocal. Lord Courtland, who never disturbed himself about any thing, was rather diverted with this juvenile attachment; and Lady Juliana, who cared little for her son, and still less for her niece, only wondered how people could be such fools as to think of marrying for love, after she had told them how miserable it would make them.

CHAPTER VI

'Unthought of frailties cheat us in the wise;
The fool lies hid in inconsistencies.'

Pope.[1]

SUCH WERE THE female members of the family to whom Mary was about to be introduced. In her mother's heart she had no place, for of her absent husband and neglected daughter she seldom thought; and their letters were scarcely read, and rarely answered. Even good Miss Grizzy's elaborate epistle, in which were curiously entwined the death of her brother, and the birth and christening of her grand-nephew, in a truly Gordian manner, remained disentangled. Had her Ladyship only read to the middle of the seventh page, she would have learned the indisposition of her daughter, with the various opinions thereupon; but poor Miss Grizzy's labours were vain, for her letter remains a dead letter to this day. Mrs. Douglas was therefore the first to convey the unwelcome intelligence, and to suggest to the mind of the mother, that her alienated daughter still retained some claims upon her care and affection; and, although this was done with all the tenderness and delicacy of a gentle and enlightened mind, it called forth the most bitter indignation from Lady Juliana.

She almost raved at what she termed the base ingratitude and hypocrisy of her sister-in-law. After the sacrifice she had made in giving up her child to her when she had none of her own, it was a pretty return to send her back only to die. But she saw through it. She did not believe a word of the girl's illness: that was all a trick to get rid of her. Now they had a child of their own, they had no use for hers; but she was not to be made a fool of in such a way, and by such people, &c. &c.

'If Mrs. Douglas is so vile a woman,' said the provok-

ing Lady Emily, 'the sooner my cousin is taken from her
the better.'

'You don't understand these things, Emily,' returned
her aunt impatiently.

'What things?'

'The trouble and annoyance it will occasion me to take
charge of the girl at this time.'

'Why at this time more than at any other?'

'Absurd, my dear! how can you ask so foolish a question? Don't you know that you and Adelaide are both to
bring out this winter, and how can I possibly do you
justice, with a dying girl upon my hands?'

'I thought you suspected it was all a trick,' continued
the persecuting Lady Emily.

'So I do; I havn't the least doubt of it. The whole
story is the most improbable stuff I ever heard.'

'Then you will have less trouble than you expect.'

'But I hate to be made a dupe of, and imposed upon
by low cunning. If Mrs. Douglas had told me candidly
she wished me to take the girl, I would have thought
nothing of it; but I can't bear to be treated like a fool.'

'I don't see any thing at all unbecoming in Mrs.
Douglas' treatment.'

'Then, what can I do with a girl who has been educated
in Scotland? She must be vulgar—all Scotchwomen are
so. They have red hands and rough voices; they yawn,
and blow their noses, and talk, and laugh loud, and do a
thousand shocking things. Then, to hear the Scotch
brogue—oh, heavens! I should expire every time she
opened her mouth!'

'Perhaps my sister may not speak so *very* broad,' kindly
suggested Adelaide in her sweetest accents.

'You are very good, my love, to think so; but nobody
can live in that odious country without being infected
with its *patois*. I really thought I should have caught it
myself; and Mr. Douglas (no longer Henry) became

quite gross in his language, after living amongst his relations.'

'This is really too bad,' cried Lady Emily indignantly. 'If a person speaks sense and truth, what does it signify how it is spoken? And whether your Ladyship chooses to receive your daughter here or not, I shall, at any rate, invite my cousin to my father's house.' And, snatching up a pen, she instantly began a letter to Mary.

Lady Juliana was highly incensed at this freedom of her niece; but she was a little afraid of her, and therefore, after some sharp altercation, and with infinite violence done to her feelings, she was prevailed upon to write a decently civil sort of a letter to Mrs. Douglas, consenting to receive her daughter for a *few months*; firmly resolving in her own mind to conceal her from all eyes and ears while she remained, and to return her to her Scotch relations early in the summer.

This worthy resolution formed, she became more serene, and awaited the arrival of her daughter with as much firmness as could reasonably have been expected.

CHAPTER VII

'And for unfelt imaginations
They often feel a world of restless cares.'
Shakespeare.[1]

LITTLE WEENED THE good ladies of Glenfern the ungracious reception their *protégé* was likely to experience from her mother; for in spite of the defects of her education, Mary was a general favourite in the family; and however they might solace themselves by depreciating her to Mrs. Douglas, to the world in general, and their young female acquaintances in particular, she was upheld as an epitome of every perfection above and below the sun. Had it been possible for them to conceive that Mary could have been received with any thing short of rapture, Lady Juliana's letter might, in some measure, have opened the eyes of their understanding; but to the guileless sisters, it seemed every thing that was proper. Sorry for the necessity Mrs. Douglas felt under of parting with her adopted daughter—was 'prettily expressed'—had no doubt it was merely a slight nervous affection, 'was kind and soothing;' and the assurance, more than once repeated, that her friends might rely upon her being returned to them in the course of a very few months, 'shewed a great deal of feeling and consideration.' But as their minds never maintained a just equilibrium long upon any subject, but, like falsely adjusted scales, were ever hovering and vibrating at either extreme—so they could not rest satisfied in the belief that Mary was to be happy—there must be something to counteract that stilling sentiment; and that was the apprehension that Mary would be spoilt. This, for the present, was the pendulum of their imaginations.

'I declare, Mary, my sisters, and I, could get no sleep last night for thinking of you,' said Miss Grizzy; 'we are all certain that Lady Juliana especially, but indeed all your English relations, will think so much of you—from not knowing you, you know—which will be quite natural, that my sisters and I have taken it into our heads—but I hope it won't be the case, as you have a great deal of good sense of your own—that they will quite turn your head.'

'Mary's head is on her shoulders to little purpose,' followed up Miss Jacky, 'if she can't stand being made of when she goes amongst strangers; and she ought to know by this time, that a mother's partiality is no proof of a child's merit.'

'You hear that, Mary,' rejoined Miss Grizzy: 'So I'm sure I hope you won't mind a word that your mother says to you, I mean about yourself; for, of course, you know, she can't be such a good judge of you as us, who have known you all your life. As to other things, I daresay she is very well informed about the country, and politics, and these sort of things—I'm certain Lady Juliana knows a great deal.'

'And I hope, Mary, you will take care and not get into the daadlin'[1] handless ways of the English women,' said Miss Nicky; 'I wouldn't give a pin for an English-woman.'

'And I hope you will never look at an Englishman, Mary,' said Miss Grizzy, with equal earnestness; 'take my word for it, they are a very dissipated unprincipled set. They all drink, and game,[2] and keep race-horses; and many of them, I'm told, even keep play-actresses— So you may think what it would be for all of us, if you was to marry any of them,'—and tears streamed from the good spinster's eyes, at the bare supposition of such a calamity.

'Don't be afraid, my dear aunt,' said Mary, with a kind caress, 'I shall come back to you your own "High-land Mary."[3] No Englishman, with his round face and trim meadows, shall ever captivate me. Heath-covered hills, and high cheek bones, are the charms that must win my heart.'

'I'm delighted to hear you say so, my dear Mary,' said the literal minded Grizzy: 'Certainly nothing can be prettier than the heather when it's in flower; and there is something very manly—nobody can dispute that—in high cheek bones: and besides, to tell you a secret, Lady Maclaughlan has a husband in her eye for you—We, none of us, can conceive who it is, but, of course, he must be suitable in every respect; for you know Lady Maclaughlan has had three husbands herself, so, of course, she must be an excellent judge of a good husband.'

'Or a bad one,' said Mary, 'which is the same thing. Warning is as good as example.'

Mrs. Douglas' ideas and those of her aunts, did not coincide upon this occasion more than upon most others. In her sister-in-law's letter, she flattered herself she saw only fashionable indifference; and she fondly hoped that would soon give way to a tenderer sentiment, as her daughter became known to her. At any rate, it was proper that Mary should make the trial, and which ever way it ended, it must be for her advantage.

'Mary has already lived too long in these mountain solitudes,' thought she; 'her ideas will become romantic, and her taste fastidious. If it is dangerous to be too early initiated into the ways of the world, it is perhaps equally so to live too long secluded from it. Should she make herself a place in the heart of her mother and sister, it will be so much happiness gained; and should it prove otherwise, it will be a lesson learnt—a hard one indeed! but hard are the lessons we must all learn in the school of life!' Yet Mrs. Douglas' fortitude almost failed her, as the period of separation approached.

It had been arranged by Lady Emily, that a carriage and servants should meet Mary at Edinburgh, whither Mr. Douglas was to convey her. The cruel moment came; and mother, sister, relations, friends, all the bright visions which Mary's sanguine spirit had conjured up to soften the parting pang, all were absorbed in one agonizing feeling—one overwhelming thought. O, who that for the first time has parted from the parent, whose tenderness and love were entwined with our earliest recollections, whose sympathy had soothed our infant sufferings, whose fondness had brightened our infant felicity;—who that has a heart, but must have felt it sink beneath the anguish of a first farewell! Yet bitterer still must be the feelings

of the parent upon committing the cherished object of
their cares and affections to the stormy ocean of life.
When experience points to the gathering cloud and rising
surge which soon may assail their defenceless child, what
can support the mother's heart, but trust in Him, whose
eye slumbereth not, and whose power extendeth over
all! It was this pious hope, this holy confidence, that
enabled this more than mother to part from her adopted
child with a resignation which no earthly motive could
have imparted to her mind. It seems almost profanation,
to mingle with her elevated feelings, the coarse, yet
simple sorrows of the aunts, old and young, as they
clung around the nearly lifeless Mary, each tendering
the parting gift they had kept as a solace for the last.

Poor Miss Grizzy was more than usually incoherent,
as she displayed 'a nice new umbrella that could be
turned into a nice walking-stick, or any thing;' and a
dressing-box, with a little of every thing in it; and, with
a fresh burst of tears, Mary was directed where she
would *not* find eye ointment, and where she was *not* to
look for sticking-plaister.

Miss Jacky was more composed, as she presented a
flaming copy of Fordyce's Sermons to Young Women,[1]
with a few suitable observations; but Miss Nicky could
scarcely find voice to tell, that the house-wife she now
tendered, had once been Lady Girnachgowl's, and that
it contained Whitechapel needles of every size and
number. The younger ladies had clubbed for the purchase of a large locket, in which was enshrined a lock
from each subscriber, tastefully arranged by the ———
jeweller, in the form of a wheat sheaf, upon a blue
ground. Even old Donald had his offering, and, as he
stood tottering at the chaise door, he contrived to get a
'bit snishin mull'[2] laid on Mary's lap, with a 'God bless
her bonny face, an' may she ne'er want a good sneesh!'[3]

The carriage drove off, and for a while Mary's eyes
were closed in despair.

CHAPTER VIII

'Farewell to the mountains, high covered with snow;
Farewell to the straths,[1] and green vallies below;
Farewell to the forests, and wild hanging woods,
Farewell to the torrents, and loud roaring floods!'

Scotch Song.[2]

HAPPILY IN THE moral world, as in the material one, the warring elements have their prescribed bounds, and 'the flood of grief decreaseth, when it can swell no higher;'[3] but it is only by retrospection we can bring ourselves to believe in this obvious truth. The young and untried heart hugs itself in the bitterness of its emotions, and takes a pride in believing, that its anguish can end but with its existence; and it is not till time hath almost steeped our senses in forgetfulness, that we discover the mutability of all human passions.

But Mary left it not to the slow hand of time to subdue in some measure the grief that swelled her heart. Had she given way to selfishness, she would have sought the free indulgence of her sorrow as the only mitigation of it; but she felt also for her uncle. He was depressed at parting with his wife and child, and he was taking a long and dreary journey entirely upon her account. Could she therefore be so selfish as to add to his uneasiness by a display of her sufferings? No—she would strive to conceal it from his observation, though to overcome it was impossible. Her feelings must ever remain the same, but she would confine them to her own breast; and she began to converse with, and even strove to amuse her kind-hearted companion. Ever and anon, indeed, a rush of tender recollections came across her mind, and the soft voice, and the bland countenance of her maternal friend, seemed for a moment present to her senses; and then the dreariness and desolation that succeeded as the delusion vanished, and all was stillness and vacuity! Even self-reproach shot its piercing sting into her ingenuous heart; levities on which, in her usual gaiety of spirit, she had never bestowed a thought, now appeared to her as crimes of the deepest dye. She thought how often she had slighted the counsels and neglected the wishes of her gentle monitress; how she had wearied of her good old aunts, their cracked voices, and the everlasting *tic-a-tic* of their knitting needles; how coarse and vulgar she had sometimes deemed the younger ones; how she had mimicked Lady Maclaughlan, and caricatured Sir Sampson, and 'even poor dear old Donald,' said she, as she summed up the catalogue of her crimes, 'could not escape my insolence and ill nature. How clever I thought it to sing "Haud awa frae me, Donald,"[1] and how affectedly I shuddered at every thing he touched;' and the 'sneeshin mull' was bedewed with tears of affectionate contrition. But every painful sentiment was for a while suspended in admiration of the magnificent scenery that was spread around them. Though summer had fled, and few even of autumn's graces remained, yet over the august features of mountain scenery the seasons have little controul. Their charms depend not upon richness of verdure, or luxuriance of foliage, or any of the mere prettinesses of nature; but whether wrapped in snow, or veiled in mist, or glowing in sunshine, their lonely grandeur remains the same; and the same feelings fill and elevate the soul in contemplating these mighty works of an Almighty hand. The eye is never weary in watching the thousand varieties of light and shade, as they flit over the mountain, and gleam upon the lake; and the ear is satisfied with the awful stillness of nature in her solitude.

Others besides Mary seemed to have taken a fanciful pleasure in combining the ideas of the mental and elemental world, for in the dreary dwelling where they were destined to pass the night, she found inscribed the following lines:—

The busy winds war mid the waving boughs,
And darkly rolls the heaving surge to land;
Among the flying clouds the moon-beam glows
With colours foreign to its softness bland.

Here, one dark shadow melts, in gloom profound,
The towering Alps—the guardians of the Lake;
There, one bright gleam sheds silver light around,
And shews the threat'ning strife that tempests wake.

Thus o'er my mind a busy memory plays,
That shakes the feelings to their inmost core;
Thus beams the light of Hope's fallacious rays,
When simple confidence can trust no more.

So one dark shadow shrouds each by-gone hour,
So one bright gleam the coming tempest shews;
That tells of sorrows, which, though past, still lower,
And *this* reveals th' approach of future woes.[1]

While Mary was trying to decypher these somewhat mystic lines, her uncle was carrying on a colloquy in Gaelic with their hostess. The consequences of the consultation were not of the choicest description, consisting of braxy* mutton, raw potatoes, wet bannocks, hard cheese, and whisky. Very differently would the travellers have fared, had the good Nicky's intentions been fulfilled. She had prepared with her own hands a moorfowl-pye and potted nowt's head,[2] besides a profusion of what she termed 'trifles, just for Mary, poor thing! to divert herself with upon the road.' But alas! in the anguish of separation, the covered basket had been forgot, and the labour of Miss Nicky's hands fell to be consumed by the family, though Miss Grizzy protested, with tears in her eyes, 'that it went to her heart like a knife, to eat poor Mary's puffs and snaps.'[3]

* Sheep that have died a natural death, and been salted.[4]

Change of air, and variety of scene, failed not to produce the happiest effects upon Mary's languid frame and drooping spirits. Her cheek already glowed with health, and was sometimes dimpled with smiles. She still wept indeed as she thought of those she had left; but often while the tear trembled in her eye, its course was arrested by wonder, or admiration, or delight; for every object had its charms for her. Her cultivated taste and unsophisticated mind could descry beauty in the form of a hill, and grandeur in the foam of the wave, and elegance in the weeping birch, as it dipped its now almost leafless boughs in the mountain stream. These simple pleasures, unknown alike to the sordid mind and vitiated taste, are ever exquisitely enjoyed by the refined yet unsophisticated child of nature.

CHAPTER IX

'Her native sense improved by reading,
Her native sweetness by good breeding.'[1]

DURING THEIR PROGRESS through the Highlands, the travellers were hospitably entertained at the mansions of the country gentlemen, where old fashioned courtesy, and modern comfort, combined to cheer the stranger guest. But upon *coming out*, as it is significantly expressed by the natives of these mountain regions, viz. entering the low country, they found they had only made a change of difficulties. In the Highlands they were always sure, that wherever there was a house, that house would be to them a home; but on a fair-day in the little town of G. they found themselves in the midst of houses, and surrounded by people, yet unable to procure rest or shelter.

At the only inn the place afforded, they were informed, 'The horses were baith oot, an' the ludgin' a' tane up,[1] an' mair tu;' while the driver asserted, what indeed was apparent, 'that his beasts war nae fit to gang the length o' their tae farrer[2]—no for the king himsel'.'

At this moment, a stout, florid, good-humoured-looking man passed whistling 'Roy's Wife'[3] with all his heart; and just as Mr. Douglas was stepping out of the carriage to try what could be done, the same person, evidently attracted by curiosity, repassed, changing his tune to 'There's cauld kail in Aberdeen.'[4]

He started at sight of Mr. Douglas; then eagerly grasping his hand, 'Ah! Archie Douglas, is this you?' exclaimed he with a loud laugh, and hearty shake. 'What! you haven't forgot your old schoolfellow Bob Gawffaw?'

A mutual recognition now took place, and much pleasure was manifested on both sides at this unexpected rencontre. No time was allowed to explain their embarrassments, for Mr. Gawffaw had already tipped the post-boy the wink (which he seemed easily to comprehend); and forcing Mr. Douglas to resume his seat in the carriage, he jumped in himself.

'Now for Howffend, and Mrs. Gawffaw! ha, ha, ha! This will be a surprise upon her. She thinks I'm in my barn all this time—ha, ha, ha!'

Mr. Douglas here began to express his astonishment at his friend's precipitation, and his apprehensions as to the trouble they might occasion Mrs. Gawffaw; but bursts of laughter and broken expressions of delight were the only replies he could procure from his friend.

After jolting over half a mile of very bad road, the carriage stopped at a mean vulgar-looking mansion, with dirty windows, ruinous thatched offices,[1] and broken fences.

Such was the picture of still life. That of animated nature was not less picturesque. Cows bellowed, and cart horses neighed, and pigs grunted, and geese gabbled, and ducks quacked, and cocks and hens flapped and fluttered promiscuously, as they mingled, in a sort of yard, divided from the house by a low dyke, possessing the accommodation of a crazy gate, which was bestrode by a parcel of bare-legged boys.

'What are you about, you confounded rascals!' called Mr. Gawffaw to them.

'Naething,' answered one.

'We're just takin' a heize on the yett,'[2] answered another.

'I'll heize ye,[3] ye scoundrels!' exclaimed the incensed Mr. Gawffaw, as he burst from the carriage; and, snatching the driver's whip from his hand, flew after the more nimble-footed culprits.

Finding his efforts to overtake them in vain, he returned to the door of his mansion, where stood his guests, waiting to be ushered in. He opened the door himself, and led the way to the parlour, which was quite of a piece with the exterior of the dwelling. A dim dusty table stood in the middle of the floor, heaped with a variety of heterogeneous articles of dress: an exceeding dirty volume of a novel lay open amongst them. The floor was littered with shapings of flannel, and shreds of gauzes, ribbons, &c. The fire was almost out, and the hearth was covered with ashes.

After insisting upon his guests being seated, Mr. Gawffaw walked to the door of the apartment, and hallooed out, 'Mrs. Gawffaw—ho! May, my dear!—I say, Mrs. Gawffaw!'

A low, croaking, querulous voice was now heard in reply, 'For heaven's sake, Mr. Gawffaw, make less noise!

For God's sake, have mercy on the walls of your house, if you've none on my poor head!' And thereupon entered Mrs. Gawffaw, a cap in one hand, which she appeared to have been trying on—a smelling-bottle in the other.

She possessed a considerable share of insipid, and somewhat faded, beauty, but disguised by a tawdry trumpery style of dress, and rendered almost disgusting by the air of affectation, folly, and peevishness, that overspread her whole person and deportment. She testified the utmost surprise and coldness at sight of her guests; and, as she entered, Mr. Gawffaw rushed out, having descried something passing in the yard that called for his interposition. Mr. Douglas was therefore under the necessity of introducing himself and Mary to their ungracious hostess; briefly stating the circumstances that had led them to be her guests, and dwelling, with much warmth, on the kindness and hospitality of her husband in having relieved them from their embarrassment. A gracious smile, or what was intended as such, beamed over Mrs. Gawffaw's face at first mention of their names.

'Excuse me, Mr. Douglas,' said she, making a profound reverence to him, and another to Mary, while she waved her hand for them to be seated. 'Excuse me, Miss Douglas; but, situated as I am, I find it necessary to be very distant to Mr. Gawffaw's friends sometimes. He is a thoughtless man, Mr. Douglas; a very thoughtless man. He makes a perfect inn of his house. He never lies out of the town, trying who he can pick up, and bring home with him. It is seldom I am so fortunate as to see such guests as Mr. and Miss Douglas of Glenfern Castle in my house,' with an elegant bow to each, which, of course, was duly returned. 'But Mr. Gawffaw would have shewn more consideration, both for you and me, had he apprised me of the honour of your visit, instead of bringing you here in this ill-bred, unceremonious manner. As for me, I am too well accustomed to him to be hurt at these things now. He has kept me in hot water, I may say, since the day I married him!'

In spite of the conciliatory manner in which this agreeable address was made, Mr. Douglas felt considerably disconcerted, and again renewed his apologies, adding something about hopes of being able to proceed.

'Make no apologies, my dear sir,' said the lady, with what she deemed a most bewitching manner, 'it affords me the greatest pleasure to see any of your family under my roof. I meant no reflection on you, it is entirely Mr. Gawffaw that is to blame, in not having apprised me of the honour of this visit, that I might not have been caught in this *déshabille*; but I was really so engaged by my studies,' pointing to the dirty novel, 'that I was quite unconscious of the lapse of time.' The guests felt more and more at a loss what to say. But the lady was at none. Seeing Mr. Douglas still standing with his hat in his hand, and his eye directed towards the door, she resumed her discourse.

'Pray be seated, Mr. Douglas—I beg you will sit off the door. Miss Douglas, I entreat you will walk into the fire[1]—I hope you will consider yourself as quite at home' —another elegant bend to each. 'I only regret that Mr. Gawffaw's folly and ill-breeding should have brought you into this disagreeable situation, Mr. Douglas. He is a well meaning man, Mr. Douglas, and a good hearted man; but he is very deficient in other respects, Mr. Douglas.'

Mr. Douglas, happy to find any thing to which he could assent, warmly joined in the eulogium on the excellence of his friend's heart. It did not appear, however, to give the satisfaction he expected. The lady resumed with a sigh, 'Nobody can know Mr. Gawffaw's heart better than I do, Mr. Douglas. It *is* a good one, but it is far from being an elegant one; it is one in which I find no congeniality of sentiment with my own. Indeed Mr. Gawffaw is no companion for me, nor I for him, Mr. Douglas—he is never happy in my society, and I really believe he would rather sit down with the tinklers[1] on the road side, as spend a day in my company.'

A deep sigh followed; but its pathos was drowned in the obstreperous ha, ha, ha! of her joyous helpmate, as he bounced into the room, wiping his forehead.

'Why, May, my dear, what have you been about to-day; things have been all going to the deuce. Why didn't you hinder these boys from sweeing'[2] the gate off its hinges, and—'

'Me hinder boys from sweein' gates, Mr. Gawffaw! Do I look like as if I was capable of hindering boys from sweein' gates, Miss Douglas?'

'Well, my dear, you ought to look after your pigs a little better. That jade, black Jess, has trod a parcel of them to death, ha, ha, ha! and—'

'Me look after pigs, Mr. Gawffaw! I'm really astonished at you!' again interrupted the lady, turning pale with vexation. Then, with an affected giggle, appealing to Mary, 'I leave you to judge, Miss Douglas, if I look like a person made for running after pigs!'

'Indeed,' thought Mary, 'you don't look like as if you could do any thing half so useful.'

'Well, never mind the pigs, my dear; only don't give us any of them for dinner—ha, ha, ha!—and, May, when will you let us have it?'

'Me let you have it, Mr. Gawffaw! I'm sure I don't hinder you from having it when you please, only you know I prefer late hours myself. I was always accustomed to them in my poor father's lifetime—he never dined before four o'clock; and I seldom knew what it was to be in my bed before twelve o'clock at night, Miss Douglas, till I married Mr. Gawffaw!'

Mary tried to look sorrowful, to hide the smile that was dimpling her cheek.

'Come, let us have something to eat in the meantime, my dear.'

'I'm sure you may eat the house, if you please, for me, Mr. Gawffaw! What would you take, Miss Douglas? pull the bell—Softly, Mr. Gawffaw! you do every thing so violently.'

A dirty maid-servant, with bare feet, answered the summons.

'Where's Tom?' demanded the lady, well knowing that Tom was afar off at some of the farm operations.

'I ken nae[1] whar he's. He'll be aether at the patatees, or the horses. I'se warran.[2] Div[3] ye want him?'

'Bring some glasses,' said her mistress, with an air of great dignity. 'Mr. Gawffaw, you must see about the wine yourself, since you have sent Tom out of the way.'

Mr. Gawffaw and his handmaid were soon heard in an adjoining closet; the one wondering where the screw was, the other vociferating for a knife to cut the bread; while the mistress of this well-regulated mansion sought to divert her guests' attention from what was passing, by entertaining them with complaints of Mr. Gawffaw's noise, and her maid's insolence, till the parties appeared to speak for themselves.

After being refreshed with some very bad wine, and old baked bread, the gentlemen set off on a survey of the farm, and the ladies repaired to their toilettes. Mary's simple dress was quickly adjusted; and, upon descending, she found her uncle alone in what Mrs. Gawffaw had shewn to her as the drawing-room. He guessed her curiosity to know something of her hosts; and therefore briefly informed her that Mrs. Gawffaw was the daughter of a trader in some manufacturing town, who had lived in opulence, and died insolvent. During his life, his daughter had eloped with Bob Gawffaw, then a gay

lieutenant in a marching regiment, who had been
esteemed a very lucky fellow in getting the pretty Miss
Croaker, with the prospect of ten thousand pounds.
None thought more highly of her husband's good fortune
than the lady herself; and though *her* fortune never was
realized, she gave herself all the airs of having been the
making of his. At this time, Mr. Gawffaw was a reduced
lieutenant,[1] living upon a small paternal property,
which he pretended to farm; but the habits of a military
life, joined to a naturally social disposition, were rather
inimical to the pursuits of agriculture, and most of his
time was spent in loitering about the village of G. where
he generally continued either to pick up a guest, or
procure a dinner.

Mrs. Gawffaw despised her husband—had weak
nerves and headaches—was above managing her house—
read novels—dyed ribbons—and altered her gowns
according to every pattern she could see or hear of.

Such were Mr. and Mrs. Gawffaw—one of the many
ill-assorted couples in this world—joined, not matched.
A sensible man would have curbed her folly and peevishness: A good tempered woman would have made his
home comfortable, and rendered him more domestic.

The dinner was such as might have been expected
from the previous specimens—bad of its kind, cold, ill
dressed, and slovenly set down; but Mrs. Gawffaw seemed
satisfied with herself and it.

'This is very fine mutton, Mr. Douglas, and not under-
done to most people's tastes—and this fowl, I have no
doubt will eat well, Miss Douglas, though it is not so
white as some I have seen.'

'The fowl, my dear, looks as if it had been the great-
grandmother of this sheep, ha, ha, ha!'

'For heaven's sake, Mr. Gawffaw, make less noise, or
my head will split in a thousand pieces!' putting her
hands to it, as if to hold the frail tenement together. This

was always her refuge when at a loss for a reply.

A very ill-concocted pudding next called forth her approbation.

'This pudding should be good; for it is the same I used to be so partial to in my poor father's life time! when I was used to every delicacy, Miss Douglas, that money could purchase.'

'But you thought me the greatest delicacy of all, my dear, ha, ha, ha! for you left all your other delicacies for me, ha, ha, ha!—what do you say to that May?— ha, ha, ha!'

May's reply consisted in putting her hands to her head, with an air of inexpressible vexation; and finding all her endeavours to be elegant, frustrated by the over-powering vulgarity of her husband, she remained silent during the remainder of the repast; solacing herself with complacent glances at her yellow silk gown, and adjusting the gold chains and necklaces that adorned her bosom.

Poor Mary was doomed to a *tête-à-tête* with her during the whole evening; for Mr. Gawffaw was too happy *with* his friend, and *without* his wife, to quit the dining-room till a late hour; and then he was so much exhilarated, that she could almost have joined Mrs. Gawffaw in her exclamation of 'For heaven's sake, Mr. Gawffaw, have mercy on my head!'

The night, however, like all other nights, had a close; and Mrs. Gawffaw, having once more enjoyed the felicity of finding herself in company at twelve o'clock at night, at length withdrew; and having apologised, and hoped, and feared, for another hour in Mary's apartment, she finally left her to the blessings of solitude and repose.

As Mr. Douglas was desirous of reaching Edinburgh the following day, he had, in spite of the urgent remonstrances of his friendly host, and the elegant importunities of his lady, ordered the carriage at an early hour; and Mary was too eager to quit Howffend to keep it waiting.

Mr. Gawffaw was in readiness to hand her in, but fortunately Mrs. Gawffaw's head did not permit of her rising. With much the same hearty laugh that had welcomed their meeting, honest Gawffaw now saluted the departure of his friend; and as he leant whistling over his gate, he ruminated sweet and bitter thoughts as to the destinies of the day—whether he should solace himself with a good dinner, and the company of Bailie Merrythought, at the Cross Keys in G. or put up with cold mutton, and May, at home.

CHAPTER X

'Edina! Scotia's darling seat!
All hail thy palaces and tow'rs,
Where once, beneath a monarch's feet,
Sat legislation's sov'reign pow'rs!'

Burns.[1]

ALL MARY'S SENSATIONS of admiration were faint, compared to those she experienced as she viewed the Scottish metropolis. It was associated in her mind, with all the local prepossessions to which youth and enthusiasm love to give 'a local habitation and a name;'[2] and visions of olden times floated o'er her mind, as she gazed on its rocky battlements, and traversed the lonely arcades of its deserted palace.

'And this was once a gay court!' thought she, as she listened to the dreary echo of her own footsteps; 'and this very ground on which I now stand, was trod by the hapless Mary Stuart! Her eye beheld the same objects that mine now rests upon; her hand has touched the draperies I now hold in mine. These frail memorials remain; but what remains of Scotland's Queen but a blighted name!'

Even the blood-stained chamber possessed a nameless charm for Mary's vivid imagination. She had not entirely escaped the superstitions of the country in which she had lived; and she readily yielded her assent to the asseverations of her guide, as to its being the *bona fide*[1] blood of David Rizzio, which, for nearly three hundred years, had resisted all human efforts to efface.

'My credulity is so harmless,' said she in answer to her uncle's attempt to laugh her out of her belief, 'that I surely may be permitted to indulge it—especially since, I confess, I feel a sort of indescribable pleasure in it.'

'You take a pleasure in the sight of blood!' exclaimed Mr. Douglas in astonishment, 'you who turn pale at sight of a cut finger, and shudder at a leg of mutton with the juice in it!'

'Oh! mere modern vulgar blood is very shocking,' answered Mary with a smile; 'but observe how this is mellowed by time into a tint that could not offend the most fastidious fine lady; besides,' added she in a graver tone, 'I own I love to believe in things supernatural; it seems to connect us more with another world, than when every thing is seen to proceed in the mere ordinary course of nature, as it is called. I cannot bear to imagine a dreary chasm betwixt the inhabitants of this world, and beings of a higher sphere; I love to fancy myself surrounded by——'

'I wish to heaven you would remember you are surrounded by rational beings, and not fall into such rhapsodies,' said her uncle, glancing at a party, who stood near them, jesting upon all the objects which Mary had been regarding with so much veneration. 'But, come, you have been long enough here. Let us try whether a breeze on the Calton Hill will not dispel these cobwebs from your brain.'

The day, though cold, was clear and sunny; and the lovely spectacle before them shone forth in all its gay magnificence. The blue waters lay calm and motionless. The opposite shores glowed in a thousand varied tints of wood and plain, rock and mountain, cultured field, and purple moor. Beneath, the old town reared its dark brow, and the new one stretched its golden lines; while, all around, the varied charms of nature lay scattered in that profusion, which nature's hand alone can bestow.

'Oh! this is exquisite!' exclaimed Mary after a long pause, in which she had been rivetted in admiration of the scene before her. 'And you are in the right, my dear uncle. The ideas which are inspired by the contemplation of such a spectacle as this are far—oh how far!—superior to those excited by the mere works of art. There, I can, at best, think but of the inferior agents of Providence: Here, the soul rises from nature up to nature's God.'

'Upon my soul, you will be taken for a Methodist, Mary, if you talk in this manner,' said Mr. Douglas, with some marks of disquiet, as he turned round at the salutation of a fat elderly gentleman, whom he presently recognised as Bailie[1] Broadfoot.

The first salutations over, Mr. Douglas' fears of Mary having been overheard recurred, and he felt anxious to remove any unfavourable impression with regard to his own principles, at least, from the mind of the enlightened magistrate.

'Your fine views here have set my niece absolutely raving,' said he with a smile; 'but I tell her it is only in romantic minds that fine scenery inspires romantic ideas. I daresay many of the worthy inhabitants of Edinburgh walk here with no other idea than that of sharpening their appetites for dinner.'

'Nae doot,' said the Bailie, 'it's a most capital place for that. Were it no' for that, I ken nae muckle[2] use it would be of.'

'You speak from experience of its virtues in that respect, I suppose?' said Mr. Douglas gravely.

''Deed, as to that I canna compleen. At times, to be
sure, I am troubled with a little kind of a squeamishness
after our public interteenments; but three rounds o' the
hill sets a' to rights.' Then observing Mary's eyes explor-
ing, as he supposed, the town of Leith, 'You see that
prospeck to nae advantage the day,[1] Miss,' said he. 'If
the glass-houses had been workin', it would have looked
as weel again. Ye hae nae glass-houses in the Highlands;
na, na.'

The Bailie had a share in the concern; and the volcanic
clouds of smoke that issued from thence were far more
interesting subjects of speculation to him than all the
eruptions of Vesuvius or Etna. But there was nothing to
charm the lingering view to-day; and he therefore proposed their taking a look at Bridewell,[2] which, next to
the smoke from the glass-houses, he reckoned the object
most worthy of notice. It was, indeed, deserving of the
praises bestowed upon it; and Mary was giving her whole
attention to the details of it, when she was suddenly
startled by hearing her own name wailed in piteous
accents from one of the lower cells, and, upon turning
round, she discovered in the prisoner the son of one of the
tenants of Glenfern. Duncan M'Free had been always
looked upon as a very honest lad in the Highlands, but he
had left home to push his fortune as a pedlar; and the
temptations of the low country having proved too much
for his virtue, poor Duncan was now expiating his offence
in durance vile.

'I shall have a pretty account of you to carry to Glenfern,' said Mr. Douglas, regarding the culprit with his
sternest look.

'O deed, Sir, it's no' my faut!' answered Duncan,
blubbering bitterly; 'but there's nae freedom at a' in
this country. Lord, an' I war oot o't![3] Ane canna ca'
their head their ain in't; for ye canna lift the bouk o' a
prin,[4] but they're a' upon ye.' And a fresh burst of

sorrow ensued.

Finding the *peccadillo* was of a venial nature, Mr. Douglas besought the Bailie to use his interest to procure the enfranchisement of this his vassal, which Mr. Broadfoot, happy to oblige a good customer, promised should be obtained on the following day; and Duncan's emotions being rather clamorous, the party found it necessary to withdraw.

'And noo,' said the Bailie, as they emerged from this place of dole and durance, 'will ye step up to the monument,[1] and tak a rest and some refreshment?'

'Rest and refreshment in a monument!' exclaimed Mr. Douglas. 'Excuse me, my good friend, but we are not inclined to bait there[2] yet a while.'

The Bailie did not comprehend the joke; and he proceeded in his own drawling humdrum accent, to assure them, that the monument was a most convenient place.

'It was erected in honor of Lord Neilson's memory,' said he, 'and is let aff to a pastry cook and confectioner, where you can always find some trifles to treat the ladies, such as pies and custards, and berries, and these sort of things: but we passed an order in the coonncil, that there should be naething of a spirituous nature introduced; for, if ance spirits got admittance, there's no saying what might happen.'

This was a fact which none of the party were disposed to dispute; and the Bailie, triumphing in his dominion over the spirits, shuffled on before to do the honours of this place, appropriated at one and the same time to the manes[3] of a hero, and the making of minced pies. The regale was admirable, and Mary could not help thinking times were improved, and that it was a better thing to eat tarts in Lord Nelson's Monument, than to have been poisoned in Julius Caesar's.[4]

CHAPTER XI

'Having a tongue rough as a cat, and biting like an adder, and all their reproofs are direct scoldings, their common intercourse is open contumely.'

Jeremy Taylor.[1]

'Though last, not least[2] of nature's works, I must now introduce you to a friend of mine,' said Mr. Douglas, as, the Bailie having made his bow, they bent their steps towards the Castle Hill. 'Mrs. Violet Macshake is an aunt of my mother's, whom you must often have heard of, and the last remaining branch of the noble race of Girnachgowl.'

'I am afraid she is rather a formidable person, then?' said Mary.

Her uncle hesitated—'No, not formidable—only rather particular, as all old people are; but she is very good-hearted.'

'I understand, in other words, she is very disagreeable. All ill-tempered people, I observe, have the character of being good-hearted; or else all good-hearted people are ill-tempered, I can't tell which.'

'It is more than reputation with her,' said Mr. Douglas, somewhat angrily; 'for she is, in reality, a very good-hearted woman, as I experienced when a boy at college. Many a crown piece and half-guinea I used to get from her. Many a scold, to be sure, went along with them; but that, I daresay, I deserved. Besides, she is very rich, and I am her reputed heir; therefore gratitude and self-interest combine to render her extremely amiable in my estimation.'

They had now reached the airy dwelling where Mrs. Macshake resided, and having rung, the door was at length most deliberately opened, by an ancient, sour visaged, long waisted female, who ushered them into an apartment, the *coup d'œil* of which struck a chill to Mary's heart. It was a good sized room, with a bare sufficiency of small legged dining tables, and lank hair-cloth chairs, ranged in high order round the walls. Although the season was advanced, and the air piercing cold, the grate stood smiling in all the charms of polished steel; and the mistress of the mansion was seated by the side of it in an arm-chair, still in its summer position. She appeared to have no other occupation than what her own meditations afforded; for a single glance sufficed to shew, that not a vestige of book or work was harboured there. She was a tall, large boned woman, whom even Time's iron hand scarcely bent, as she merely stooped at the shoulders. She had a drooping snuffy nose—a long turned-up chin —small quick grey eyes, and her face projected far beyond her figure, with an expression of shrewd restless curiosity. She wore a mode,[1] (not *à-la-mode*,) bonnet, and cardinal[2] of the same; a pair of clogs[3] over her shoes, and black silk mittens[4] on her arms.

As soon as she recognised Mr. Douglas, she welcomed him with much cordiality, shook him long and heartily by the hand—patted him on the back—looked into his face with much seeming satisfaction; and in short, gave all the demonstrations of gladness usual with gentle-women of a certain age. Her pleasure, however, appeared to be rather an *impromptu* than an habitual feeling; for as the surprise wore off, her visage resumed its harsh and sarcastic expression, and she seemed eager to efface any agreeable impression her reception might have excited.

'An' wha thought o' seein' ye enoo,'[5] said she, in a quick gabbling voice; 'what's brought you to the toon? are ye come to spend your honest faither's siller, ere he's weel cauld in his grave, puir man.'

Mr. Douglas explained, that it was upon account of his niece's health.

'Health!' repeated she, with a sardonic smile, 'it wad

mak an ool[1] laugh to hear the wark that's made aboot young fowk's health noo-a-days. I wonder what ye're aw made o',' grasping Mary's arm in her great bony hand—'a wheen puir feckless windlestraes[2]—ye maun awa to Ingland for yere healths.—Set ye up![3] I wunder what cam o' the lasses i' my time, that bute[4] to bide at hame? And whilk o' ye,[5] I sude like to ken, 'll e'er leive to see ninety-sax, like me—Health! he, he!'

Mary, glad of a pretence to indulge the mirth the old lady's manner and appearance had excited, joined most heartily in the laugh.

'Tak aff yere bannet, bairn, an' let me see yere face; wha can tell what like ye are wi' that snule[6] o' a thing on yere head.' Then after taking an accurate survey of her face, she pushed aside her pelisse—'Weel, it's ae mercy, I see ye hae neither the red heed, nor the muckle cuits[7] o' the Douglasses. I ken nae whuther yere faither has them or no. I ne'er set een on him: neither him, nor his braw leddie, thought it worth their while to speer[8] after me; but I was at nae loss, by aw accounts.'

'You have not asked after any of your Glenfern friends,' said Mr. Douglas, hoping to touch a more sympathetic chord.

'Time eneugh—wull ye let me draw my breath, man —fowk canna say aw thing at ance.—An' ye bute to hae an Inglish wife tu, a Scotch lass was nae serr ye—An' yere wean,[9] I'se warran', it's ane o' the warld's wonders— it's been unca lang o' cummin'[10]—he, he!'

'He has begun life under very melancholy auspices, poor fellow!' said Mr. Douglas, in allusion to his father's death.

'An' whas faut was that?—I ne'er heard tell the like o't, to hae the bairn kirsened[11] an' its grandfaither deein'!—But fowk are naither born, nor kirsened, nor do they wad or dee[12] as they used to du—aw thing's changed.'

'You must, indeed, have witnessed many changes,' observed Mr. Douglas, rather at a loss how to utter any thing of a conciliatory nature.

'Changes!—weel a waat,[1] I sometimes wunder if it's the same waurld, an' if it's my ain heed that's upon my shoothers.'

'But with these changes, you must also have seen many improvements?' said Mary, in a tone of diffidence.

'Impruvements!' turning sharply round upon her, 'what ken ye about impruvements, bairn? A bonny impruvement or ens no,[2] to see tyleyors and sclaters leavin', whar I mind Jewks an' Yerls[3]—An' that great glowrin'[4] new toon there,' pointing out of her windows, 'whar I used to sit an' luck oot at bonny green parks, and see the coos milket, and the bits o' bairnys rowin' an' tummlin',[5] an' the lasses trampin'[6] i' their tubs—What see I noo, but stane an' lime, an' stoor[7] an' dirt, an' idle cheels,[8] an' dinket-oot[9] madams prancin'.—Impruvements indeed!'

Mary found she was not likely to advance her uncle's fortune by the judiciousness of her remarks, therefore prudently resolved to hazard no more. Mr. Douglas, who was more *au fait* to the prejudices of old age, and who was always amused with her bitter remarks, when they did not touch himself, encouraged her to continue the conversation by some observation on the prevailing manners.

'Mainars!' repeated she, with a contemptuous laugh, 'what caw ye mainars noo, for I dinna ken;[10] ilk ane gangs bang in till their neebor's hooss,[11] an' bang oot o't as it war a chynge hooss; an' as for the maister o't he's no o' sae muckle vaalu as the flunky ahint his chyre.[12] I' my grandfaither's time, as I hae heard him tell, ilka maister o' a faamily had his ain sate in his ain hooss, ay! an' sat wi' his hat on his heed afore the best o' the land, an' had his ain dish, an' was aye helpit

first, an' keepit up his owthority as a man sude du.
Paurents war paurents than—bairnes dardna set up
their gabs[1] afore them than as they du noo. They ne'er
presumed to say their heeds war their ain i' thae days—
wife an' servants—reteeners an' childer, aw trummelt[2] i'
the presence o' their heed.'

Here a long pinch of snuff caused a pause in the old
lady's harangue; but after having duly wiped her nose
with her coloured handkerchief, and shook off all the
particles that might be presumed to have lodged upon her
cardinal, she resumed—

'An' nae word o' ony o' your sisters gawn to get
husbands yet? They tell me they're but coorse lasses: an'
wha'll tak ill-farred tocherless queans,[3] when there's
walth o' bonny faces an' lang purses[4] i' the market—
He, he!' Then resuming her scrutiny of Mary—'An'
I'se warran' ye'll be lucken for an Inglish sweetheart tu;
that'll be what's takin' ye awa to Ingland.'

'On the contrary,' said Mr. Douglas, seeing Mary was
too much frightened to answer for herself—'On the
contrary, Mary declares she will never marry any but a
true Highlander; one who wears the dirk and plaid, and
has the second-sight. And the nuptials are to be celebrated with all the pomp of feudal times; with bagpipes,
and bonfires, and gatherings of clans, and roasted sheep,
and barrels of whisky, and ————'

'Weel a wat an' she's i' the right there,' interrupted
Mrs. Macshake, with more complacency than she had
yet shewn.—'They may caw them what they like, but
there's nae waddins noo. Wha's the better o' them but
innkeepers and chise-drivers? I wud nae count mysel
married i' the hiddlins[5] way they gang aboot it noo.'

'I daresay you remember these things done in a very
different style?' said Mr. Douglas.

'I dinna mind them whan they war at the best; but I
hae heard my mither tell what a bonny ploy[6] was at her

waddin':[1] I canna tell ye hoo mony was at it; mair nor
the room wad haud, ye may be sure, for every relation an'
freend o' baith sides war there, as well they sude; an'
aw in full dress; the leddies in their hoops roond them,
an' some o' them had sutten up aw night till[2] hae their
heads drest; for they hadnae thae pooket-like taps[3] ye
hae noo,' looking with contempt at Mary's Grecian
contour. 'An' the bride's goon was aw shewed ow'r wi'
favors,[4] frae the tap doon to the tail, an' aw roond the
neck, an' aboot the sleeves; and, as shune as the ceremony
was ow'r, ilk ane ran till her an' rugget an' rave at her
for the favors, till they hardly left the claise[5] upon her
back. Than they did nae run awa as they du noo, but
sax an' thretty o' them[6] sat doon till[7] a graund denner,
and there was a ball at night, an' ilka[8] night till Sabbath
cam roond; an' than the bride an' the bridegroom, drest
in their waddin' suits, and aw their friends in theirs, wi'
their favors on their breests, walkit in procession till the
kirk. An' was nae that something like a waddin'? It was
worth while to be married i' thae[9] days—He, he!'

'The wedding seems to have been admirably conducted,' said Mr. Douglas, with much solemnity. 'The
christening, I presume, would be the next distinguished
event in the family?'

'Troth, Archie—an' ye sude keep your thoomb upon
kirsnins as lang's ye leeve; yours was a bonnie kirsnin' or
ens no! I hae heard o' mony things, but a bairn kirsened
whan its grandfaither was i' the deed-thraw, I ne'er
heard tell o' before.'—Then observing the indignation
that spread over Mr. Douglas' face, she quickly resumed,
'An' so ye think the kirsnin' was the neist ploy?—He, he!
Na; the crying[10] was a ploy, for the leddies did nae keep
themsels up than as they do noo; but the day after the
bairn was born, the leddy sat up i' her bed, wi' her fan
intill[11] her hand; an' aw her freends cam an' stud roond
her, an' drank her health an' the bairn's. Than at the

leddy's recovery, there was a graund supper gien that they caw'd the *cummerfeals*,[1] an' there was a great pyramid o' hens at the tap o' the table, an' anither pyramid o' ducks at the fit, an' a muckle stoup fu' o' posset[2] i' the middle, an' aw kinds o' sweeties doon the sides; an' as sune as ilk ane had eatin their fill, they aw flew till the sweeties, an' fought, an' strave, an' wrastled for them, leddies an' gentlemen an' aw; for the brag was, wha could pocket maist; an' whiles[3] they wad hae the claith aff the table, an' aw thing i' the middle i' the floor, an' the chyres upside doon. Oo! muckle gude diversion, I'se warran', was at the *cummerfeals*—Than whan they had drank the stoup dry, that ended the ploy. As for the kirsnin', that was aye whar it sude be—i' the hooss o' God, an' aw the kith an' kin bye in full dress, an' a band o' maiden cimmers[4] aw in white; an' a bonny sight it was, as I've heard my mither tell.'

Mr. Douglas, who was now rather tired of the old lady's reminiscences, availed himself of the opportunity of a fresh pinch, to rise and take leave.

'Oo, what's takin' ye awa, Archie, in sic a hurry? Sit doon there,' laying her hand upon his arm, 'an' rest ye, an' tak a glass o' wine, an' a bit breed;[5] or may be,' turning to Mary, 'ye wad rather hae a drap broth[6] to warm ye. What gars ye luck sae blae,[7] bairn? I'm sure it's no cauld; but ye're just like the lave:[8] ye gang aw skiltin' aboot[9] the streets half naked, an' than ye maun sit an' birsle yoursels[10] afore the fire at hame.'

She had now shuffled along to the further end of the room, and opening a press, took out wine, and a plateful of various-shaped articles of bread, which she handed to Mary.

'Hae, bairn—tak a cookie[11]—tak it up—what are you fear'd for?—it'll no bite ye. Here's t'ye, Glenfern, an' your wife, an' your wean, puir tead,[12] it's no had a very chancy ootset,[13] weel a wat.'

The wine being drank, and the cookies discussed, Mr. Douglas made another attempt to withdraw, but in vain.

'Canna ye sit still a wee, man, an' let me spear after my auld freens at Glenfern? Hoo's Grizzy, an' Jacky, an' Nicky?—aye workin' awa at the peels an' the drogs —he, he! I ne'er swallowed a peel, nor gied a doit[1] for drogs aw my days, an' see an[2] ony of them'll rin a race wi' me whan they're naur[3] five score.'

Mr. Douglas here paid her some compliments upon her appearance, which were pretty graciously received; and added that he was the bearer of a letter from his aunt Grizzy, which he would send along with a roebuck and brace of moor-game.

'Gin[4] your roebuck's nae better than your last, atweel[5] it's no worth the sendin'; poor dry fisinless[6] dirt, no worth the chowin'; weel a wat, I begrudged my teeth on't. Your muirfowl war na that ill, but they're no worth the carryin'; they're dong cheap[7] i' the market enoo,[8] so it's nae great compliment. Gin ye had brought me a leg o' gude mutton, or a cauler sawmont,[9] there would hae been some sense in't; but ye're ane o' the fowk that'll ne'er harry yoursel wi' your presents; it's but the pickle poother[10] they cost you, an' I'se warran' ye're thinkin' mair o' your ain diversion than o' my stamick, when ye're at the shootin' o' them, puir beasts.'

Mr. Douglas had borne the various indignities levelled against himself and his family with a philosophy that had no parallel in his life before; but to this attack upon his game, he was not proof. His colour rose, his eyes flashed fire, and something resembling an oath burst from his lips, as he strode indignantly towards the door.

His friend, however, was too nimble for him. She stepped before him, and, breaking into a discordant laugh, as she patted him on the back, 'So I see ye're just the auld man, Archie,—aye ready to tak the strums,[11] an ye dinna get a' thing yere ain wye. Mony a time I had

to fleech ye oot o' the dorts[1] whan ye was a callant.[2]
Div[3] ye mind hoo ye was affronted because I set ye doon
to cauld pigeon-pye, an' a tanker o' tippenny[4] ae night
to yere fowerhoors,[5] afore some leddies—he, he, he!
Weel a wat, yere wife maun hae her ain adoos to
manage ye, for ye're a cumstairy[6] chield, Archie.'

Mr. Douglas still looked as if he was irresolute whether
to laugh or be angry.

'Come, come, sit ye doon there till I speak to this
bairn,' said she, as she pulled Mary into an adjoining
bed-chamber, which wore the same aspect of chilly
neatness as the one they had quitted. Then pulling a
huge bunch of keys from her pocket, she opened a
drawer, out of which she took a pair of diamond ear-
rings. 'Hae, bairn,' said she as she stuffed them into
Mary's hand; 'they belanged to your faither's grandmother. She was a gude woman, an' had four-an'-twenty
sons an' dochter, an' I wiss ye nae war fortin[7] than just
to hae as mony. But mind ye,' with a shake of her bony
finger, 'they maun a' be Scots. Gin I thought ye wad
mairry ony pock-puddin,'[8] fient haed[9] wad ye hae gotten
frae me.—Noo, had yere tongue, and dinna deive[10] me
wi' thanks,' almost pushing her into the parlour again,
'and sin ye're gawn awa' the morn, I'll see nae mair o'ye
enoo[11]—so fare ye weel. But, Archie, ye main come an'
tak your breakfast wi' me. I hae muckle to say to you;
but ye manna be sae hard upon my baps,[12] as ye used to
be,' with a facetious grin to her mollified favourite, as
they shook hands and parted.

'Well, how do you like Mrs. Macshake, Mary?' asked
her uncle as they walked home.

'That is a cruel question, uncle,' answered she with a
smile. 'My gratitude and my taste are at such variance,'
displaying her splendid gift, 'that I know not how to
reconcile them.'

'That is always the case with those whom Mrs.

Macshake has obliged,' returned Mr. Douglas: 'She does many liberal things, but in so ungracious a manner, that people are never sure whether they are obliged or insulted by her. But the way in which she receives kindness is still worse. Could any thing equal her impertinence about my roebuck?—Faith, I've a good mind never to enter her door again!'

Mary could scarcely preserve her gravity at her uncle's indignation, which seemed so disproportioned to the cause. But, to turn the current of his ideas, she remarked, that he had certainly been at pains to select two admirable specimens of her countrywomen for her.

'I don't think I shall soon forget either Mrs. Gawffaw or Mrs. Macshake,' said she, laughing.

'I hope you won't carry away the impression, that these two *lusus naturæ*[1] are specimens of Scotchwomen?' said her uncle. 'The former, indeed, is rather a sort of weed that infests every soil—the latter, to be sure, is an indigenous plant. I question if she would have arrived at such perfection in a more cultivated field, or genial clime. She was born at a time when Scotland was very different from what it is now. Female education was little attended to, even in families of the highest rank; consequently, the ladies of those days possess a *raciness* in their manners and ideas that we should vainly seek for in this age of cultivation and refinement. Had your time permitted, you could have seen much good society here, superior, perhaps, to what is to be found any where else, as far as mental cultivation is concerned. But you will have leisure for that when you return.'

Mary acquiesced with a sigh. *Return* was to her still a melancholy sounding word. It reminded her of all she had left—of the anguish of separation—the dreariness of absence; and all these painful feelings were renewed, in their utmost bitterness, when the time approached for her to bid adieu to her uncle. Lord Courtland's carriage, and two respectable looking servants, awaited her; and the following morning she commenced her journey, in all the agony of a heart that fondly clings to its native home.

CHAPTER XII

————'Nor only by the warmth
And soothing sunshine of delightful things,
Do minds grow up and flourish.'

Akenside.[1]

AFTER PARTING WITH the last of her beloved relatives, Mary tried to think only of the happiness that awaited her in a re-union with her mother and sister; and she gave herself up to the blissful reveries of a young and ardent imagination. Mrs. Douglas had sought to repress, rather than excite, her sanguine expectations; but vainly is the experience of others employed in moderating the enthusiasm of a glowing heart—Experience *cannot* be imparted: We may render the youthful mind prematurely cautious, or meanly suspicious; but the experience of a pure and enlightened mind is the result of observation, matured by time.

The journey, like most modern journies, was performed in comfort and safety; and, late one evening, Mary found herself at the goal of her wishes—at the threshold of the house that contained her mother! One idea filled her mind; but that idea called up a thousand emotions.

'I am now to meet my mother!' thought she; and, unconscious of every thing else, she was assisted from the carriage, and conducted into the house. A door was thrown open; but shrinking from the glare of light and sound of voices that assailed her, she stood dazzled and dismayed, till she beheld a figure approaching that she guessed to be her mother. Her heart beat violently—a film was upon her eyes—she made an effort to reach her mother's arms, and sunk lifeless on her bosom!

Lady Juliana, for such it was, doubted not but that her daughter was really dead; for, though she talked of fainting every hour of the day herself, still what is emphatically called a *dead-faint*,[1] was a spectacle no less strange than shocking to her. She was, therefore, sufficiently alarmed and overcome to behave in a very interesting manner; and some yearnings of pity even possessed her heart, as she beheld her daughter's lifeless form extended before her—her beautiful, though inanimate features, half hid by the profusion of golden ringlets that fell around her. But these kindly feelings were of short duration; for no sooner was the nature of her daughter's insensibility ascertained, than all her former hostility returned, as she found every one's attention directed to Mary, and she herself entirely overlooked in the general interest she had excited; and her displeasure was still further increased, as Mary, at length slowly unclosing her eyes, stretched out her hands, and faintly articulated, 'My mother!'

'Mother! What a hideous vulgar appellation!' thought the fashionable parent to herself; and, instead of answering her daughter's appeal, she hastily proposed that she should be conveyed to her own apartment: then, summoning her maid, she consigned her to her care, slightly touching her cheek as she wished her good night, and returned to the card table. Adelaide too resumed her station at the harp, as if nothing had happened; but Lady Emily attended her cousin to her room—embraced her again and again, as she assured her she loved her already, she was so like her dear Edward: then, after satisfying herself that every thing was comfortable, affectionately kissed her, and withdrew.

Bodily fatigue got the better of mental agitation; and Mary slept soundly, and awoke refreshed.

'Can it be,' thought she, as she tried to collect her bewildered thoughts, 'can it be that I have really beheld my mother—that I have been pressed to her heart—that she has shed tears over me while I lay unconscious in her arms? Mother! What a delightful sound; and how beautiful she seemed! yet I have no distinct idea of her, my head was so confused; but I have a vague recollection of something very fair, and beautiful, and seraph-like, covered with silver drapery, and flowers, and with the sweetest voice in the world.—Yet that must be too young for my mother—Perhaps it was my sister; and my mother was too much overcome to meet her stranger child. Oh! how happy must I be with such a mother and sister!'

In these delightful cogitations, Mary remained till Lady Emily entered.

'How well you look this morning, my dear cousin,' said she, flying to her; 'you are much more like my Edward than you were last night. Ah! and you have got his smile too! You must let me see that very often.'

'I am sure I shall have cause,' said Mary, returning her cousin's affectionate embrace, 'but at present I feel anxious about my mother and sister. The agitation of our meeting, and my weakness, I fear it has been too much for them;' and she looked earnestly in Lady Emily's face for a confirmation of her fears.

'Indeed, you need be under no uneasiness on their account,' returned her cousin, with her usual bluntness, 'their feelings are not so easily disturbed; you will see them both at breakfast, so come along.'

The room was empty; and again Mary's sensitive heart trembled for the welfare of those already so dear to her; but Lady Emily did not appear to understand the nature of her feelings.

'Have a little patience, my dear!' said she, with something of an impatient tone, as she rung for breakfast, 'they will be here at their usual time. Nobody in this house is a slave to hours, or *gêné*[1] with each other's society. Liberty is the motto here; every body breakfasts when and where they please. Lady Juliana, I believe, frequently takes hers in her dressing-room: Papa never is visible till two or three o'clock; and Adelaide is always late.'

'What a selfish cold-hearted thing is grandeur!' thought Mary, as Lady Emily and she sat like two specks in the splendid saloon, surrounded by all that wealth could purchase, or luxury invent; and her thoughts reverted to the pious thanksgiving, and affectionate meeting that graced their social meal in the sweet sunny parlour at Lochmarlie.

Some of those airy nothings, without a local habitation,[2] who are always to be found flitting about the mansions of the great, now lounged into the room; and soon after Adelaide made her *entrée*. Mary, trembling violently, was ready to fall upon her sister's neck; but Adelaide seemed prepared to repel every thing like a *scène;* for, with a cold but sweet, 'I hope you are better this morning?' she seated herself at the opposite side of the table. Mary's blood rushed back to her heart—her eyes filled with tears, she knew not why; for she could not analyse the feelings that swelled in her bosom. She would have shuddered to *think* her sister unkind, but she *felt* she was so.

'It can only be the difference of our manners,' sighed she to herself; 'I am sure my sister loves me, though she does not shew it in the same way I should have done;' and she gazed with the purest admiration and tenderness on the matchless beauty of her face and form. Never had she beheld any thing so exquisitely beautiful; and she longed to throw herself into her sister's arms, and tell her how she loved her. But Adelaide seemed to think the present company wholly unworthy of her regard; for, after having received the adulation of the gentlemen, as they severally paid her a profusion of compliments upon her appearance, 'Desire Tomkins,' said she to a footman, 'to ask Lady Juliana for the "Morning Post,"[1] and the second volume of "Le ———," of the French novel I am reading; and say she shall have it again when I have finished it.'

'In what different terms people may express the same meaning,' thought Mary; 'had I been sending a message to my mother, I should have expressed myself quite differently; but no doubt my sister's meaning is the same, though she may not use the same words.'

The servant returned with the newspaper, and the novel would be sent when it could be found.

'Lady Juliana never reads like any body else,' said her daughter; 'she is for ever mislaying books. She has lost the first volumes of the two last novels that came from town, before I had even seen them.'

This was uttered in the softest, sweetest tone imaginable, and as if she had been pronouncing a panegyric.

Mary was more and more puzzled.

'What can be my sister's meaning here?' thought she; 'the words seem almost to imply censure; but that voice and smile speak the sweetest praise. How truly Mrs. Douglas warned me never to judge of people by their words.'

At that moment the door opened, and three or four dogs rushed in, followed by Lady Juliana, with a volume of a novel in her hand. Again Mary found herself assailed by a variety of powerful emotions—she attempted to rise; but, pale and breathless, she sunk back in her chair.

Her agitation was unmarked by her mother, who did not even appear to be sensible of her presence; for, with a graceful bend of her head to the company in general, she approached Adelaide, and putting her lips to her forehead, 'How do you do, love? I'm afraid you are very angry with me, about that teazing Le ———. I can't conceive where it can be; but here is the third volume, which is much prettier than the second.'

'I certainly shall not read the third volume before the second,' said Adelaide with her usual serenity.

'Then I shall order another copy from town, my love; or I daresay I could tell you the story of the second volume: it is not at all interesting, I assure you. Hermisilde,[1] you know—but I forget where the first volume left off.'—Then directing her eyes to Mary, who had summoned strength to rise, and was slowly venturing to approach her, she extended a finger towards her. Mary eagerly seized her mother's hand, and pressed it with fervour to her lips; then hid her face on her shoulder to conceal the tears that burst from her eyes.

'Absurd, my dear!' said her Ladyship in a peevish tone, as she disengaged herself from her daughter; 'you must really get the better of this foolish weakness; these *scènes* are too much for me. I was most excessively shocked last night, I assure you, and you ought not to have quitted your room to-day.'

Poor Mary's tears congealed in her eyes at this tender salutation; and she raised her head, as if to ascertain whether it really proceeded from her mother; but instead of the angelic vision she had pictured to herself, she beheld a face which, though once handsome, now conveyed no pleasurable feeling to the heart.

Late hours, bad temper, and rouge, had done much to impair Lady Juliana's beauty. There still remained enough to dazzle a superficial observer; but not to satisfy the eye used to the expression of all the best affections of the soul. Mary almost shrank from the peevish inanity pourtrayed on her mother's visage, as a glance of the mind contrasted it with the mild eloquence of Mrs.

Douglas' countenance; and, abashed and disappointed, she remained mournfully silent.

'Where is Dr. Redgill?' demanded Lady Juliana of the company in general.

'He has got scent of a turtle at Admiral Yellowchops',' answered Mr. P.

'How vastly provoking,' rejoined her Ladyship, 'that he should be out of the way the only time I have wished to see him since he came to the house!'

'Who is this favoured individual, whose absence you are so pathetically lamenting, Julia?' asked Lord Courtland, as he indolently sauntered into the room.

'That disagreeable Dr. Redgill. He has gone somewhere to eat turtle, at the very time I wished to consult him about—'

'The propriety of introducing a new niece to your Lordship,' said Lady Emily, as, with affected solemnity, she introduced Mary to her uncle. Lady Juliana frowned —the Earl smiled—saluted his niece—hoped she had recovered the fatigue of the journey—remarked it was very cold; and then turned to a parrot, humming 'Pretty Poll, say,'[1] &c.

Such was Mary's first introduction to her family; and those only who have felt what it was to have the genial current of their souls chilled by neglect, or changed by unkindness, can sympathise in the feelings of wounded affection—when the overflowings of a generous heart are confined within the narrow limits of its own bosom, and the offerings of love are rudely rejected by the hand most dear to us.

Mary was too much intimidated by her mother's manner towards her, to give way, in her presence, to the emotions that agitated her; but she followed her sister's steps as she quitted the room, and, throwing her arms around her, sobbed in a voice almost choked with the excess of her feelings, 'My sister, love me!—oh! love

me!' But Adelaide's heart, seared by selfishness and
vanity, was incapable of loving any thing in which self
had no share; and, for the first time in her life, she felt
awkward and embarrassed. Her sister's streaming eyes
and supplicating voice spoke a language to which she
was a stranger; for art is ever averse to recognise the
accents of nature. Still less is it capable of replying to
them; and Adelaide could only wonder at her sister's
agitation, and think how unpleasant it was; and say
something about overcome, and *eau-de-luce*,[1] and composure; which was all lost upon Mary as she hung upon
her neck, every feeling wrought to its highest tone by the
complicated nature of those emotions which swelled her
heart. At length, making an effort to regain her composure, 'Forgive me, my sister!' said she. 'This is very
foolish—to weep when I ought to rejoice—and I do
rejoice—and I know I shall be so happy yet!' but in
spite of the faint smile that accompanied her words, tears
again burst from her eyes.

'I am sure I shall have infinite pleasure in your
society,' replied Adelaide, with her usual sweetness and
placidity, as she replaced a ringlet in its proper position;
'but I have unluckily an engagement at this time. You
will, however, be at no loss for amusement; you will
find musical instruments there,' pointing to an adjacent
apartment; 'and here are new publications, and *porte
feuilles*[2] of drawings you will perhaps like to look over;'
and so saying, she disappeared.

'Musical instruments and new publications!' repeated
Mary mechanically to herself: 'what have I to do with
them?—Oh! for one kind word from my mother's lips!
—one kind glance from my sister's eye!'

And she remained overwhelmed with the weight of
those emotions, which, instead of pouring into the hearts
of others, she was compelled to concentrate in her own.
Her mournful reveries were interrupted by her kind

friend Lady Emily; but Mary deemed her sorrow too
sacred to be betrayed even to her, and therefore rallying
her spirits, she strove to enter into those schemes of
amusement suggested by her cousin for passing the day.
But she found herself unable for such continued exertion;
and hearing a large party was expected to dinner, she
retired, in spite of Lady Emily's remonstrance, to her
own apartment, where she sought a refuge from her
thoughts, in writing to her friends at Glenfern.

Lady Juliana looked in upon her as she passed to
dinner. She was in a better humour, for she had received
a new dress which was particularly becoming, as both
her maid and her glass had attested.

Again Mary's heart bounded towards the being to
whom she owed her birth; yet afraid to give utterance
to her feelings, she could only regard her with silent
admiration, till a moment's consideration converted that
into a less pleasing feeling, as she observed for the first
time, that her mother wore no mourning.

Lady Juliana saw her astonishment, and, little guessing
the cause, was flattered by it. 'Your style of dress is very
obsolete, my dear,' said she, as she contrasted the effect
of her own figure and her daughter's in a large mirror;
'and there's no occasion for you to wear black here. I
shall desire my woman to order some things for you;
though perhaps there won't be much occasion, as your
stay here is to be short; and, of course, you won't think
of going out at all. *Apropos*, you will find it dull here by
yourself, won't you? I shall leave you my darling Blanche
for a companion,' kissing a little French lap-dog, as she
laid it in Mary's lap; 'only you must be very careful of
her, and coax her, and be very, very good to her; for I
would not have my sweetest Blanche vexed, not for
the world!' And, with another long and tender salute
to her dog, and a 'Good bye, my dear!' to her daughter,
she quitted her to display her charms to a brilliant

drawing-room, leaving Mary to solace herself in her solitary chamber with the whines of a discontented lap-dog.

CHAPTER XIII

'C'est un personnage illustre dans son genre, et qui a porté le talent de se bien nourrir jusques où il pouvoit aller; ———— il ne semble né que pour la digestion.'

La Bruyère.[1]

IN EVERY SEASON of life, grief brings its own peculiar antidote along with it. The buoyancy of youth soon repels its deadening weight—the firmness of manhood resists its weakening influence—the torpor of old age is insensible to its most acute pangs.

In spite of the disappointment she had experienced the preceding day, Mary arose the following morning with fresh hopes of happiness springing in her heart.

'What a fool I was,' thought she, 'to view so seriously what, after all, must be merely difference of manner; and how illiberal to expect every one's manners should accord exactly with my ideas; but now that I have got over the first impression, I dare say I shall find every body quite amiable and delightful!'

And Mary quickly reasoned herself into the belief, that she only could have been to blame. With renovated spirits she therefore joined her cousin, and accompanied her to the breakfasting saloon. The visitors had all departed, but Dr. Redgill had returned, and seemed to be at the winding up of a solitary but voluminous meal. He was a very tall corpulent man, with a projecting front, large purple nose, and a profusion of chin.

'Good morning, ladies,' mumbled he with a full mouth, as he made a feint of half-rising from his chair. 'Lady Emily, your servant—Miss Douglas, I presume— hem! allow me to pull the bell for your Ladyship,' as he sat without stirring hand or foot; then after it was done—''pon my honour, Lady Emily, this is not using me well. Why did you not desire me?—and you are so nimble—I defy any man to get the start of you.'

'I know you have been upon hard service, Doctor, and therefore I humanely wished to spare you any additional fatigue,' replied Lady Emily.

'Fatigue, phoo! I'm sure I mind fatigue as little as any man; besides it's really nothing to speak of. I have merely rode from my friend Admiral Yellowchops' this morning.'

'I hope you passed a pleasant day there yesterday?'

'So, so—very so, so,' returned the Doctor drily.

'Only so, so, and a turtle in the case!' exclaimed Lady Emily.

'Phoo!—as to that, the turtle was neither here nor there. I value turtle as little as any man. You may be sure it wasn't for that I went to see my old friend Yellowchops. It happened, indeed, that there *was* a turtle, and a very well dressed one too; but where five and thirty people (one half of them ladies, who, of course, are always helped first,) sit down to dinner, there's an end of all rational happiness in my opinion.'

'But at a turtle feast you have surely something much better. You know you may have rational happiness any day over a beef-steak.'

'I beg your pardon—that's not such an easy matter. I can assure you it is a work of no small skill to dress a beef-steak handsomely; and, moreover, to eat it in perfection, a man must eat it by himself. If once you come to exchange words over it, it is useless. I once saw the finest steak I ever clapt my eyes upon, completely ruined by one silly scoundrel asking another if he liked fat. If he liked fat!—what a question for one rational being to ask another! The fact is, a beef-steak is like a woman's reputation, if once it is breathed upon it's good for nothing!'[1]

'One of the stories with which my nurse used to amuse my childhood,' said Mary, 'was that of having seen an itinerant conjurer dress a beef-steak on his tongue.'

The Doctor suspended the morsel he was carrying to his mouth, and for the first time regarded Mary with looks of unfeigned admiration.

''Pon my honour, and that was as clever a trick as ever I heard of! You are a wonderful people, you Scotch —a very wonderful people—but, pray, was she at any pains to examine the fellow's tongue?'

'I imagine not,' said Mary; 'I suppose the love of science was not strong enough to make her run the risk of burning her fingers.'

'It's a thousand pities,' said the Doctor, as he dropped his chin with an air of disappointment. 'I am surprised none of your Scotch *sçavans*[2] got hold of the fellow, and squeezed the secret out of him. It might have proved an important discovery—a very important discovery;—and your Scotch are not apt to let any thing escape them—a very searching shrewd people as ever I knew—and that's the only way to arrive at knowledge. A man must be of a stirring mind, if he expects to do good.'

'A poor woman below wishes to see you, Sir,' said a servant.

'These poor women are perfect pests to society,' said the Doctor, as his nose assumed a still darker hue; 'there is no resting upon one's seat for them—always something the matter! They burn, and bruise, and hack themselves, and their brats, one would really think, on purpose to give trouble.'

'I have not the least doubt of it,' said Lady Emily;

'they must find your sympathy so soothing.'

'As to that, Lady Emily, if you knew as much about poor women as I do, you wouldn't think so much of them as you do. Take my word for it—they are one and all of them a very greedy ungrateful set, and require to be kept at a distance.'

'And also to be kept waiting. As poor people's time is their only wealth, I observe you generally make them pay a pretty large fee in that way.'

'That is really not what I should have expected from you, Lady Emily. I must take the liberty to say, your Ladyship does me the greatest injustice. You must be sensible how ready I am to fly,' rising as if he had been glued to his chair, 'when there is any real danger. I'm sure it was only last week I got up as soon as I had swallowed my dinner, to see a man who had fallen down in a fit; and now I am going to this woman, who, I dare say, has nothing the matter with her, before my breakfast is well down my throat.'

'Who is that gentleman?' asked Mary, as the Doctor at length, with much reluctance, shuffled out of the room.

'He is a sort of medical aid-de-camp of papa's,' answered Lady Emily; 'who, for the sake of good living, has got himself completely domesticated here. He is vulgar, selfish, and *gourmand*, as you must already have discovered; but these are accounted his greatest perfections, as papa, like all indolent people, must be diverted —and *that* he never is by genteel sensible people. He requires something more *piquant*, and nothing fatigues him so much as the conversation of a common-place sensible man—one who has the skill to keep his foibles out of sight. Now, what delights him in Dr. Redgill, there is no *retenu*[1]—any child who runs may read his character at a glance.'

'It certainly does not require much penetration,' said

Mary, 'to discover the Doctor's master passion;[1] love of ease, and self-indulgence, seem to be the predominant features of his mind; and he looks as if, when he sat in an arm-chair, with his toes on the fender, and his hands crossed, he would not have an idea beyond "I wonder what we shall have for dinner to-day."'

'I'm glad to hear you say so, Miss Douglas,' said the Doctor, catching the last words as he entered the room, and taking them to be the spontaneous effusions of the speaker's own heart; 'I rejoice to hear you say so. Suppose we send for the bill of fare,'—pulling the bell; and then to the servant, who answered the summons, 'Desire Grillade to send up his bill—Miss Douglas wishes to see it.'

'Young ladies are much more housewifely in Scotland than they are in this country,' continued the Doctor, seating himself as close as possible to Mary,—'at least they were when I knew Scotland; but that's not yesterday, and it's much changed since then, I dare say. I studied physic in Edinburgh, and went upon a *tower*[2] through the Highlands. I was very much pleased with what I saw, I assure you. Fine country in some respects —nature has been very liberal.'

Mary's heart leapt within her at hearing her dear native land praised even by Dr. Redgill, and her conscience smote her for the harsh and hasty censure she had passed upon him. 'One who can admire the scenery of the Highlands,' thought she, 'must have a mind. It has always been observed, that only persons of taste were capable of appreciating the peculiar charms of mountain scenery. A London citizen, or a Lincolnshire grazier, sees nothing but deformity in the sublime works of nature,' *ergo*, reasoned Mary, 'Dr. Redgill must be of a more elevated way of thinking than I had supposed.' The entrance of Lady Juliana prevented her expressing the feelings that were upon her lips; but she thought what pleasure she would have in resuming the delightful theme at another opportunity.

After slightly noticing her daughter, and carefully adjusting her favourites, Lady Juliana began:—

'I am anxious to consult you, Dr. Redgill, upon the state of this young person's health.—You have been excessively ill, my dear, Have you not? (My sweetest Blanche, do be quiet!) You had a cough I think, and every thing that was bad.—And as her friends in Scotland have sent her to me for a short time, entirely on account of her health, (My charming Frisk, your spirits are really too much!) I think it quite proper that she should be confined to her own apartment during the winter, that she may get quite well and strong against spring. As to visiting, or going into company, that of course must be quite out of the question. You can tell Dr. Redgill, my dear, all about your complaints yourself.'

Mary tried to articulate, but her feelings rose almost to suffocation, and the words died upon her lips.

'Your Ladyship confounds me,' said the Doctor, pulling out his spectacles, which, after duly wiping, he adjusted on his nose, and turned their beams full on Mary's face—'I really never should have guessed there was any thing the matter with the young lady.—She does look a *leetle* delicate, to be sure—changing colour, too—but hand cool—eye clear—pulse steady, a *leetle* impetuous, but that's nothing, and the appetite good. I own I was surprised to see you cut so good a figure after the delicious meals you have been accustomed to in the north: you must find it miserable picking here. An English breakfast,' glancing with contempt at the eggs, muffins, toast, preserves, &c. &c. he had collected round him, 'is really a most insipid meal: if I did not make a rule of rising early and taking regular exercise, I doubt very much if I should be able to swallow a mouthful—there's nothing to whet the appetite here; and it's the same every where; as Yellowchops says, our breakfasts are a disgrace to England. One would think the whole nation was upon a regimen of tea and toast—from the Land's End to Berwick-upon-Tweed, nothing but tea and toast—Your Ladyship must really acknowledge the prodigious advantage the Scotch possess over us in that respect.'[1]

'I thought the breakfasts like every thing else in Scotland, extremely disgusting,' replied her Ladyship, with indignation.

'Ha! well, that really amazes me.—The people I give up—they are dirty and greedy —the country, too, is a perfect mass of rubbish—and the dinners not fit for dogs—the cookery, I mean; as to the materials, they are admirable—But the breakfasts! that's what redeems the land—and every county has its own peculiar excellence.[2] In Argyleshire you have the Lochfine herring, fat, luscious, and delicious, just out of the water, falling to pieces with its own richness—melting away like butter in your mouth. In Aberdeenshire, you have the Finnan haddo'[3] with a flavour all its own, vastly relishing—just salt enough to be *piquant*, without parching you up with thirst. In Perthshire, there is the Tay salmon, kippered, crisp and juicy—a very magnificent morsel—a *leetle* heavy, but that's easily counteracted by a tea-spoonful of the Athole whisky. In other places, you have the exquisite mutton of the country made into hams of a most delicate flavour; flour scones, soft and white; oatcake, thin and crisp; marmalade and jams of every description; and—But I beg pardon—your Ladyship was upon the subject of this young lady's health.—'Pon my honour! I can see little the matter—We were just going to look over the bill together when your Ladyship entered. I see it begins with that eternal *soupe santé*, and that paltry *potage-au-riz*—this is the second day within a week Monsieur Grillade has thought fit to treat us with them; and it's a fortnight yesterday since I have seen either oyster or turtle soup upon the table. 'Pon my honour! such inattention is infamous. I know Lord Courtland detests *soupe santé*, or, what's the same thing, he's quite indifferent to it—for I take indifference and dislike to be much the same: a man's indifference to his dinner is a serious thing, and so I shall let Monsieur Grillade know.'—And the Doctor's chin rose and fell like the waves of the sea.

'What is the name of the physician at Bristol, who is so celebrated for consumption complaints?' asked Lady Juliana of Adelaide. 'I shall send for him; he is the only person I have any reliance upon. I know he always recommends confinement for consumption.'

Tears dropped from Mary's eyes. Lady Juliana regarded her with surprise and severity.

'How very tiresome! I really can't stand these perpetual *scènes*. Adelaide, my love, pull the bell for my *eau de luce*.[1] Dr. Redgill, place the screen there. This room is insufferably hot. My dogs will literally be roasted alive;' and her Ladyship fretted about in all the perturbation of ill humour.

'Pon my honour! I don't think the room hot,' said the Doctor, who, from a certain want of tact and opacity of intellect, never comprehended the feelings of others: 'I declare I have felt it much hotter, when your Ladyship has complained of the cold: but there's no accounting for people's feelings. If you would move your seat a *leetle* this way, I think you would be cooler; and as to your daughter——'

'I have repeatedly desired, Dr. Redgill, that you will not use these familiar appellations when you address me or any of my family,' interrupted Lady Juliana with haughty indignation.

'I beg pardon,' said the Doctor, nowise discomposed at this rebuff.—'Well, with regard to Miss—Miss—this young lady, I assure your Ladyship, you need be under no apprehensions on her account. She's a *leetle* nervous, that's all—take her about by all means—all young ladies love to go about and see sights. Shew her the pump-room,[1] and the ball-room, and the shops, and the rope-dancers, and the wild beasts, and there's no fear of her. I never recommend confinement to man, woman, or child. It destroys the appetite—and our appetite is the best part of us—What would we be without appetites? Miserable beings! worse than the beasts of the field!'—And away shuffled the Doctor to admonish Monsieur Grillade on the iniquity of neglecting this the noblest attribute of man.

'It appears to me excessively extraordinary,' said Lady Juliana, addressing Mary, 'that Mrs. Douglas should have alarmed me so much about your health, when it seems, there's nothing the matter with you. She certainly shewed very little regard for my feelings. I can't understand it; and I must say, if you are not ill, I have been most excessively ill used by your Scotch friends.' And, with an air of great indignation, her Ladyship swept out of the room, regardless of the state into which she had thrown her daughter.

Poor Mary's feelings were now at their climax, and she gave way to all the repressed agony that swelled her heart. Lady Emily, who had been amusing herself at the other end of the saloon, and had heard nothing of what had passed, flew towards her at sight of her suffering, and eagerly demanded of Adelaide the cause.

'I really don't know,' answered Adelaide, lifting her beautiful eyes from her book, with the greatest composure, 'Lady Juliana is always cross of a morning.'

'Oh, no!' exclaimed Mary, trying to regain her composure, 'the fault is mine. I—I have offended my mother, I know not how. Tell me—O tell me, how I can obtain her forgiveness?'

'Obtain her forgiveness!' repeated Lady Emily indignantly, 'for what?'

'Alas! I know not; but in some way I have displeased my mother: her looks—her words—her manner—all tell me how dissatisfied she is with me; while to my sister, and even to her very dogs—' Here Mary's agitation choked her utterance.

'If you expect to be treated like a dog, you will certainly be disappointed,' said Lady Emily. 'I wonder Mrs. Douglas did not warn you of what you had to expect. She must have known something of Lady Juliana's ways; and it would have been as well had you been better prepared to encounter them.'

Mary looked hurt, and making an effort to conquer her emotion, she said, 'Mrs. Douglas never spoke of my mother with disrespect; but she did warn me against expecting too much from her affection. She said I had been too long estranged from her, to have retained my place in her heart; but still—'

'You could not foresee the reception you have met with?—Nor I neither. Did you, Adelaide?'

'Lady Juliana is sometimes so odd,' answered her daughter, in her sweetest tone, 'that I really am seldom surprised at any thing she does; but all this fracas appears to me perfectly absurd, as nobody minds any thing she says.'

'Impossible!' exclaimed Mary; 'my duty must ever be to reverence my mother. My study should be to please her, if I only knew how; and oh! would she but suffer me to love her!'

Adelaide regarded her sister for a moment with a look of surprise; then rose and left the room, humming an Italian air.

Lady Emily remained with her cousin; but she was a bad comforter: her indignation against the oppressor was always much stronger than her sympathy with the oppressed; and she would have been more in her element scolding the mother than soothing the daughter.

But Mary had not been taught to trust to mortals weak as herself for support in the hour of trial: She knew her aid must come from a higher source; and in solitude she sought for consolation.

'This must be all for my good,' sighed she, 'else it would not be. I had drawn too bright a picture of happiness—already it is blotted out with my tears. I must set about replacing it with one of soberer colours.'

Alas! Mary knew not how many a fair picture of human felicity had shared the same fate as hers!

CHAPTER XIV

'They were in sooth a most enchanting train;
————————————skilful to unite
With evil good, and strew with pleasure pain.'
Castle of Indolence.[1]

IN WRITING TO her maternal friend, Mary did not follow the mode usually adopted by young ladies of the heroic cast, viz. that of giving a minute and circumstantial detail of their own complete wretchedness; and abusing, in terms highly sentimental, every member of the family with whom they are associated. Mary knew, that to breathe a hint of her own unhappiness would be to embitter the peace of those she loved; and she therefore strove to conceal from their observation the disappointment she had experienced. Many a sigh was heaved, however, and many a tear was wiped away ere a letter could be composed that would carry pleasure to the dear group at Glenfern. She could say nothing of her mother's tenderness, or her sister's affection; but she dwelt upon the elegance of the one, and the beauty of the other. She could not boast of the warmth of her uncle's reception, but she praised his good humour, and enlarged upon Lady Emily's kindness and attention. Even Dr. Redgill's admiration of Scotch breakfasts, was given as a *bonne bouche*[1] for her good old aunts.

'I declare,' said Miss Grizzy, as she ended her fifth perusal of the letter, 'Mary must be a happy creature! Every body must allow—indeed I never heard it disputed that Lady Juliana is a most elegant being; and I daresay she is greatly improved since we saw her, for you know that is a long time ago.'

'The mind may improve after a certain age,' replied Jacky, with one of her wisest looks, 'but I doubt very much if the person does.'

'If the inside had been like the out, there would have been no need for improvement,' observed Nicky.

'I'm sure you are both perfectly right,' resumed the sapient Grizzy, 'and I have not the least doubt but that our dear niece is a great deal wiser than when we knew her; nobody can deny but she is a great deal older; and you know people always grow wiser as they grow older of course.'

'They *ought* to do it,' said Jacky with emphasis.

'But there's no fool like an old fool,' quoth Nicky.

'What a delightful creature our charming niece Adelaide must be, from Mary's account,' said Grizzy; 'only I can't conceive how her eyes come to be black. I'm sure there's not a black eye amongst us. The Kilnacroish family are black to be sure; and Kilnacroish's great-grandmother was first cousin, once removed, to our grandfather's aunt, by the mother's side: it's wonderful the length that resemblances run in some old families; and I really can't account for our niece Adelaide's black eyes naturally, any other way than just through the Kilnacroish family; for I'm quite convinced it's from us she takes them, children always take their eyes from their father's side; every body knows that Becky's, and Bella's, and Babby's, are all as like their poor father's as they can stare.'

'There's no accounting for the varieties of the human species,' said Jacky.

'And like's an ill mark,'[1] observed Nicky.

'And only think of her being so much taller than Mary, and twins! I declare it's wonderful—I should have thought, indeed I never doubted, that they would have been exactly the same size—And such a beautiful colour too, when we used to think Mary rather pale—it's very unaccountable!'

'You forget,' said Jacky, who had not forgot the insult offered to her nursing system eighteen years before; 'you forget that I always predicted what would happen.'

'I never knew any good come of changes,'[2] said Nicky.

'I'm sure that's very true,' rejoined Grizzy; 'and we have great reason to thank our stars, that Mary is not a perfect dwarf; which I really thought she would have been for long, till she took a shooting,—summer was a year.'

'But she'll shoot no more,' said Jacky, with a shake of the head that might have vied with Jove's imperial nod;[3] 'England's not the place for shooting.'

'The Englishwomen are all poor droichs,'[4] said Nicky, who had seen three in the course of her life.

'It's a great matter to us all, however, and to herself too, poor thing! that Mary should be so happy,' resumed Grizzy. 'I'm sure I don't know what she would have done, if Lord Courtland had been an ill-tempered harsh man, which, you know, he might just as easily have been; and it would really have been very hard upon poor Mary—and Lady Emily such a sweet creature too! I'm sure we must all allow we have the greatest reason to be thankful.'

'I don't know,' said Jacky; 'Mary was petted enough before, I wish she may have a head to stand any more.'

'She'll be ten times nicer than ever,' quoth Nicky.

'There is some reason, to be sure, that can't be denied, to be afraid of that; at the same time, Mary has a great deal of sense of her own when she chooses; and it's a great matter for her, and indeed for all of us, that she is under the eye of such a sensible worthy man, as that Dr. Redgill. Of course, we may be sure, Lord Courtland will keep a most elegant table, and have a great variety of sweet things, which are certainly very tempting for young people; but I have no doubt but Dr. Redgill will look after Mary, and see that she doesn't eat too many of them.'

'Dr. Redgill must be a very superior man,' pronounced Jacky, in her most magisterial manner.

'If I could hear of a private opportunity,' exclaimed Nicky, in a transport of generosity, 'I would send them one of our hams, and a nice little pig* of butter—the English are all great people for butter.'

The proposal was hailed with rapture by both sisters in a breath; and it was finally settled, that to those tender pledges of Nicky's, Grizzy should add a box of Lady Maclaughlan's latest invented pills, while Miss Jacky was to compose the epistle that was to accompany them.

The younger set of aunts were astonished that Mary had said nothing about lovers and offers of marriage, as they had always considered going to England as synonimous with going to be married.

To Mrs. Douglas' more discerning eye, Mary's happiness did not appear in so dazzling a light, as to the weaker optics of her aunts.

'It is not like my Mary,' thought she, 'to rest so much

* Jar.

on mere external advantages; surely her warm affectionate heart cannot be satisfied with the *grace* of a mother, and the *beauty* of a sister: these she might admire in a stranger; but where we seek for happiness, we better prize more homely attributes. Yet Mary is so open and confiding, I think she could not have concealed from me, had she experienced a disappointment.'

Mrs. Douglas was not aware of the effect of her own practical lessons; and that, while she was almost unconsciously practising the quiet virtues of patience, and fortitude, and self-denial, and unostentatiously sacrificing her own wishes, to promote the comfort of others—her example, like a kindly dew, was shedding its silent influence on the embryo blossoms of her pupil's heart.

CHAPTER XV

> ——'So the devil prevails often; *opponit nubem*, he claps a
> cloud between;[1] some little objection; a stranger is come; or my
> head aches; or the church is too cold; or I have letters to write;
> or I am not disposed; or it is not yet time; or the time is past:
> these, and such as these, are the clouds the devil claps between
> heaven and us; but these are such impotent objections, that they
> were as soon confuted, as pretended, by all men that are not
> fools, or professed enemies of religion.'
>
> *Jeremy Taylor.*[2]

LADY JULIANA HAD, in vain, endeavoured to obtain a sick certificate for her daughter, that would have authorised her consigning her to the oblivion of her own apartment. The physicians, whom she consulted, all agreed, for once, in recommending a totally different system to be pursued; and her displeasure, in consequence, was violently excited against the medical tribe in general, and Dr. Redgill in particular. For that worthy, she had, indeed, always entertained a most thorough contempt and aversion; for he was poor, ugly, and vulgar, and these were the three most deadly sins in her calendar. The object of her detestation was, however, completely insensible to its effects. The Doctor, like Achilles, was vulnerable but in one part, and over that she could exercise no controul. She had nothing to do with the *menage*—possessed no influence over Lord Courtland, nor authority over Monsieur Grillade. She differed from himself as to the dressing of certain dishes; and, in short, he summed up her character in one emphatic sentence, that, in his idea, conveyed severer censure than all that Pope or Young[1] ever wrote—'I don't think she has the taste of her mouth!'

Thus thwarted in her scheme, Lady Juliana's dislike to her daughter rather increased than diminished: and it was well for Mary, that lessons of forbearance had been early infused into her mind; for her spirit was naturally high, and would have revolted from the tyranny and injustice with which she was treated, had she not been taught the practical duties of Christianity, and that 'patience, with all its appendages, is the sum-total of all our duty that is proper to the day of sorrow.'

Not that Mary sought, by a blind compliance with all her mother's follies and caprices, to ingratiate herself into her favour—even the motive she would have deemed insufficient to have sanctified the deed. And the only arts she employed to win a place in her parent's heart, were ready obedience, unvarying sweetness, and uncomplaining submission.

Although Mary possessed none of the sour bigotry of a narrow mind, she was yet punctual in the discharge of her religious duties; and the Sunday following her arrival, as they sat at breakfast, she inquired of her cousin, at what time the church-service began.

'I really am not certain—I believe it is late,' replied her cousin carelessly. 'But why do you ask?'

'Because I wish to be there in proper time.'

'But we scarcely ever go—never, indeed, to the parish church—and we are rather distant from any other; so you must say your prayers at home.'

'I would certainly prefer going to church,' said Mary.

'Going to church!' exclaimed Dr. Redgill, in amazement. 'I wonder what makes people so keen of going to church! I'm sure there's little good to be got there. For my part, I declare I would just as soon think of going into my grave. Take my word for it, churches and church-yards are rather too nearly related.'

'In such a day as this,' said Mary, 'so dry and sunny, I am sure there can be no danger.'

'Take your own way, Miss Mary,' said the Doctor; 'but I think it my duty to let you know my opinion of churches. I look upon them as extremely prejudicial to the health. They are, invariably, either too hot or too cold; you are either stewed or starved in them; and, till some improvement takes place, I assure you my foot shall never enter one of them. In fact, they are perfect receptacles of human infirmities. I can tell one of your church-going ladies at a glance: they have all rheumatisms in their shoulders, and colds in their heads, and swelled faces. Besides, it's a poor country church—there's nothing to be seen after you do go.'

'I assure you, Lady Juliana will be excessively annoyed if you go,' said Lady Emily, as Mary rose to leave the room.

'Surely my mother cannot be displeased at my attending church!' said Mary, in astonishment.

'Yes, she can, and most certainly will. She never goes herself now, since she had a quarrel with Dr. Barlow, the clergyman; and she can't bear any of the family to attend him.'

'And you have my sanction for staying away, Miss Mary,' added the Doctor.

'Is he a man of bad character?' asked Mary, as she stood irresolute whether to proceed.

'Quite the reverse. He is a very good man; but he was scandalized at Lady Juliana's bringing her dogs to church one day, and wrote her what she conceived a most insolent letter about it.—But here comes your lady-mamma, and the culprits in question.'

'Your Ladyship is just come in time to settle a dispute here,' said the Doctor, anxious to turn her attention from a hot muffin, which had just been brought in, and which he meditated appropriating to himself: 'I have said all I can—(Was you looking at the toast, Lady Emily?)—I must now leave it to your Ladyship to convince this young lady of the folly of going to church.'

The Doctor gained his point. The muffin was upon his own plate, while Lady Juliana directed her angry look towards her daughter.

'Who talks of going to church?' demanded she.

Mary gently expressed her wish to be permitted to attend divine service.

'I won't permit it. I don't approve of girls going about by themselves. It is vastly improper, and I won't hear of it.'

'It is the only place I shall ask to go to,' said Mary, timidly; 'but I have always been accustomed to attend church, and—'

'That is a sufficient reason for my choosing that you should not attend it here. I won't suffer a Methodist in the house.'

'I assure you, the Methodists are gaining ground very fast,' said the Doctor, with his mouth full. ''Pon my soul, I think it's very alarming!'

'Pray, what is so alarming in the apprehension?' asked Lady Emily.

'What is so alarming! 'Pon my honour, Lady Emily, I'm astonished to hear you ask such a question!'—muttering to himself, 'zealots—fanatics—enthusiasts—bedlamites! I'm sure every body knows what Methodists are!'

'There has been quite enough said upon the subject,' said Lady Juliana.

'There are plenty of sermons in the house, Miss Mary,' continued the Doctor, who, like many other people, thought he was always doing a meritorious action when he could dissuade any body from going to church. 'I saw a volume somewhere not long ago; and, at any rate, there's the Spectator,[1] if you want Sunday's reading—some of the papers there are as good as any sermon you'll get from Dr. Barlow.'

Mary, with fear and hesitation, made another attempt to overcome her mother's prejudice; but in vain.

'I desire I may hear no more about it!'cried she, raising her voice. 'The clergyman is a most improper person. I won't suffer any of my family to attend his church; and therefore, once for all, I won't hear another syllable on the subject.'

This was said in a tone and manner not to be disputed, and Mary felt her resolution give way before the displeasure of her mother. A contest of duties was new to her, and she could not all at once resolve upon fulfilling one duty at the expense of another. 'Besides,' thought she, 'my mother thinks she is in the right. Perhaps, by degrees, I may bring her to think otherwise; and it is surely safer to try to conciliate than to determine to oppose.'

But another Sabbath came, and Mary found she had made no progress in obtaining the desired permission. She therefore began seriously to commune with her own heart, as to the course she ought to pursue.

The commandment of 'Honour thy father and thy mother,'[2] had been deeply imprinted on her mind, and

few possessed higher notions of filial reverence; but there
was another precept, which also came to her recollection. 'Whosoever loveth father and mother more than
me, cannot be my disciple.'[1] 'But I may honour and
obey my parent without loving her more than my
Saviour,' argued she with herself, in hopes of lulling her
conscience by this reflection. 'But again,' thought she,
'the Scripture saith, "He that keepeth my command-
ments, he it is that loveth me."'[2] Then she felt the necessity of owning, that if she obeyed the commands of her
mother, when in opposition to the will of her God, she
gave one of the Scripture proofs of either loving or fearing
her parent upon earth more than her father which is in
heaven. But Mary, eager to reconcile impossibilities,
viz. the will of an ungodly parent with the holy commands
of her Maker, thought now of another argument to calm
her conscience. 'The Scripture,' said she, 'says nothing
positive about attending public worship; and, as Lady
Emily says, I may say my prayers just as well at home.'
But the passages of Scripture were too deeply imprinted
on her mind to admit of this subterfuge. 'Forsake not the
assembling of yourselves together.'[3] 'Where two or three
are gathered together in my name, there will I be in the
midst of them,'[4] &c. &c.—But, alas! two or three never
were gathered together at Beech Park, except upon
parties of pleasure, games of hazard, or purposes of
conviviality.

The result of Mary's deliberations was, a firm determination to do what she deemed her duty, however
painful. And she went in search of Lady Emily, hoping
to prevail upon her to use her influence with Lady
Juliana to grant the desired permission; or should she
fail in obtaining it, she trusted her resolution would
continue strong enough to enable her to brave her
mother's displeasure in this act of conscientious disobedience. She met her cousin, with her bonnet on,

prepared to go out.

'Dear Lady Emily,' said she, 'let me entreat of you to use your influence with my mother, to persuade her to allow me to go to church.'

'In the first place,' answered her cousin, 'you may know that I have no influence;—in the second, that Lady Juliana is never to be persuaded into any thing;— in the third, I really can't suppose you are serious in thinking it a matter of such vast moment, whether or not you go to church.'

'Indeed I do,' answered Mary, earnestly. 'I have been taught to consider it as such; and—'

'Pshaw! nonsense! these are some of your stiff-necked Presbyterian notions. I shall really begin to suspect you are a Methodist; and yet you are not at all like one.'

'Pray, tell me,' said Mary, with a smile, 'what are your ideas of a Methodist?'

'Oh! thank heaven, I know little about them!—almost as little as Dr. Redgill, who, I verily believe, could scarcely tell the difference betwixt a Catholic and a Methodist, except that the one dances, and t'other prays. But I am rather inclined to believe it is a sort of a scowling, black-browed, hard-favoured creature, with its greasy hair combed straight upon its flat forehead, and that twirls its thumbs, and turns up its eyes, and speaks through its nose; and, in short, is every thing that you are not, except in this matter—of going to church. So, to avert all these evil signs from falling upon you, I shall make a point of your keeping company with me for the rest of the day.'

Again Mary became serious, as she renewed her entreaties to her cousin to intercede with Lady Juliana, that she might be allowed to attend *any* church.[1]

'Not for kingdoms!' exclaimed she. 'Her Ladyship is in one of her most detestable humours to day; not that I should mind that, if it was any thing of real consequence that I had to compass for you. A ball, for instance—I should certainly stand by you there; but I am really not so fond of mischief as to enrage her for nothing!'

'Then I fear I must go to church without leave,' said Mary, in a melancholy tone.

'If you are to go at all, it must certainly be without it. And here is the carriage—get your bonnet, and come along with me. You shall, at least, have a sight of the church.'

Mary went to put on her pelisse; and, descending to join her cousin in the drawing-room, she found her engaged in an argument with Dr. Redgill. How it had commenced, did not appear; but the Doctor's voice was raised as if to bring it to a decided termination.

'The French, Madam, in spite of your prejudices, are a very superior nation to us. Their skill and knowledge are both infinitely higher. Every man in France is a first rate cook—in fact they are a nation of cooks; and one of our late travellers assures us, that they have discovered three hundred methods of dressing eggs, for one thing.'

'That is just two hundred and ninety-nine ways more than enough,' said Lady Emily; 'give me a plain boiled egg, and I desire no other variety of the produce of a hen, till it takes the form of a chicken.'

Dr. Redgill lowered his eye-brows, and drew up his chin, but disdained to waste more arguments upon so tasteless a being. 'To talk sense to a woman is like feeding chickens upon turtle soup,' thought he to himself.

As for Lady Juliana, she exulted in the wise and judicious manner in which she had exercised her authority, and felt her consequence greatly increased by a public display of it; power being an attribute she was very seldom invested with now. Indeed, to do her Lady-ship justice, she was most feelingly alive to the duty due to parents, though that such a commandment existed seemed quite unknown to her till she became a mother. But she made ample amends for former deficiencies now; as to hear her expatiate on the subject, one would have deemed it the only duty necessary to be practised, either by Christian or heathen, and that, like charity, it comprehended every virtue, and was a covering for every sin. But there are many more sensible people than her Ladyship, who entertain the same sentiments, and, by way of variety, reverse the time and place of their duties. When they are children, they make many judicious reflections on the duties of parents; when they become parents, they then acquire a wonderful insight into the duties of children. In the same manner, husbands and wives are completely alive to the duties incumbent upon each other; and the most ignorant servant is fully instructed in the duty of a master. But we shall leave Lady Juliana to pass over the duties of parents, and ponder upon those of children, while we follow Lady Emily and Mary in their airing.

The road lay by the side of a river; and though Mary's taste had been formed upon the wild romantic scenery of the Highlands, she yet looked with pleasure on the tamer beauties of an English landscape. And, though accustomed to admire even 'rocks where the snow flake reposes;'[1] she had also taste, though of a less enthusiastic kind, for the 'gay landscapes and gardens or roses,'[2] which, in this more genial clime, bloomed even under winter's sway. The carriage drove smoothly along, and the sound of the church bell fell at intervals on the ear, 'in cadence sweet, now dying all away;'[3] and, at the holy sound, Mary's heart flew back to the peaceful vale and primitive kirk of Lochmarlie, where all her happy Sabbaths had been spent. The view now opened upon the village church, beautifully situated on the slope of a green hill. Parties of straggling villagers, in their holiday suits, were descried in all directions, some already assembled in the church-yard, others traversing the neat foot-paths that led through the meadows. But, to Mary's eyes, the well dressed English rustic, trudging along the smooth path, was a far less picturesque object, than the bare-footed Highland girl, bounding over trackless heath-covered hills; and the well preserved glossy blue coat, seemed a poor substitute for the varied drapery of the graceful plaid.

So much do early associations tincture all our future ideas.

They had now reached the church, and as Mary adhered to her resolution of attending divine worship, Lady Emily declared her intention of accompanying her, that she might come in for her share of Lady Juliana's displeasure; but, in spite of her levity, the reverend aspect, and meek, yet fervent piety of Dr. Burley,[1] impressed her with better feelings; and she joined in the service with outward decorum, if not with inward devotion. The music consisted of an organ, simply but well played; and to Mary, unaccustomed to any sacred sounds, save those twanged through the nose of a Highland *precentor*,[2] it seemed the music of the spheres.

Far different sounds than those of peace and praise awaited her return. Lady Juliana, apprized of this open act of rebellion, was in all the paroxysms incident to a little mind, on discovering the impotence of its power. She rejected all attempts at reconciliation; raved about ingratitude and disobedience; declared her determination of sending Mary back to her vulgar Scotch relations one moment—the next protested she should never see those odious Methodists again—then she was to take her to France, and shut her up in a convent, &c. till after uttering all the incoherencies usual with ladies in a passion, she at last succeeded in raving herself into a fit of hysterics.

Poor Mary was deeply affected at this (to her)

tremendous display of passion. She who had always been used to the mild placidity of Mrs. Douglas, and who had seen her face sometimes clouded with sorrow, but never deformed by anger—what a spectacle! to behold a parent subject to the degrading influence of an ungovernable temper! Her very soul sickened at the sight; and while she wept over her mother's weakness, she prayed that the power which stayed the ocean's wave would mercifully vouchsafe to still the wilder tempests of human passion.

CHAPTER XVI

'Why, all delights are vain; but that most vain,
Which, with pain purchased, doth inherit pain.'
                                        Shakespeare.[1]

IN ADDITION TO her mother's implacable wrath and unceasing animadversion, Mary found she was looked upon as a sort of alarming character by the whole family. Lord Courtland seemed afraid of being drawn into a religious controversy every time he addressed her. Dr. Redgill retreated at her approach, and eyed her askance, as much as to say, "Pon my honour, a young lady that can fly in her mother's face about such a trifle as going to church, is not very safe company.' And Adelaide shunned her more than ever, as if afraid of coming in contact with a professed Methodist. Lady Emily, how-ever, remained staunch to her; and though she had her own private misgivings as to her cousin's creed, she yet stoutly defended her from the charge of Methodism, and maintained that, in many respects, Mary was no better than her neighbours.

'Well Mary,' cried she, as she entered her room one day with an air of exultation, 'here is an opportunity for you to redeem your character—There,' throwing down a card, 'is an invitation for you to a fancy ball.'[1]

Mary's heart bounded at the mention of a ball. She had never been at one, and it was pictured in her imagination in all the glowing colours with which youth and inexperience deck untried pleasures.

'O how charming!' exclaimed she, with sparkling eyes, 'how my aunts Becky and Bella, will love to hear an account of a ball—And a fancy ball!—what is that?'

Lady Emily explained to her the nature of the entertainment, and Mary was in still greater raptures.

'It will be a perfect scene of enchantment, I have no doubt,' continued her cousin, 'for Lady M. understands giving balls, which is what every one does not; for there are dull balls as well as dull everythings else in the world. But come, I have left Lady Juliana and Adelaide in grand debate as to their dresses. We must also hold a cabinet council upon ours. Shall I summon the inimitable Slash to preside?'

The mention of her mother recalled Mary's thoughts from the festive scene to which they had already flown.

'But are you *quite* sure,' said she, 'that I shall have my mother's consent to go?'

'Quite the contrary,' answered her cousin coolly: 'She won't hear of your going. But what signifies that; you could go to church in spite of her, and surely you can't think her consent of much consequence to a ball?'

Poor Mary's countenance fell, as the bright vision of her imagination melted into air.

'Without my mother's permission,' said she, 'I shall certainly not think of, or even wish,' with a sigh, 'to go to the ball; and if she has already refused it, that is enough.'

Lady Emily regarded her with astonishment. 'Pray, is it only on Sundays you make a point of disobeying your mother?'

'It is only when I conceive a higher duty is required of me,' answered Mary.

'Why, I confess I used to think, that, to honour one's father and mother, *was* a duty, till you shewed me the contrary. I have to thank you for ridding me of that vulgar prejudice. And now, after setting me such a noble example of independence, you seem to have got a new light on the subject yourself.'

'My obedience and disobedience both proceed from the same source,' answered Mary. 'My first duty I have been taught is to worship my Maker—my next to obey my mother. My own gratification never can come in competition with either.'

'Well, I really can't enter into a religious controversy with you; but it seems to me, the sin, if it is one, is precisely the same, whether you play the naughty girl in going to one place or another. I can see no difference.'

'To me it appears very different,' said Mary; 'and therefore I should be inexcusable, were I to choose the evil believing it to be such.'

'Say what you will,' cried her cousin pettishly, 'you never will convince me there can be any harm in disobeying such a mother as yours—so unreasonable—so—.'

'The Bible makes no exceptions,' interrupted Mary, gently; 'it is not because of the reasonableness of our parents' commands that we are required to obey them, but because it is the will of God.'

'You certainly are a Methodist—there's no denying it. I have fought some hard battles for you, but I see I must give you up. The thing won't conceal.'—This was said with such an air of vexation, that Mary burst into a fit of laughter.

'And yet you are the oddest compound,' continued her cousin, 'so gay and comical, and so little given to be shocked and scandalized at the wicked ways of others; or to find fault and lecture; or, in short, to do any of the insufferable things that your good people are so addicted to. I really don't know what to think of you.'

'Think of me as a creature with too many faults of her own, to presume to meddle with those of others,' replied Mary, smiling at her cousin's perplexity.

'Well, if all good people were like you, I do believe I should become a saint myself. If you are right, I must be wrong; but fifty years hence we shall settle that matter with spectacles on nose over our family Bibles. In the mean time, the business of the ball room is much more pressing.—We really must decide upon something. Will you choose your own style, or shall I leave it to Madame Trieur to do us up exactly alike?'

'You have only to choose for yourself, my dear cousin,' answered Mary. 'You know I have no interest in it—at least not till I have received my mother's permission.'

'I have told you already there is no chance of obtaining it. I had a *brouillerie*[1] with her on the subject before I came to you.'

'Then I entreat you will not say another word. It is a thing of so little consequence, that I am quite vexed to think that my mother should have been disturbed about it. Dear Lady Emily, if you love me, promise that you will not say another syllable on the subject.'

'And this is all the thanks I get for my trouble and vexation,' exclaimed Lady Emily, angrily; 'but the truth is, I believe you think it would be a sin to go to a ball—and as for dancing—Oh shocking! that would be absolute ————. I really can't say the bad word you good people are so fond of using.'

'I understand your meaning,' answered Mary, laughing; 'but, indeed, I have no such apprehensions. On the contrary, I am very fond of dancing; so fond, that I have often taken aunt Nicky for my partner in a Strathspey[2] rather than sit still—and, to confess my weakness, I should like very much to go to a ball.'

'Then you must and shall go to this one. It is really a pity that you should have enraged Lady Juliana so much by that unfortunate church-going; but for that, I think she might have been managed; and even now, I should not despair, if you would, like a good girl, beg pardon for what is past, and promise never to do so any more.'

'Impossible!' replied Mary. 'You surely cannot be serious in supposing I would barter a positive duty for a trifling amusement?'

'O hang duties! they are odious things. And as for your amiable, dutiful, virtuous Goody Two-Shoes[1] characters, I detest them. They never would go down with me, even in the nursery, with all the attractions of a gold watch, and coach and six. They were ever my abhorrence, as every species of canting and hypocrisy still is—'

Then, struck with a sense of her own violence and impetuosity, contrasted with her cousin's meek unreproving manner, Lady Emily threw her arms around her, begging pardon, and assuring her she did not mean her.

'If you had,' said Mary, returning her embrace, 'you would only have told me what I am in some respects. Dull and childish, I know I am; for I am not the same creature I was at Lochmarlie'—and a tear trembled in her eye as she spoke—'and troublesome, I am sure, you have found me.'

'No, no!' eagerly interrupted Lady Emily; 'you are the reverse of all that. You are the picture of my Edward, and every thing that is excellent and engaging; and I see, by that smile, you will go to the ball—there's a darling!'

Mary shook her head.

'I'll tell you what we can do,' cried her persevering patroness, 'We can go as masks, and Lady Juliana shall know nothing about it. That will save the scandal of an

open revolt, or a tiresome dispute. Half the company
will be masked; so, if you keep your own secret, nobody
will find it out. Come, what characters shall we choose?'

'That of Janus,[1] I think, would be the most suitable
for me,' said Mary. Then, in a serious tone, she added,
'I can neither disobey nor deceive my mother. Therefore, once for all, my dear cousin, let me entreat of you
to be silent on a subject on which my mind is made up.
I am perfectly sensible of your kindness, but any further
discussion will be very painful to me.'

Lady Emily was now too indignant to stoop to remonstrance. She quitted her cousin in great anger, and poor
Mary felt as if she had lost her only friend.

'Alas!' sighed she, 'how difficult it is to do right, when
even the virtues of others throw obstacles in our way!
and how easy our duties would be, could we kindly aid
one another in the performance of them!'

But such is human nature. The real evils of life, of
which we so loudly complain, are few in number, compared to the daily, hourly pangs we inflict on one another.

Lady Emily's resentment, though violent, was short-
lived; and, in the certainty that either the mother would
relent, or the daughter rebel, she ordered a dress for
Mary; but the night of the ball arrived, and both
remained unshaken in their resolution. With a few words,
Adelaide might have obtained the desired permission
for her sister; but she chose to remain neuter, coldly
declaring she never interfered in quarrels.

Mary beheld the splendid dresses and gay countenances
of the party for the ball with feelings free from envy,
though perhaps not wholly unmixed with regret. She
gazed with the purest admiration on the extreme beauty
of her sister, heightened as it was by the fantastic
elegance of her dress, and contrasted with her own pale
visage, and mourning habiliments.

'Indeed,' thought she, as she turned from the mirror,

with rather a mournful smile, 'my aunt Nicky was in the right: I certainly am a poor *shilpit*[1] thing.'

As she looked again at her sister, she observed, that her ear-rings were not so handsome as those she had received from Mrs. Macshake; and she instantly brought them, and requested Adelaide would wear them for that night.

Adelaide took them with her usual coolness—remarked how very magnificent they were—wished some old woman would take it into her head to make her such a present; and, as she clasped them in her ears, regarded herself with increased complacency. The hour of departure arrived; Lord Courtland and Lady Juliana were at length ready, and Mary found herself left to a *tête-à-tête* with Dr. Redgill; and, strange as it may seem, neither in a sullen nor melancholy mood. But after a single sigh, as the carriage drove off, she sat down with a cheerful countenance to play backgammon[2] with the Doctor.

The following day, she heard of nothing but the ball and its delights; for both her mother and cousin sought (though from different motives) to heighten her regret at not having been there. But Mary listened to the details of all she had missed with perfect fortitude, and only rejoiced to hear they had all been so happy.

CHAPTER XVII

'Day follows night. The clouds return again
After the falling of the latter rain;
But to the aged blind shall ne'er return
Grateful vicissitude: She still must mourn
The sun, and moon, and every starry light,
Eclipsed to her, and lost in everlasting night.'

Prior.[1]

AMONGST THE NUMEROUS letters and parcels with
which Mary had been entrusted by the whole county
of ———, there was one she had received from the
hands of Lady Maclaughlan, with a strict injunction to
be the bearer of it herself; and, as even Lady Maclaughlan's wishes now wore an almost sacred character in
Mary's estimation, she was very desirous of fulfilling
this her parting charge. But, in the thraldom in which
she was kept, she knew not how that was to be accomplished. She could not venture to wait upon the lady
to whom it was addressed, without her mother's permission; and she was aware, that to ask was upon every
occasion only to be refused. In this dilemma, she had
recourse to Lady Emily; and, shewing her the letter,
craved her advice and assistance.

'Mrs. Lennox, Rose Hall,' said her cousin, reading
the superscription. 'Oh! I don't think Lady Juliana will
care a straw about your going there. She is merely an
unfortunate blind old lady, whom every body thinks it a
bore to visit—myself, I'm afraid, amongst the number.
We ought to have called upon her ages ago—so I shall
go with you now.'

Permission for Mary to accompany her was easily
obtained; for Lady Juliana considered a visit to Mrs.
Lennox as an act of penance rather than of pleasure;
and Adelaide protested the very mention of her name
gave her the vapours.[2] There certainly was nothing that
promised much gratification in what Mary had heard;

and yet she already felt interested in this unfortunate blind lady, whom every body thought it a bore to visit, and she sought to gain some more information respecting her. But Lady Emily, though possessed of warm feelings, and kindly affections, was little given to frequent the house of mourning, or sympathise with the wounded spirit; and she yawned, as she declared she was very sorry for poor Mrs. Lennox, and would have made a point of seeing her oftener, could she have done her any good.

'But what can I possibly say to her,' continued she, 'after losing her husband, and having I don't know how many sons killed in battle, and her only daughter dying of a consumption, and herself going blind in consequence of her grief for all these misfortunes—What can I possibly do for her, or say to her? Were I in her situation, I'm sure I should hate the sight and sound of any human being, and should give myself up entirely to despair.'

'That would be but a pagan sacrifice,' said Mary.

'What would you do in such desperate circumstances?' demanded Lady Emily.

'I would hope,' answered Mary, meekly.

'But, in poor Mrs. Lennox's case, that would be to hope, though hope were lost; for what can she hope for now? She has still something to fear, however, as I believe she has one son remaining, who is in the brunt of every battle; of course, she has nothing to expect but accounts of his death.'

'But she may hope that heaven will preserve him, and—'

'That you will marry him. That would do excellently well, for he is as brave as a real Highlander, though he has the misfortune to be only half a one. His father, General Lennox, was a true Scot to the very tip of his tongue, and as proud and fiery as any chieftain need be. *His* death, certainly, was an improvement in the family.

But there is Rose Hall, with its pretty shrubberies, and nice parterres,[1] what do you say to becoming its mistress?'

'If I am to lay snares,' answered Mary, laughing, 'it must be for nobler objects than hedge-row elms and hillocks green.'[2]

'O! it must be for black crags and naked hills! Your country really does vastly well to rave about! Lofty mountains and deep glens, and blue lakes and roaring rivers, are mighty fine sounding things; but I suspect corn fields and barn yards are quite as comfortable neighbours: so take my advice and marry Charles Lennox.'

Mary only answered by singing, 'My heart's in the Highlands, my heart is not here,'[3] &c. as the carriage drew up.

'This is the property of Mrs. Lennox,' said Lady Emily, in answer to some remark of her companion's: 'she is the last of some ancient stock; and you see the family taste has been treated with all due respect.'

Rose Hall was indeed perfectly English: it was a description of place of which there are none in Scotland; for it wore the appearance of antiquity, without the too usual accompaniments of devastation or decay; neither did any incongruities betray vicissitude of fortune, or change of owner; but the taste of the primitive possessor seemed to have been respected through ages, by his descendants; and the ponds remained as round, and the hedges as square, and the grass walks as straight, as the day they had been planned. The same old-fashioned respectability was also apparent in the interior of the mansion: The broad heavy oaken stair-case, shone in all the lustre of bees wax;[4] and the spacious sitting room, into which they were ushered, had its due allowance of Vandyke[5] portraits, massive chairs, and china jars, standing much in the same positions they had been placed in a hundred years before.

To the delicate mind the unfortunate are always objects of respect: as the ancients held sacred those places which had been blasted by lightning,[1] so the feeling heart considers the afflicted as having been touched by the hand of God himself. Such were the sensations with which Mary found herself in the presence of the venerable Mrs. Lennox—venerable rather through affliction than age; for sorrow, more than time, had dimmed the beauty of former days, though enough still remained to excite interest and engage affection, in the mournful, yet gentle expression of her countenance, and the speaking silence of her darkened eyes. On hearing the names of her visitors, she arose, and, guided by a little girl, who had been sitting at her feet, advanced to meet them, and welcomed them with a kindness and simplicity of manner, that reminded Mary of the home she had left, and the maternal tenderness of her beloved aunt. She delivered her credentials, which Mrs. Lennox received with visible surprise; but laid the letter aside without any comments.

Lady Emily began some self-accusing apologies for the length of time that had intervened since her last visit; but Mrs. Lennox gently interrupted her.

'Do not blame yourself, my dear Lady Emily,' said she, 'for what is so natural at your age; and do not suppose I am so unreasonable, as to expect that the young and the gay should seek for pleasure in the company of an old blind woman; at your time of life, I would not have courted distress any more than you.'

'At every time of life,' said Lady Emily, 'I am sure you must have been a very different being from what I am, or ever shall be.'

'Ah! you little know what changes adversity makes in the character,' said Mrs. Lennox mournfully; 'and may you never know—unless it is for your good.'

'I doubt much if I shall ever be good on any terms,'

answered Lady Emily, in a half melancholy tone; 'I
don't think I have the elements of goodness in my
composition; but here is my cousin, who is fit to stand
proxy for all the virtues.'

Mrs. Lennox involuntarily turned her mild but sight-
less eyes towards Mary, then heaved a sigh, and shook
her head, as she was reminded of her deprivation. Mary
was too much affected to speak; but the hand that was
extended to her, she pressed with fervour to her lips,
while her eyes overflowed with tears. The language of
sympathy is soon understood. Mrs. Lennox seemed to
feel the tribute of pity and respect that flowed from Mary's
warm heart, and from that moment they felt towards
each other that indefinite attraction, which however it
may be ridiculed, certainly does sometimes influence our
affections.

'That is a picture of your son, Colonel Lennox, is it not?'
asked Lady Emily, 'I mean the one that hangs below
the lady in the satin gown with the bird on her hand.'

Mrs. Lennox answered in the affirmative; then added,
with a sigh, 'and when I *could* look on that face, I forgot
all I had lost; but I was too fond, too proud a mother.
Look at it, my dear,' taking Mary's hand, and leading
her to the well known spot, while her features brightened
with an expression which shewed maternal vanity was
not yet extinct in the mourner's heart. 'He was only
eighteen,' continued she, 'when that was done; and many
a hot sun has burned on the fair brow; and many a
fearful sight has met these sweet eyes since then; and
sadly that face may be changed; but I shall never see it
more!'

'Indeed,' said Lady Emily, affecting to be gay, while
a tear stood in her eye, 'it is a very dangerous face to
look on; and I should be afraid to trust myself with it,
were not my heart already pledged; as for my cousin
there, there is no fear of her falling a sacrifice to hazel

eyes and chesnut hair—her imagination is all on the side of sandy locks and frosty grey eyes; and I should doubt if Cupid himself would have any chance with her, unless he appeared in tartan plaid and Highland bonnet.'

'Then my Charles would have some,' said Mrs. Lennox, with a faint smile, 'for he has lately been promoted to the command of a Highland regiment.'

'Indeed!' said Lady Emily, 'that is very gratifying, and you have reason to be proud of Colonel Lennox; he has distinguished himself upon every occasion.'

'Ah! the days of my pride are now past,' replied Mrs. Lennox, with a sigh; ''tis only the more honour, the greater danger, and I am weary of such bloody honours. See there!' pointing to another part of the room, where hung a group of five lovely children, 'three of these cherub heads were laid low in battle; the fourth, my Louisa, died of a broken heart for the loss of her brothers. Oh! what can human power, or earthly honours do, to cheer the mother who has wept o'er her children's graves! But there *is* a power,' raising her darkened eyes to heaven, 'that can sustain even a mother's heart; and here,' laying her hand upon an open Bible, 'is the balm he has graciously vouchsafed to pour into the wounded spirit. My comfort is not that my boys died nobly, but that they died Christians.'

Lady Emily and Mary were both silent from different causes. The former was at a loss what to say—the latter felt too much affected to trust her voice with the words of sympathy that hovered on her lips.

'I ought to beg your pardon, my dears,' said Mrs. Lennox, after a pause, 'for talking in this serious manner to you, who cannot be supposed to enter into sorrows to which you are strangers. But you must excuse me, though my heart does sometimes run over.'

'Oh do not suppose,' said Mary, making an effort to conquer her feelings, 'that we are so heartless as to refuse to take a part in the afflictions of others—surely none can be so selfish—and might I be allowed to come often —very often—' She stopped and blushed; for she felt that her feelings were carrying her farther than she was warranted to go.

Mrs. Lennox kindly pressed her hand.—'Ah! God hath, indeed, sent some into the world, whose province it is to refresh the afflicted, and lighten the eyes of the disconsolate—such, I am sure, you would be to me—for I feel my heart revive at the sound of your voice; it reminds me of my heart's darling, my Louisa! and the remembrance of her, though sad, is still sweet. Come to me, then, when you will, and God's blessing, and the blessing of the blind and desolate, will reward you.'

Lady Emily turned away, and it was not till they had been some time in the carriage, that Mary was able to express the interest this visit had excited, and her anxious desire to be permitted to renew it.

'It is really an extraordinary kind of delight, Mary, that you take in being made miserable,' said her cousin, wiping her eyes; 'for my part, it makes me quite wretched to witness suffering that I can't relieve; and how can you or I possibly do poor Mrs. Lennox any good? We can't bring back her sons.'

'No; but we can bestow our sympathy, and that, I have been taught, is always a consolation to the afflicted.'

'I don't quite understand the nature of that mysterious feeling called sympathy. When I go to visit Mrs. Lennox, she always sets me a crying, and I try to set her a laughing —Is that what you call sympathy?'

Mary smiled, and shook her head.

'Then, I suppose, it is sympathy to blow one's nose— and—and read the Bible. Is that it? or what is it?'

Mary declared, she could not define it; and Lady Emily insisted she could not comprehend it.

'You will some day or other,' said Mary; 'for none, I

believe, have ever passed through life without feeling, or at least requiring its support; and it is well, perhaps, that we should know betimes, how to receive, as well as how to bestow it.'

'I don't see the necessity at all. I know I should hate mortally to be what you call sympathised with; indeed it appears to me the height of selfishness in any body to like it. If I am wretched, it would be no comfort to me to make every body else wretched; and were I in Mrs. Lennox's place, I would have more spirit than to speak about my misfortunes.'

'But Mrs. Lennox does not appear to be what you call a spirited creature. She seems all sweetness, and—'

'O sweet enough, certainly!—But hers is a sort of Eolian harp,[1] sweetness that lulls me to sleep. I tire to death of people, who have only two or three notes in their character. By the bye, Mary, you have a tolerable compass yourself, when you choose; though I don't think you have science enough for a *bravura: there* I certainly have the advantage of you, as I flatter myself my mind is a full band in itself. My kettle drums and trumpets I keep for Lady Juliana, and I am quite in the humour for giving her a flourish to-day. I really require something of an exhilarating nature after Mrs. Lennox's dead march.'

An unusual bustle seemed to pervade Beech Park as the carriage stopped, and augured well for its mistress' intention of being more than usually vivacious. It was found to be occasioned by the arrival of her brother Lord Lindore's servants and horses, with the interesting intelligence that his Lordship would immediately follow; and Lady Emily, wild with delight, forgot every thing in the prospect of embracing her brother.

'How does it happen,' said Mary, when her cousin's transports had a little subsided, 'that you, who are in such ecstacies at the idea of seeing your brother, have scarcely mentioned his name to me?'

'Why, to tell you the truth, I fear I was beginning to forget there was such a person in the world. I have not seen him since I was ten years old. At that time he went to college, and from thence to the Continent. So all I remember of him is, that he was very handsome, and very good humoured; and all that I have heard of him is, that wherever he goes he is the "glass of fashion, and the mould of form"[1]—not that he is much of a Hamlet, I've a notion, in other respects: So pray put off that Ophelia phiz,[2] and don't look as if you were of ladies most deject and wretched,[3] when every body else is gay and happy. Come, give your last sigh to the Lennox, and your first smile to Lindore.'

'That is sympathy,' said Mary.

CHAPTER XVIII

'Quelle fureur, dit-il, quel aveugle caprice
Quand le dîner est prêt.————'

Boileau.[4]

'I HOPE YOUR Lordship has no thoughts of waiting dinner for Lord Lindore?' asked Dr. Redgill, with a face of alarm, as seven o'clock struck, and neither dinner nor Lord Lindore appeared.

'I have no thoughts upon the subject,' answered Lord Courtland, as he turned over some new caricatures, with as much *nonchalance* as if it had been mid-day.

'That's enough, my Lord; but I suspect Mr. Marshall, in his officiousness, takes the liberty of thinking for you, and that we shall have no dinner without orders,' rising to pull the bell.

'We ought undoubtedly to wait for Frederick,' said

Lady Juliana; 'it is of no consequence when we sit down to table.'

A violent yell from the sleeping Beauty on the rug, sounded like a summary judgment on her mistress.

'What is the meaning of this?' cried her Ladyship, flying to the offended fair one, in all the transports of pity and indignation; 'how can you, Dr. Redgill, presume to treat my dog in such a manner?'

'Me treat your Ladyship's dog!' exclaimed the Doctor, in well-feigned astonishment—"Pon my honour!—I'm quite at a loss!—I'm absolutely confounded!'

'Yes! I saw you plainly give her a kick, and—'

'Me kick Beauty!—after that!—'Pon my soul, I should just as soon have thought of kicking my own grandmother. I did give her a *leetle*—a very *leetle* shove, just with the point of my toe, as I was going to pull the bell; but it couldn't have hurt a fly. I assure you it would be one of the last actions of my life to treat Beauty ill— Beauty!—poor Beauty!'—affecting to pat and soothe, by way of covering his transgression. But neither Beauty nor her mistress were to be taken in by the Doctor's cajoleries. The one felt, and the other saw the indignity he had committed; and his caresses and protestations were all in vain. The fact was, the Doctor's indignation was so raised by Lady Juliana's remark, made in all the plenitude of a late luncheon, that, had it been herself instead of her favourite, he could scarcely have refrained from this testimony of his detestation and contempt. But much as he despised her, he felt the necessity of propitiating her at this moment, when dinner itself depended upon her decision; for Lord Courtland was perfectly neutral, Lady Emily was not present, and a servant waited to receive orders.

'I really believe it's hunger that's vexing her, poor brute!' continued he, with an air of unfeigned sympathy; 'she knows the dinner hour as well as any of us. Indeed

the instinct of dogs in that respect is wonderful—
Providence has really—a—hem!—indeed it's no joke to
tamper with dogs, when they've got the notion of dinner
in their heads. A friend of mine had a very fine animal—
just such another as poor Beauty there—she had always
been accustomed, like Beauty, to attend the family to
dinner at a particular hour; but one day, by some
accident, instead of sitting down at five, she was kept
waiting till half past six; the consequence was, the
disappointment operating upon an empty stomach,
brought on an attack of the hydrophobia, and the poor
thing was obliged to be shot the following morning. I
think your Lordship said—Dinner,' in a loud voice to
the servant; and Lady Juliana, though still sullen, did
not dissent.

For an hour the Doctor's soul was in a paradise still
more substantial than a Turk's;[1] for it was lapt in the
richest of soups and *ragoûts*, and, secure of their existence,
it smiled at ladies of quality, and defied their lap-dogs.

Dinner passed away, and supper succeeded; and
breakfast, dinner and supper revolved, and still no Lord
Lindore appeared. But this excited no alarm in the
family: It was Lord Courtland's way, and it was Lady
Juliana's way, and it was all their ways, not to keep to
their appointed time, and they therefore experienced
none of the vulgar consternation incident to common
minds, when the expected guest fails to appear. Lady
Emily indeed wondered, and was provoked, and impatient; but she was not alarmed; and Mary amused herself
with contrasting in her own mind the difference of her
aunts' feelings in similar circumstances.

'Dear aunt Grizzy would certainly have been in tears
these two days, fancying the thousand deaths Lord
Lindore must have died; and aunt Jacky would have
been inveighing from morning till night against the
irregularities of young men. And aunt Nicky would

have been lamenting that the black cock had been roasted yesterday, or that there would be no fish for to-morrow.' And the result of Mary's comparison was, that her aunts' feelings, however troublesome, were better than no feelings at all. 'They are, to be sure, something like brambles,' thought she; 'they fasten upon one in every possible way, but still they are better than the faded exotics of fashionable life.'

At last, on the third day, when dinner was nearly over, and Dr. Redgill was about to remark for the third time, 'I think it's as well we didn't wait for Lord Lindore;' the door opened, and, without warning or bustle, Lord Lindore walked calmly into the room.

Lady Emily, uttering an exclamation of joy, threw herself into his arms. Lord Courtland was roused to something like animation, as he cordially shook hands with his son; Lady Juliana flew into raptures at the beauty of his Italian greyhound; Adelaide, at the first glance, decided, that her cousin was worthy of falling in love with her; Mary thought on the happiness of the family re-union; and Dr. Redgill offered up a silent thanksgiving, that this fracas had not happened ten minutes sooner, otherwise the woodcocks would have been as cold as death. Chairs were placed by the officious attendants in every possible direction; and the discarded first course was threatening to displace the third: But Lord Lindore seemed quite insensible to all these attentions; he stood surveying the company with a *nonchalance*, that had nothing of rudeness in it, but seemed merely the result of high-bred ease. His eye, for a moment, rested upon Adelaide. He then slightly bowed and smiled, as in recognition of their juvenile acquaintance.

'I really can't recommend either the turtle soup, or the venison, to your Lordship to-day,' said Dr. Redgill, who experienced certain uneasy sensations at the idea of beholding them resume their stations, something

resembling those which Macbeth testified at sight of
Banquo's ghost, or Hamlet on contemplating Yorick's
skull—'after travelling, there is nothing like a light
dinner, allow me to recommend this *pretty leetle cuisse de
poulet en papillote*—and here are some fascinating *beignets
d'abricots*—quite foreign.'

'If there is any roast beef or boiled mutton to be had,
pray let me have it,' said Lord Lindore, waving off the
zealous *maître d'hotel*, as he kept placing dish after dish
before him.

'Roast beef, or boiled mutton!' ejaculated the Doctor,
with a sort of internal convulsion; 'he is certainly mad.'

'How did you contrive to arrive without being heard
by me, Frederick?' asked Lady Emily; 'my ears have
been wide open these two days and three nights watching
your approach.'

'I walked from Newberry house,' answered he, carelessly: 'I met Lord Newberry two days ago, as I was
coming here, and he persuaded me to alter my course,
and accompany him home.'

'Vastly flattering to your friends here,' said Lady
Emily, in a tone of pique.

'What! you walked all the way from Newberry,'
exclaimed the Earl, 'and the ground covered with snow.
How could you do so foolish a thing?'

'Simply because, as the children say, I liked it,' replied
Lord Lindore, with a smile.

'That's just of a piece with his liking to eat boiled
mutton,' muttered the Doctor to Mary; 'and yet to look
at him, one would really not expect such gross stupidity.'

There certainly was nothing in Lord Lindore's appearance, that denoted either coarseness of taste or imbecility
of mind. On the contrary, he was an elegant looking
young man, rather slightly formed, and of the middle
size, possessing that ease and grace in all his movements,
which a perfect proportion alone can bestow. There was

nothing foreign or *recherché*,[1] either in his dress or deportment; both were plain, even to simplicity; yet an almost imperceptible air of *hauteur* was mingled with the good-humoured indifference of his manner. He spoke little, and seemed rather to endure, than to be gratified by attentions; his own were chiefly directed to his dog, as he was more intent on feeding it, than on answering the questions that were put to him. There never was any thing to be called conversation at the dinner table at Beech Park; and the general practice was in no danger of being departed from on the present occasion. The Earl hated to converse—it was a bore; and he now merely exchanged a few desultory sentences with his son, as he ate his olives and drank his claret. Lady Juliana, indeed, spoke even more than her usual quantity of nonsense, but nobody listened to it. Lady Emily was somewhat perplexed in her notions about her brother. He was handsome and elegant, and appeared good-humoured and gentle; yet something was wanting to fill up the measure of her expectations, and a latent feeling of disappointment lurked in her heart. Adelaide was indignant that he had not instantly paid her the most marked attention, and revenged herself by her silence. In short, Lord Lindore's arrival seemed to have added little or nothing to the general stock of pleasure; and the effervescence of joy—the rapture of *sensation*, like some subtle essence, had escaped almost as soon as it was perceived.

'How stupid every body always is at a dinner table!' exclaimed Lady Emily, rising abruptly with an air of chagrin. 'I believe it is the fumes[2] of the meat that dulls one's senses, and renders them so detestable. I long to see you in the drawing-room, Frederick. I've a notion you are more of a carpet knight, than a knight of the round table; so pray,' in a whisper as she passed, 'leave papa to be snored asleep by Dr. Redgill, and do you follow us—here's metal more attractive,'[1] pointing to the sisters, as they quitted the room;—and she followed without waiting for her brother's reply.

CHAPTER XIX

'Io dubito, Signor M. Pietro che il mio Cortegiano non sarà stato altro che fatica mia, e fastidio degli amici.'
Baldassarre Castiglione.[2]

LORD LINDORE WAS in no haste to avail himself of his sister's invitation; and when he did, it was evident his was a 'mind not to be changed by place;'[3] for he entered more with the air of one who was tired of the company he had left, than expecting pleasure from the society he sought.

'Do come and entertain us, Lindore,' cried Lady Emily, as he entered, 'for we are all heartily sick of one another. A snow storm, and a lack of company, are things hard to be borne; it is only the expectancy of your arrival that has kept us alive these two days, and now pray don't let us die away of the reality.'

'You have certainly taken a most effectual method of sealing my lips,' said her brother with a smile.

'How so?'

'By telling me that I am expected to be vastly entertaining, since every word I utter can only serve to dispel the illusion, and prove that I am gifted with no such miraculous power.'

'I don't think it requires any miraculous power, either to entertain or be entertained. For my part, I flatter myself I can entertain any man, woman, or child, in the kingdom, when I choose; and as for being entertained, that is still an easier matter. I seldom meet with any body who is not entertaining, either from their folly, or their affectation, or their stupidity, or their vanity; or, in short, something of the ridiculous, that renders them not merely supportable, but positively amusing.'

'How extremely happy you must be,' said Lord Lindore.

'Happy! no—I don't know that my feelings precisely amount to happiness neither; for at the very time I'm most diverted, I'm sometimes disgusted too, and often provoked. My spirit gets chafed, and—'

'You long to box the ears of all your acquaintances,' said her brother, laughing. 'Well, no matter—there is nothing so enviable as a facility of being amused, and even the excitement of anger is perhaps preferable to the stagnation of indifference.'

'O, thank heaven! I know nothing about indifference —I leave that to Adelaide.'

Lord Lindore turned his eyes with more animation than he had yet evinced towards his cousin, who sat reading, apparently paying no attention to what was going on. He regarded her for a considerable time with an expression of admiration; but Adelaide, though she was conscious of his gaze, calmly pursued her studies.

'Come, you positively must do something to signalize yourself. I assure you, it is expected of you, that you should be the soul of the company. Here is Adelaide waltzes like an angel, when she can get a partner to her liking.'

'But I waltz like a mere mortal,' said Lord Lindore, seating himself at a table, and turning over the leaves of a book.

'And I am engaged to play billiards with my uncle,' said Adelaide, rising with a blush of indignation.

'Shall we have some music then? Can you bear to listen to our croakings, after the warbling of your Italian nightingales?' asked Lady Emily.

'I should like very much to hear you sing,' answered her brother, with an air of the most perfect indifference.

'Come then, Mary, do you be the one to "untwist the chains that tie the hidden soul of harmony."[1] Give us your Scotch Exile, pray? it is tolerably appropriate to the occasion, though an English one would have been still more so; but, as you say, there is nothing in this country to make a song about.'

Mary would rather have declined, but she saw a refusal would displease her cousin; and she was not accustomed to consult her own inclination in such frivolous matters: She therefore seated herself at the harp, and sung the following verses:—

THE EXILE

The weary wanderer may roam
    To seek for bliss in change of scene;
Yet still the loved idea of his home,
    And of the days he there has seen,
Pursue him with a fond regret,
Like rays from suns that long have set.

'Tis not the sculptor's magic art,
    'Tis not th' heroic deeds of yore,
That fill and gratify the heart.
    No! 'tis affection's tender lore—
The thought-of friends, and love's first sigh,
When youth, and hope, and health were nigh.

What though on classic ground we tread,[2]
    What though we breathe a genial air—
Can these restore the bliss that's fled?
    Is not remembrance ever there?
Can any soil protect from grief,
Or any air breathe soft relief?

No! the sick soul, that wounded flies
   From all its early thoughts held dear,
Will more some gleam of memory prize,
   That draws the long lost treasure near;
And warmly presses to its breast
The very thought that mars its rest.

Some mossy stone, some torrent rude,
   Some moor unknown to worldly ken,
Some weeping birches, fragrant wood,
   Or some wild roebuck's fern-clad glen.
Yes! these his aching heart delight,
These bring his country to his sight.[1]

Ere the song was ended, Lord Lindore had sauntered away to the billiard-room, singing, 'Oh! Giove Omnipotente!'[2] and seemingly quite unconscious that any attentions were due from him in return. But there, even Adelaide's charms failed to attract. In spite of the variety of graceful movements practised before him—the beauty of the extended arm, the majestic step, and the exclamations of the enchanting voice, Lord Lindore kept his station by the fire, in a musing attitude, from which he was only roused occasionally by the caresses of his dog. At supper, it was still worse: He placed himself by Mary, and when he spoke, it was only of Scotland.

'Well—what do you think of Lindore?' demanded Lady Emily of her aunt and cousins, as they were about to separate for the night. 'Is he not divine?'

'Perfectly so!' replied Lady Juliana, with all the self-importance of a fool. 'I assure you, I think very highly of him. He is a vastly charming, clever young man—perfectly beautiful, and excessively amiable; and his attention to his dog is quite delightful—it is so uncommon to see men at all kind to their dogs. I assure you, I have known many who were absolutely cruel to them—beat them, and starved them, and did a thousand shocking things; and—'

'Pray, Adelaide, what is your opinion of my brother?'

'Oh! I—I—have no doubt he is extremely amiable,' replied Adelaide, with a gentle yawn. 'As mamma says, his attentions to his dog prove it.'

'And you, Mary, are your remarks to be equally judicious and polite?'

Mary, in all the sincerity of her heart, said, she thought him by much the handsomest and most elegant-looking man she had ever seen. And there she stopped.

'Yes; I know all that. But—however, no matter—I only wish he may have sense enough to fall in love with you, Mary. How happy I should be to see you Lady Lindore!—*En attendant*—you must take care of your heart; for I hear he is *un peu volage*[1]—and, moreover, that he admires none but *les dames Mariées*. As for Adelaide, there is no fear of her: She will never cast such a pearl away[2] upon one who is merely, no doubt, extremely amiable,' retorting Adelaide's ironical tone.

'Then you may feel equally secure upon my account,' said Mary, 'as I assure you I am in still less danger of losing mine, after the warning you have given.'

This off-hand sketch of her brother's character, which Lady Emily had thoughtlessly given, produced the most opposite effects on the minds of the sisters. With Adelaide, it increased his consequence, and enhanced his value. It would be no vulgar conquest to fix and reform one who was notorious for his inconstancy and libertine principles; and, from that moment, she resolved to use all the influence of her charms to captivate and secure the heart of her cousin. In Mary's well regulated mind other feelings arose. Although she was not one of the out-rageously virtuous, who storm and rail at the very men-tion of vice, and deem it contamination to hold any intercourse with the vicious, she yet possessed proper ideas of the distinction to be drawn; and the hope of finding a friend and brother in her cousin, now gave way to the feeling, that in future she could only consider him as a mere common acquaintance.

CHAPTER XX

'On sera ridicule et je n'oserai rire!'

Boileau.[1]

IN HONOUR OF her brother's return, Lady Emily resolved to celebrate it with a ball; and always prompt in following up her plans, she fell to work immediately with her visiting list.

'Certainly,' said she, as she scanned it over, 'there never was any family so afflicted in their acquaintances as we are. At least one half of the names here belong to the most insufferable people on the face of the earth. The Claremonts, and the Edgefields, and the Bouveries, and the Sedleys, and a few more, are very well; but can any thing, in human form, be more insupportable than the rest; for instance, that wretch Lady Placid?'

'Does her merit lie only in her name then?' asked Mary.

'You shall judge for yourself, when I have given you a slight sketch of her character. Lady Placid, in the opinion of all sensible persons in general, and myself in particular, is a vain, weak, conceited, vulgar egotist. In her own eyes she is a clever, well-informed, elegant, amiable woman; and though I have spared no pains to let her know how detestable I think her, it is all in vain: she remains as firmly entrenched in her own good opinion, as folly and conceit can make her; and I have

the despair of seeing all my buffetings fall blunted to the
ground. She reminds me of some odious fairy or genii I
have read of, who possessed such a power in their person,
that every hostile weapon levelled against them was
immediately turned into some agreeable present—stones
became balls of silk—arrows, flowers—swords, feathers,
&c. Even so it is with Lady Placid: The grossest insult
that could be offered, she would construe into an
elegant compliment—the very crimes of others, she
seems to consider as so much incense offered up at the
shrine of her own immaculate virtue. I'm certain she
thinks she deserves to be canonized for having kept out
of Doctors' Commons.[1] Never is any affair of that sort
alluded to, that she does not cast such a triumphant look
towards her husband, as much as to say, "Here am I, the
paragon of faithful wives and virtuous matrons!" Were
I in his place, I should certainly throw a plate at her
head. And here, you may take this passing remark—
How much more odious people are who have radical
faults, than those who commit, I do not say positive
crimes, but occasional weaknesses. Even a noble nature
may fall into a great error; but what is that to the ever-
enduring pride, envy, malice, and conceit of a little
mind. Yes—I would, at any time, rather be the fallen, as
the one to exult over the fall of another. Then, as a
mother, she is, if possible, still more meritorious. "A
woman, (this is the way she talks,) a woman has nobly
performed her part to her country, and for posterity,
when she has brought a family of fine healthy children
into the world." "I can't agree with you," I reply;
"I think many mothers have brought children into the
world, who would have been much better out of it. A
mother's merit must depend solely upon how she brings
up her children," (hers are the most spoiled brats in
Christendom.) "There I perfectly agree with you, Lady
Emily. As you observe, it is not every mother who does

her duty by her children. Indeed, I may say to you, it is not every one that will make the sacrifices for their family I have done; but thank God! I am richly repaid. My children are every thing I could wish them to be!"—Every thing of hers, as a matter of course, must be superior to every other person's, and even what she is obliged to share in common with others, acquires some miraculous charm in operating upon her. Thus it is impossible for any one to imagine the delight she takes in bathing; and as for the sun, no mortal can conceive the effect it has upon her. If she was to have the plague, she would assure you it was owing to some peculiar virtue in her blood; and if she was to be put in the pillory, she would ascribe it entirely to her great merit. If her coachman was to make her a declaration of love, she would impute it to the boundless influence of her charms; that every man who sees her does not declare his passion, is entirely owing to the well-known severity of her morals, and the dignity of her deportment. If she is amongst the first invited to my ball, that will be my eagerness to secure her; if the very last, it will be a mark of my friendship, and the easy footing we are upon. If not invited at all, then it will be my jealousy. In short, the united strength of worlds, would not shake that woman's good opinion of herself; and the intolerable part of it is, there are so many fools in this one, that she actually passes with the multitude for being a charming sweet-tempered woman—always the same—always pleased and contented. Contented! just as like contentment as the light emitted by putridity resembles the divine halo! But too much of her—Let her have a card however.'

'Then comes Mrs. Wiseacre, that renowned lawgiver, who lavishes her advice on all who will receive it, without hope of fee or reward, except that of being thought wiser than any body else. But, like many more deserving characters, she meets with nothing but ingratitude in return; and the wise sentences that are for ever hovering around her pursed-up mouth, have only served to render her insupportable. This is her mode of proceeding—"If I might presume to advise Lady Emily;" or, "if my opinion could be supposed to have any weight," or, "if my experience goes for any thing;" or, "I'm an old woman now, but I think I know something of the world;" or, "if a friendly hint of mine would be of any service:"—then when very desperate, it is, "however averse I am to obtrude my advice, yet as I consider it my duty, I must for once;" or, "it certainly is no affair of mine, at the same time I must just observe," &c. &c. I don't say that she insists, however, upon your swallowing all the advice she crams you with; for provided she has the luxury of giving it, it can make little difference how it is taken; because whatever befalls you, be it good or bad, it is equally a matter of exultation to her. Thus she has the satisfaction of saying, "if poor Mrs. Dabble had but followed my advice, and not have taken these pills of Dr. Doolittle's, she would have been alive to-day, depend upon it;" or, "if Sir Thomas Speckle had but taken advantage of a friendly hint I threw out some time ago, about the purchase of the Drawrent estate, he might have been a man worth ten thousand a-year at this moment;" or, "if Lady Dull hadn't been so infatuated as to neglect the caution I gave her about Bob Squander, her daughter might have been married to Nabob Gull."[1]

'But there is a strange contradiction about Mrs. Wiseacre, for though it appears that all her friends' misfortunes proceed from neglecting her advice, it is no less apparent, by her account, that her own are all occasioned by following the advice of others. She is for ever doing foolish things, and laying the blame upon her neighbours. Thus, "had it not been for my friend Mrs. Jobbs there, I never would have parted with my house for an old song as I did;" or, "it was entirely owing to Miss Glue's obstinacy, that I was robbed of my diamond necklace;" or, "I have to thank my friend, Colonel Crack, for getting my carriage smashed to pieces." In short, she has the most comfortable repository of stupid friends to have recourse to, of any body I ever knew. Now what I have to warn you against, Mary, is the sin of ever listening to any of her advices. She will preach to you about the pinning of your gown, and the curling of your hair, till you would think it impossible not to do exactly what she wants you to do. She will inquire with the greatest solicitude what shoemaker you employ, and will shake her head most significantly when she hears it is any other than her own. But if ever I detect you paying the smallest attention to any of her recommendations, positively I shall have done with you.'

Mary laughingly promised to turn a deaf ear to all Mrs. Wiseacre's wisdom; and her cousin proceeded:

'Then here follows a swarm "as thick as idle motes in sunny ray,"[1] and much of the same importance, methinks, in the scale of being. Married ladies only celebrated for their good dinners, or their pretty equipages, or their fine jewels. How I should scorn to be talked of as the appendage to any soups or pearls! Then there are the daughters of these ladies— Misses, who are mere misses, and nothing more. Oh! the insipidity of a mere Miss! a soft simpering thing with pink cheeks, and pretty hair, and fashionable clothes;—*sans* eyes[2] for any thing but lovers—*sans* ears for any thing but flattery—*sans* taste for any thing but balls—*sans* brains for any thing at all! Then there are ladies who are neither married nor young, and who strive with all their might to talk most delightfully, that the charms of their conversation may efface the marks of the crows feet; but "all these I passen by, and nameless numbers moe."[3] And now comes the Hon. Mrs. Downe Wright, a person of considerable shrewdness and penetration—vulgar, but unaffected. There is no politeness, no gentleness in her heart; but she possesses some warmth, much honesty, and great hospitality. She has acquired the character of being, Oh, odious thing! a clever woman! There are two descriptions of clever women, observe; the one is endowed with corporeal cleverness—the other with mental; and I don't know which of the two is the greater nuisance to society; the one torments you with her management—the other with her smart sayings; the one is for ever rattling her bunch of keys in your ears—the other electrifies you with the shock of her wit; and both talk *so* much and *so* loud, and are such egotists, that I rather think a clever woman is even a greater term of reproach than a good creature. But to return to that clever woman, Mrs. Downe Wright: she is a widow, left with the management of an only son—a common place, weak young man. No one, I believe, is more sensible of his mental deficiencies than his mother; but she knows that a man of fortune is, in the eyes of the many, a man of consequence; and she therefore wisely talks of it as his chief characteristic. To keep him in good company, and get him well-married, is all her aim; and this, she thinks, will not be difficult, as he is very handsome—possesses an estate of ten thousand a-year—and succeeds to some Scotch Lord Something's title—There's for you, Mary! She once had views of Adelaide, but Adelaide met the advances with so much scorn, that Mrs. Downe Wright declared she was thankful she had shewn the cloven foot in time; for that she never would have done for a wife to her William. Now you are the very thing to suit, for you have no cloven feet to shew.'

'Or, at least, you are not so quick-sighted as Mrs. Downe Wright. You have not spied them yet, it seems,' said Mary, with a smile.

'O, as to that, if you had them, I should defy you, or

any one, to hide them from me. When I reflect upon the characters of most of my acquaintances, I sometimes think nature has formed my optics only to see disagreeables.'

'That must be a still more painful faculty of vision than even the second sight,' said Mary; 'but I should think it depended very much upon yourself to counteract it.'

'Impossible! my perceptions are so peculiarly alive to all that is obnoxious to them, that I could as soon preach my eyes into blindness, or my ears into deafness, as put down my feelings with chopping logic. If people *will* be affected and ridiculous, why must I live in a state of warfare with myself, on account of the feelings they rouse within me?'

'If people *will* be irritable,' said Mary, laughing, 'why must others sacrifice their feelings to gratify them?'

'Because mine are natural feelings, and theirs are artificial. A very saint must sicken at sight of affectation, you'll allow. Vulgarity, even innate vulgarity, is bearable—stupidity itself is pardonable—but affectation is never to be endured or forgiven.'

'It admits of palliation, at least,' answered Mary. 'I daresay there are many people who would have been pleasing and natural in their manners, had not their parents and teachers interfered. There are many, I believe, who have not courage to shew themselves such as they are—some who are naturally affected—and many, very many, who have been taught affectation as a necessary branch of education.'

'Yes—as my governesses would have taught me; but, thank heaven! I got the better of them. *Fascinating* was what they wanted to make me; but whenever the word was mentioned, I used to knit my brows, and frown upon them in such a sort. The frown, I know, sticks by me; but no matter, a frowning brow is better than a false heart, and I defy any one to say that I am fascinating.'

'There certainly must be some fascination about you, otherwise I should never have sat so long listening to you,' said Mary, as she rose from the table at which she had been assisting to dash off the at-homes.

'But you must listen to me a little longer,' cried her cousin, seizing her hand to detain her: 'I have not got half through my detestables yet; but, to humour you, I shall let them go for the present. And now, that you mayn't suppose I am utterly insensible to excellence, you must suffer me to shew you, that I can and do appreciate worth, when I can find it. I confess, my talent lies fully as much in discovering the ridiculous as the amiable; and I am equally ready to acknowledge it is a fault, and no mark of superior wit or understanding; since it is much easier to hit off the glaring caricature lines of deformity, than the finer and more exquisite touches of beauty, especially for one who reads as he runs—the sign-posts are sure to catch the eye. But now for my favourite— no matter for her name—it would frighten you were you to hear it. In the first place, she is, as some of your old divines say, *hugely religious*; but then she keeps her piety in its proper place, and where it ought to be—in her very soul. It is never a stumbling block in other people's way, or interfering with other people's affairs. Her object is to *be*, not to *seem*, religious; and there is neither hypocrisy nor austerity necessary for that. She is forbearing, without meanness—gentle, without insipidity —sincere, without rudeness. She practises all the virtues herself, and seems quite unconscious that others don't do the same. She is, if I may trust the expression of her eye, almost as much alive to the ridiculous as I am; but she is only diverted where I am provoked. She never bestows false praise, even upon her friends; but a simple approval from her is of more value than the finest panegyric from another. She never finds occasion to censure or condemn the conduct of any one, however flagrant it may be in the eyes of others; because she seems to think virtue is better expressed by her own actions than by her neighbour's vices. She cares not for admiration, but is anxious to do good and give pleasure. To sum up the whole, she could listen with patience to Lady Placid; she could bear to be advised by Mrs. Wiseacre; she could stand the scrutiny of Mrs. Downe Wright; and, hardest task of all, (throwing her arms around Mary's neck,) she can bear with all my ill-humour and impertinence.'

CHAPTER XXI

> 'Have I then no tears for thee, my *mother*?
> Can I forget they cares, from helpless years—
> Thy tenderness for me? an eye still beamed
> With love?'
>
> *Thomson.*[1]

THE ARRIVAL OF Lord Lindore brought an influx of visitors to Beech Park; and, in the unceasing round of amusement that went on, Mary found herself completely overlooked. She therefore gladly took advantage of her insignificance to pay frequent visits to Mrs. Lennox, and easily prevailed with Lady Juliana to allow her to spend a week there occasionally. In this way, the acquaintance soon ripened into the warmest affection on both sides. The day seemed doubly dark to Mrs. Lennox that was not brightened by Mary's presence; and Mary felt all the drooping energies of her heart revive in the delight of administering to the happiness of another.

Mrs. Lennox was one of those gentle, amiable beings, who engage our affections far more powerfully than many possessed of higher attributes. Her understanding was not strong—neither had it been highly cultivated according to the ideas of the present time; but she had a benevolence of heart, and a guileless simplicity of thought, that shamed the pride of wit, and pomp of learning. Bereft of all external enjoyments, and destitute of great mental resources, it was retrospection and futurity that gilded the dark evening of her days, and shed their light on the dreary realities of life. She loved to recall the remembrance of her children—to tell of their infant beauties, their growing virtues—and to retrace scenes of past felicity which memory loves to treasure in the heart.

'Oh! none but a mother can tell,' she would exclaim, 'the bitterness of those tears which fall from a mother's eyes!—all other sorrows seem natural, but—God forgive me!—surely it is not natural that the old should weep for the young. Oh! when I saw myself surrounded by my children, little did I think that death was so soon to seal their eyes! Sorrow mine! and yet methinks I would rather have suffered all than have stood in the world a lonely being.—Yes—my children revered His power and believed in His name, and, thanks to His mercy, I feel assured they are now angels in heaven! Here,' taking some papers from a writing-box, 'my Louisa speaks to me even from the tomb!—These are the words she wrote but a few hours before her death. Read them to me; for it is not every voice I can bear to hear uttering her last thoughts.'—Mary read as follows:

FOR EVER GONE

> For ever gone! oh, chilling sound!
>   That tolls the knell of hope and joy!
> Potent with torturing pang to wound,
>   But not in mercy to destroy.

For ever gone! What words of grief—
    Replete with wild mysterious woe!
The Christian kneels to seek relief—
    A Saviour died——It is not so.

For a brief space we sojourn here,
    And life's rough path we journey o'er;
Thus was it with the friend so dear,
    That is not lost, but sped before.

For ever gone! oh, madness wild
    Dwells in that drear and Atheist doom!
But death of horror is despoiled,
    When heaven shines forth beyond the tomb.

For ever gone! oh, dreadful fate!
    Go visit nature—gather thence
The symbols of man's happier state,
    Which speak to every mortal sense.

The leafless spray, the withered flower,
    Alike with man, owns death's embrace;
But bursting forth, in summer hour,
    Prepare anew to run life's race.

And shall it be, that man alone
    Dies, never more to rise again?
Of all creation, highest one,
    Created but to live in vain?

For ever gone! oh, dire despair!—
    Look to the heavens, the earth, the sea—
Go, read a Saviour's promise there—
    Go, heir of Immortality![1]

From such communings as these the selfish would have
turned with indifference; but Mary's generous heart was
ever open to the overflowings of the wounded spirit.
She had never been accustomed to lavish the best feelings

of her nature on frivolous pursuits, or fictitious distresses; but had early been taught to consecrate them to the best, the most ennobling purposes of humanity—even to the comforting of the weary soul—the binding of the bruised heart. Yet Mary was no rigid moralist. She loved amusement as the *amusement* of an imperfect existence, though her good sense, and still better principles, taught her to reject it as the *business* of an immortal being.

Several weeks passed away, during which Mary had been an almost constant inmate at Rose Hall; but the day of Lady Emily's *fête* arrived, and with something of hope and expectation fluttering at her heart, she anticipated her *début* in the ball-room. She repaired to the breakfast-table of her venerable friend, with even more than usual hilarity; but, upon entering the apartment, her gaiety fled; for she was struck with the emotion visible on the countenance of Mrs. Lennox: her meek, but tearful eyes, were raised to heaven, and her hands were crossed on her bosom, as if to subdue the agitation of her heart. Her faithful attendant stood by her with an open letter in her hand.

Mary flew towards her; and as her light step and soft accents met her ear, she extended her arms towards her.

'Mary, my child, where are you,' exclaimed she, as she pressed her with convulsive eagerness to her heart—'My son!—my Charles!—to-morrow I shall see him—See him! oh, God help me! I shall never see him more!' And she wept in all the agony of contending emotions, suddenly and powerfully excited.

'But you will hear him—you will hold him to your heart—you will be conscious that he is beside you,' said Mary.

'Yes, thank God! I shall once more hear the voice of a living child! Oh, how often do those voices ring in my heart, that are all hushed in the grave! I am used to it now—but to think of his returning to this wilderness!

When last he left it, he had father, brothers, sisters—
and to find all gone!'

'Indeed it will be a sad return,' said the old housekeeper, as she wiped her eyes; 'for the Colonel doated
on his sister, and she on him, and his brothers too!
Dearly they all loved one another. How in this very
room have I seen them chace each other up and down
in their pretty plays, with their papa's cap and sword,
and say they would be soldiers!'

Mary motioned the good woman to be silent; then
turning to Mrs. Lennox, she sought to soothe her into
composure, and turned, as she always did, the bright
side of the picture to view, by dwelling on the joy her
son would experience in seeing her. Mrs. Lennox shook
her head mournfully.

'Alas! he cannot joy in seeing me, such as I am. I
have too long concealed from him my dreary doom:
he knows not that these poor eyes are sealed in darkness!
Oh! he will seek to read a mother's fondness there, and
he will find all cold and silent.'

'But he will also find you resigned—even contented,'
said Mary, while her tears dropped on the hand she
held to her lips.

'Yes; God knows, I do not repine at his will. It is not
for myself these tears fall; but my son!—How will he
bear to behold the mother he so loved and honoured,
now blind. bereft, and helpless!' And the wounds of her
heart seemed to bleed afresh at the excitement of even its
happiest emotions—the return of a long absent, much-
loved son.

Mary exerted all the powers of her understanding, all
the tenderness of her heart, to dispel the mournful
images that pressed on the mind of her friend; but she
found it was not so much her *arguments* as her *presence*
that produced that effect; and to leave her in her present
situation seemed impossible. In the agitation of her spirits,

she had wholly forgotten the occasion that called for
Mary's absence, and she implored her to remain with
her till the arrival of her son, with an earnestness that
was irresistible.

The thoughts of her cousin's displeasure, should she
absent herself upon such an occasion, caused Mary to
hesitate; yet her feelings would not allow her to name the
cause.

'How unfeeling it would sound to talk of balls at such
a time,' thought she; 'what a painful contrast must it
present! surely Lady Emily will not blame me, and
no one will miss me——' And, in the ardour of her feelings, she promised to remain. Yet she sighed as she sent
off her excuse, and thought of the pleasures she had
renounced; but the sacrifice made, the regrets were soon
past; and she devoted herself entirely to soothing the
agitated spirits of her venerable friend.

It is perhaps the simplest and most obvious truth, skil-
fully administered, that, in the season of affliction,
produces the most salutary effects upon our mind. Mary
was certainly no logician, and all that she could say
might have been said by another; but there is something
in the voice and manner that carries an irresistible
influence along with it—something that tells us our
sorrows are felt and understood, not coldly seen and
heard. Mary's well-directed exertions were repaid with
success; she read, talked, played, and sung, not in her
gayest manner; but in that subdued strain which har-
monized with the feelings, while it won upon the attention, and she had at length the satisfaction of seeing the
object of her solicitude, restored to her usual state of
calm confiding acquiescence.

'God bless you, my dear Mary!' said she, as they were
about to separate for the night; 'He only can repay you
for the good you have done me this day!'

'Ah!' thought Mary, as she tenderly embraced her,

'such a blessing is worth a dozen balls!'

At that moment the sound of a carriage was heard, and an unusual bustle took place below; but scarcely had they time to notice it, ere the door flew open, and Mrs. Lennox found herself locked in the arms of her son.

For some minutes the tide of feeling was too strong for utterance, and 'My mother!' 'My son!' were the only words that either could articulate. At length, raising his head, Colonel Lennox fixed his eyes on his mother's face, with a gaze of deep and fearful inquiry—but no returning glance spoke there. With that mournful vacuity, peculiar to the blind, which is a thousand times more touching than all the varied expression of the living orb, she continued to regard the vacant space which imagination had filled, with the image she sought in vain to behold.

At this confirmation of his worst fears, a shade of the deepest anguish overspread the visage of her son. He raised his eyes, as in agony, to heaven—then threw himself on his mother's bosom; and as Mary hurried from the apartment, she heard the sob which burst from his manly heart, as he exclaimed, 'My dear mother, do I indeed find you thus!'

CHAPTER XXII

> 'There is more complacency[1] in the negligence of some men, than in what is called the good breeding of others; and the little absences of the heart are often more interesting and engaging than the punctilious attention of a thousand professed sacrificers to the graces.'
>
> *Mackenzie.*[2]

POWERFUL EMOTIONS ARE the certain levellers of ordinary feelings. When Mary met Colonel Lennox in the breakfast room the following morning, he accosted her, not with the ceremony of a stranger, but with the frankness of a heart careless of common forms; and spoke of his mother with indications of sensibility, which he vainly strove to repress. Mary knew that she had sought to conceal her real situation from him; but it seemed a vague suspicion of the truth had crossed his mind, and having, with difficulty, obtained a short leave of absence, he had hastened to have either his hopes or fears realized.

'And, now that I know the worst,' said he, 'I know it only to deplore it. Far from alleviating, my presence seems rather to aggravate my poor mother's misfortune. Oh! it is heart-rending to see the strivings of these longing eyes to look upon the face of those she loves!'

'Ah!' thought Mary, 'were they to behold that face now, how changed would it appear!' as she contrasted it with the portrait that hung immediately over the head of the original. The one in all the brightness of youth— the radiant eyes—the rounded cheek—the fair open brow—spoke only of hope, and health, and joy. Those eyes were now dimmed by sorrow; the cheek was wasted with toil; the brow was clouded by cares. Yet, 'as it is the best part of beauty which a picture cannot express,'*[1] so there is something superior to the mere charms of form and colour; and an air of high-toned feeling, of mingled vivacity and sensibility, gave a grandeur to the form, and an expression to the countenance, which more than atoned for the want of youth's more brilliant attributes.

At least so thought Mary; but her comparisons were interrupted by the entrance of Mrs. Lennox. Her son flew towards her, and taking her arm from that of her attendant, led her to her seat, and sought to render her those little offices which her helplessness required.

'My dear Charles,' said she, with a smile, as he tried

* Lord Bacon.

to adjust her cushions, 'your hands have not been used to this work. Your arm is my best support, but a gentler hand must smooth my pillow. Mary, my love, where are you? Give me your hand.' Then placing it in that of her son—'Many a tear has this hand wiped from your mother's eyes!'

Mary, blushing deeply, hastily withdrew it. She felt it as a sort of appeal to Colonel Lennox's feelings; and a sense of wounded delicacy made her shrink from being thus recommended to his gratitude. But Colonel Lennox seemed too much absorbed in his own painful reflections to attach such a meaning to his mother's words; and though they excited him to regard Mary for a moment with peculiar interest, yet, in a little while, he relapsed into the mournful reverie from which he had been roused.

Colonel Lennox was evidently not a shew-off character. He seemed superior to the mere vulgar aim of making himself agreeable—an aim which has much oftener its source in vanity than in benevolence. Yet he exerted himself to meet his mother's cheerfulness; though as often as he looked at her, or raised his eyes to the youthful group that hung before them, his changing hue and quivering lip betrayed the anguish he strove to hide.

Breakfast ended, Mary rose to prepare for her departure, in spite of the solicitations of her friend, that she should remain till the following day.

'Surely, my dear Mary,' said she, in an imploring accent, 'you will not refuse to bestow one day of happiness upon me?—and it is *such* a happiness to see my Charles and you together. I little thought that ever I should have been so blessed. Ah! I begin to think God has yet some good in store for my last days! Do not then leave me just when I am beginning to taste of joy!'— And she clung to her with that pathetic look which Mary had ever found irresistible.

But, upon this occasion, she steeled her heart against

all supplication. It was the first time she had ever turned from the entreaty of old age or infirmity; and those only who have lived in the habitual practice of administering to the happiness of others, can conceive how much it costs the generous heart to resist even the weaknesses of those it loves. But Mary felt she had already sacrificed too much to affection, and she feared the reproaches and ridicule that awaited her return to Beech Park. She therefore gently, though steadily, adhered to her resolution, only softening it by a promise of returning soon.

'What an angel goes there!' exclaimed Mrs. Lennox to her son, as Mary left the room to prepare for her departure. 'Ah! Charles, could I but hope to see her yours!'

Colonel Lennox smiled—'That must be when I am an angel myself then. A poor weather-beaten soldier like me must be satisfied with something less.'

'But is she not a lovely creature?' asked his mother, with some solicitude.

'Angels, you know, are always fair,' replied Colonel Lennox, laughingly, trying to parry this attack upon his heart.

'Ah! Charles, that is not being serious! But young people now are different from what they were in my day. There is no such thing as falling in love now, you are all so cautious.'

And the good old lady's thoughts reverted to the time when the gay and gallant Captain Lennox had fallen desperately in love with her, as she danced a minuet in a blue satin sack,[1] and Bologna hat,[2] at a county ball.

'You forget, my dear mother, what a knack I had at falling in love ten years ago. Since then, I confess I have got rather out of the way of it; but a little, a very little practice, I am sure, will make me as expert as ever;— and then I promise you shall have no cause to complain of my caution.'

Mrs. Lennox sighed, and shook her head. She had long cherished the hope, that if ever her son came home, it would be to fall in love with and marry her beloved Mary; and she had dwelt upon this favourite scheme till it had taken entire possession of her mind. In the simplicity of her heart, she also imagined that it would greatly help to accelerate the event, were she to suggest the idea to her son, as she had no doubt but that the object of her affections must necessarily become the idol of his. So little did she know of human nature, that the very means she used to accomplish her purpose were the most effectual she could have contrived to defeat it. Such is man, that his pride revolts from all attempts to influence his affections. The weak and the undiscerning, indeed, are often led to 'choose love by another's eyes;'[1] but the lofty and independent spirit loves to create for itself those feelings, which lose half their charms when their source is not in the depths of their own heart.

It was with no slight mortification that Mrs. Lennox saw Mary depart without having made the desired impression on the heart of her son; or, what was still more to be feared, of his having secured himself a place in her favour. But, again and again, she made Mary repeat her promise of returning soon, and spending some days with her. 'And then,' thought she, 'things will all come right. When they live together, and see each other constantly, they cannot possibly avoid loving each other, and all will be as it should be. God grant I may live to see it!'

And hope softened the pang of disappointment.

CHAPTER XXIII

'Qui vous a pu plonger dans cette humeur chagrine,
A-t-on par quelque edit réformé la cuisine?'

Boileau.[1]

MARY'S INEXPERIENCED MIND expected to find, on
her return to Beech Park, some vestige of the pleasures
of the preceding night—some shadows, at least, of
gaiety, to shew what happiness she had sacrificed—what
delight her friends had enjoyed; but, for the first time,
she beheld the hideous aspect of departed pleasure.
Drooping evergreens, dying lamps, dim transparencies,[2]
and faded flowers, met her view as she crossed the hall;
while the public rooms[3] were covered with dust from the
chalked floors,[4] and wax from the droppings of the candles.
Every thing, in short, looked tawdry and forlorn. Nothing was in its place—nothing looked as it used to do—
and she stood amazed at the disagreeable metamorphose
all things had undergone.

Hearing some one approach, she turned, and beheld
Dr. Redgill enter.

'So—it's only you, Miss Mary!' exclaimed he, in a
tone of chagrin. 'I was in hopes it was some of the
women-servants. 'Pon my soul, it's disgraceful to think
that, in this house, there is not a woman stirring yet!
I have sent five messages, by my man, to let Mrs. Brown
know that I have been waiting for my breakfast these
two hours; but this confounded ball has turned every
thing upside down!—You are come to a pretty scene,'
continued he, looking round with a mixture of fury and
contempt,—'a very pretty scene! 'Pon my honour, I
blush to see myself standing here! Just look at these
rag!' kicking a festoon of artificial roses that had fallen
to the ground. 'Can any thing be more despicable?—
and to think that rational creatures in possession of their

senses should take pleasure in the sight of such trumpery!
—'Pon my soul, I—I—declare it confounds me! I
really used to think Lady Emily (for this is all her doing)
had some sense—but such a display of folly as this!'

'Pshaw!' said Mary, 'it is not fair in us to stand here
analysing the dregs of gaiety after the essence is gone. I
daresay this was a very brilliant scene last night.'

'Brilliant scene, indeed!' repeated the Doctor, in a
most wrathful accent: 'I really am amazed—I—yes—
brilliant enough—if you mean, that there was a glare
of light, enough to blind the devil. I thought my eyes
would have been put out, the short time I staid; indeed,
I don't think this one has recovered it yet,' advancing
a fierce blood-shot eye almost close to Mary's. 'Don't
you think it looks a *leetle* inflamed, Miss Mary?'

Mary gave it as her opinion that it did.

'Well, that's all I've got by this business; but I never
was consulted about it. I thought it my duty, however, to
give a *leetle* hint to the Earl, when the thing was proposed.
"My Lord," says I, "your house is your own; you have a
right to do what you please with it; burn it; pull it
down; make a purgatory of it; but, for God's sake, don't
give a ball in it!" The ball was given, and you see the
consequences. A ball! and what's a ball, that a whole
family should be thrown into disorder for it?'

'I daresay to those who are engaged in it, it is a very
delightful amusement at the time.'

'Delightful fiddlestick! 'Pon my soul, I'm surprised
at you, Miss Mary! I thought your staying away was a
pretty strong proof of your good sense; but I—hem!
Delightful amusement, indeed! to see human creatures
twirling one another about all night like so many monkies
—making perfect mountebanks of themselves. Really, I
look upon dancing as a most degrading and a most
immoral practice. 'Pon my soul, I—I couldn't have the
face to waltz, I know; and it's all on account of this

delightful amusement,' with a convulsive shake of his chin, 'that things are in this state—myself kept waiting for my breakfast two hours and a half beyond my natural time: not that I mind myself at all—that's neither here nor there—and if I was the only sufferer, I'm sure I should be the very last to complain—but I own it vexes —it distresses me—'pon my honour, I can't stand seeing a whole family going to destruction!'

The Doctor's agitation was so great, that Mary really pitied him.

'It is rather hard that you cannot get any breakfast, since you had no enjoyment in the ball,' said she. 'I daresay, were I to apply to Mrs. Brown, she would trust me with her keys; and I shall be happy to officiate for her in making your tea.'

'Thank you, Miss Mary,' replied the Doctor coldly. 'I'm very much obliged to you. It is really a very polite offer on your part; but—hem!—you might have observed, that I never take tea to breakfast. I keep that for the evening: most people, I know, do the reverse, but they're in the wrong. Coffee is too nutritive for the evening. The French themselves are in an error there. That woman, that Mrs. Brown knows what I like; in fact, she's the only woman I ever met with, who could make coffee—coffee that I thought drinkable. She knows that—and she knows that I like it to a moment—and yet—'

Here the Doctor blew his nose, and Mary thought she perceived a tear twinkle in his eye. Finding she was incapable of administering consolation, she was about to quit the room, when the Doctor, recovering himself, called after her.

'If you happen to be going the way of Mrs. Brown's room, Miss Mary, I would take it very kind, if you could just contrive to let her know what time of day it is; and that I have not tasted a mouthful of any thing since last

night at twelve o'clock, when I took a *leetle* morsel of
supper in my own room.'

Mary took advantage of the deep sigh that followed
to make her escape; and as she crossed the vestibule, she
descried the Doctor's man, hurrying along with a coffee
pot, which she had no doubt would pour consolation into
his master's soul.

As Mary was aware of her mother's dislike to introduce
her into company, she flattered herself she had for once
done something to merit her approbation, by having
absented herself on this occasion. But Mary was a novice
in the ways of temper, and had yet to learn, that to study
to please, and to succeed, are very different things. Lady
Juliana had been decidedly averse to her appearing at the
ball, but she was equally disposed to take offence at her
having staid away; besides, she had not been pleased
herself, and her glass told her she looked jaded and ill.
She was, therefore, as her maid expressed it, in a most
particular bad temper; and Mary had to endure
reproaches, of which she could only make out, that
although she ought not to have been present, she was
much to blame in having been absent. Lady Emily's
indignation was in a different style. There was a heat and
energy in her anger, that never failed to overwhelm her
victim at once. But it was more tolerable than the tedious,
fretful, ill humour of the other; and after she had fairly
exhausted herself in invective, and ridicule, and insolence,
and drawn tears from her cousin's eyes by the bitterness
of her language, she heartily embraced her—vowed she
liked her better than any body in the world—and that
she was a fool for minding any thing she said to her.

'I assure you,' said she, 'I was only tormenting you a
little, and you must own you deserve that; but you can't
suppose I meant half what I said; that is a *bêtise*[1] I can't
conceive you guilty of. You see I am much more charitable in my conclusions than you. You have no scruple in

thinking me a wretch, though I'm too good natured to set you down for a fool. Come, brighten up, and I'll tell you all about the ball.—How I hate it, were it only for having made your nose red! But really, the thing in itself was detestable. Job himself must have gone mad at the provocations I met with. In the first place, I had set my heart upon introducing you with *eclât*, and instead of which you preferred psalm singing with Mrs. Lennox, or sentiment with her son—I don't know which. In the next place, there was a dinner in Bath, that kept away some of the best men; then, after waiting an hour and a half for Frederick to begin the ball with Lady Charlotte M. I went myself to his room, and found him lounging by the fire with a volume of Rousseau in his hand, not dressed, and quite surprised that I should think his presence at all necessary; and when he did make his *entré*, conceive my feelings at seeing him single out Lady Placid as his partner! I certainly would rather have seen him waltzing with a hyena! I don't believe he knew or cared whom he danced with—unless, perhaps, it had been Adelaide, but she was engaged—and, by-the-bye, there certainly is some sort of a *liaison* there—how it will end I don't know—it depends upon themselves—for I'm sure the course of their love may run smooth if they choose— I know nothing to interrupt it. Perhaps, indeed, it may become stagnate from that very circumstance—for you know, or perhaps you don't know, "there is no spirit under heaven that works with such delusion".'[1]

Mary would have felt rather uneasy at this intelligence, had she believed it possible for her sister to be in love; but she had ever appeared to her so insensible to every tender emotion and generous affection, that she could not suppose even love itself was capable of making any impression on her heart. When, however, she saw them together, she began to waver in her opinion. Adelaide, silent and disdainful to others, was now gay and enchanting to Lord Lindore, and looked as if she triumphed in the victory she had already won. It was not so easy to ascertain the nature of Lord Lindore's feelings towards his cousin, and time only developed them.

END OF VOLUME SECOND

VOLUME III

CHAPTER I

*'Les douleurs muettes et stupides sont hors d'usage; on
pleure, on récite, on répète, on est si touchée de la mort de son
mari, qu'on n'en oublie pas la moindre circonstance.'*

La Bruyère.[1]

'PRAY PUT ON your Lennox face this morning, Mary,'
said Lady Emily one day to her cousin, 'for I want you to
go and pay a funeral visit with me to a distant relation,
but unhappily a near neighbour of ours, who has lately
lost her husband. Lady Juliana and Adelaide ought to go,
but they won't, so you and I must celebrate, as we best
can, the obsequies of the Honourable Mr. Sufton.'

Mary readily assented; and when they were seated in
the carriage, her cousin began—

'Since I am going to put you in the way of a trap, I
think it but fair to warn you of it. All traps are odious
things, and I make it my business to expose them where-
ever I find them. I own it chafes my spirit to see even
sensible people taken in by the clumsy machinery of such
a woman as Lady Matilda Sufton. So here she is in her
true colours. Lady Matilda is descended from the ancient
and illustrious family of Altamont. To have a fair character is, in her eyes, much more important than to deserve
it. She has prepared speeches for every occasion; and she

expects they are all to be believed—she has studied
attitudes, and imagines they are to pass for *impromptu*
feelings—in short, she is a *shew* woman—the world is her
theatre, and from it she looks for the plaudits due to her
virtue—for with her, the reality and the semblance are
synonimous. She has a grave and imposing air, which
keeps the timid at a distance; and she delivers the most
common truths as if they were the most profound
aphorisms. To degrade herself is her greatest fear; or, to
use her own expression, there is nothing so degrading as
associating with our inferiors—that is, our inferiors in
rank and wealth—for with her all other gradations are
incomprehensible. With the lower orders of society she is
totally unacquainted—she knows they are meanly
clothed and coarsely fed—consequently they are mean.
She is proud, both from nature and principle; for she
thinks it is the duty of every woman of family to be proud,
and that humility is only a virtue in the *canaille*. Proper
pride she calls it, though I rather think it ought to be
pride *proper*,[1] as I imagine it is a distinction that was
unknown before the introduction of heraldry. The only
true knowledge, according to her creed, is the knowledge
of the world, by which she means a knowledge of the
most courtly etiquette—the manners and habits of the
great, and the newest fashions in dress. Ignoramuses
might suppose she entered deeply into things, and was
thoroughly acquainted with human nature—no such
thing—the only wisdom she possesses, like the owl, is the
look of wisdom, and that is the very part of it which I
detest. Passions or feelings she has none; and to love, she
is an utter stranger. When, somewhat "in the sear and
yellow leaf,"[2] she married Mr. Sufton, a silly old man,
who had been dead to the world for many years. But
after having had him buried alive in his own chamber till
his existence was forgot, she had him disinterred for
the purpose of giving him a splendid burial in good

earnest. That done, her duty is now to mourn, or appear to mourn, for the approbation of the world. And now you shall judge for yourself, for here is Sufton-House. Now for the trappings and the weeds of woe.'[1]

Aware of her cousin's satirical turn, Mary was not disposed to yield conviction to her representation, but entered Lady Matilda's drawing-room with a mind sufficiently unbiassed to allow her to form her own judgment; but a very slight survey satisfied her that the picture was not over-charged. Lady Matilda sat in an attitude of woe—a crape-fan and open prayer-book lay before her —her cambric handkerchief was in her hand—her mourning-ring[2] was upon her finger—and the tear, not unbidden, stood in her eye. On the same sofa, and side by side, sat a tall, awkward, vapid looking personage, whom she introduced as her brother, the Duke of Altamont. His Grace was flanked by an obsequious looking gentleman, who was slightly named, as General Carver; and at a respectful distance was seated a sort of half-cast gentlewoman, something betwixt the confidential friend and humble companion, who was incidentally mentioned as 'my good Mrs. Finch.'

Her Ladyship pressed Lady Emily's hand—

'I did not expect, my dearest young friend, after the blow I have experienced—I did not expect I should so soon have been enabled to see my friends; but I have made a great exertion. Had I consulted my own feelings, indeed!—but there is a duty we owe to the world—there is an example we are all bound to shew—but such a blow!' Here she had recourse to her handkerchief.

'Such a blow!' echoed the Duke.

'Such a blow!' re-echoed the General.

'Such a blow!' reverberated Mrs. Finch.

'The most doating husband! I may say he lived but in my sight. Such a man!'

'Such a man!' said the Duke.

'Such a man!' exclaimed the General.

'Oh! such a man!' sobbed Mrs. Finch, as she complacently dropped a few tears. At that moment, sacred to tender remembrance, the door opened, and Mrs. Downe Wright was announced. She entered the room as if she had come to profane the ashes of the dead, and insult the feelings of the living. A smile was upon her face; and, in place of the silent pressure, she shook her Ladyship heartily by the hand, as she expressed her pleasure at seeing her look so well.

'Well!' replied the Lady, 'that is wonderful, after what I have suffered—but grief, it seems, will not kill!'

'I never thought it would,' said Mrs. Downe Wright; 'but I thought your having been confined to the house so long might have affected your looks. However, I'm happy to see that is not the case, as I don't recollect ever to have seen you so fat.'

Lady Matilda tried to look her into decency, but in vain. She sighed, and even groaned; but Mrs. Downe Wright would not be dolorous, and was not to be taken in, either by sigh or groan, crape-fan, or prayer-book. There was nobody her Ladyship stood so much in awe of as Mrs. Downe Wright. She had an instinctive knowledge that she knew her, and she felt her genius repressed by her, as Julius Caesar's was by Cassius.[1] They had been very old acquaintances, but never were cordial friends, though many worthy people are very apt to confound the two. Upon this occasion, Mrs. Downe Wright certainly did; for, availing herself of this privilege, she took off her cloak, and said, ''Tis so long since I have seen you, my dear; and since I see you so well, and able to enjoy the society of your friends, I shall delay the rest of my visits, and spend the morning with you.'

'That is truly kind of you, my dear Mrs. Downe Wright,' returned the mourner, with a countenance in which real woe was now plainly depicted; 'but I cannot be so selfish as to claim such a sacrifice from you.'

'There is no sacrifice in the case, I assure you, my dear,' returned Mrs. Downe Wright: 'This is a most comfortable room: and I could go nowhere, that I would meet a pleasanter little circle,' looking round.

Lady Matilda thought herself undone. Looking well—fat—comfortable room—pleasant circle—rung in her ears, and caused almost as great a whirl in her brain as noses, lips, handkerchiefs,[1] did in Othello's. Mrs. Downe Wright, always disagreeable, was now perfectly insupportable. She had disconcerted all her plans—she was a bar to all her studied speeches—even an obstacle to all her sentimental looks—yet to get rid of her was impossible. In fact, Mrs. Downe Wright was far from being an amiable woman. She took a malicious pleasure in tormenting those she did not like; and her skill in this art was so great, that she even deprived the tormented of the privilege of complaint. She had a great insight into character, and she might be said to read the very thoughts of her victims. Making a desperate effort to be herself again, Lady Matilda turned to her two young visitors, with whom she had still some hopes of success.

'I cannot express how much I feel indebted to the sympathy of my friends upon this trying occasion—an occasion, indeed, that called for sympathy.'

'A most melancholy occasion!' said the Duke.

'A most distressing occasion!' exclaimed the General.

'Never was greater occasion!' moaned Mrs. Finch.

Her Ladyship wiped her eyes, and resumed.

'I feel that I act but a melancholy part, in spite of every exertion. But my kind friend, Mrs. Downe Wright's spirits will, I trust, support me. She knows what it is to lose—'

Again her voice was buried in her handkerchief, and again she recovered and proceeded.

'I ought to apologize for being thus overcome; but my

friends, I hope, will make due allowance for my situation.
It cannot be expected that I should at all times find myself able for company.'

'Not at all!' said the Duke; and the two satellites
uttered their responses.

'You are able for a great deal, my dear!' said the provoking Mrs. Downe Wright; 'and I have no doubt but,
with a very little exertion, you could behave as if nothing
had happened.'

'Your partiality makes you suppose me capable of a
great deal more than I am equal to,' answered her Ladyship, with a real hysteric sob. 'It is not every one who is
blessed with the spirits of Mrs. Downe Wright.'

'What woman can do, you dare; who dares do more,
is none!'[1] said the General, bowing with a delighted air
at this brilliant application.

Mrs. Downe Wright charitably allowed it to pass, as
she thought it might be construed either as a compliment or a banter. Visitors flocked in, and the insufferable
Mrs. Downe Wright declared to all, that her Ladyship
was astonishingly well; but without the appropriate
whine, which gives proper pathos, and generally accom-
panies this hackneyed speech. Mrs. Finch indeed
laboured hard to counteract the effect of this injudicious
cheerfulness, by the most orthodox sighs, shakes of the
head, and confidential whispers, in which 'wonderful
woman!'—'prodigious exertion!'—'perfectly overcome!'
—'suffer for this afterwards,'—were audibly heard by all
present; but even then Mrs. Downe Wright's drawn up
lip, and curled nose, spoke daggers. At length, the tor-
mentor recollected an engagement she had made elsewhere, and took leave, promising to return, if possible,
the following day. Her friend, in her own mind, took her
measures accordingly. She resolved to order her own
carriage to be in waiting, and if Mrs. Downe Wright put
her threat in execution, she would take an airing. True,

she had not intended to have been able for such an exertion for at least a week longer; but, with the blinds down, she thought it might have an interesting effect.

The enemy fairly gone, Lady Matilda seemed to feel like a person suddenly relieved from the night-mare;[1] and she was beginning to give a fair specimen of her scenic powers, when Lady Emily, seeing the game was up with Mrs. Downe Wright, abruptly rose to depart.

'This has been a trying scene for you, my sweet young friends!' said her Ladyship, taking a hand of each.

'It has indeed!' replied Lady Emily, in a tone so significant as made Mary start.

'I know it would—youth is always so full of sympathy. I own I have a preference for the society of my young friends on that account. My good Mrs. Finch, indeed, is an exception; but worthy Mrs. Downe Wright has been almost too much for me.'

'She *is* too much!' said the Duke.

'She is a great deal too much!' said the General.

'She is a vast deal too much!' said Mrs. Finch.

'I own I have been rather overcome by her!' with a deep-drawn sigh, which her visitors hastily availed themselves of to make their retreat. The Duke and the General handed Lady Emily and Mary to their carriage.

'You find my poor sister wonderfully composed,' said the former.

'Charming woman, Lady Matilda!' ejaculated the latter; 'her feelings do honour to her head and heart!'

Mary sprung into the carriage as quick as possible to be saved the embarrassment of a reply; and it was not till they were fairly out of sight, that she ventured to raise her eyes to her cousin's face. There the expression of ill humour and disgust was so strongly depicted, that she could not longer repress her risible emotions, but gave way to a violent fit of laughter.

'How!' exclaimed her companion, 'is this the only

effect "Matilda's moan" has produced upon you? I expected your taste for grief would have been highly gratified by this affecting representation.'

'My appetite, you ought rather to say,' replied Mary; 'taste implies some discrimination which you seem to deny me.'

'Why, to tell you the truth, I do look upon you as a sort of intellectual goule—you really do remind me of the lady in the Arabian Nights,[1] whose taste or appetite, which you will, led her to scorn every thing that did not savour of the church-yard.'

'The delicacy of your comparison is highly flattering,' said Mary; 'but I must be duller than the fat weed,[2] were I to give my sympathy to such as Lady Matilda Surface.'

'Well, I'm glad to hear you say so; for I assure you, I was in pain lest you should have been taken in, notwithstanding my warning to say something *larmoyante*—or join the soft echo—or heave a sigh—or drop a tear—or do something, in short, that would have disgraced you with me for ever. At one time I must do you the justice to own, I thought I saw you with difficulty repress a smile, and then you blushed so, for fear you had betrayed yourself! The smile I suppose has gained you one conquest—the blush another. How happy you, who can hit the various tastes so easily! Mrs. Downe Wright whispered me as she left the room, "What a charming intelligent countenance your cousin has!" While my Lord Duke of Altamont observed, as he handed me along, "What a very sweet modest looking girl, Miss Douglas was!" So take your choice—Mrs. William Downe Wright, or Duchess of Altamont!'

'Duchess of Altamont, to be sure,' said Mary: 'and then such a man! Oh! such a man!'

CHAPTER II

'For marriage is a matter of more worth
Than to be dealt with in attorneyship.'

Shakespeare.[1]

'ALLOW ME TO introduce to you, ladies, that most high and puissant[2] Princess, her Grace the Duchess of Altamont, Marchioness of Norwood, Countess of Penrose, Baroness of, &c. &c.' cried Lady Emily, as she threw open the drawing-room door, and ushered Mary into the presence of her mother and sister, with all the demonstrations of ceremony and respect. The one frowned—the other coloured.

'How vastly absurd!' cried Lady Juliana, angrily.

'How vastly amusing!' cried Adelaide, contemptuously.

'How vastly annoying!' cried Lady Emily; 'to think that this little Highlander should bear aloft the Ducal crown, while you and I, Adelaide, must sneak about in shabby straw bonnets,' throwing down her own in pretended indignation. 'Then to think, which is almost certain, of her Viceroying it some day; and you and I, and all of us, being presented to her Majesty—having the honour of her hand to kiss—retreating from the Royal presence upon our heels. Oh! ye Sylphs and Gnomes!'[3] and she pretended to sink down overwhelmed with mortification.

Lady Emily delighted in tormenting her aunt and cousin, and she saw that she had completely succeeded. Mary was disliked by her mother, and despised by her sister; and any attempt to bring her forward, or raise her to a level with themselves, never failed to excite the indignation of both. The consequences were always felt by her, in the increased ill humour and disdainful indifference with which she was treated; and, on the present occasion, her injudicious friend was only brewing phials of wrath[4] for her. But Lady Emily never looked to future consequences—present effect was all she cared for; and she went on to relate seriously, as she called it, but in the most exaggerated terms, the admiration which the Duke had expressed for Mary, and her own firm belief that she might be Duchess when she chose; 'that is, after the expiry of his mourning for the late Duchess. Every one knows that he is desirous of having a family, and is determined to marry the moment propriety permits—he is now decidedly on the look-out, for the year must be very near a close; and then, hail Duchess of Altamont!'[1]

'I must desire, Lady Emily, you will find some other subject for your wit, and not fill the girl's head with folly and nonsense—there is a great deal too much of both already.'

'Take care what you say of the future representative of majesty; this may be high treason yet; only I trust your Grace will be as generous as Henry the Fifth[2] was, and that the Duchess of Altamont will not remember the offences committed against Mary Douglas.'

Lady Juliana, to whom a jest was an outrage, and raillery incomprehensible, now started up, and, as she passionately swept out of the room, threw down a stand of hyacinths, which, for the present, put a stop to Lady Emily's diversion.

The following day Mrs. Downe Wright arrived with her son, evidently primed for falling in love at first sight. He was a very handsome young man, gentle, and rather pleasing in his manners; and Mary, to whom his intentions were not so palpable, thought him by no means deserving of the contempt her cousin had expressed for him.

'Well!' cried Lady Emily, after they were gone, 'the plot begins to thicken[3]—lovers begin to pour in, but all for Mary—how mortifying to you and me, Adelaide! At this rate, we shall have nothing to boast of in the way of disinterested attachment—nobody refused!—nothing renounced!—By and bye Edward will be reckoned a very good match for *me*, and *you* will be thought greatly married, if you succeed in securing Lindore: *poor* Lord Lindore, as it seems that wretch Placid calls him.'

Adelaide heard all her cousin's taunts in silence, and with apparent coolness; but they rankled deep in a heart already festering with pride, envy, and ambition. The thoughts of her sister—and that sister so inferior to herself—attaining a more splendid alliance, was not to be endured.—True, she loved Lord Lindore, and imagined herself beloved in return; but even that was not sufficient to satisfy the craving passions of a perverted mind. She did not, indeed, attach implicit belief to all that her cousin said on the subject; but she was provoked and irritated at the mere supposition of such a thing being possible; for it is not merely the jealous whose happiness is the sport of trifles light as air[1]—every evil thought, every unamiable feeling, bears about with it the bane of that enjoyment after which it vainly aspires.

Mary felt the increasing ill humour which this subject drew upon her, without being able to penetrate the cause of it; but she saw that it was displeasing to her mother and sister, and that was sufficient to make her wish to put a stop to it. She, therefore, earnestly entreated Lady Emily to end the joke.

'Excuse me,' replied her Ladyship, 'I shall do no such thing. In the first place, there happens to be no joke in the matter: I'm certain, seriously certain, or certainly serious, which you like, that you may be Duchess of Altamont, if you please. It could be no common admiration that prompted his Grace to an original and spontaneous effusion of it. I have met with him before, and never suspected that he had an innate idea in his head. I certainly never heard him utter any thing half so brilliant before—it seemed quite like the effect of inspiration.'

'But I cannot conceive, even were it as you say, why

my mother should be so displeased about it. She surely cannot suppose me so silly, as to be elated by the unmeaning admiration of any one, or so meanly aspiring as to marry a man I could not love, merely because he is a Duke: She was incapable of such a thing herself, she cannot then suspect me.'

'It seems as impossible to make you enter into the characters of your mother and sister, as it would be to teach them to comprehend yours, and far be it from me to act as interpreter betwixt your understandings. If you can't even imagine such things as prejudice, narrow-mindedness, envy, hatred, and malice, your ignorance is bliss,[1] and you had better remain in it. But you may take my word for one thing, and that is, that 'tis a much wiser thing to resist tyranny, than to submit to it. Your patient Grizzles[2] make nothing of it, except in little books: in real life they become perfect pack-horses, saddled with the whole offences of the family. Such will you become unless you pluck up spirit, and dash out. Marry the Duke, and drive over the necks of all your relations; that's my advice to you.'

'And you may rest assured, that when I follow your advice, it shall be in whole, not in part.'

'Well, situated so detestably as you are, I rather think the best thing you could do, would be to make yourself Duchess of Altamont. How disdainful you look! Come, tell me honestly now, would you really refuse to be Your Grace, with ninety thousand a year, and remain simple Mary Douglas, passing rich with perhaps forty?'

'Unquestionably,' said Mary.

'What! you really pretend to say you would not marry the Duke of Altamont?' cried Lady Emily. 'Not that I would take him myself; but as you and I, though the best of friends, differ widely in our sentiments on most subjects, I should really like to know how it happens that we coincide in this one. Very different reasons, I

dare say, lead to the same conclusion; but I shall
generously give you the advantage of hearing mine first.
I shall say nothing of being engaged—I shall even banish
that idea from my thoughts; but were I free as air[1]—
unloving and unloved—I would refuse the Duke of Altamont; first, because he is old—no, first, because he is
stupid; second, because he is formal; third, because he
swallows all Lady Matilda's flummery; fourth, because
he is more than double my age; fifth, because he is not
handsome; and, to sum up the whole in the sixth, he
wants that inimitable *Je ne sçais quoi*, which I consider as
a necessary ingredient in the matrimonial cup. I shall
not, in addition to these defects, dwell upon his unmeaning stare—his formal bow—his little senseless simper,
&c. &c. &c. All these enormities, and many more of the
same stamp, I shall pass by, as I have no doubt they had
their due effect upon you as well as me; but then I am
not, like you, under the torments of Lady Juliana's
authority: Were that the case, I should certainly think it
a blessing to become Duchess of any body tomorrow.'

'And can you really imagine,' said Mary, 'that for the
sake of shaking off a parent's authority, I would impose
upon myself chains still heavier, and even more binding?
Can you suppose I would so far forfeit my honour and
truth, as that I would swear to love, honour, and obey,
where I could feel neither love nor respect; and where
cold constrained obedience would be all of my duty I
could hope to fulfil?'

'Love!' exclaimed Lady Emily; 'can I credit my ears?
Love! did you say? I thought that had only been for
naughty ones, such as me; and that saints like you would
have married for any thing and every thing but love!
Prudence, I thought, had been the word with you proper
ladies—a prudent marriage! Come, confess, is not that
the climax of virtue in the creed of your school?'

'I never learnt the creed of any school,' said Mary,

'nor ever heard any one's sentiments on the subject, except my dear Mrs. Douglas.'

'Well, I should like to hear your oracle's opinion, if you can give it in short hand.'

'She warned me there was a passion, which was very fashionable, and which I should hear a great deal of, both in conversation and books, that was the result of indulged fancy, warm imaginations, and ill regulated minds; that many had fallen into its snares, deceived by its glowing colours and alluring name; that————'

'A very good sermon, indeed!' interrupted Lady Emily; 'but, no offence to Mrs. Douglas, I think I could preach a better myself. Love is a passion that has been much talked of, often described, and little understood. Cupid has many counterfeits going about the world, who pass very well with those whose minds are capable of passion, but not of love. These Birmingham Cupids[1] have many votaries amongst boarding school misses, militia officers, and milliners' apprentices; who marry upon the mutual faith of blue eyes and scarlet coats: have dirty houses and squalling children, and hate each other most delectably. Then there is another species for more refined souls, which owes its birth to the works of Rousseau, Goethe, Cottin,[2] &c.: its success depends very much upon rocks, woods, and waterfalls; and it generally ends in daggers, pistols, poison, or Doctors' Commons. But there, I think, Lindore would be more eloquent than me, so I shall leave it for him to discuss that chapter with you. But, to return to your own immediate concerns— Pray, are you then positively prohibited from falling in love? Did Mrs. Douglas only dress up a scarecrow to frighten you, or had she the candour to shew you Love himself in all his majesty?'

'She told me,' said Mary, 'that there was a love which even the wisest and most virtuous need not blush to entertain—the love of a virtuous object, founded upon esteem, and heightened by similarity of tastes, and sympathy of feelings, into a pure and devoted attachment: unless I feel all this, I shall never fancy myself in love.'

'Humph! I can't say much as to the similarity of tastes and sympathy of souls between the Duke and you, but surely you might contrive to feel some love and esteem for a coronet and ninety thousand a year.'

'Suppose I did,' said Mary, with a smile, 'the next point is to honour; and surely he is as unlikely to excite that sentiment as the other. Honour—'

'I can't have a second sermon upon honour. "Can honour take away the grief of a wound?"[1] as Falstaff says. Love is the only subject I care to preach about; though, unlike many young ladies, we can talk about other things too; but as to this Duke, *I* certainly "had rather live on cheese and garlic, in a windmill far, than feed on cates,[2] and have him talk to me in any summer-house in Christendom;"[3] and now I have had Mrs. Douglas' second hand sentiments upon the subject—I should like to hear your own.'

'I have never thought much upon the subject,' said Mary; 'my sentiments are therefore all at second hand, but I shall repeat to you what I think is *not* love, and what *is*.'—And she repeated these pretty and well known lines:—

CARELESS AND FAITHFUL LOVE

> To sigh—yet feel no pain—
> To weep—yet scarce know why,
> To sport an hour with beauty's chain,
> Then throw it idly by:
> To kneel at many a shrine,
> Yet lay the heart on none;
> To think all other charms divine,
> But those we just have won:—

This is love—careless love—
Such as kindleth hearts that rove.

———

To keep one sacred flame
Through life, unchill'd, unmov'd;
To love in wint'ry age the same
That first in youth we loved:
To feel that we adore
With such refined excess,
That though the heart would break with more,
We could not love with less.—
This is love—faithful love,
Such as saints might feel above.[1]

'And such as I do feel, and will always feel, for my Edward,' said Lady Emily—'But there is the dressing bell!' And she flew off, singing,

'To keep one sacred flame,' &c.

CHAPTER III

'Some, when they write to their friends, are all affection; some are wise and sententious; some strain their powers for efforts of gaiety; some write news, and some write secrets—but to make a letter without affection, without wisdom, without gaiety, without news, and without a secret, is doubtless the great epistolic art.'

Dr. Johnson.[2]

AN UNUSUAL LENGTH of time had elapsed since Mary had heard from Glenfern, and she was beginning to feel some anxiety on account of her friends there, when her apprehensions were dispelled by the arrival of a large packet, containing letters from Mrs. Douglas and aunt Jacky. The former, although the one that conveyed the greatest degree of pleasure, was perhaps not the one that would be most acceptable to the reader. Indeed, it is generally admitted, that the letters of single ladies are infinitely more lively and entertaining than those of married ones—a fact which can neither be denied nor accounted for. The following is a faithful transcript from the original letter in question.

'Glenfern Castle, ———*shire, N.B.*[1]
Feb. 19*th,* 18——.

'MY DEAR MARY,

'YOURS was *received* with *much* pleasure, as it is *always* a satisfaction to your friends *here* to know that you are *well* and doing *well*. We all *take* the most *sincere* interest in your *health,* and also in your *improvements* in other *respects*. But I am *sorry* to say they do not quite *keep* pace with *our* expectations. I must therefore *take* this opportunity of *mentioning* to you a *fault* of yours, *which,* though a very great *one* in itself, is one *that* a very slight *degree* of attention on your *part,* will, I have *no* doubt, enable you to *get* entirely the *better of.* It is fortunate for *you,* my dear Mary, that you have *friends* who are always ready to point *out* your errors to you. For *want* of that *most* invaluable *blessing,* viz. a sincere *friend,* many a *one* has gone out of the *world,* no wiser in many *respects,* than when they *came* into it. But that, I flatter *myself,* will not be your *case,* as you cannot *but* be sensible of the great *pains* my sister and I have *taken* to point out your *faults* to you from the *hour* of your birth. The *one* to which I particularly *allude* at present is, the constant omission of *proper* dates to your *letters,* by which means we are all of us very often *brought* into *most* unpleasant *situations.* As an *instance* of it, our *worthy* minister, Mr. M'Drone, happened to be *calling* here the very *day* we received your last *letter*. After *hearing* it read, he most *naturally* inquired the date of it; and I *cannot* tell you how *awkward* we all *felt* when we were *obliged* to confess it had *none!* And since I am *upon* that subject, I think it much *better* to tell you candidly that I *do* not think your *hand* of write by any *means* improved. It does not *look* as if you *bestowed* that pains upon it which you *undoubtedly* ought to do; for without *pains*, I can assure you, Mary, you *will* never do any *thing* well. As our admirable *grandmother*, good Lady Girnachgowl, *used* to say, pains *makes* gains;[1] and so it was *seen* upon her; for it was entirely *owing* to her *pains* that the Girnachgowl estate was relieved, and *came* to be what it is now, viz. a most valuable and *highly* productive *property*.

'I know there are *many* young *people* who are very *apt* to think it *beneath* them to take *pains;* but I sincerely trust, my dear Mary, you have *more* sense than to be so very *foolish*. Next to a good distinct *hand* of write, and *proper* stops (which I observe you never *put*) the thing *most* to be attended to is your style, *which* we all think might *be* greatly *improved* by a *little* reflection on your *part*, joined to a *few* judicious *hints* from your friends. We are *all* of opinion, that your *periods* are too short, and also *that* your expressions are *deficient* in dignity. *Neither* are you sufficiently circumstantial in your *intelligence*, even upon subjects of the highest *importance*. Indeed, upon some *subjects*, you *communicate* no information whatever, which is *certainly* very extraordinary in a *young* person, who ought to be naturally extremely communicative. Miss M'Pry, who is here upon a *visit* to us at *present*, is perfectly *astonished* at the total *want* of news in your *letters*. She has a *niece* residing in the neighbourhood of *Bath*, who sends her regular lists of the company there, and also an *account* of the most *remarkable* events that take *place* there. Indeed, had it not *been* for Patty M'Pry, we never would have *heard* a *syllable* of the celebrated *Lady* Travers' elopement with *Sir* John Conquest; and, indeed, I cannot *conceal* from you, that we have heard more as to what goes on in

Lord Courtland's *family*, through Miss Patty M'Pry, than *ever* we have heard from you, *Mary*.

'In short, I *must* plainly tell you, *however* painful you may *feel* it, that not one of us is ever a *whit* the wiser after reading your *letters* than we *were* before. But I am *sorry* to say this is not the *most* serious part of the *complaint* we have to *make* against you. We are all *willing* to find excuses for you, even *upon* these points, but I must *confess*, your neglecting to *return* any answers to certain inquiries of your aunts', *appears* to me perfectly inexcusable. Of *course*, you must *understand* that I allude to that *letter* of your aunt Grizzy's, dated the 17th of December, wherein she *expressed* a strong desire that you should endeavour to make yourself *mistress* of Dr. Redgill's opinion with *respect* to lumbago, as she is extremely anxious to *know* whether he *considers* the seat of the disorder to be in the bones or the sinews; and undoubtedly it is of the greatest *consequence* to procure the *opinion* of a sensible well-informed English *physician*, upon a subject of such vital *importance*. Your aunt Nicky, also, in a letter, *dated* the 22d of December, requested to be *informed* whether Lord Courtland (like our *great* landholders) killed his own *mutton*, as Miss P. M'P. insinuates in a *letter* to her aunt, that the *servants* there are suspected of being *guilty* of great *abuses* on that *score;* but there you also *preserve* a most unbecoming, and I own I think *somewhat* mysterious *silence.*

'And now, my dear Mary, *having* said all that *I* trust is necessary to *recal* you to a sense of *your* duty, I *shall* now communicate to you a *piece* of intelligence, *which*, I am certain, will *occasion* you the *most* unfeigned pleasure, viz. the prospect there is of your soon *beholding* some of your friends from this *quarter* in Bath. Our valuable friend and *neighbour*, Sir Sampson, has been rather (we think) worse than *better* since you left us. He is now *deprived* of the entire use of one leg. He *himself* calls his *complaint* a morbid rheumatism; but Lady Maclaughlan *assures* us it is a rheumatic palsy,[1] and she has now *formed* the resolution of *taking* him up to Bath early in the ensuing *spring*. And not only that, but she has most considerately *invited* your aunt Grizzy to accompany them, *which*, of course, she is to do with the greatest *pleasure*. We are therefore all extremely *occupied* in getting your aunt's things *put* in order for such an *occasion;* and you must *accept* of that as an apology for none of the girls *being* at leisure to write *you* at present, and *likewise* for the shortness of *this* letter. But be assured we will all *write* you fully by Grizzy. Meantime, all *unite* in kind remembrance to *you*. And I *am*, my dear Mary, your most affectionate aunt,

'JOAN DOUGLAS.

'P. S. Upon *looking* over your letter, I am much *struck* with your X's. You surely *cannot* be so ignorant as *not* to know that a well *made x* is neither more nor *less* than *two* c's joined together back to back, *instead* of these senseless crosses you *seem* so fond of; and as to *your z*'s, I defy any *one* to distinguish them *from* your *y*'s. I trust you will *attend* to this, and shew that it *proceeds* rather from want of proper *attention* than *from* wilful airs.

'J. D.

'P. S. Miss P. M'Pry *writes* her aunt that *there* is a strong *report* of Lord Lindore's marriage to our *niece* Adelaide; but *we* think that is *impossible*, as you certainly *never* could have omitted to *inform* us of a circumstance *which* so deeply concerns *us*. If so, I must *own* I shall think you quite *unpardonable*. At the *same* time, it *appears* extremely improbable *that* Miss M'P. *would* have mentioned *such* a thing to her *aunt*, without having good *grounds* to *go* upon.

'J. D.'

Mary could not entirely repress her mirth while she read this catalogue of her crimes; but she was, at the same time, eager to expiate her offences, real or imaginary, in the sight of her good old aunt; and she immediately sat down to the construction of a letter after the model prescribed;—though with little expectation of being able to cope with the intelligent Miss P. M'P. in the extent of her communications. Her heart warmed at the thoughts of seeing again the dear familiar face of aunt Grizzy, and of hearing the tones of that voice, which, though sharp and cracked, still sounded sweet in memory's ear. Such is the power that early associations ever retain over the kind and unsophisticated heart. But she was aware how differently her mother would feel on the subject, as she never alluded to her husband's family, but with indignation or contempt; and she therefore resolved to be silent with regard to aunt Grizzy's prospects for the present.

CHAPTER IV

———'As in apothecaries' shops all sorts of drugs are permitted to be, so may all sorts of books be in the library; and as they out of vipers, and scorpions, and poisonous vegetables, extract often wholesome medicaments for the life of mankind, so out of whatsoever book, good instruction and examples may be acquired.'

Drummond of Hawthornden.[1]

MARY'S THOUGHTS HAD often reverted to Rose Hall since the day she had last quitted it, and she longed to fulfil her promise to her venerable friend; but a feeling of delicacy, unknown to herself, withheld her. 'She will not miss me while she has her son with her,' said she to herself; but, in reality, she dreaded her cousin's raillery should she continue to visit there as frequently as before. At length a favourable opportunity occurred: Lady Emily, with great exultation, told her the Duke of Altamont was to dine at Beech Park the following day, but that she was to conceal it from Lady Juliana and Adelaide; 'for assuredly,' said she, 'if they were apprised of it, they would send you up to the nursery as a naughty girl, or, perhaps, down to the scullery, and make a Cinderella of you. Depend upon it, you would not get leave to shew your face in the drawing-room.'

'Do you really think so?' asked Mary.

'I know it. I know Lady Juliana would torment you till she had set you a crying; and then she would tell you, you had made yourself such a fright, that you were not fit to be seen, and so order you to your own room. You know very well it would not be the first time that such a thing has happened.'

Mary could not deny the fact; but, sick of idle altercation, she resolved to say nothing, but walk over to Rose Hall the following morning. And this she did, leaving a note for her cousin, apologizing for her flight.

She was received with rapture by Mrs. Lennox.

'Ah! my dear Mary,' said she, as she tenderly embraced her, 'you know not, you cannot, conceive, what a blank your absence makes in my life! When you open your eyes in the morning, it is to see the light of day, and the faces you love, and all is brightness around you. But, when I wake, it is still to darkness. My night knows no end. 'Tis only when I listen to your dear voice that I forget I am blind.'

'I should not have staid so long from you,' said Mary, 'but I knew you had Colonel Lennox with you, and I could not flatter myself you would have even a thought to bestow upon me.'

'My Charles is, indeed, every thing that is kind and

devoted to me. He walks with me, reads to me, talks to me, sits with me for hours, and bears with all my little weaknesses as a mother would with her sick child; but still there are a thousand little feminine attentions he cannot understand. I would not that he did. And then to have him always with me seems so selfish; for, gentle and tender-hearted as he is, I know he bears the spirit of an eagle within him; and the tame monotony of my life can ill accord with the nobler habits of his. Yet he says he is happy with me, and I try to make myself believe him.'

'Indeed,' said Mary, 'I cannot doubt it. It is always a happiness to be with those we love, and whom we know love us, under any circumstances; and it is for that reason I love so much to come to my dear Mrs. Lennox,' caressing her as she spoke.

'Dearest Mary, who would not love you? Oh! could I but see—could I but hope—'

'You must hope every thing you desire,' said Mary, gaily, and little guessing the nature of her good friend's hopes; 'I do nothing but hope.' And she tried to check a sigh, as she thought how some of her best hopes had been already blighted by the unkindness of those whose love she had vainly strove to win.

Mrs. Lennox's hopes were already upon her lips, when the entrance of her son fortunately prevented their being for ever destroyed by a premature disclosure. He welcomed Mary with an appearance of the greatest pleasure, and looked so much happier and more animated than when she last saw him, that she was struck with the change, and began to think he might almost stand a comparison with his picture.

'You find me still here, Miss Douglas,' said he, 'although my mother gives me many hints to be gone, by insinuating what, indeed, cannot be doubted, how very ill I supply your place; but,' turning to his mother, 'you are not likely to be rid of me for some time, as I have just received an additional leave of absence; but for that, I must have left you to-morrow.'[1]

'Dear Charles! you never told me so. How could you conceal it from me! how wretched I should have been had I dreamed of such a thing!'

'That is the very reason for which I concealed it, and yet you reproach me. Had I told you there was a chance of my going, you would assuredly have set it down for a certainty, and so have been vexed for no purpose.'

'But your remaining was a chance too,' said Mrs. Lennox, who could not all at once reconcile herself even to an *escape* from danger; 'and think, had you been called away from me without any preparation!—Indeed, Charles, it was very imprudent.'

'My dearest mother, I meant it in kindness: I could not bear to give you a moment's certain uneasiness for an uncertain evil. I really cannot discover either the use or the virtue of tormenting one's self by anticipation. I should think it quite as rational to case myself in a suit of mail, by way of security to my person, as to keep my mind perpetually on the rack of anticipating evil. I perfectly agree with that philosopher who says, if we confine ourselves to general reflections on the evils of life, *that* can have no effect in preparing us for them; and if we bring them home to us, *that* is the certain means of rendering ourselves miserable.'

'But they will come, Charles,' said his mother mournfully, 'whether we bring them or not.'

'True, my dear mother; but when misfortune does come, it comes commissioned from a higher power, and it will ever find a well-regulated mind ready to receive it with reverence, and submit to it with resignation. There is something, too, in real sorrow, that tends to enlarge and exalt the soul; but the imaginary evils of our own creating, can only serve to contract and depress it.'

Mrs. Lennox shook her head—'Ah! Charles, you may

depend upon it your reasoning is wrong, and you will be convinced of it some day.'

'I am convinced of it already. I begin to fear this discussion will frighten Miss Douglas away from us. *There* is an evil anticipated! Now, do you, my dear mother, help me to avert it; where that can be done, it cannot be too soon apprehended.'

As Colonel Lennox's character unfolded itself, Mary saw much to admire in it; and it is more than probable the admiration would soon have been reciprocal, had it been allowed to take its course. But good Mrs. Lennox would force it into a thousand little channels prepared by herself, and love itself must have been quickly exhausted by the perpetual demands that were made upon it. Mary would have been deeply mortified had she suspected the cause of her friend's solicitude to shew her off; but she was a stranger to match-making in all its bearings—had scarcely ever read a novel in her life, and was, consequently, not at all aware of the necessity there was for her falling in love with all convenient speed. She was, therefore, sometimes amused, though oftener ashamed, at Mrs. Lennox's panegyrics, and could not but smile as she thought how aunt Jacky's wrath would have been kindled, had she heard the extravagant praises that were bestowed on her most trifling accomplish-ments.

'You must sing my favourite song to Charles, my love —he has never heard you sing. Pray do: you did not use to require any entreaty from me, Mary! Many a time you have gladdened my heart with your songs, when, but for you, it would have been filled with mournful thoughts!'

Mary finding, whatever she did or did *not*, she was destined to hear only her own praises, was glad to take refuge at the harp, to which she sung the following ancient ditty:—

'Sweet day! so cool, so calm, so bright,
The bridal of the earth and sky,
Sweet dews shall weep thy fall to night,
                    For thou must die.

'Sweet rose! whose hue, angry and brave,
Bids the rash gazer wipe his eye,
Thy root is ever in its grave;
                    And thou must die.

'Sweet spring! full of sweet days and roses,
A box where sweets compacted lie,
My music shews you have your closes,
                    And all must die.

'Only a sweet and virtuous soul,
Like season'd timber, never gives;
But when the whole world turns to coal,
                    Then chiefly lives.'[1]

'That,' said Colonel Lennox, 'is one of the many
exquisite little pieces of poetry which are to be found,
like jewels in an Ethiop's ear,[2] in my favourite Isaac
Walton. The title of the book offers no encouragement to
female readers, but I know few works from which I rise
with such renovated feelings of benevolence and good will.
Indeed, I know no author who has given, with so much
naïveté, so enchanting a picture of a pious and contented
mind. Here,' taking the book from a shelf, and turning
over the leaves, 'is one of the passages which has so often
charmed me:— "That very hour which you were absent
from me, I sat down under a willow by the waterside,
and considered what you had told me of the owner of that
pleasant meadow in which you left me—that he has a
plentiful estate, and not a heart to think so; that he has
at this time many law-suits depending[3]—and that they
both damped his mirth, and took up so much of his time
and thoughts, that he himself had not leisure to take that

sweet comfort, I, who pretended no title to them, took in his fields; for I could there sit quietly, and, looking in the water, see some fishes sport themselves in the silver streams, others leaping at flies of several shapes and colours. Looking on the hills, I could behold them spotted with woods and groves; looking down upon the meadows, I could see, here a boy gathering lilies and lady-smocks,[1] and there a girl cropping culverkeys[2] and cowslips, all to make garlands suitable to this present month of May. These, and many other field flowers, so perfumed the air, that I thought that very meadow like that field in Sicily, of which Diodorus speaks,[3] where the perfumes arising from the place make all dogs that hunt in it to fall off and lose their scent. I say, as I thus sat joying in my own happy condition, and pitying this poor rich man, that owned this and many other pleasant groves and meadows about me, I did then thankfully remember what my Saviour said, that the *meek possess the earth*[4]—or, rather, they enjoy what the others possess and enjoy not; for anglers and meek-spirited men are free from those high, those restless thoughts, which corrode the sweets of life; and they, and they only, can say, as the poet has happily expressed it—

> "Hail, blest estate of lowliness!
> Happy enjoyments of such minds
> As, rich in self-contentedness,
> Can, like the reeds in roughest winds,
> By yielding, make that blow but small,
> By which proud oaks and cedars fall.'"[5]

'There is both poetry and painting in such prose as this,' said Mary; 'but I should certainly as soon have thought of looking for a pearl necklace in a fish pond, as of finding pretty poetry in a treatise upon the art of angling.'

'That book was a favourite of your father's, Charles,' said Mrs. Lennox; 'and I remember, in our happiest days, he used to read parts of it to me. One passage, in particular, made a strong impression upon me, though I little thought then it would ever apply to me. It is upon the blessings of sight. Indulge me by reading it to me once again.'

Colonel Lennox made an effort to conquer his feelings, while he read as follows:

'What would a blind man give to see the pleasant rivers, and meadows, and flowers, and fountains, that we have met with! I have been told, that if a man that was born blind could attain to have his sight for *but only one hour* during his whole life, and should, at the first opening of his eyes, fix his sight upon the sun when it was in its full glory, either at the rising or the setting, he would be so transported and amazed, and so admire the glory of it, that he would not willingly turn his eyes from that first ravishing object, to behold all the other various beauties this world could present to them. And this, and many other like objects, we enjoy daily————'[1]

A deep sigh from Mrs. Lennox made her son look up: Her eyes were bathed in tears.

He threw his arms around her. 'My dearest mother!' cried he, in a voice choked with agitation, 'how cruel— how unthinking—thus to remind you————'

'Do not reproach yourself for my weakness, dear Charles; but I was thinking, how much rather, could I have my sight but for one hour, I would look upon the face of my own child, than on all the glories of the creation!'

Colonel Lennox was too deeply affected to speak: He pressed his mother's hand to his lips—then rose abruptly, and quitted the room. Mary succeeded in soothing her weak and agitated spirits into composure; but the chord of feeling had been jarred, and all her efforts to restore it to its former tone, proved abortive for the rest of the day.

CHAPTER V

'Friendship is constant in all other things
Save in the office and affairs of love:
Therefore all hearts in love use their own tongues;
Let every eye negociate for itself,
And trust no agent.'

Much Ado about Nothing.[1]

THERE WAS SOMETHING so refreshing in the domestic peacefulness of Rose Hall, when contrasted with the heartless bustle of Beech Park, that Mary felt too happy in the change to be in any hurry to quit it. But an unfortunate discovery soon turned all her enjoyment into bitterness of heart; and Rose Hall, from being to her a place of rest, was suddenly transformed into an abode too hateful to be endured.

It happened, one day as she entered the drawing-room, Mrs. Lennox was, as usual, assailing the heart of her son in her behalf. A large Indian screen divided the room, and Mary's entrance was neither seen nor heard till she was close by them.

'O, certainly, Miss Douglas is all that you say—very pretty—very amiable—and very accomplished,' said Colonel Lennox, with a sort of half-suppressed yawn, in answer to an eulogium of his mother's.

'Then why not love her? Ah! Charles, promise me that you will at least try!' said the good old lady, laying her hand upon his with the greatest earnestness.

This was said when Mary was actually standing before her. To hear the words, and to feel their application, was a flash of lightning; and, for a moment, she felt as if her brain were on fire. She was alive but to one idea, and that the most painful that could be suggested to a delicate mind. She had heard herself recommended to the love of a man who was indifferent to her. Could there be such a humiliation—such a degradation? Colonel Lennox's embarrassment was scarcely less; but his mother saw not the mischief she had done, and she continued to speak without his having the power to interrupt her. But her words fell unheeded on Mary's ear—she could hear nothing but what she had already heard. Colonel Lennox rose and respectfully placed a chair for her, but the action was unnoticed—she saw only herself a suppliant for his love; and, insensible to every thing but her own feelings, she turned and hastily quitted the room without uttering a syllable. To fly from Rose Hall, never again to enter it, was her first resolution; yet how was she to do so without coming to an explanation, worse even than the cause itself; for she had that very morning yielded to the solicitations of Mrs. Lennox, and consented to remain till the following day.

'Oh!' thought she, as the scalding tears of shame, for the first time, dropped from her eyes, 'what a situation am I placed in! To continue to live under the same roof with the man whom I have heard solicited to love me; and how mean—how despicable must I appear in his eyes—thus offered—rejected! How shall I ever be able to convince him that I care not for his love—that I wished it not—that I would refuse, scorn it to-morrow were it offered to me. Oh! could I but tell him so; but he must ever remain a stranger to my real sentiments—*he* might reject—but *I* cannot disavow! And yet, to have him think, that I have all this while been laying snares for him—that all this parade of my acquirements was for the purpose of gaining his affections! Oh! how blind and stupid I was, not to see through the injudicious praises of Mrs. Lennox! I should not then have suffered this degradation in the eyes of her son!'

Hours passed away unheeded by Mary, while she was giving way to the wounded sensibility of a naturally high spirit and acute feelings, thus violently excited in all their first ardour. At length, she was recalled to herself, by hearing the sound of a carriage, as it passed under her window; and, immediately after, she received a message to repair to the drawing-room to her cousin, Lady Emily.

'How fortunate!' though she; 'I shall now get away—no matter how or where, I shall go never again to return.'

And, unconscious of the agitation visible in her countenance, she hastily descended, impatient to bid an eternal adieu to her once loved Rose Hall. She found Lady Emily and Colonel Lennox together. Eyes less penetrating than her cousin's, would easily have discovered the state of poor Mary's mind, as she entered the room; her beating heart—her flushed cheek and averted eye, all declared the perturbation of her spirits; and Lady Emily regarded her, for a moment, with an expression of surprise that served to heighten her confusion.

'I have no doubt, I am a very unwelcome visitor here to all parties,' said she; 'for I come—how shall I declare it!—to carry you home, Mary, by command of Lady Juliana.'

'No, no!' exclaimed Mary eagerly; 'you are quite welcome. I am quite ready. I was wishing—I was waiting.' —Then, recollecting herself, she blushed still deeper at her own precipitation.

'There is no occasion to be so vehemently obedient,' said her cousin; '*I* am not quite ready, neither am I wishing, or waiting to be off in such a hurry. Colonel Lennox and I had just set about reviving an old acquaintance; begun, I can't tell when—and broken off, when I was a thing in the nursery, with a blue sash and red fingers. I have promised him, that when he comes to Beech Park, you shall sing him my favourite Scotch song, "Should auld acquaintance be forgot."[1] I would sing it myself if I could; but I think every English woman, who pretends to sing Scotch songs, ought to have the bow-string;'[2] then turning to the harpsichord, she began to play it with exquisite taste and feeling.

'There,' said she, rising with equal levity; 'is not that worth all the formal bows— and "recollects to have had the pleasure"—and "long time since I had the honour" —and such sort of hateful reminiscences, that make one feel nothing, but that they are a great deal older, and uglier, stupider, and more formal than they were so many years before.'

'Where the early ties of the heart remain unbroken,' said Colonel Lennox, with some emotion, 'such remembrances do indeed give it back all its first freshness; but it cannot be to every one a pleasure to have its feelings awakened, even by tones such as these.'

There was nothing of austerity in this; on the contrary, there was so much sweetness mingled with the melancholy which shaded his countenance, that even Lady Emily was touched, and for a moment silent. The entrance of Mrs. Lennox relieved her from her embarrassment. She flew towards her, and taking her hand, 'My dear Mrs. Lennox, I feel very much as if I were come here in the capacity of an executioner;—no, not exactly that, but rather a sort of constable or bailiff;—for I am come on the part of Lady Juliana Douglas, to summon you to surrender the person of her well-beloved daughter, to be disposed of as she in her wisdom may think fit.'

'Not to-day, surely,' cried Mrs. Lennox in alarm; 'to-morrow—'

'My orders are peremptory—the suit is pressing,' with a significant smile to Mary; 'this day—oh, ye hours!' looking at a time piece, 'this very minute, come Mary— are you ready—*cap-a-pee*?'[1]

At another time Mary would have thought only of the regrets of her venerable friend at parting with her; but now she felt only her own impatience to be gone, and she hastily quitted the room to prepare for her departure.

On returning to it, Colonel Lennox advanced to meet

her, evidently desirous of saying something, yet labouring under great embarrassment.

'Were it not too selfish and presumptuous,' said he, while his heightened colour spoke his confusion, 'I would venture to express a hope that your absence will not be very long from my poor mother.'

Mary pretended to be very busy collecting her work, drawings, &c. which lay scattered about, and merely bent her head in acknowledgement. Colonel Lennox proceeded—

'I am aware of the sacrifice it must be to such as Miss Douglas, to devote her time and talents to the comforting of the blind and desolate; and I cannot express—she cannot conceive—the gratitude—the respect—the admiration, with which my heart is filled at such proofs of noble disinterested benevolence on her part.'

Had Mary raised her eyes to those that vainly sought to meet hers, she would there have read all, and more than had been expressed; but she could only think, 'he has been entreated to love!' and at that humiliating idea, she bent her head still lower to hide the colour that dyed her cheek to an almost painful degree, while a sense of suffocation at her throat prevented her disclaiming, as she wished to do, the merit of any sacrifice. Some sketches of Lochmarlie lay upon a table, at which she had been drawing the day before; they had ever been precious in her sight till now; but they only excited feelings of mortification, as she recollected having taken them from her *porte feuille*,[1] at Mrs. Lennox's request to shew to her son.

'This was part of the parade by which I was to win him,' thought she with bitterness; and scarcely conscious of what she did, she crushed them together, and threw them into the fire. Then hastily advancing to Mrs. Lennox, she tried to bid her farewell; but, as she thought it was for the last time, tears of tenderness as well as pride stood in her eyes.

'God bless you, my dear child!' said the unsuspecting Mrs. Lennox, as she held her in her arms. 'And God *will* bless you in his way—though his ways are not as our ways. I cannot urge you to return to this dreary abode. But oh, Mary! think sometimes in your gaiety, that when you do come, you bring gladness to a mournful heart, and lighten eyes that never see the sun!'

Mary, too much affected to reply, could only wring the hand of her venerable friend, as she tore herself from her embrace, and followed Lady Emily to the carriage. For some time they proceeded in silence. Mary dreaded to encounter her cousin's eyes, which she was aware were fixed upon her with more than their usual scrutiny. She therefore kept hers steadily employed in surveying the well-known objects the road presented. At length her Ladyship began in a grave tone.

'You appear to have had very stormy weather at Rose Hall?'

'Very much so,' replied Mary, without knowing very well what she said.

'And we have had nothing but calms and sun-shine at Beech Park. Is not that strange?'

'Very singular indeed.'

'I left the barometer very high—not quite at *settled calm*—that would be too much; but I find it very low indeed—absolutely below nothing.'

Mary now did look up in some surprise; but she hastily withdrew from the intolerable expression of her cousin's eyes.

'Dear Lady Emily!' cried she, in a deprecating tone.

'Well—what more? You can't suppose I'm to put up with hearing my own name; I've heard that fifty times to-day already from Lady Juliana's parrot—come, your face speaks volumes. I read a declaration of love in the colour of your cheeks—a refusal in the height of your nose—remorse in the twinkling of your eye—and a sort of general agitation in the quiver of your lip—and the *déréglement* of your hair. Now for your pulse—a *leetle* hasty, as Dr. Redgill would say; but let your tongue declare the rest.'

Mary would fain have concealed the cause of her distress from every human being, as she felt as if degraded still lower by repeating it to another; and she remained silent, struggling with her emotions.

''Pon my honour, Mary, you really do use great liberties with my patience and good nature. I appeal to yourself whether I might not just as well have been reading one of Tully's[1] orations to a mule all this while. Come, you must really make haste to tell your tale, for I am dying to disclose mine. Or shall I begin? No—that would be inverting the order of nature or custom, which is the same thing—beginning with the farce and ending with the tragedy—so *commencez au commencement, m'amie*.'

Thus urged, Mary at length, and with much hesitation, related to her cousin the humiliation she had experienced. 'And after all,' said she, as she ended, 'I am afraid I behaved very like a fool—and yet what could I do? In my situation, what would you have done?'

'Done! why, I should have taken the old woman by the shoulders, and cried Boh! in her ear. And so this is the mighty matter! You happen to overhear Mrs. Lennox, good old soul! recommending you as a wife to her son—What could be more natural? except his refusing to fall head and ears in love before he had time to pull his boots off. And then to have a wife recommended to him! and all your perfections set forth, as if you had been a laundry maid: an early riser, neat worker, regular attention upon church! Ugh!—I must say, I think his conduct quite meritorious. I could almost find in my heart to fall in love with him myself, were it for no other reason than because he is not such a Tommy Goodchild[2] as to be in love at his mamma's bidding—that is, loving his mother as he does—for I see he could cut off a hand, or pluck out an eye, to please her, though he can't or won't give her his heart and soul to dispose of as she thinks proper.'

'You quite misunderstand me,' said Mary, with increasing vexation. 'I did not mean to say any thing against Colonel Lennox. I did not wish—I never once thought whether he liked me or not.'

'That says very little for you: You must have a very bad taste if you care more for the mother's liking than the son's. Then, what vexes you so much? Is it at having made the discovery, that your good old friend is a—a—I beg your pardon—a bit of a goose? Well, never mind—since you don't care for the man, there's no mischief done. You have only to change the *dramatis personæ*. Fancy that you overheard me recommending you to Dr. Redgill for your skill in cookery—you'd only have laughed at that—so why should you weep at t'other. However, one thing I must tell you, whether it adds to your grief or not, I did remark that Charles Lennox looked very lover-like towards you; and, indeed, this sentimental passion he has put you in, becomes you excessively. I really never saw you look so handsome before—it has given an energy and *esprit* to your countenance, which is the only thing it wants. You are very much obliged to him, were it only for having kindled such a fire in your eyes, and raised such a carnation in your cheek. It would have been long before good *larmoyante* Mrs. Lennox would have done as much for you. I shouldn't wonder were he to fall in love with you after all.'

Lady Emily little thought how near she was to the truth when she talked in this random way. Colonel Lennox saw the wound he had innocently inflicted on Mary's feelings, and a warmer sentiment than any he had hitherto experienced had sprung up in his heart. Formerly, he had merely looked upon her as an amiable

sweet-tempered girl; but when he saw her roused to a
sense of her own dignity, and marked the struggle
betwixt tender affection and offended delicacy, he formed
a higher estimate of her character, and a spark was kindled that wanted but opportunity to blaze into a flame,
pure and bright as the shrine on which it burned. Such
is the waywardness and caprice of even the best affections of the human breast.

CHAPTER VI

—'C'est à moi de *choisir* mon gendre;
Toi, tel qu'il est, c'est à toi de le prendre;
De vous aimer, si vous pouvez tous deux,
Et d'obéir à tout ce que je veux.'

L'Enfant Prodigue.[1]

'AND NOW,' SAID Lady Emily, 'that I have listened to
your story, which after all is really a very poor affair, do
you listen to mine. The heroine in both is the same, but
the hero differs by some degrees. Know, then, as the
ladies in novels say, that the day which saw you depart
from Beech Park was the day destined to decide your
fate, and dash your hopes, if ever you had any, of becoming Duchess of Altamont. The Duke arrived, I know, for
the express purpose of being enamoured of you; but,
alas! you were not. And there was Adelaide so sweet—so
gracious—so beautiful—the poor gull was caught, and is
now, I really believe, as much in love as it is in the nature
of a stupid man to be. I must own she has played her part
admirably, and has made more use of her time than I,
with all my rapidity, could have thought possible. In fact,

the Duke is now all but her declared lover, and that merely stands upon a point of punctilio.'

'But Lord Lindore!' exclaimed Mary, in astonishment.

'Why, that part of the story is what I don't quite comprehend. Sometimes I think it is a struggle with Adelaide. Lindore, poor, handsome, captivating, on one hand; his Grace, rich, stupid, magnificent, on the other. As for Lindore, he seems to stand quite aloof. Formerly, you know, he never used to stir from her side, or notice any one else. Now he scarcely notices her, at least, in presence of the Duke. Sometimes he affects to look unhappy, but I believe it is mere affectation. I doubt if he ever thought seriously of Adelaide, or indeed any body else, that he could have in a straight forward Ally Croker[1] sort of a way—but something too much of this. While all this has been going on in one corner, there comes regularly every day Mr. William Downe Wright, looking very much as if he had lost his shoe-string, or pocket handkerchief, and had come there to look for it. I had some suspicion of the nature of the loss, but was hopeful he would have the sense to keep it to himself. No such thing: he yesterday stumbled upon Lady Juliana all alone, and, in the weakest of his weak moments, informed her that the loss he had sustained was no less than the loss of that precious jewel his heart;[2] and that the object of his search was no other than that of Miss Mary Douglas to replace it! He even carried his *bêtise*[3] so far as to request her permission, or her influence, or, in short, something that her Ladyship never was asked for by any mortal in their senses before to aid him in his pursuit. You know how it delights her to be dressed in a little brief authority; so you may conceive her transports at seeing the sceptre of power thus placed in her hands. In the heat of her pride, she makes the matter known to the whole household. Redgills, cooks, stable-boys, scullions, all are quite *au fait* to your marriage with Mr. Downe Wright; so I hope you'll allow that it was about time you should be made acquainted with it yourself. But why so pale and frightened-looking?'[1]

Poor Mary was, indeed, shocked at her cousin's intelligence. With the highest feelings of filial reverence, she found herself perpetually called upon, either to sacrifice her own principles, or to act in direct opposition to her mother's will; and, upon this occasion, she saw nothing but endless altercation awaiting her: for her heart revolted from the indelicacy of such measures, and she could not for a moment brook the idea of being *bestowed* in marriage. But she had little time for reflection. They were now at Beech Park; and, as she alighted, a servant informed her, Lady Juliana wished to see her in her dressing room immediately. Thither she repaired with a beating heart and agitated step. She was received with greater kindness than she had ever yet experienced from her mother.

'Come in, my dear,' cried she, as she extended two fingers to her, and slightly touched her cheek. 'You look very well this morning—much better than usual. Your complexion is much improved. At the same time, you must be sensible how few girls are married merely for their looks—that is, married well—unless, to be sure, their beauty is something *à merveilleuse*—such as your sister's for instance. I assure you, it is an extraordinary piece of good fortune in a merely pretty girl to make what is vulgarly called a good match. I know, at least, twenty really nice young women at this moment who cannot get themselves established.'

Mary was silent; and her mother, delighted at her own good sense, and judicious observations, went on—

'That being the case, you may judge how very comfortable I must feel at having managed to procure for you a most excessive good establishment—just the very thing I have long wished, as I have felt quite at a loss about you of late, my dear. When your sister marries, I shall, of course, reside with her; and, as I consider your *liaison* with those Scotch people as completely at an end, I have really been quite wretched as to what was to become of you. I can't tell you, therefore, how excessively relieved I was when Mr. Downe Wright yesterday asked my permission to address you. Of course, I could not hesitate an instant; so you will meet him at dinner as your accepted. By the bye, your hair is rather blown. I shall send Fanchon to dress it for you. You have really got very pretty hair; I wonder I never remarked it before. Oh! and Mrs. Downe Wright is to wait upon me to-morrow, I think; and then, I believe, we must return the visit. There is a sort of etiquette, you know, in all these matters: that is the most unpleasant part of it; but when that is over, you will have nothing to think of but order-ing your things.'

For a few minutes, Mary was too much confounded by her mother's rapidity to reply. She had expected to be urged to accept of Mr. Downe Wright; but to be told that was actually done for her was more than she was prepared for. At length she found voice to say, that Mr. Downe Wright was almost a stranger to her, and she must therefore be excused from receiving his addresses at present.

'How excessively childish!' exclaimed Lady Juliana, angrily. 'I won't hear of any thing so perfectly foolish. You know (or, at any rate, I do,) all that is necessary to know. I know that he is a man of family and fortune, heir to a title, uncommonly handsome, and remarkably sensible and well-informed. I can't conceive what more you would wish to know!'

'I would wish to know something of his character—his principles—his habits—temper, talents—in short, all those things on which my happiness would depend.'

'Character and principles!—one would suppose you

were talking of your footman! Mr. Downe Wright's character is perfectly good. I never heard any thing against it. As to what you call his principles, I must profess my ignorance. I really can't tell whether he is a Methodist; but I know he is a gentleman—has a large fortune—is very good-looking—and is not at all dissipated, I believe. In short, you are most excessively fortunate in meeting with such a man.'

'But I have not the slightest partiality for him,' said Mary, colouring. 'It cannot be expected that I should, when I have not been half a dozen times in his company. I must be allowed some time before I can consent even to consider—'

'I don't mean that you are to marry to-morrow. It may probably be six weeks, or two months, before every thing can be arranged.'

Mary saw she must speak boldly.

'But I must be allowed much longer time before I can consider myself as sufficiently acquainted with Mr. Downe Wright, to think of him at all in that light. And even then—he may be very amiable, and yet'—hesitating—'I may not be able to love him as I ought.'

'Love!' exclaimed Lady Juliana, her eyes sparkling with anger; 'I desire I may never hear that word again from any daughter of mine. I am determined I shall have no disgraceful love-marriages in the family. No well educated young woman ever thinks of such a thing now, and I won't hear a syllable on the subject.'

'I shall never marry any body, I am sure, that you disapprove of,' said Mary, timidly.

'No; I shall take care of that. I consider it the duty of parents to establish their children properly in the world, without any regard to their ideas on the subject. I think, I must be rather a better judge of the matter than you can possibly be, and I shall therefore make a point of your forming what I consider a proper alliance. Your sister, I know, won't hesitate to sacrifice her own affections to please me. She was most excessively attached to Lord Lindore—every body knew that; but she is convinced of the propriety of preferring the Duke of Altamont, and won't hesitate in sacrificing her own feelings to mine. But, indeed, she has ever been all that I could wish—so perfectly beautiful, and, at the same time, so excessively affectionate and obedient. She approves entirely of your marriage with Mr. Downe Wright, as, indeed, all your friends do. I don't include *your* friend Lady Emily in that number. I look upon her as a most improper companion for you; and the sooner you are separated from her the better. So now, good bye for the present: You have only to behave as other young ladies do upon those occasions, which, by the bye, is generally to give as much trouble to their friends as they possibly can.'

There are some people who, furious themselves at opposition, cannot understand the possibility of others being equally firm and decided in a gentle manner. Lady Juliana was one of those who always expect to carry their point by a raised voice and sparkling eyes; and it was with difficulty Mary, with her timid air, and gentle accents, could convince her that she was determined to judge for herself in a matter in which her happiness was so deeply involved. When at last brought to comprehend it, her Ladyship's indignation knew no bounds: and Mary was accused in the same breath with having formed some low connection in Scotland, and of seeking to supplant her sister, by aspiring to the Duke of Altamont. And, at length, the conference ended pretty much where it began—Lady Juliana resolved that her daughter should marry to please her, and her daughter equally resolved not to be driven into an engagement from which her heart recoiled.

CHAPTER VII

Qu'on vante en lui la foi, l'honneur, la probité;
Qu'on prise sa candeur et sa civilité;
Qu'il soit doux, complaisant, officieux, sincère:
On le veut, j'y souscris, et suis prêt à me taire.'
Boileau.[1]

WHEN MARY ENTERED the drawing-room, she found
herself, without knowing how, by the side of Mr. Downe
Wright. At dinner it was the same; and, in short, it
seemed an understood thing, that they were to be constantly together.

There was something so gentle and unassuming in his
manner, that, almost provoked as she was by the folly of
his proceedings, she found it impossible to resent it by
her behaviour towards him; and, indeed, without being
guilty of actual rudeness, of which she was incapable, it
would not have been easy to have made him comprehend
the nature of her sentiments. He appeared perfectly
satisfied with the toleration he met with; and, compared
to Adelaide's disdainful glances, and Lady Emily's biting
sarcasms, Mary's gentleness and civility might well be
mistaken for encouragement. But even under the exhilarating influence of hope and high spirits, his conversation was so insipid and common-place, that Mary found
it a relief to turn even to Dr. Redgill. It was evident the
Doctor was aware of what was going on, for he regarded
her with that increased respect due to the future mistress
of a splendid establishment. Between the courses he made
some complimentary allusions to Highland mutton and
red deer; and he even carried his attentions so far as to
whisper, at the very first mouthful, that *les côtellettes de
saumon* were superb, when he had never been known to
commend any thing to another, until he had fully dis-

cussed it himself. On the opposite side of the table sat
Adelaide and the Duke of Altamont, the latter looking
still more heavy and inanimate than ever. The operation
of eating over, he seemed unable to keep himself awake,
and every now and then yielded to a gentle slumber,
from which, however, he was instantly recalled at the
sound of Adelaide's voice, when he exclaimed, 'Ah!
charming—very charming, ah!'—Lady Emily looked
from them as she hummed some part of Dryden's Ode—

> 'Aloft in awful state
> The godlike hero sate, &c.
> The lovely Thais by his side,
> Look'd like a blooming eastern bride.'[1]

Then, as his Grace closed his eyes, and his head sunk on
his shoulder—

> 'With ravish'd ears
> The monarch hears,
> Assumes the god,
> Affects to nod.'[1]

Lady Juliana, who would have been highly incensed, had
she suspected the application of the words, was so unconscious of it, as to join occasionally in singing them, to
Mary's great confusion, and Adelaide's manifest displeasure.

When they returned to the drawing-room, 'Heavens!
Adelaide,' exclaimed her cousin, in an affected manner,
'what are you made of? Semele[3] herself was but a mere
cinder-wench to you! How can you stand such a Jupiter
—and not scorched! not even singed, I protest!' pretending to examine her all over. 'I vow, I trembled at your
temerity—your familiarity with the imperial nod was

fearful. I every instant expected to see you turned into a live coal.'

'I did burn,' said Adelaide, 'with shame, to see the mistress of a house forget what was due to her father's guests.'

'There's a slap on the cheek for me! Mercy! how it burns!—No, I did not forget what was due to my father's guests; on the contrary, I consider it due to them to save them, if I can, from the snares that I see set for them. I have told you that I abhor all traps, whether for the poor simple mouse that comes to steal its bit of cheese, or for the dull elderly gentleman who falls asleep with a star on his breast.'

'This is one of the many kind and polite allusions for which I am indebted to your Ladyship,' said Adelaide, haughtily; 'but I trust the day will come when I shall be able to discharge what I owe you.'

And she quitted the room, followed by Lady Juliana, who could only make out that Lady Emily had been insolent, and that Adelaide was offended. A pause followed.

'I see you think I am in the wrong, Mary; I can read that in the little reproachful glance you gave me just now. Well, perhaps I am; but I own it chafes my spirit to sit and look on such a scene of iniquity—Yes, iniquity I call it, for a woman to be in love with one man, and at the same time laying snares for another. You may think, perhaps, that Adelaide has no heart to love any thing; but she has a heart, such as it is, though it is much too fine for every day use, and therefore it is kept locked up in a marble casket, quite out of reach of you or me. But I'm mistaken if Frederick has not made himself master of it! Not that I should blame her for that, if she would be honestly and downrightly in love with him. But how despicable to see her, with her affections placed upon one man, at the same time lavishing all her attentions on another—and that other, if he had been plain John Altamont, Esq. she would not have been commonly civil to! And, *apropos* of civility—I must tell you, if you mean to refuse your hero, you were too civil by half to him. I observed you at dinner, you sat perfectly straight, and answered every thing he said to you.'

'What could I do?' asked Mary, in some surprise.

'I'll tell you what I would have done, and have thought the most honourable mode of proceeding; I should have turned my back upon him, and have merely thrown him a monosyllable now and then over my shoulder.'

'I could not be less than civil to him, and I am sure I was not more.'

'Civility is too much for a man one means to refuse. You'll never get rid of a stupid man by civility. Whenever I had any reason to apprehend a lover, I thought it my duty to turn short upon him and give him a snarl at the outset, which rid me of him at once. But I really begin to think I manage these matters better than any body else—"Where I love, I profess it: where I hate, in every circumstance I dare proclaim it." '[1]

Mary tried to defend her sister, in the first place; but though her charity would not allow her to censure, her conscience whispered there was much to condemn; and she was relieved from what she felt a difficult task, when the gentlemen began to drop in.

In spite of all her manœuvres, Mr. Downe Wright contrived to be next her, and whenever she changed her seat, she was sure of his following her. She had also the mortification of overhearing Lady Juliana tell the Duke, that Mr. Downe Wright was the accepted lover of her youngest daughter—that he was a man of large fortune—and heir to his uncle, Lord Glenallan!

'Ah! a nephew of my Lord Glenallan's! Indeed—a pretty young man—like the family!—Poor Lord Glenallan! I knew him very well: He has had the palsy since then, poor man—ah!'

The following day Mary was compelled to receive Mrs. Downe Wright's visit; but she was scarcely conscious of what passed, for Colonel Lennox arrived at the same time; and it was equally evident that his visit was also intended for her. She felt that she ought to appear unconcerned in his presence, and she tried to be so; but still the painful idea would recur, that he had been solicited to love her, and, unskilled in the arts of even innocent deception, she could only try to hide the agitation under the coldness of her manner.

'Come, Mary,' cried Lady Emily, as if in answer to something Colonel Lennox had addressed to her in a low voice, 'do you remember the promise I made Colonel Lennox, and which it rests with you to perform?'

'I never consider myself bound to perform the promises of others,' replied Mary, gravely.

'In some cases that may be a prudent resolution, but, in the present, it is surely an unfriendly one,' said Colonel Lennox.

'A most inhuman one!' cried Lady Emily, 'since you and I, it seems, cannot commence our friendship without something sentimental to set us agoing. It rests with you, Mary, to be the founder of our friendship; and if you manage the matter well, that is, sing in your best manner, we shall perhaps make it a triple alliance, and admit you as third.'

'As every man is said to be the artificer of his own fortune,[1] so every one, I think, had best be the artificer of their own friendship,' said Mary, trying to smile, as she pulled her embroidery frame towards her, and began to work.

'Neither can be the worse of a good friend to help them on,' observed Mrs. Downe Wright.

'But both may be materially injured by an injudicious

one,' said Colonel Lennox; 'and although, on this occasion, I am the greatest sufferer by it, I must acknowledge the truth of Miss Douglas' observation: Friendship and love, I believe, will always be found to thrive best when left to themselves.'

'And so ends my novel, elegant, and original plan, for striking up a sudden friendship,' cried Lady Emily. 'Pray, Mr. Downe Wright, can you suggest any thing better for the purpose than an old song?'

Mr. Downe Wright, who was not at all given to suggesting, looked a little embarrassed.

'Pull the bell, William, for the carriage,' said his mother; 'we must now be moving.' And with a general obeisance to the company, and a significant pressure of the hand to Mary, she withdrew her son from his dilemma. Although a shrewd, penetrating woman, she did not possess that tact and delicacy necessary to comprehend the finer feelings of a mind superior to her own; and in Mary's averted looks and constrained manner, she saw nothing but what she thought quite proper and natural in her situation. 'As for Lady Emily,' she observed, 'there would be news of her and that fine dashing looking Colonel yet, and Miss Adelaide would, perhaps, come down a pin before long.'

Soon after Colonel Lennox took his leave, in spite of Lady Emily's pressing invitation for him to spend the day there, and meet her brother, who had been absent for some days, but was now expected home. He promised to return again soon, and departed.

'How prodigiously handsome Colonel Lennox looked to-day,' said she, addressing Mary; 'and how perfectly unconscious, at least indifferent, he seems about it. It is quite refreshing to see a handsome man that is neither a fool nor a coxcomb.'

'Handsome! no, I don't think he is very handsome,' said Lady Juliana: 'Rather dark, don't you think, my love?' turning to Adelaide, who sat apart at a table writing, and had scarcely deigned to lift her head all the time.

'Who do you mean? The man who has just gone out? Is his name Lennox?—Yes, he is rather handsome.'

'I believe you are right; he certainly is good looking, but in a peculiar style. I don't quite like the expression of his eye, and he wants that air *distingué*, which, indeed, belongs exclusively to persons of birth.'

'He has perfectly the air of a man of fashion,' said Adelaide, in a decided tone, as if ashamed to agree with her mother. 'Perhaps *un peu militaire*, but nothing at all professional.'

'Lennox!—it is a Scotch name,' observed Lady Juliana contemptuously.

'And, to cut the matter short,' said Lady Emily, as she was quitting the room, 'the man who has just gone out is Colonel Lennox, and not the Duke of Altamont.'

After a few more awkward, indefinite sorts of visits, in which Mary found it impossible to come to an explanation, she was relieved, for the present, from the assiduities of her lover. Lady Juliana received a note from Mrs. Downe Wright, apologizing for what she termed her son's unfortunate absence at such a critical time; but he had received accounts of the alarming illness of his uncle Lord Glenallan, and had, in consequence, set off instantly for Scotland, where she was preparing to follow; concluding with particular regards to Miss Mary—hopes of being soon able to resume their pleasant footing in the family, &c. &c.

'How excessively well arranged it will be that old man's dying at this time,' said her Ladyship, as she tossed the note to her daughter; 'Lord Glenallan will sound so much better than Mr. Downe Wright. The name I have always considered as the only objectionable part: You are really most prodigiously fortunate.'

Mary was now aware of the folly of talking reason to her mother, and remained silent; thankful for the present peace this event would ensure her, and almost tempted to wish that Lord Glenallan's doom might not speedily be decided.

CHAPTER VIII

'It seems it is as proper to our age,
To cast beyond ourselves in our opinions,
As it is common for the younger sort
To lack discretion.'

Hamlet.[1]

LORD LINDORE AND Colonel Lennox had been boyish acquaintances, and a sort of superficial intimacy was soon established between them, which served as the ostensible cause of his frequent visits at Beech Park. But to Mary, who was more alive to the difference of their characters and sentiments than any other member of the family, this appeared very improbable, and she could not help suspecting, that love for the sister, rather than friendship for the brother, was the real motive by which he was actuated. In a half jesting manner she mentioned her suspicions to Lady Emily, who treated the idea with her usual ridicule.

'I really could not have supposed you so extremely missy-ish, Mary,' said she, 'as to imagine, that because two people like each other's society, and talk, and laugh together a little more than usual, that they must needs be in love! I believe Charles Lennox loves me much the same as he did eleven years ago, when I was a little wretch, that used to pull his hair, and spoil his watch. And as for me, you know that I consider myself quite as an old woman—at least as a married one; and he is perfectly *au fait* to my engagement with Edward. I have even shewn him his picture, and some of his letters.'

Mary looked incredulous.

'You may think as you please, but I tell you it is so. In my situation, I should scorn to have Colonel Lennox, or any body else, in love with me. As to his liking to talk to me, pray, who else can he talk to? Adelaide would sometimes *condescend* indeed; but he won't be condescended to, that's clear, not even by a Duchess. With what mock humility he meets her airs! how I adore him for it! Then you are such a pillar of ice!—so shy and unsociable when he is present!—and, by the bye, if I did not despise recrimination as the *pis aller* of all conscious Misses, I would say you are much more the object of his *attention*, at least, than I am. Several times I have caught him looking very earnestly at you, when, by the laws of good breeding, his eyes ought to have been fixed exclusively upon me; and—'

'Pshaw!' interrupted Mary, colouring, 'that is mere absence—nothing to the purpose—or perhaps,' forcing a smile, 'he may be *trying* to love me!'

Mary thought of her poor old friend, as she said this, with bitterness of heart. It was long since she had seen her; and when she had last inquired for her, her son had said he did not think her well, with a look Mary could not misunderstand. She had heard him make an appointment with Lord Lindore for the following day, and she took the opportunity of his certain absence to visit his mother. Mrs. Lennox, indeed, looked ill, and seemed more than usually depressed. She welcomed Mary with her usual tenderness, but even her presence seemed to fail of inspiring her with gladness.

Mary found she was totally unsuspicious of the cause of her estrangement, and imputed it to a very different one.

'You have been a great stranger, my dear!' said she, as she affectionately embraced her; 'but at such a time I could not expect you to think of me.'

'Indeed,' answered Mary, equally unconscious of her meaning, 'I have thought much and often, very often, upon you, and wished I could have come to you; but—' she stopped for she could not tell the truth, and would not utter a falsehood.

'I understand it all,' said Mrs. Lennox, with a sigh. 'Well—well—God's will be done!' Then trying to be more cheerful, 'Had you come a little sooner, you would have met Charles. He is just gone out with Lord Lindore. He was unwilling to leave me, as he always is, and when he does, I believe it is as much to please me as himself. Ah! Mary, I once hoped that I might have lived to see you the happy wife of the best of sons. I may speak out now, since that is all over. God has willed otherwise, and may you be rewarded in the choice you have made!'

Mary was struck with consternation to find that her supposed engagement with Mr. Downe Wright, had spread even to Rose Hall; and in the greatest confusion she attempted to deny it. But after the acknowledgment she had just heard, she acquitted herself awkwardly; for she felt as if an open explanation would only serve to revive hopes that never could be realized, and subject Colonel Lennox and herself to future perplexities. Nothing but the whole truth would have sufficed to undeceive Mrs. Lennox, for she had had the intelligence of Mary's engagement from Mrs. Downe Wright herself, who, for better security of what she already considered her son's property, had taken care to spread the report of his being the accepted lover before she left the country. Mary felt all the unpleasantness of her situation. Although detesting deceit and artifice of every kind, her confused and stammering denials seemed rather to corroborate the fact; but she felt that she could not declare her resolution of never bestowing her hand upon Mr. Downe Wright, without seeming at the same time, to court the addresses of Colonel Lennox. Then how painful—how unjust to herself, as well as cruel to him, to have it for an instant believed, that she was the betrothed of one whose wife she was resolved she never would be!

In short, poor Mary's mind was a complete chaos; and, for the first time in her life, she found it impossible to determine which was the right course for her to pursue. Even in the midst of her distress, however, she could not help smiling at the *naïveté* of the good old lady's remarks.

'He is a handsome young man, I hear,' said she, still in allusion to Mr. Downe Wright: 'has a fine fortune, and as easy temper. All these things help people's happiness, though they cannot make it; and his choice of you, my dear Mary, shews that he has some sense.'

'What an eulogium!' said Mary, laughing and blushing. 'Were he really to me what you suppose, I must be highly flattered; but I must again assure you, it is not using Mr. Downe Wright well to talk of him as any thing to me. My mother, indeed——'

'Ah! Mary, my dear, let me advise you to beware of being led, even by a mother, in such a matter as this. God forbid that I should ever recommend disobedience towards a parent's will; but I fear you have yielded too much to yours. I said, indeed, when I heard it, that I feared undue influence had been used; for that[1] I could not think William Downe Wright would ever have been the choice of your heart. Surely parents have much to answer for, who mislead their children in such an awful step as marriage!'

This was the severest censure Mary had ever heard drop from Mrs. Lennox's lips; and she could not but marvel at the self-delusion that led her thus to condemn in another the very error she had committed herself; but under such different circumstances, that she would not easily have admitted it to be the same. She sought for the happiness of her son, while Lady Juliana, she was convinced, wished only her own aggrandizement.

'Yes, indeed,' said Mary, in answer to her friend's observation, 'parents ought, if possible, to avoid even forming wishes for their children. Hearts are wayward things, even the best of them.' Then more seriously she added, 'and dear Mrs. Lennox, do not either blame my mother nor pity me; for be assured, with my heart only will I give my hand; or rather, I should say, with my hand only will I give my heart: And now good bye,' cried she, starting up and hurrying away, as she heard Colonel Lennox's voice in the hall.

She met him on the stair, and would have passed on with a slight remark, but he turned with her, and finding she had dismissed the carriage, intending to walk home, he requested permission to attend her. Mary declined; but, snatching up his hat, and whistling his dogs, he set out with her in spite of her remonstrances to the contrary.

'If you persist in refusing my attendance,' said he, 'you will inflict an incurable wound upon my vanity. I shall suspect you are ashamed of being seen in such company. To be sure, myself, with my shabby jacket, and my spattered dogs, do form rather a ruffian-like escort; and I should not have dared to have offered my services to a fine lady—but you are not a fine lady, I know;' and he gently drew her arm within his as they began to ascend a hill.

This was the first time Mary had found herself alone with Colonel Lennox, since that fatal day which seemed to have divided them for ever. At first she felt uneasy and embarrassed, but there was so much good sense and good feeling in the tone of his conversation; it was so far removed either from pedantry or frivolity, that all disagreeable ideas soon gave way to the pleasure she had in conversing with one whose turn of mind seemed so similar to her own; and it was not till she had parted from him at the gate of Beech Park, she had time to wonder, how she could possibly have walked two miles *tête-à-tête* with a man whom she had heard solicited to love her!

From that day Colonel Lennox's visits insensibly increased in length and number; but Lady Emily seemed to appropriate them entirely to herself; and certainly all the flow of his conversation, the brilliancy of his wit, were directed to her; but Mary could not but be conscious that his looks were much oftener rivetted on herself, and if his attentions were not such as to attract general observation, they were such as she could not fail of perceiving and being unconsciously gratified by.

'How I admire Charles Lennox's manner to you, Mary,' said her cousin; 'after the awkward dilemma you were both in, it was no easy matter to know how to proceed; a vulgar-minded man would either have oppressed you with his attentions, or insulted you by his neglect, while he steers so gracefully free from either extreme; and I observe, you are the only woman upon whom he designs to bestow *les petits soins*. How I despise a man who is ever on the watch to pick up every silly Miss's fan or glove, that she thinks it pretty to drop! No— the woman he loves, whether his mother or his wife, will always be distinguished by him, were she amongst queens and empresses; not by his silly vanity or vulgar fondness, but by his marked and gentlemanlike attentions towards her. In short, the best thing you can do, is to make up your quarrel with him—take him for all in all[1]—you won't meet with such another—certainly not amongst your Highland lairds, by all that I can learn; and, by the bye, I do suspect, he is now, as you say, trying to love you; and let him—you will be very well repaid if he succeeds.'

Mary's heart swelled at the thoughts of submitting to

such an indignity, especially as she was beginning to feel
conscious that Colonel Lennox was not quite the object
of indifference to her that he ought to be; but her cousin's
remarks only served to render her more distant and
reserved to him than ever.

CHAPTER IX

'What dangers ought'st thou not to dread,
When Love, that's blind, is by blind Fortune led?'
                                        Cowley.[1]

AT LENGTH THE long-looked for day arrived. The Duke
of Altamont's proposals were made in due form, and in
due form accepted. Lady Juliana seemed now touching
the pinnacle of earthly joy; for, next to being greatly
married herself, her happiness centred in seeing her
daughter at the head of a splendid establishment. Again
visions of bliss hovered around her, and 'Peers, and
Dukes, and all their sweeping train,'[2] swam before her
eyes, as she anticipated the brilliant results to herself
from so noble an alliance; for self was still, as it had ever
been, her ruling star, and her affection for her daughter
was the mere result of vanity and ambition.

The ensuing weeks were passed in all the bustle of
preparations necessarily attendant on the nuptials of the
great. Every morning brought from Town, dresses, jewels,
patterns, and packages of all descriptions. Lady Juliana
was in ecstasies, even though it was but happiness in the
second person. Mary watched her sister's looks with the
most painful solicitude; for from her lips she knew she
never would learn the sentiments of her heart. But
Adelaide was aware she had a part to act, and she went
through it with an ease and self-possession that seemed

to defy all scrutiny. Once or twice, indeed, her deepening
colour and darkening brow, betrayed the feelings of her
heart, as the Duke of Altamont and Lord Lindore were
brought into comparison; and Mary shuddered to think
that her sister was even now ashamed of the man whom
she was so soon to vow to love, honour, and obey. She
had vainly tried to lead Adelaide to the subject. Adelaide
would listen to nothing which she had reason to suppose
was addressed to herself; but either with cool contempt
took up a book, or left the room, or, with insolent
affectation, would put her hands to her head, exclaiming,
'*mes oreilles n'etoient pas faites pour les entretiens serieux.*'

All Mary's worst fears were confirmed a few days
before that fixed for the marriage. As she entered the
music-room, she was startled to find Lord Lindore and
Adelaide alone. Unwilling to suppose that her presence
would be considered as an interruption, she seated herself
at a little distance from them, and was soon engrossed
by her task, that of copying music. Adelaide, too, had the
air of being deeply intent upon some trifling employment;
and Lord Lindore, as he sat opposite to her, with his
head resting upon his hands, had the appearance of being
engaged in reading. All were silent for some time; but
as Mary happened to look up, she saw Lord Lindore's
eyes fixed earnestly upon her sister, and with a voice of
repressed feeling he repeated, '*Ah! je le sens, ma Julie! s'il
falloit renoncer à vous, il n'y auroit plus pour moi d'autre sejour
ni d'autre saison;*'[1] and throwing down the book, he
quitted the room. Adelaide, pale and agitated, rose as if
to follow him; then, recollecting herself, she rushed from
the apartment by an opposite door. Mary followed,
vainly hoping that, in this moment of excited feeling, she
might be induced to open her heart to the voice of
affection—but Adelaide was a stranger to sympathy,
and saw only the degradation of confessing the struggle
she endured in choosing betwixt love and ambition. That

her heart was Lord Lindore's, she could not conceal from herself, though she would not confess it to another; and that other, the tenderest of sisters, whose only wish was to serve her. Mary's tears and entreaties were therefore in vain, and at Adelaide's repeated desire, she at length quitted her, and returned to the room she had left.

She found Lady Emily there with a paper in her hand. 'Lend me your ears, Mary,' cried she, 'while I read these lines to you. Don't be afraid, there are no secrets in them, or at least none that you or I will be a whit the wiser for, as they are truly in a most mystic strain. I found them lying upon this table, and they are in Frederick's hand-writing, for I see he affects the *soupirant*[1] at present; and it seems there has been a sort of a sentimental farce acted between Adelaide and him. He pretends, that although distractedly in love with her, he is not so selfish as even to wish her to marry him in preference to the Duke of Altamont; and Adelaide, not to be outdone in heroics, has also made it out, that it is the height of virtue in her to espouse the Duke of Altamont, and sacrifice all the tenderest affections of her heart to duty!—Duty! yes, the duty of being a Duchess, and of living in state and splendour with the man she secretly despises, to the pleasure of renouncing both for the man she loves; and so they have parted, and here, I suppose, is Lindore's lucubrations upon it, intended as a *souvenir* for Adelaide, I presume. Now, night visions befriend me![2]

> 'The time returns when o'er my wilder'd mind,
> A thraldom came which did each sense enshroud;
> Not that I bowed in willing chain confined,
> But that a soften'd atmosphere of cloud
> Veiled every sense—conceal'd th' impending doom.
> 'Twas mystic night, and I seem'd borne along
> By pleasing dread—and in a doubtful gloom,
> Where fragrant incense and the sound of song,
> And all fair things we dream of, floated by,

Lulling my fancy like a cradled child,
Till that the dear and guileless treachery,
Made me the wretch I am—so lost, so wild—
A mingled feeling, neither joy or grief,
Dwelt in my heart—I knew not whence it came,
And—but that woe is me! 'twas passing brief,
Even at this hour I fain would feel the same!
I track'd a path of flowers—but flowers among
Were hissing serpents and drear birds of night,
That shot across and scared with boding cries;
And yet deep interest lurked in that affright,
Something endearing in those mysteries,
Which bade me still the desperate joy pursue,
Heedless of what might come—when from mine eyes
The clouds should pass, or what might then accrue.
The cloud *has* passed—the blissful power is flown,
The flowers are wither'd—wither'd all the scene.
But ah! the dear delusions I have known,
Are present still, with loved though altered mien:
I tread the self-same path in heart unchanged;
But changed now is all that path to me,
For where 'mong flowers and fountains once I ranged,
Are barren rocks and savage scenery!'

Mary felt it was in vain to attempt to win her sister's
confidence, and she was too delicate to seek to wrest her
secrets from her; she therefore took no notice of this
effusion of love and disappointment, which she concluded
it to be.

Adelaide appeared at dinner as usual. All traces of
agitation had vanished; and her manner was as cool and
collected, as if all had been peace and tranquillity at
heart. Lord Lindore's departure was slightly noticed. It
was generally understood, that he had been rejected by
his cousin; and his absence at such a time was thought
perfectly natural. The Duke merely remarking, with a
vacant simper, 'So Lord Lindore is gone—Ah! poor Lord
Lindore.'

Lady Juliana had, in a very early stage of the business, fixed in her own mind, that she, as a matter of course, would be invited to accompany her daughter upon her marriage; indeed, she had always looked upon it as a sort of triple alliance, that was to unite her as indissolubly to the fortunes of the Duke of Altamont, as though she had been his wedded wife. But the time drew near, and in spite of all her hints and manœuvres, no invitation had yet been extorted from Adelaide. The Duke had proposed to her to invite her sister, and even expressed something like a wish to that effect; for though he felt no positive pleasure in Mary's society, he was yet conscious of a void in her absence.—She was always in good humour—always gentle and polite—and, without being able to tell why, his Grace always felt more at ease with her than with any body else. But his selfish bride seemed to think that the joys of her elevation would be diminished, if shared even by her own sister, and she coldly rejected the proposal. Lady Juliana was next suggested— for the Duke had a sort of vague understanding that his safety lay in a multitude. With him, as with all stupid people, company was society, words were conversation— and all the gradations of intellect, from Sir Isaac Newton, down to Dr. Redgill, were to him unknown. But although, as with most weak people, obstinacy was his *forte*, he was here again compelled to yield to the will of his bride, as she also declined the company of her mother for the present. The disappointment was somewhat softened to Lady Juliana, by the sort of indefinite hopes that were expressed by her daughter of seeing her in town when they were fairly established; but until she had seen Altamont House, and knew its accommodations, she could fix nothing; and Lady Juliana was fain to solace herself with this dim perspective, instead of the brilliant reality her imagination had placed within her grasp. She felt, too, without comprehending, the imperfectness of all earthly felicity. As she witnessed the magnificent preparations for her daughter's marriage, it recalled the bitter remembrance of her own—and many a sigh burst from her heart as she thought, 'Such as Adelaide is, I might have been, had I been blest with such a mother, and brought up to know what was for my good!'

The die was cast[1]—Amidst pomp and magnificence, elate with pride, and sparkling with jewels, Adelaide Douglas reversed the fate of her mother; and while her affections were bestowed on another, she vowed, in the face of heaven, to belong only to the Duke of Altamont!

'Good bye, my dearest love!' said her mother, as she embraced her with transport, 'and I shall be with you very soon; and, above all things, try to secure a good opera-box for the season. I assure you it is of the greatest consequence.'

The Duchess impatiently hurried from the congratulations of her family, and throwing herself into the splendid equipage that awaited her, was soon lost to their view.

CHAPTER X

'Every white will have its black,
And every sweet its sour:'[2]

As LADY JULIANA experienced. Her daughter was Duchess of Altamont, but Grizzy Douglas had arrived in Bath!—The intelligence was communicated to Mary in a letter. It had no date, but was as follows:

'MY DEAR MARY,

'You will See from the Date of this, that we are at
last Arrived here, after a very long journey, which, you
of Course Know it is from this to our Part of the country;
at the same Time, it was uncommonly Pleasant, and we
all enjoyed it very Much, only poor Sir Sampson was so
ill that we Expected him to Expire every minute, which
would have made it Extremely unpleasant for dear Lady
Maclaughlan. He is now, I am Happy to say, greatly
Better, though still so Poorly, that I am much Afraid you
will see a very Considerable change upon him. I sincerely
hope, my dear Mary, that you will make a proper
Apology to Lady Juliana for my not going to Beech Park
(where I know I would be made most Welcome) directly
—but I am Certain she will Agree with me that it would
be Highly Improper in me to leave Lady Maclaughlan
when she is not at all Sure how long Sir Sampson may
Live; and it would Appear very Odd if I was to be out
of the way at such a time as That. But you may Assure
her, with my Kind love, and indeed all our Loves (as I
am sure None of us can ever forget the Pleasant time she
spent with us at Glenfern in my Poor brother's lifetime,
before you was Born) that I will Take the very first
Opportunity of Spending some time at Beech Park before
leaving Bath, as we Expect the Waters will set Sir
Sampson quite on his Feet again. It will be a happy
Meeting, I am certain, with Lady Juliana and all of us,
as it is Eighteen years this spring since we have Met. You
may be sure I have a great Deal to tell you and Lady
Juliana too, about all Friends at Glenfern, whom I left all
quite Well. Of course, the Report of Bella's and Betsy's
marriages Must have reached Bath by this time, as it will
be three Weeks to day since we left our part of the country;
but in case it has not reached you, Lady Maclaughlan
is of opinion that the Sooner you are made Acquainted

with it the Better, especially as there is no doubt of it.
Bella's marriage, which is in a manner fixed by this time,
I daresay, though of Course it will not take place for
some time, is to Capt. M'Nab of some Regiment, but
I'm sure I Forget which, for there are so many Regiments,
you know, it is Impossible to remember them All; but
he is quite a Hero, I know that, as he has been in Several
battles, and had Two of his front teeth Knocked out at
one of them, and was Much complimented about it; and
he Says, he is quite Certain of getting Great promotion—
at any Rate a pension for it, so there is no Fear of him.

'Betsy has, if Possible, been still More fortunate than
her Sister, although you know Bella was always reckoned the Beauty of the Family, though some People
certainly preferred Betsy's Looks too. She has made a
Complete conquest of Major M'Tavish, of the Militia,
who, Independent of his rank, which is certainly very
High, has also distinguished himself very Much, and
shewed the Greatest bravery once when there was a Very
serious Riot about the raising the Potatoes a penny a peck,
when there was no Occasion for it, in the town of
Dunoon; and it was very much talked of at the Time, as
well as Being in all the Newspapers. This gives us all the
Greatest Pleasure, as I am certain it will also Do Lady
Juliana, and you, my dear Mary. At the same time, we
Feel very much for poor Babby, and Beenie, and Becky,
as they Naturally, and indeed all of us, Expected they
would, of Course, be married first; and it is certainly a
great Trial for them to See their younger sisters married
before them. At the same Time, they are Wonderfully
supported, and Behave with Astonishing firmness; and I
Trust, my dear Mary, you will do the Same, as I have
no doubt you will All be married yet, as I am sure you
Richly deserve it when it Comes. I hope I will see you
Very soon, as Lady Maclaughlan, I am certain, will
Make you most Welcome to call. We are living in Most

elegant Lodgings—all the Furniture is quite New, and perfectly Good. I do not know the Name of the street yet, as Lady Maclaughlan, which is no wonder, is not fond of being Asked questions when she is Upon a Journey; and, indeed, makes a Point of never Answering any, which, I daresay, is the Best way. But, of Course, any body will Tell you where Sir Sampson Maclaughlan, Baronet, of Lochmarlie Castle, Perthshire,[1] N. B., lives; and, if You are at any Loss, it has a Green door, and a most Elegant Balcony. I must now bid you adieu, my dear Mary, as I Am so soon to See yourself. Sir Sampson and Lady Maclaughlan unite with Me in Best compliments to the Family at Beech Park. And, in kind love to Lady Juliana and you, I remain, My dear Mary, your most affectionate Aunt,

'GRIZZEL DOUGLAS.

'P. S. I have a long letter for you, from Mrs. Douglas, which is in my Trunk, that is Coming by the Perth Carrier, and unless he is stopped by the Snow, I Expect he will be here in ten days.'

With the idea of Grizzy was associated in Mary's mind all the dear familiar objects of her happiest days, and her eyes sparkled with delight at the thoughts of again beholding her.

'Oh! when may I go to Bath to dear aunt Grizzy?' exclaimed she, as she finished the letter. Lady Juliana looked petrified. Then recollecting that this was the first intimation her mother had received of such an event being even in contemplation, she made haste to exculpate her aunt at her own expense, by informing her of the truth. But nothing could be more unpalatable than the truth; and poor Mary's short-lived joy was soon turned into the bitterest sorrow at the reproaches that were showered upon her by the incensed Lady Juliana. But for her these people never would have thought of coming to Bath; or if they did, she should have had no connection with them. She had been most excessively ill-used by Mr. Douglas' family, and had long since resolved to have no farther intercourse with them—they were nothing to her, &c. &c.—The whole concluding with a positive prohibition against Mary's taking any notice of her aunt.

'From all that has been said, Mary,' said Lady Emily, gravely, 'there can be no doubt but that you are the origin of Lady Juliana's unfortunate connection with the family of Douglas.'

'Undoubtedly,' said her Ladyship.

'But for you, it appears that she would not have known—certainly never would have acknowledged— that her husband had an aunt?'

'Certainly not,' said Lady Juliana warmly.

'It is a most admirable plan,' continued Lady Emily, in the same manner, 'and I shall certainly adopt it. When I have children I am determined they shall be answerable for my making a foolish marriage; and it shall be their fault if my husband has a mother.—*En attendant*, I am determined to patronize Edward's relations to the last degree; and therefore, unless Mary is permitted to visit her aunt as often as she pleases, I shall make a point of bringing the dear aunt Grizzy here. Yes,' (putting her hand to the bell,) 'I shall order my carriage this instant, and set off. To-morrow, you know, we give a grand dinner in honour of Adelaide's marriage. Aunt Grizzy shall be queen of the feast.'

Lady Juliana was almost suffocated with passion; but she knew her niece too well to doubt her putting her threat in execution, and there was distraction in the idea of the vulgar obscure Grizzy Douglas being presented to a fashionable party as her aunt. After a violent altercation, in which Mary took no part, an ungracious permission was at length extorted, which Mary eagerly availed herself of; and, charged with kind messages from Lady Emily, set off in quest of aunt Grizzy, and the green door.

After much trouble, and many unsuccessful attacks upon green doors and balconies, she was going to give up the search in despair, when her eye was attracted by the figure of aunt Grizzy herself at full length, stationed at a window, in an old-fashioned riding-habit, and spectacles. The carriage was stopped; and in an instant Mary was in the arms of her aunt, all agitation, as Lochmarlie flashed on her fancy, at again hearing its native accents uttered by the voice familiar to her from infancy. Yet the truth must be owned. Mary's taste was somewhat startled, even while her heart warmed at the sight of the good old aunt. Association and affection still retained their magic influence over her; but absence had dispelled the blest illusions of habitual intercourse; and, for the first time, she beheld her aunt freed from its softening spell. Still her heart clung to her as to one known and loved from infancy; and she soon rose superior to the weakness she felt was besetting her, in the slight sensation of shame as she contrasted her awkward manner and uncouth accent with the graceful refinement of those with whom she associated.

Far different were the sensations with which the good spinster regarded her niece. She could not often enough declare her admiration of the improvements that had taken place. Mary was grown taller, and stouter, and fairer, and fatter, and her back was a straight as an arrow, and her carriage would even surprise Miss Macgowk herself. It was quite astonishing to see her, for she had always understood Scotland was the place for beauty, and that nobody ever came to any thing in England. Even Sir Sampson and Lady Maclaughlan were forgot as she stood rivetted in admiration, and Mary was the first to recall her recollection to them. Sir

Sampson, indeed, might well have been overlooked by a more accurate observer;[1] for, as Grizzy observed, he was worn away to nothing, and the little that remained seemed as if it might have gone too without being any loss. He was now deaf, paralytic, and childish, and the only symptom of life he shewed was an increased restlessness and peevishness. His lady sat by him calmly pursuing her work, and, without relaxing from it, merely held up her face to salute Mary as she approached her.

'So, I'm glad you are no worse than you was, dear child,' surveying her from head to foot; 'that's more than *we* can say. You see these poor creatures,' pointing to Sir Sampson and aunt Grizzy: 'They are much about it now. Well, we know what we are, but God knows what we shall be[2]—humph!'

Sir Sampson shewed no signs of recognizing her, but seemed pleased when Grizzy resumed her station beside him; and, began, for the five hundredth time, to tell him why he was not in Lochmarlie Castle, and why he was in Bath.

Mary now saw, that there are situations in which a weak capacity has its uses, and that the most foolish chat may sometimes impart greater pleasure than all the wisdom of the schools, even when proceeding from a benevolent heart.

Sir Sampson and Grizzy were so much upon a par in intellect, that they were reciprocally happy in each other. This the strong sense of Lady Maclaughlan had long perceived, and was the principal reason of her selecting so weak a woman as her companion; though, at the same time, in justice to her Ladyship's heart, as well as head, she had that partiality for her friend, for which no other reason can be assigned than that given by Montaigne: 'Je l'amais parceque c'étoit *elle*, parceque c'étoit moi.'[3]

Mary paid a long visit to her aunt, and then took leave, promising to return the following day to take Miss Grizzy to deliver a letter of introduction she had received, and which had not been left to the chance of the carrier and the snow.

CHAPTER XI

'This sort of person is skilled to assume the appearance of all virtues, and all good qualities; but their favourite mask is universal benevolence. And the reason why they prefer this disguise to all others, is, that it tends most effectively to conceal its opposite, which is, indeed, their true character—an universal selfishness.'

Knox's Essays.[1]

ALTHOUGH, ON HER return, Mary read her mother's displeasure in her looks, and was grieved at again having incurred it, she yet felt it a duty towards her father to persevere in her attentions to his aunt. She was old, poor, and unknown—plain in her person—weak in her intellects—vulgar in her manners; but she was related to her by ties more binding than the laws of fashion or the rules of taste. Even these disadvantages, which, to a worldly mind, would have served as excuses for neglecting her, to Mary's generous nature, were so many incentives to treat her with kindness and attention. Faithful to her promise, therefore, she repaired to Milsom Street, and found her aunt all impatience for her arrival, with the letter so firmly grasped in both hands, that she seemed almost afraid to trust any one with a glance at the direction.

'This letter, Mary,' said she, when they were seated in the carriage, 'will be a great thing for me, and especially for you. I got it from Mrs. Menzies, through Mrs. M'Drone, whose friend, Mrs. Campbell's half-sister, Miss Grant, is a great friend of Mrs. Fox's, and she says, she is a most charming woman. Of course she is no friend to the great Fox;[1] or, you know, it would have been very odd in me, with Sir Sampson's principles, and my poor brother's principles, and all our own principles, to have visited her. But she's quite of a different family of Foxes: she's a Fox of Peckwell, it seems—a most amiable woman, very rich, and prodigiously charitable. I am sure we have been most fortunate in getting a letter to such a woman.' And, with this heartfelt ejaculation, they found themselves at Mrs. Fox's.

Every thing corresponded with the account of this lady's wealth and cosnequence; the house was spacious, and handsomely furnished, with its due proportion of livery servants; and they were ushered into a sitting-room, which was filled with all the wonders of nature and art, —Indian shells—inlaid cabinets—ivory boxes—stuffed birds—old china—Chinese mandarins—stood disclosed in all their charms. The lady of the mansion was seated at a table covered with works of a different description: it exhibited the various arts of woman, in regular gradation, from the painted card-rack and gilded fire-screen, to the humble thread-paper[2] and shirt-button. Mrs. Fox was a fine, fashionable looking woman, with a smooth countenance, and still smoother address. She received her visitors with that overstrained complaisance, which, to Mary's nicer tact, at once discovered that all was hollow; but poor Miss Grizzy was scarcely seated, before she was already transfixed with admiration at Mrs. Fox's politeness, and felt as if her whole life would be too short to repay such kindness. Compliments over —the weather, &c. discussed, Mrs. Fox began:

'You must be surprised, ladies, to see me in the midst of such a litter, but you find me busy arranging the works of some poor *protégés* of mine. A most unfortunate family!—I have given them what little instruction I could in these little female works; and you see,' putting a gaudy work-basket into Grizzy's hands, 'it is astonishing what progress they have made. My friends have been most liberal in their purchases of these trifles, but I own I am a wretched beggar: They are in bad hands when they are in mine, poor souls! The fact is, I can give, but I cannot beg. I tell them, they really must find somebody else to dispose of their little labours—somebody who has more of what I call the gift of begging, than I am blest with.'

Tears of admiration stood in Grizzy's eye—her hand was in her pocket. She looked to Mary, but Mary's hands and eyes betrayed no corresponding emotions; she felt only disgust at the meanness and indelicacy of the mistress of such a mansion levying contributions from the stranger within her door.

Mrs. Fox proceeded: 'That most benevolent woman, Miss Gull, was here this morning, and bought no less than seven of these sweet little pin-cushions. I would fain have dissuaded her from taking so many—it really seemed such a stretch of virtue; but she said, "My dear Mrs. Fox, how can one possibly spend their money better than in doing a good action, and at the same time enriching themselves."'

Grizzy's purse was in her hand. 'I declare that's very true. I never thought of that before; and I'm certain Lady Maclaughlan will say the very same; and I'm sure she will be delighted—I've no doubt of that—to take a pin-cushion; and each of my sisters, I'm certain, will take one, though we have all plenty of pin-cushions; and I'll take one to myself, though I have three, I'm sure, that I've never used yet.'

'My dear Miss Douglas, you really are, I could almost say, *too* good. Two and two's four, and one's five—five half crowns! My poor *protégés*! you will really be the making of their fortune!'

Grizzy, with trembling hands, and a face flushed with

conscious virtue, drew forth the money from her little hoard.

But Mrs. Fox did not quit her prey so easily. 'If any of your friends are in want of shirt-buttons, Miss Douglas, I would fain recommend those to them. They are made by a poor woman in whom I take some interest, and are far superior to any that are to be had from the shops. They are made from the very best materials. Indeed, I take care of that, as' (in a modest whisper) 'I furnish her with the materials myself; but the generality of those you get to purchase are made from old materials. I've ascertained that, and it's a fact you may rely upon.'

Poor Grizzy's hair stood on end, to hear of such depravity in a sphere where she had never even suspected it; but, for the honour of her country, she flattered herself such practices were there unknown; and she was entering upon a warm vindication of the integrity of Scotch shirt-buttons, when Mrs. Fox coolly observed:

'Indeed, our friend Miss Grant was so conscious of the great superiority of these buttons over any others, that she bespoke thirty-six dozen of them to take to Scotland with her. In fact, they are the real good old-fashioned shirt-buttons, such as I have heard my mother talk of; and for all that, I make a point of my poor woman selling them a penny a dozen below the shop price; so that, in taking twelve dozen, which is the common quantity, there is a shilling saved at once.'

Grizzy felt as if she would be the saving of the family by the purchase of these incomparable shirt-buttons, and, putting down her five shillings, became the happy possessor of twelve dozen of them.

Fresh expressions of gratitude and admiration ensued, till Grizzy's brain began to whirl, even more rapidly than usual, at the thought of the deeds she had done.

'And now,' said Mrs. Fox, observing her eyes in a fine frenzy rolling[1] from her lapful of pin-cushions and shirt-buttons, to a mandarin nearly as large as life, 'perhaps, my dear Miss Douglas, you will do me the favour to take a look of my little collection.'

'Favour!' thought Grizzy; 'what politeness!' and she protested there was nothing she liked so much as to look at every thing, and that it would be the greatest favour to shew her any thing. The mandarin was made to shake his head—a musical snuff-box played its part—and a variety of other expensive toys were also exhibited.

Mary's disgust increased. 'And this woman,' thought she, 'professes to be charitable amidst all this display of selfish extravagance. Probably the price of one of these costly baubles would have provided for the whole of these poor people, for whom she affects so much compassion, without subjecting her to the meanness of turning her house into a beggar's repository.' And she walked away to the other end of the room, to examine some fine scriptural paintings.

'Here,' said Mrs. Fox to her victim, as she unlocked a superb cabinet, 'is what I value more than my whole collection put together: It is my specimens of Scotch pebbles[1]; and I owe them solely to the generosity and good will of my Scotch friends. I assure you, that is a proud reflection to me. I am a perfect enthusiast in Scotch pebbles, and, I may say, in Scotch people. In fact, I am an enthusiast in whatever I am interested in; and at present, I must own, my heart is set upon making a complete collection of Scotch pebbles.'

Grizzy began to feel a sort of tightness at her throat, at which was affixed a very fine pebble brooch pertaining to Nicky, but lent to Grizzy, to enable her to make a more distinguished figure in the gay world. 'Oh!' thought she, 'what a pity this brooch is Nicky's, and not mine; I would have given it to this charming Mrs. Fox. Indeed, I don't see how I can be off giving it to her, even although it is Nicky's.'

'And, by the bye,' exclaimed Mrs. Fox, as if suddenly struck with the sight of the brooch, 'that seems a very fine stone of yours. I wonder I did not observe it sooner; but, indeed, pebbles are thrown away in dress. May I beg a nearer view of it?'

Grizzy's brain was now all on fire. On the one hand, there was the glory of presenting the brooch to such a polite, charitable, charming woman; on the other, there was the fear of Nicky's indignation: But then it was quite thrown away upon Nicky—she had no cabinet, and Mrs. Fox had declared that pebbles were quite lost any where but in cabinets, and it was a thousand pities that Nicky's brooch should be lost. All these thoughts Grizzy revolved with her usual clearness, as she unclasped the brooch, and gave it into the hand of the collector.

'Bless me, my dear Miss Douglas, this is really a very fine stone! I had no conception of it when I saw it sticking in your throat. It looks quite a different thing in the hand: It is a species I am really not acquainted with. I have nothing at all similar to it in my poor collection. Pray, can you tell me the name of it, and where it is found, that I may at least endeavour to procure a piece of it.'

'I'm sure, I wish to goodness my sister Nicky was here —I'm certain she would—though, to be sure, she has a great regard for it; for it was found on the Glenfern estate, the very day my grandfather won his plea against Drimsydie: and we always called it the lucky stone from that.'

'The lucky stone! what a delightful name! I shall never think myself in luck till I can procure a piece of your lucky stone. I protest, I could almost go to Scotland on purpose. Oh, you dear lucky stone!' kissing it with rapture.

'I'm sure—I'm almost certain—indeed I'm convinced, if my sister Nicky was here, she would be delighted to offer——It would certainly be doing my sister Nicky the greatest favour, since you think it would be seen to so much greater advantage in your cabinet, which, for my own part, I have not the least doubt of, as certainly my sister Nicky very seldom wears it for fear of losing it, and it would be a thousand pities if it was lost; and, to be sure, it will be much safer locked up—nobody can dispute that—so I am sure it's by far the best thing my sister Nicky can do—for certainly a pebble brooch is quite lost as a brooch.'

'My dear Miss Douglas! I am really quite ashamed! This is a perfect robbery, I protest! But I must insist upon your accepting some little token of my regard for Miss Nicky in return.' Going to her charity-table, and returning with a set of painted thread papers, 'I must request the favour of you to present these to Miss Nicky, with my kind regards, and assure her I shall consider her lucky stone as the most precious jewel in my possession.'

The whole of this scene had been performed with such rapidity, that poor Grizzy was not prepared for the sudden metamorphose of Nicky's pebble brooch into a set of painted thread papers, and some vague alarms began to float through her brain.

Mary now advanced, quite unconscious of what had been going on; and having whispered her aunt to take leave, they departed. They returned in silence. Grizzy was so occupied in examining her pin-cushions, and counting her buttons, that she never looked up till the carriage stopped in Milsom street.

Mary accompanied her in. Grizzy was all impatience to display her treasures; and as she hastily unfolded them, began to relate her achievements. Lady Maclaughlan heard her in silence, and a deep groan was all that she uttered; but Grizzy was too well accustomed to be groaned at, to be at all appalled, and went on, 'But all that's nothing to the shirt-buttons, made of Mrs. Fox's own linen, and only five shillings the twelve dozen; and considering what tricks are played with shirt-buttons now—I assure you people require to be on their guard with shirt-buttons now.'

'Pray, my dear, did you ever read the Vicar of Wakefield?'

'The Vicar of Wakefield? I—I think always I must have read it;—at any rate, I'm certain I've heard of it.'

'Moses and his green spectacles[1] was as one of the acts of Solomon compared to you and your shirt-buttons. Pray, which of you is it that wears shirts?'

'I declare that's very true—I wonder I did not think of that sooner—to be sure none of us wear shirts since my poor brother died.'

'And what's become of her brooch?' turning to Mary, who for the first time observed the departure of Nicky's crown jewel.

'O, as to the brooch,' cried Grizzy, 'I'm certain you'll all think that well bestowed, and certainly it has been the saving of it.' Upon which she commenced a most entangled narrative, from which the truth was at length extracted.

'Well,' said Lady Maclaughlan, 'there are two things, God grant I may never become, an *amateur* in charity, and a collector of curiosities. No Christian can be either—both are pick-pockets. I would'nt keep company with my own mother were she either one or other—humph!'

Mary was grieved at the loss of the brooch; but Grizzy seemed more than ever satisfied with the exchange, as Sir Sampson had taken a fancy for the thread papers, and it would amuse him for the rest of the day to be told every two minutes what they were intended for. Mary, therefore, left her quite happy, and returned to Beech Park.

CHAPTER XII

'He either fears his fate too much,
   Or his deserts are small,
Who dares not put it to the touch,
   To gain or lose it all.'

Marquis of Montrose.[1]

TIME ROLLED ON, but no event occurred in Grizzy's life worthy of being commemorated. Lady Juliana began to recover from the shock of her arrival, and at length was even prevailed upon to pay her a visit, and actually spent five minutes in the same room with her. All her Ladyship's plans seemed now on the point of being accomplished. Mr. Downe Wright was now Lord Glenallan, with an additional fifteen thousand per annum, and by wiser heads than hers, would have been thought an unexceptionable match for any young woman. Leaving his mother to settle his affairs in Scotland, to which she was much more *au fait* than himself, he hastened to Beech Park to claim Mary's promised hand.

But neither wealth nor grandeur possessed any sway over Mary's well-regulated mind, and she turned from that species of happiness which she felt would be insufficient to satisfy the best affections of her heart. 'No,' thought she, 'it is not in splendour and distinction that I shall find happiness; it is in the cultivation of the domestic virtues—the peaceful joys of a happy home, and a loved companion, that my felicity must consist. Without these, I feel that I should still be poor, were I mistress of millions;' and she took the first opportunity of acquainting Lord Glenallan with the nature of her sentiments.

He received the communication with painful surprise; but as he was one of those who do not easily divest themselves of an idea that has once taken possession of their brain, he seemed resolved to persevere in his quiet, though pointed attentions.

Lady Juliana's anger at the discovery of her daughter's refusal, it is needless to describe—it may easily be imagined; and poor Mary was almost heart-broken by the violence and duration of it. Sometimes she wavered in her ideas, as to whether she was doing right in thus resisting her mother's wishes; and in the utmost distress she mentioned her scruples to Lady Emily.

'As to Lady Juliana's wishes,' said her cousin, 'they are mere soap bubbles; but as to your own views—why, really you are somewhat of a riddle to me. I rather think, were I such a quiet, civil, well disposed person as you, I could have married Lord Glenallan well enough. He is handsome, good-natured, and rich; and though "he is but a Lord, and nothing but a Lord,"[1] still there is a dash and bustle in twenty thousand a year, that takes off from the *ennui* of a dull companion. With five hundred a year, I grant you, he would be execrable.'

'Then I shall never marry a man with twenty thousand a year, whom I would not have with five hundred.'

'In short, you are to marry for love—that's the old story, which, with all your wisdom, you wise, well educated girls always end in. Where shall I find a hero upon five hundred a year for you? Of course he must be virtuous, noble, dignified, handsome, brave, witty. What would you think of Charles Lennox?'

Mary coloured. 'After what passed, I would not marry Colonel Lennox—no,' affecting to smile, 'not if he were to ask me, which is certainly the most unlikely of all things.'

'Ah! true, I had forgot that scrape. No, that won't do —it certainly would be most pitiful in you, after what passed—Well, I don't know what's to be done with you: There's nothing for it but that you should take Lord Glenallan, with all his imperfections on his head; and, after all, I really see nothing that he wants but a little more brain, and, as you'll have the managing of him, you can easily supply that deficiency.'

'Indeed,' answered Mary, 'I find I have quite little
enough for myself, and I have no genius whatever for
managing. I shall, therefore, never marry, unless I marry
a man on whose judgment I could rely for advice and
assistance, and for whom I could feel a certain deference,
that I consider due from a wife to her husband.'

'I see what you would be at,' said Lady Emily; 'you
mean to model yourself upon the behaviour of Mrs.
Tooley, who has such a deference for the judgment of her
better half, that she consults him even about the tying of
her shoes, and would not presume to give her child a
few grains of magnesia[1] without his full and unqualified
approbation. Now, I flatter myself, my husband and I
shall have a more equitable division; for, though man is
a reasonable being, he shall know and own that woman
is so too—sometimes. All things that men ought to know
better I shall yield: Whatever may belong to either sex, I
either seize upon as my prerogative, or scrupulously
divide; for which reason, I should like the profession of
my husband to be something in which I could not
possibly interfere. How difficult must it be for a woman
in the lower ranks of life to avoid teaching her husband
how to sew, if he is a tailor; or how to bake, if he is a
baker,' &c.

'Nature seems to have provided for this tendency of
both sexes, by making your sensible men—that is, men
who think themselves sensible, and wish every body else
to think the same—incline to foolish women. I can detect
one of these sensible husbands at a glance, by the pomp
and formality visible in every word, look, or action: Men,
whose "visages do cream and mantle like a standing
pond;"[2] who are perfect Joves in their own houses—who
speak their will by a nod, and lay down the law by the
motion of their eye-brow—and who attach prodigious
ideas of dignity to frightening their children, and being

worshipped by their wives, till you see one of these wiseacres looking as if he thought himself, and his obsequious helpmate, were exact personifications of Adam and Eve—"he for God only, she for God in him."[1] Now, I am much afraid, Mary, with all your sanctity, you are in some danger of becoming one of these idolatresses.'

'I hope not,' replied Mary, laughing; 'but if I should, that seems scarcely so bad as the sect of Independents in the marriage state; for example, there is Mrs. Boston, who by all strangers is taken for a widow, such emphasis does she lay upon the personal pronoun—with her, 'tis always, *I* do this, or *I* do that, without the slightest reference to her husband; and she talks of *my* house, *my* gardens, *my* carriage, *my* children, as if there were no copartnery in the case.'

'Ah, she is very odious,' cried Lady Emily, 'she is both master and mistress, and more if possible—she makes her husband look like her footman; but she is a fool, as every woman must needs be, who thinks she can raise herself by lowering her husband. Then, there is the sect of the Wranglers, whose marriage is only one continued dispute: But, in short, I see it is reserved for me to set a perfect example to my sex in the married state. But I'm more reasonable than you, I suspect, for I don't insist upon having a bright genius for my mate.'

'I confess, I should like that my husband's genius was at least as bright as my own,' said Mary, 'and I can't think there is any thing unreasonable in that; or rather, I should say, were I a genius myself, I could better dispense with a certain portion of intellect in my husband; as it has been generally remarked, that those who are largely endowed themselves, can easier dispense with talents in their companions, than others of more moderate endowments can do; but virtue and talents on the one side, virtue and tenderness on the other, I look upon as the principal ingredients in a happy union.'

'Well, I intend to be excessively happy; and yet, I don't think Edward will ever find the longitude. And, as for my tenderness—humph!—as your Lady Maclaughlan says; but as for you—I rather think you're in some danger of turning into an aunt Grizzy, with a long waist and large pockets, peppermint drops, and powdered curls; but, whatever you do, for heaven's sake, let us have no more human sacrifices—if you do, I shall certainly appear at your wedding in sackcloth.'—And this was all of comfort or advice that her Ladyship could bestow.

As Lady Emily was not a person who concealed either her own secrets or those of others, Colonel Lennox was not long of hearing from her what had passed, and of being made thoroughly acquainted with Mary's sentiments on love and marriage. 'Such a heart must be worth winning,' thought he; but he sighed to think that he had less chance for the prize than another. Independent of his narrow fortune, which, he was aware, would be an insuperable bar to obtaining Lady Juliana's consent, Mary's coldness and reserve towards him, seemed to increase rather than diminish. Or if she sometimes gave way to the natural frankness and gaiety of her disposition before him, a word or look expressive of admiration on his part, instantly recalled to her those painful ideas which had been for a moment forgot, and seemed to throw him at a greater distance than ever.

Colonel Lennox was too noble minded himself, to suppose, for an instant, that Mary actually felt dislike towards him; because, at the commencement of their acquaintance, he had not done justice to her merits; but he was also aware, that, until he had explained to her the nature of his sentiments, she must naturally regard his attentions with suspicion, and consider them rather as acts of duty towards his mother, than as the spontaneous expression of his own attachment. He therefore in the most simple and candid manner, laid open to her the secret of his heart, and in all the eloquence of real passion, poured forth those feelings of love and admiration, with which she had unconsciously inspired him.

For a moment, Mary's distrust was overcome by the ardour of his address, and the open manly manner in which he had avowed the rise and progress of his attachment; and she yielded herself up to the delightful conviction of loving and being beloved.

But soon that gave way to the mortifying reflection that rushed over her mind. 'He *has* tried to love me!' thought she; 'but it is in obedience to his mother's wish, and he thinks he has succeeded. No, no; I cannot be the dupe of his delusion—I will not give myself to one who has been solicited to love me!' And again wounded delicacy and woman's pride resumed their empire over her, and she rejected the idea of *ever* receiving Colonel Lennox as a lover. He heard her determination with the deepest anguish, and used every argument and entreaty to soften her resolution; but Mary had wrought herself up to a pitch of heroism—she had rejected the man she loved—the only man she ever *could* love—that done, to persist in the sacrifice seemed easy; and they parted with increased attachment in their hearts, even though those hearts seemed severed for ever.

Soon after he set off to join his regiment; and it was only in saying farewell! that Mary felt how deeply her happiness was involved in the fate of the man she had for ever renounced. To no one did she impart what had passed; and Lady Emily was too dull herself, for some days after the departure of her friend, to take any notice of Mary's dejection.

CHAPTER XIII

'What taught the parrot to cry, hail?
What taught the chattering pie his tale?
Hunger; that sharpener of the wits,
Which gives e'en fools some thinking fits.'
Drummond's Persius.[1]

MARY FOUND HERSELF bereft of both her lovers nearly at the same time. Lord Glenallan, after formally renewing his suit, at length took a final leave, and returned to Scotland. Lady Juliana's indignation could only be equalled by Dr. Redgill's upon the occasion. He had planned a snug retreat for himself during the game season at Glenallan Castle; where, from the good nature and easy temper of both master and mistress, he had no doubt but that he should in time come to *rule the roast,*[2] and be lord paramount over kitchen and larder. His disappointment was therefore great at finding all the solid joys of red deer and moor-game, kippered salmon and mutton hams, 'vanish like the baseless fabric of a vision,'[3] leaving not a wreck behind.

'Refused Lord Glenallan!' exclaimed he to Lady Emily, upon first hearing of it. 'The thing's incredible—absolutely impossible—I won't believe it!'

'That's right, Doctor; who is it that says "and still believe the story false that *ought* not to be true!"[4] I admire your candour, and wish I could imitate it.'

'Then your Ladyship really believes it. 'Pon my soul, I—I—it's really a very vexatious affair. I feel for Lady Juliana, poor woman! No wonder she's hysterical—five and twenty thousand a year[5] refused! What is it she would have? The finest deer park in Scotland! Every sort of game upon the estate! A salmon fishing at the very door! —I should just like to know what *is* the meaning of it?'

'Cannot you guess, Doctor?' asked Lady Emily.

'Guess! No, 'pon my soul! I defy any man to guess

what could tempt a woman to refuse five and twenty thousand a year; unless, indeed, she has something higher in view, and even then she should be pretty sure of her mark. But I suppose, because Miss Adelaide has got a Duke, she thinks she must have one too. I suppose that's the story; but I can tell her Dukes are not so plenty; and she's by no means so fine a woman as her sister, and her market's spoilt, or I'm much mistaken. What man in his senses would ever ask a woman, who had been such an idiot as to refuse five and twenty thousand a year?'

'I see, Doctor, you are quite a novice in the tender passion. Cannot you make allowance for a young lady's not being in love?'

'In what?' demanded the Doctor.

'In love,' repeated Lady Emily.

'Love! Bah—nonsense—no mortal in their senses ever thinks of such stuff now.'

'Then you think love and madness are one and the same thing it seems?'

'I think the man or woman who could let their love stand in the way of five and twenty thousand a year, is the next thing to being mad,' said the Doctor warmly; 'and in this case I can see no difference.'

'But you'll allow there are some sorts of love that may be indulged, without casting any shade upon the understanding?'

'I really can't tell what your Ladyship means,' said the Doctor impatiently.

'I mean, for example, the love one may feel towards a turtle, such as we had lately.'

'That's quite a different thing,' interrupted the Doctor.

'Pardon 'me, but whatever the consequence may be, the effects in both cases were very similar, as exemplified in yourself. Pray, what difference did it make to your friends, who were deprived of your society, whether you spent your time in walking with "even step, and musing gait,"[1] before your dulcinea's window, or the turtle's cistern?[2]—whether you were engrossed in composing a sonnet to your mistress' eye-brow,[3] or in contriving a new method of heightening the enjoyments of *calipash*?[4]—whether you expatiated with greater rapture on the charms of a white skin, or green fat?—whether you were most devoted to a languishing or a lively beauty?—whether——'

"Pon my honour, Lady Emily, I really—I—I—can't conceive what it is you mean. There's a time for every thing; and I'm sure nobody but yourself would ever have thought of bringing in a turtle to a conversation upon marriage.'

'On the contrary, Doctor, I thought it had been upon love; and I was endeavouring to convince you, that even the wisest of men may be susceptible of certain tender emotions towards a beloved object.'

'You'll never convince me that any but a fool can be in love,' cried the Doctor, his visage assuming a darker purple as the argument advanced.

'Then you must rank Lord Glenallan, with his five and twenty thousand a year, amongst the number, for he is desperately in love, I assure you.'

'As to that, Lord Glenallan, or any man with his fortune, may be whatever he chooses. He has right to be in love. He can afford to be in love.'

'I have heard much of the torments of love,' said Lady Emily; 'but I never heard it rated as a luxury before. I hope there is no chance of your being made premier, otherwise I fear we should have a tax upon love-marriages[5] immediately.'

'It would be greatly for the advantage of the nation, as well as the comfort of individuals, if there was,' returned the Doctor. 'Many a pleasant fellow has been lost to society, by what you call a love-marriage. I speak from experience. I was obliged to drop the oldest friend

I had, upon his making one of your love-marriages.'

'What! were you afraid of the effects of evil example?' asked Lady Emily.

'No—it was not for that; but he asked me to take a family dinner with him one day, and I, without knowing any thing of the character of the woman he had married, was weak enough to go. I found a very so so table-cloth, and a shoulder of mutton, which ended our acquaintance. I never entered his door after it. In fact, no man's happiness is proof against dirty table-cloths and bad dinners; and you may take my word for it, Lady Emily, these are the invariable accompaniments of your love-marriages.'

'Pshaw! that is only amongst the *bourgeois*,' said Lady Emily affectedly; 'that is not the sort of *ménage* I mean to have. Here is to be the style of my domestic establishment;' and she repeated Shenstone's beautiful pastoral—

'My banks they are furnished with bees,'[1] &c.

till she came to—

'I have found out a gift for my fair,
I have found where the wood-pigeons breed.'[2]

'There's some sense in that,' cried the Doctor, who had been listening with great weariness. 'You may have a good pigeon pye, or *un sauté de pigeons au sang*, which is still better when well dressed.'

'Shocking!' exclaimed Lady Emily; 'to mention pigeon-pies in the same breath with nightingales and roses!'

'I'll tell you what, Lady Emily, it's just these sort of nonsensical descriptions that do all the mischief amongst you young ladies. It's these confounded poets that turn all your heads, and make you think you have nothing to

do after you are married, but sit beside fountains and
grottos, and divert yourself with birds and flowers, instead of looking after your servants, and paying your
butcher's bills; and, after all, what is the substance of that
trash you have just been reading, but to say that the man
was a substantial farmer and grazier, and had bees;
though I never heard of any man in his senses going to
sleep amongst his bee-hives before. 'Pon my soul! if I had
my will, I would burn every line of poetry that ever was
written. A good recipe for a pudding is worth all that
your Shenstones, and the whole set of them, ever wrote;
and there's more good sense and useful information in
this book,' rapping his knuckles against a volume he held
in his hand, 'than in all your poets, ancient and modern.'

Lady Emily took it out of his hand and opened it.

'And some very poetical description too, Doctor;
although you affect to despise it so much. Here is an
eulogium on the partridge. I doubt much if St. Preux
ever made a finer on his adorable Julie;'[1] and she read as
follows:—

'La Perdrix tient le premier rang après la Bécasse, dans
la cathégorie des gibiers à plumes. C'est, lorsqu'elle est
rouge, l'un des plus honorables et des meilleurs rôtis qui
puissent être étalés sur une table gourmande. Sa forme
appétissante, sa taille élégante et svelte, quoiqu' arrondie,
son embonpoint modéré, ses jambes d'écarlate; enfin,
son fumet divin et ses qualités restaurantes, tout con-
court à la faire rechercher des vrais amateurs. D'autres
gibiers sont plus rares, plus chers, mieux accueillis par la
vanité, le préjugé, et la mode; la Perdrix rouge, belle
de sa propre beauté, dont les qualités sont indépendantes
de la fantaisie, qui réunit en sa personne tout ce qui peut
charmer les yeux, délecter le palais, stimuler l'appétit, et
ranimer les forces, plaira dans tous les temps, et con-
courra à l'honneur de tous les festins, sous quelque
forme qu'elle y paroisse.'*[2]

* Manuel des Amphitryons.

The Doctor sighed: 'That's nothing to what he says of the woodcock:' and with trembling hands he turned over the leaves, till he found the place. 'Here it is,' said he, 'page 88, chap. xvi. Just be so good as read that, Lady Emily, and say, whether it is not infamous that Monsieur Grillade has never even attempted to make it.'

With an air of melancholy enthusiasm she read—'Dans les pays où les Bécasses sont communes, on obtient, de leurs carcasses pilées dans un mortier, une purée sur laquelle on dresse diverses entrées, telles que de petites côtelettes de mouton, &c. Cette purée est l'une des plus délicieuses choses qui puisse être introduite dans le palais d'un gourmand, et l'on peut assurer que quiconque n'en a point mangé n'a point connu les joies du paradis terrestre. Une purée de Bécasse, bien faite, est le *ne plus ultrâ* des jouissances humaines. Il faut mourir après l'avoir gôutée, car toutes les autres alors ne paroitront plus qu'insipides.'[1]

'And these *bécasses*, these woodcocks, perfectly swarm on the Glenallan estate in the season,' cried the Doctor; 'and to think that such a man should have been refused —But Miss Mary will repent this the longest day she lives. I had a cook in my eye for them, too—one who is quite up to the making of this *purée*. 'Pon my soul! she deserves to live upon sheep's head[2] and haggis for the rest of her life; and if I was Lady Juliana, I would try the effect of bread and water.'

'She certainly does not aspire to such joys as are here pourtrayed in this *your* book of life,' said Lady Emily; 'for I suspect she could endure existence even upon roast mutton, with the man she loves.'

'That's nothing to the purpose, unless the man she loves, as you call it, loves to live upon roast mutton too. Take my word for it, unless she gives her husband good dinners, he'll not care twopence for her in a week's time. I look upon bad dinners to be the source of much of the misery we hear of in the married life. Women are much mistaken, if they think it's by dressing themselves they are to please their husbands.'

'Pardon me, Doctor, we must be the best judges there, and I have the authority of all ages and sages in my favour: The beauty and the charms of women have been the favourite theme, time immemorial; now, no one ever heard of a fair one being celebrated for her skill in cookery.'

'There I beg leave to differ from you,' said the Doctor, with an air of exultation, again referring to his *text-book;* 'here is the great Madame Pompadour, celebrated for a single dish: "Les tendrons d'agneau au soleil et à la Pompadour, sont sortis de l'imagination de cette dame célèbre, pour entrer dans la bouche d'un Roi." '[1]

'But it was Love that inspired her—it was Love that kindled the fire in her imagination. In short, you must acknowledge that

'Love rules the court, the camp, the grove.'[2]

'I'll acknowledge no such thing,' cried the Doctor, with indignation. 'Love rule the camp indeed! A very likely story! Don't I know that all our first Generals carry off the best cooks—that there's no such living any where as in camp—that their *aides-de-camp* are quite ruined by it—that in time of war they live at the rate of twenty thousand a year, and when they come home they can't get a dinner they can eat! As for the Court, I don't pretend to know much about it; but I suspect there's more cooks than Cupids to be seen about it. And for the groves, I shall only say I never heard of any of your *fêtes champêtre*, or *picnics*, where all the pleasure did'nt seem to consist in the eating and drinking.'

'Ah, Doctor! I perceive you have taken all your ideas on that subject from Werter, who certainly was a sort of a sentimental *gourmand*, he seems to have enjoyed so much drinking his coffee under the shade of the lime-trees, and going to the kitchen to make his own pease soup; and then he breaks out into such raptures at the idea of the illustrious lovers of Penelope killing and dressing their own meat![1] Butchers and cooks in one! only conceive them with their great knives and blue aprons, or their spits and white nightcaps! Poor Penelope! no wonder she preferred making webs to marrying one of these creatures! Faugh! I must have an ounce of civet to sweeten my imagination.'[2] And she flew off, leaving the Doctor to con over the *Manuel des Amphitryons*, and sigh at the mention of joys, sweet, yet mournful, to his soul.

CHAPTER XIV

'The ample proposition that hope makes
In all designs begun on earth below,
Fails in the promised largeness.'

Shakespeare.[3]

THERE IS NO saying whether the Doctor's system might not have been resorted to, had not Lady Juliana's wrath been for the present suspended by an invitation to Altamont House. True, nothing could be colder than the terms in which it was couched; but to that her Ladyship was insensible, and would have been equally indifferent, had she known that, such as it was, she owed it more to the obstinacy of her son-in-law, than the affection of her daughter. The Duke of Altamont was one of those who attach great ideas of dignity to always carrying their point; and though he might sometimes be obliged to suspend his plans, he never had been known to relinquish them. Had he settled in his own mind to tie his neckcloth

in a particular way, not all the eloquence of Cicero, or
the tears of O'Neil,[1] would have induced him to alter it;
and Adelaide, the haughty self-willed Adelaide, soon
found, that of all yokes, the most insupportable is the
yoke of an obstinate fool. In the thousand trifling
occurrences of domestic life (for his Grace was interested
in all the minutiæ of his establishment,) where good
sense and good humour on either side would have gracefully yielded to the other, there was a perpetual contest
for dominion, which invariably ended in Adelaide's
defeat. The Duke indeed never disputed, or reasoned, or
even replied; but the thing was done: till at the end of
six weeks, the Duchess of Altamont most heartily hated
and despised the man she had so lately vowed to love and
obey. On the present occasion, his Grace certainly
appeared in the most amiable light, in wishing to have
Lady Juliana invited to his house; but, in fact, it proceeded entirely from his besetting sin, obstinacy. He had
proposed her accompanying her daughter at the time of
her marriage, and been overruled; but with all the
pertinacity of a little mind, he had kept fast hold of the
idea, merely because it was his own, and he was now
determined to have it put in execution. In a postscript to
the letter, and in the same cordial style, the Duchess said
something of a hope, that *if* her mother did come to
town, Mary should accompany her; but this her Ladyship, to Mary's great relief, declared should not be,
although she certainly was very much at a loss how to
dispose of her. Mary timidly expressed her wish to be
permitted to return to Lochmarlie, and mentioned that
her uncle and aunt had repeatedly offered to come to
Bath for her, if she might be allowed to accompany
them home; but to this her mother also gave a decided
negative, adding that she never should see Lochmarlie
again, if she could help it. In short, she must remain
where she was, till something could be fixed as to her

future destination. 'It was most excessively tiresome to be clogged with a great unmarried daughter,' her Ladyship observed, as she sprung into the carriage, with a train of dogs, and drove off to dear delightful London.

But, alas! the insecurity of even the best laid schemes of human foresight! Lady Juliana was in the midst of arrangements for endless pleasures, when she received accounts of the death of her now almost forgotten husband! He had died from the gradual effects of the climate, and that was all that remained to be told of the unfortunate Henry Douglas! If his heartless wife shed some natural tears, she wiped them soon; but the wounds of disappointment and vanity were not so speedily effaced, as she contrasted the brilliant court-dress with the unbecoming widow's cap. Oh, she so detested black things—it was so hateful to wear mourning—she never could feel happy or comfortable in black! and, at such a time, how particularly unfortunate! Poor Douglas! she was very sorry!—And so ended the holiest and most indissoluble of human ties!

The Duchess did not think it incumbent upon her to be affected by the death of a person she had never seen; but she put on mourning; put off her presentation at Court for a week, and staid away one night from the opera.

On Mary's warm and unpolluted heart, the tidings of her father's death produced a very different effect. Though she had never known, in their fullest extent, those feelings of filial affection, whose source begins with our being, and over which memory loves to linger, as at the hallowed fount of the purest of earthly joys, she had yet been taught to cherish a fond remembrance of him to whom she owed her being. She had been brought up in the land of his birth—his image was associated in her mind with many of the scenes most dear to her—his name and his memory were familiar to those amongst

whom she dwelt, and thus her feelings of natural affection
had been preserved in all their genuine warmth and
tenderness. Many a letter, and many a little token of her
love, she had, from her earliest years, been accustomed to
send him; and she had ever fondly cherished the hope of
her father's return, and that she would yet know the
happiness of being blest in a parent's love. But now all
these hopes were extinguished; and, while she wept over
them in bitterness of heart, she yet bowed with pious
resignation to the decree of heaven.

CHAPTER XV

> ——'Shall we grieve their hovering shades,
> Which wait the revolution in our hearts?
> Shall we disdain their silent, soft address;
> Their posthumous advice and pious prayer?'
>
> > *Young.*[1]

FOR SOME MONTHS all was peaceful seclusion in Mary's
life, and the only varieties she knew were occasional
visits to aunt Grizzy's, and now and then spending some
days with Mrs. Lennox. She saw, with sorrow, the
declining health of her venerable friend, whose wasted
form and delicate features had now assumed an almost
ethereal aspect. Yet she never complained, and it was
only from her languor and weakness that Mary guessed
she suffered. When urged to have recourse to medical
advice, she only smiled and shook her head; yet, ever
gentle and complying to the wishes of others, she was at
length prevailed upon to receive the visits of a medical
attendant, and her own feelings were but too faithfully
confirmed by his opinion. Being an old friend of the
family, he took upon himself to communicate the intelli-

gence to her son, then abroad with his regiment; and in the meantime Mary took up her residence at Rose Hall, and devoted herself unceasingly to the beloved friend she felt she was so soon to lose.

'Ah! Mary,' she would sometimes say, 'God forgive me! but my heart is not yet weaned from worldly wishes. Even now, when I feel all the vanity of human happiness, I think how it would have soothed my last moments could I have but seen you my son's before I left the world! Yet, alas! our time here is so short, that it matters little whether it be spent in joy or grief, provided it be spent in innocence and virtue. Mine has been a long life compared to many; but when I look back upon it, what a span it seems! And it is not the remembrance of its brightest days that are now solace to my heart. Dearest Mary, if you live long, you will live to think of the hours you have given me, as the fairest, perhaps, of many a happy day that, I trust, heaven has yet in store for you. Yes! God has made some whose powers are chiefly ordained to comfort the afflicted, and in fulfilling his will you must surely be blest.'

Mary listened to the half-breathed wishes of her dear old friend with painful feelings of regret and self-reproach.

'Charles Lennox loved me,' thought she, 'truly, tenderly loved me; and had I but repaid his noble frankness—had I suffered him to read my heart when he laid his open before me, I might now have gladdened the last days of the mother he adores. I might have proudly avowed that affection I must now for ever hide.'

But, at the end of some weeks, Mrs. Lennox was no longer susceptible of emotions, either of joy or sorrow. She gradually sunk into a state of almost total insensibility, from which not even the arrival of her son had power to rouse her. His anguish was extreme at finding his mother in a condition so perfectly hopeless; and every other idea seemed, for the present, absorbed in his anxiety for her. As Mary witnessed his watchful cares, and tender solicitude, she could almost have envied the unconscious object of such devoted attachment.

A few days after his arrival, his leave of absence was abruptly recalled, and he was summoned to repair to head-quarters with all possible expedition. The army was on the move, and a battle was expected to be fought. At such a time, hesitation or delay, under any circumstances, would have been inevitable disgrace; and, dreadful as was the alternative, Colonel Lennox wavered not an instant in his resolution. With a look of fixed agony, but without uttering a syllable, he put the letter into Mary's hand as she sat by his mother's bedside, and then left the room to order preparations to be made for his instant departure. On his return, Mary witnessed the painful conflict of his feelings in his extreme agitation, as he approached his mother, to look, for the last time, on those features, already moulded into more than mortal beauty. A bright ray of the setting sun streamed full upon that face, now reposing in the awful but hallowed calm which is sometimes diffused around the bed of death. The sacred stillness was only broken by the evening song of the blackbird, and the distant lowing of the cattle—sounds which had often brought pleasure to that heart, now insensible to all human emotion. All nature shone forth in gaiety and splendour, but the eye and the ear were alike closed against all earthly objects. Yet who can tell the brightness of those visions with which the parting soul may be visited? Sounds and sights, alike unheard, unknown to mortal sense, may then hold divine communion with the soaring spirit, and inspire it with bliss inconceivable, ineffable!

Colonel Lennox gazed upon the countenance of his mother. Again and again he pressed her inanimate hands to his lips, and bedewed them with his tears, as about to tear himself from her for ever.—At that moment she opened her eyes, and regarded him with a look of intelligence, which spoke at once to his heart. He felt that he was seen and known.[1] Her look was long, and fondly fixed upon his face; then turned to Mary with an expression so deep and earnest, that both felt the instantaneous appeal. The veil seemed to drop from their hearts; one glance sufficed to tell that both were fondly, truly loved; and as Colonel Lennox received Mary's almost fainting form in his arms, he knelt by his mother, and implored her blessing on her children. A smile of angelic brightness beamed upon her face as she extended her hand towards them, and her lips moved as in prayer, though no sound escaped them. One long and lingering look was given to those so dear even in death. She then raised her eyes to heaven, and the spirit sought its native skies!

CHAPTER XVI

'Cette liaison n'est ni passion ni amitié pure: elle fait une classe à part.'

La Bruyère.[2]

IT WAS LONG before Mary could believe in the reality of what had passed. It appeared to her as a beautiful, yet awful, dream. Could it be, that she had plighted her faith by the bed of death; that the last look of her departed friend had hallowed the vow now registered in heaven; that Charles Lennox had claimed her as his own, even in the agony of tearing himself from all he loved; and that she had only felt how dear she was to him at the very moment when she had parted from him, perhaps for ever! But Mary strove to banish these overwhelming thoughts from her mind, as she devoted herself to the performance of the last duties to her departed friend.

These paid, she again returned to Beech Park.

Lady Emily had been a daily visitor at Rose Hall during Mrs. Lennox's illness, and had taken a lively interest in the situation of the family; but, notwithstanding, it was some time before Mary could so far subdue her feelings as to speak with composure of what had passed. She felt, too, how impossible it was, by words, to convey to her any idea of that excitement of mind, where a whole life of ordinary feeling seems concentrated in one sudden but ineffable emotion. All that had passed might be imagined, but could not be told; and she shrunk from the task of pourtraying those deep and sacred feelings, which language never could impart to the breast of another.

Yet she felt it was using her cousin unkindly to keep her in ignorance of what she was certain would give her pleasure to hear; and, summoning her resolution, she at length disclosed to her all that had taken place. Her own embarrassment was too great to allow her to remark Lady Emily's changing colour, as she listened to her communication; and after it was ended, she remained silent for some minutes, evidently struggling with her emotions.

At length she exclaimed indignantly—'And so it seems Colonel Lennox and you have all this time been playing the dying lover, and the cruel mistress to each other? How I detest such duplicity! and duplicity with me! My heart was ever open to you, to him, to the whole world; while yours—nay, your very faces were masked to me!'

Mary was too much confounded by her cousin's reproaches to be able to reply to them for some time; and when she did attempt to vindicate herself, she found it was in vain. Lady Emily refused to listen to her; and, in haughty displeasure, quitted the room, leaving poor Mary overwhelmed with sorrow and amazement.

There was a simplicity of heart, a singleness of idea in herself, that prevented her from ever attaching suspicion to others. But a sort of vague, undefined apprehension floated through her brain as she revolved the extraordinary behaviour of her cousin. Yet it was that sort of feeling to which she could not give either a local habitation or a name;[1] and she continued for some time in that most bewildering state of trying, yet not daring to think. Some time elapsed, and Mary's confusion of ideas was increasing rather than diminishing, when Lady Emily slowly entered the room, and stood some moments before her without speaking.

At length, making an effort, she abruptly said—'Pray, Mary, tell me what you think of me?'

Mary looked at her with surprise. 'I think of you, my dear cousin, as I have always done.'

'That is no answer to my question. What do you think of my behaviour just now?'

'I think,' said Mary, gently, 'that you have misunderstood me; that, open and candid yourself, almost to a fault, you readily resent the remotest appearance of duplicity in others. But you are too generous not to do me justice—'

'Ah, Mary! how little do I appear in my own eyes at this moment; and how little, with all my boasting, have I known my own heart! No! It was not because I am open and candid that I resented your engagement with Colonel Lennox; it was because I was—because—cannot you guess?'

Mary's colour rose, as she cast down her eyes, and exclaimed with agitation, 'No—no, indeed!'

Lady Emily threw her arms around her:—'Dear Mary, you are perhaps the only person upon earth I would make such a confession to—it was because I, who had plighted my faith to another—I, who piqued myself upon my openness and fidelity— I—how it chokes me to utter it! I was beginning to love him myself!—only beginning, observe, for it is already over—I needed but to be aware

of my danger to overcome it. Colonel Lennox is now no
more to me than your lover, and Edward is again all that
he ever was to me; but I—what am I—faithless and self-
deceived!' and a few tears dropped from her eyes.

Mary, too much affected to speak, could only press
her in silence to her heart.

'These are tears of shame, of penitence, though I must
own they look very like those of regret and mortification.
What a mercy it is that "the chemist's magic art" *cannot*
"crystalize these sacred treasures," '[1] said she with a
smile, as she shook a tear drop from her hand; 'they are
gems I am really not at all fond of appearing in.'

'And yet you never appeared to greater advantage,'
said Mary, as she regarded her with admiration.

'Ah! so you say; but there is, perhaps, a little woman-
ish feeling lurking there. And now you doubtless expect—
no, *you* don't, but another would—that I should begin a
sentimental description of the rise and progress of this
ill-fated attachment, as I suppose it would be styled in the
language of romance; but, in truth, I can tell you nothing
at all about it.'

'Perhaps Colonel Lennox'—said Mary, blushing, and
hesitating to name her suspicion.

'No, no—Colonel Lennox was not to blame: There was
no false play on either side; he is as much above the
meanness of coquetry, as—I must say it—as I am. His
thoughts were all along taken up with you, even while
he talked, and laughed, and quarrelled with me. While
I, so strong in the belief that worlds could not shake my
allegiance to Edward, could have challenged all mankind to win my love; and this wicked, wayward, faithless
heart, kept silent till you spoke, and then it uttered such
a fearful sound! And yet I don't think it was love, neither
—"l'on n'aime bien qu'une seule fois; c'est la première,"[2]
—it was rather a sort of an idle, childish, engrossing
sentiment, that *might* have grown to something stronger;

but 'tis past now. I have shown you all the weakness of my heart—despise me if you will.'

'Dearest Lady Emily, had I the same skill to shew the sentiments of mine, you would there see what I cannot express—how I admire this noble candour, this generous self-abasement——'

'O, as to meanly hiding my faults, that is what I scorn to do. I may be ignorant of them myself, and in ignorance I may cherish them; but, once convinced of them, I give them to the winds, and all who choose may pick them up. Violent and unjust, and self deceived, I have been, and may be again; but deceitful I never was, and never will be.'

'My dear cousin, what might you not be if you chose!'

'Ah! I know what you mean, and I begin to think you are in the right; by and bye, I believe, I shall come to be of your way of thinking, (if ever I have a daughter she certainly shall,) but not just at present, the reformation would be too sudden. All that I can promise for at present, is, that henceforth "I will chide no breather in the world but myself,"[1] against whom I know most faults; and now, from this day, from this moment, I vow——'

'No, I shall do it for you,' said Mary with a smile, as she threw her arms around her neck; 'henceforth

> 'The golden laws of love shall be
> Upon this pillar hung;
> A simple heart, a single eye,
> A true and constant tongue.
>
> 'Let no man for more love pretend
> Than he has hearts in store;
> True love begun shall never end:
> Love one, and love no more.'*[2]

* Marquis of Montrose.

M.—19

But much as Mary loved and admired her cousin, she could not be blind to the defects of her character, and she feared they might yet be productive of great unhappiness to herself. Her mind was open to the reception of every image that brought pleasure along with it; while, in the same spirit, she turned from every thing that wore an air of seriousness or self-restraint; and even the best affections of a naturally good heart were borne away by the ardour of her feelings, and the impetuosity of her temper. Mary grieved to see the graces of a noble mind thus running wild for want of early culture; and she sought, by every means, save those of lecture and admonition, to lead her to more fixed habits of reflection and self-examination.

But it required all her strength of mind to turn her thoughts, at this time, from herself to another. She, the betrothed of one who was now in the midst of danger, of whose existence she was even uncertain, but on whose fate she felt her own suspended.

'Oh!' thought she, with bitterness of heart, 'how dangerous it is to yield too much even to our best affections. I, with so many objects to share in mine, have yet pledged my happiness on a being perishable as myself!' And her soul sickened at the ills her fancy drew. But she strove to repress this strength of attachment, which she felt would otherwise become too powerful for her reason to controul; and if she did not entirely succeed, at least the efforts she made, and the continual exercise of mind, enabled her, in some degree, to counteract the baleful effects of morbid anxiety, and overweening attachment. At length her apprehensions were relieved for a time, by a letter from Colonel Lennox. An engagement with the enemy had taken place, but he had escaped unhurt: He repeated his vows of unalterable affection; and Mary felt that she was justified in receiving them. She had made Lady Juliana and Mrs. Douglas both acquainted with

her situation: the former had taken no notice of the communication, but the latter had expressed her approval,
in all the warmth and tenderness of gratified affection.

CHAPTER XVII

'Preach as I please, I doubt our curious men,
Will choose a pheasant still before a hen.'

Horace.[1]

AMONGST THE VARIOUS occupations to which Mary
devoted herself, there was none which merits to be
recorded as a greater act of immolation, than her un-
remitting attentions to aunt Grizzy. It was not merely
the sacrifice of time and talents that was required for
carrying on this intercourse; these, it is to be hoped, even
the most selfish can occasionally sacrifice to the *bienseances*
of society; but it was, as it were, a total surrender of her
whole being. To a mind of any reflection, no situation
can ever be very irksome, in which we can enjoy the
privileges of sitting still and keeping silent—but as the
companion of Miss Grizzy, quiet and reflection were
alike unattainable. When not engaged in *radotage* with
Sir Sampson, her life was spent in losing her scissars,
mislaying her spectacles, wondering what had become of
her thimble, and speculating on the disappearance of a
needle—all of which losses daily and hourly recurring,
subjected Mary to an unceasing annoyance, for she could
not be five minutes in her aunt's company without being
at least as many times disturbed, with—'Mary, my dear,
will you get up—I think my spectacles must be about
you'—or, 'Mary, my dear, your eyes are younger than
mine, will you look if you can see my needle on the
carpet'—or, 'Are you sure, Mary, that's not my thimble

you have got? it's very like it; and I'm sure I can't conceive what's become of mine, if that's not it,' &c. &c. &c.
But her idleness was, if possible, still more irritating than
her industry. When she betook herself to the window, it
was one incessant cry of 'Whose coach is that, Mary, with
the green and orange liveries? Come and look at this
lady and gentleman, Mary; I'm sure I wonder who they
are! Here's something, I declare I'm sure I don't know
what you call it—come here, Mary, and see what it is'—
and so on *ad infinitum*. Walking was still worse. Grizzy not
only stood to examine every article in the shop windows,
but actually turned round to observe every striking figure
that passed. In short, Mary could not conceal from
herself, that weak vulgar relations are an evil to those
whose taste and ideas are refined by superior intercourse.
But even this discovery she did not deem sufficient to
authorise her casting off or neglecting poor Miss Grizzy,
and she in no degree relaxed in her patient attentions
towards her.

Even the affection of her aunt, which she possessed in
the highest possible degree, far from being an alleviation,
was only an additional torment. Every meeting began
with, 'My dear Mary, how did you sleep last night? Did
you make a good breakfast this morning? I declare I
think you look a little pale. I'm sure I wish to goodness
you mayn't have got cold—colds are going very much
about just now—one of the maids in this house has a very
bad cold—I hope you will remember to bathe your feet,
and take some water gruel to night, and do every thing
that Dr. Redgill desires you, honest man!' If Mary
absented herself for a day, her salutation was, 'My dear
Mary, what became of you yesterday? I assure you I
was quite miserable about you all day, thinking, which
was quite natural, that something was the matter with
you; and I declare I never closed my eyes all night, for
thinking about you. I assure you, if it had not been that

I couldn't leave Sir Sampson, I would have taken a hackney coach, although I know what impositions they are,[1] and have gone to Beech Park to see what had come over you.'

Yet all this Mary bore with the patience of a martyr, to the admiration of Lady Maclaughlan, and the amazement of Lady Emily, who declared she could only submit to be bored as long as she was amused.

On going to Milsom Street one morning, Mary found her aunt in high delight at two invitations she had just received for herself and her niece.

'The one,' said she, 'is to dinner at Mrs. Pullens'. You can't remember her mother, Mrs. Macfuss, I daresay, Mary—she was a most excellent woman, I assure you, and got all her daughters married. And I remember Mrs. Pullens when she was Flora Macfuss; she was always thought very like her mother; and Mr. Pullens is a most worthy man, and very rich; and it was thought at the time a great marriage for Flora Macfuss, for she had no money of her own, but her mother was a very clever woman, and a most excellent manager; and I daresay so is Mrs. Pullens, for the Macfusses are all famous for their management—so it will be a great thing for you, you know, Mary, to be acquainted with Mrs. Pullens.'

Mary was obliged to break in upon the eulogium on Mrs. Pullens, by noticing the other card—This was a subject for still greater gratulation.

'This,' said she, 'is from Mrs. Bluemits, and it is for the same day with Mrs. Pullens, only it is to tea, not to dinner[2]—To be sure it will be a great pity to leave Mrs. Pullens so soon; but then it would be a great pity not to go to Mrs. Bluemits'; for I've never seen her, and her aunt, Miss Shaw, would think it very odd if I was to go back to the Highlands without seeing Nancy Shaw, now Mrs. Bluemits; and, at any rate, I assure you we may think much of being asked, for she is a very clever woman,

and makes it a point never to ask any but clever people
to her house; so it's a very great honour to be asked.'

It was an honour Mary would fain have dispensed
with. At another time she might have anticipated some
amusement from such parties, but at present her heart
was not tuned to the ridiculous, and she attempted to
decline the invitations, and get her aunt to do the same;
but she gave up the point when she saw how deeply
Grizzy's happiness, for the time being, was involved in
these invitations, and she even consented to accompany
her, conscious, as Lady Maclaughlan said, that the poor
creature required a leading string, and was not fit to go
alone. The appointed day arrived, and Mary found herself in company with aunt Grizzy, at the mansion of Mr.
Pullens, the fortunate husband of the *ci-devant* Miss Flora
Macfuss; but as Grizzy is not the best of biographers, we
must take the liberty of introducing this lady to the
acquaintance of our reader.

The domestic economy of Mrs. Pullens was her own
theme, and the theme of all her friends; and such was her
zeal in promulgating her doctrines, and her anxiety to
see them carried into effect, that she had endeavoured to
pass it into a law, that no preserves could be eatable but
those preserved in her method; no hams could be good
but those cured according to her receipt; no liquors
drinkable but such as were made from the results of her
experience; neither was it possible that any linens could
be white, or any flannels soft, or any muslins clear, unless
done up after the manner practised in her laundry. By
her own account, she was the slave of every servant within
her door, for her life seemed to be one unceasing labour
to get every thing done in her own way, to the very
blacking of Mr. Pullens' shoes, and the brushing of Mr.
Pullens' coat. But then these heroic acts of duty were
more than repaid by the noble consciousness of a life well
spent. In her own estimation, she was one of the greatest

characters that had ever lived; for, to use her own words, she passed nothing over—she saw every thing done herself—she trusted nothing to servants, &c. &c. &c.

From the contemplation of these her virtues, her face had acquired an expression of complacency foreign to her natural temper; for, after having scolded and slaved in the kitchen, she sat down to taste the fruits of her labours with far more elevated feelings of conscious virtue than ever warmed the breast of a Hampden,[1] or a Howard;[2] and when she helped Mr. Pullens to pie, made, not by the cook, but by herself, it was with an air of self-approbation that might have vied with that of the celebrated Jack Horner[3] upon a similar occasion. In many cases there might have been merit in Mrs. Pullens' doings —a narrow income, the capricious taste of a sick or a cross husband, may exalt the meanest offices which woman can render into acts of virtue, and even diffuse a dignity around them: but Mr. Pullens was rich and good-natured, and would have been happy had his cook been allowed to dress his dinner, and his barber his wig, quietly in their own way. Mrs. Pullens, therefore, only sought the indulgence of her own low inclinations, in thus interfering in every menial department; while, at the same time, she expected all the gratitude and admiration that would have been due to the sacrifice of the most refined taste and elegant pursuits.

But 'envy does merit as its shade pursue,'[4] as Mrs. Pullens experienced, for she found herself assailed by a host of house-keepers, who attempted to throw discredit on her various arts. At the head of this association was Mrs. Jekyll, whose arrangements were on a quite contrary plan. The great branch of science on which Mrs. Pullens mainly relied for fame, was her unrivalled art in keeping things long beyond the date assigned by nature; and one of her master-strokes was, in the middle of summer, to surprise a whole company with gooseberry tarts made of gooseberries of the preceding year; and her triumph was complete, when any of them were so polite as to assert that they might have passed upon them for the fruits of the present season. Another art in which she flattered herself she was unrivalled, was that of making things pass for what they were not; thus, she gave pork for lamb—common fowls for turkey poults—currant wine for champaigne—whisky with peach leaves for noyau;[1] but all these deceptions Mrs. Jekyll piqued herself in immediately detecting, and never failed to point out the difference; and, in the politest manner, to hint her preference of the real over the spurious. Many were the wonderful morsels with which poor Mr. Pullens was regaled, but he had now ceased to be surprised at any thing that appeared on his own table; and he had so often heard the merit of his wife's housekeeping extolled by herself, that, contrary to his natural conviction, he now began to think it must be true; or if he had occasionally any little private misgivings when he thought of the good dinners he used to have in his bachelor days, he comforted himself by thinking that his lot was the lot of all married men who are blest with active, managing, economical wives. Such were Mr. and Mrs. Pullens; and the appearance of the house offered no inadequate idea of the mistress: The furniture was incongruous, and every thing was ill-matched—for Mrs. Pullens was a frequenter of sales, and, like many other liberal minded ladies, never allowed a bargain to pass, whether she required the articles or not. Her dress was the same; there was always something to wonder at; caps that had been bought for nothing, because they were a little soiled, but by being taken down and washed, and new trimmed, turned out to be just as good as new—gowns that had been dyed, turned, cleaned, washed, &c.; and the great triumph was when nobody could tell the old breadth from the new.

The dinner was of course bad, the company stupid, and

the conversation turned solely upon Mrs. Pullens' exploits, with occasional attempts of Mrs. Jekyll to depreciate the merits of some of her discoveries. At length the hour of departure arrived, to Mary's great relief, as she thought any change must be for the better. Not so Grizzy, who was charmed and confounded by all she had seen, and heard, and tasted, and all of whose preconceived ideas on the subjects of washing, preserving, &c. had sustained a total *bouleversement*,[1] upon hearing of the superior methods practised by Mrs. Pullens.

'Well, certainly, Mary, you must allow Mrs. Pullens is an astonishing clever woman! Indeed, I think nobody can dispute it—only think of her never using a bit of soap in her house—every thing is washed by steam. To be sure, as Mrs. Jeckyll said, the table-linen was remarkably ill-coloured—but no wonder, considering—it must be a great saving, I'm sure—and she always stands and sees it done herself, for there's no trusting these things to servants. Once when she trusted it to them, they burned a dozen of Mr. Pullens' new shirts, just from careless-ness, which I'm sure was very provoking. To be sure, as Mrs. Jekyll said, if she had used soap like other people, that wouldn't have happened; and then it is wonderful how well she contrives to keep things. I declare I can't think enough of these green peas that we had at dinner to day, having been kept since summer was a year. To be sure, as Mrs. Jekyll said, they certainly were hard—nobody can deny that—but then, you know, any thing would be hard, that had been kept since summer was a year; and I'm sure I thought they ate wonderfully well considering—and these red currants, too—I'm afraid you didn't taste them—I wish to goodness you had tasted them, Mary. They were sour and dry, certainly, as Mrs. Jekyll said; but no wonder, any thing would be sour and dry that had been kept in bottles for three years.'

Grizzy was now obliged to change the current of her ideas, for the carriage had stopped at Mrs. Bluemits'.

CHAPTER XVIII

'It is certain, great knowledge, if it be without vanity, is the
most severe bridle of the tongue. For so have I heard, that all
the noises and prating of the pool, the croaking of frogs and
toads, is hushed and appeased upon the instant of bringing
upon them the light of a candle or torch. Every beam of reason,
and ray of knowledge, checks the dissolutions of the tongue.'

Jeremy Taylor.[1]

THEY WERE RECEIVED by Mrs. Bluemits with that air
of condescension which great souls practise towards
ordinary mortals, and which is intended, at one and the
same time, to encourage and to repel; to shew the extent
of their goodness, even while they make, or try to make,
their *protégé* feel the immeasurable distance which nature
or fortune has placed between them.

It was with this air of patronising grandeur that Mrs.
Bluemits took her guests by the hand, and introduced
them to the circle of females already assembled.

Mrs. Bluemits was not an avowed authoress; but she
was a professed critic, a well informed woman, a woman
of great conversational powers, &c. and, to use her own
phrase, nothing but conversation was spoke in her house.
Her guests were therefore always expected to be distinguished, either for some literary production, or for their
taste in the *belles lettres*. Two ladies from Scotland, the
land of poetry and romance, were consequently hailed
as new stars in Mrs. Bluemits' horizon. No sooner were
they seated, than Mrs. Bluemits began:

'As I am a friend to ease in literary society, we shall,
without ceremony, resume our conversation; for, as
Seneca observes, the "comfort of life depends upon conversation." '[2]

'I think,' said Miss Graves, 'it is Rochefoucault who
says, "the great art of conversation is to hear patiently
and answer precisely." '[3]

'A very poor definition for so profound a philosopher,' remarked Mrs. Apsley.

'The amiable author of what the gigantic Johnson styles the melancholy and angry Night Thoughts,[1] gives a nobler, a more elevated, and, in my humble opinion, a juster explication of the intercourse of mind,' said Miss Parkins: and she repeated the following lines with pompous enthusiasm:

> 'Speech ventilates our intellectual fire,
> Speech burnishes our mental magazine,
> Brightens for ornament, and whets for use.
> What numbers, sheath'd in erudition, lie,
> Plung'd to the hilts in venerable tomes,
> And rusted in, who might have borne an edge,
> And play'd a sprightly beam, if born to speech—
> If born blest heirs of half their mother's tongue![2]

Mrs. Bluemits proceeded:

> ''Tis thought's exchange, which, like the alternate push
> Of waves conflicting, breaks the learned scum,
> And defecates the student's standing pool.'[3]

'The sensitive poet of Olney, if I mistake not,' said Mrs. Dalton, 'steers a middle course, betwixt the somewhat bald maxim of the Parisian philosopher, and the mournful pruriency of the Bard of Night, when he says,

> 'Conversation, in its better part,
> May be esteem'd a gift, and not an art.'[4]

Mary had been accustomed to read, and to reflect upon what she read, and to apply it to the purpose for which it is valuable, viz. in enlarging her mind and cultivating her taste; but she had never been accustomed to prate, or quote, or sit down for the express purpose of displaying her acquirements; and she began to tremble at hearing authors' names 'familiar in their mouths as household words;'[1] but Grizzy, strong in ignorance, was nowise daunted. True, she heard what she could not comprehend, but she thought she would soon make things clear; and she therefore turned to her neighbour on her right hand, and accosted her with—'My niece and I are just come from dining at Mrs. Pullens'—I dare say you have heard of her—she was Miss Flora Macfuss; her father, Dr. Macfuss, was a most excellent preacher, and she is a remarkable clever woman.'

'Pray, Ma'am, has she come out,[2] or is she simply *bel esprit?*' inquired the lady.

Grizzy was rather at a loss; and, indeed, to answer a question put in an unknown language, would puzzle wiser brains than hers; but Grizzy was accustomed to converse, without being able to comprehend, and she therefore went on.

'Her mother, Mrs. Macfuss—but she is dead—was a very clever woman too; I'm sure, I declare, I don't know whether the Doctor or her was the cleverest; but many people, I know, think Mrs. Pullens beats them both.'

'Indeed! may I ask in what department she chiefly excels?'

'O, I really think in every thing. For one thing, every thing in her house is done by steam; and then she can keep every thing, I can't tell how long, just in paper bags and bottles; and she is going to publish a book with all her receipts in it. I'm sure it will be very interesting.'

'I beg ten thousand pardons for the interruption,' cried Mrs. Bluemits, from the opposite side of the room; 'but my ear was smote with the sounds of *publish*, and *interesting*—words which never fail to awaken a responsive chord in my bosom. Pray,' addressing Grizzy, and bringing her into the full blaze of observation, 'may I ask, was it of *the* Campbell[3] these electric words were spoken? To you, Madam, I am sure I need not apologize for my enthusiasm—You who claim the proud distinction of being a countrywoman, need I ask—an acquaintance?'

All that poor Grizzy could comprehend of this harangue, was, that it was reckoned a great honour to be acquainted with a Campbell; and chuckling with delight at the idea of her own consequence, she briskly replied—

'O, I know plenty of Campbells; there's the Campbells of Mireside, relations of ours; and there's the Campbells of Blackbrae, married into our family; and there's the Campbells of Windlestrae Glen, are not very distant by my mother's side.'

Mary felt as if perforated by bullets in all directions, as she encountered the eyes of the company, turned alternately upon her aunt and her; but they were on opposite sides of the room; therefore to interpose betwixt Grizzy and her assailants was impossible.

'Possibly,' suggested Mrs. Dalton, 'Miss Douglas prefers the loftier strains of the mighty Minstrel of the Mountains,[1] to the more polished periods of the Poet of the Transatlantic Plain.'[2]

'Or perhaps,' said Miss Crick, 'Miss Douglas prefers nature in its simplest, homeliest form; pray Ma'am,' turning full upon the now bewildered Grizzy, 'are you an admirer of Crabbe's Tales?'[3] 'Crabs' tails!' repeated Grizzy in astonishment, 'I don't think ever I tasted them—Indeed I don't think our Crabs have tails; but I am very fond of crabs' claws when there's any thing in them.' Fortunately, the confusion of tongues was at this moment so great, that Grizzy's *lapsus* passed unnoticed by all but Mary, whose ears tingled at every word she uttered.

'Without either a possibility or a perhaps,' said Mrs. Apsley, 'the probability is, Miss Douglas prefers the author of The Giaour to all the rest of her poetical countrymen. Where, in either Walter Scott or Thomas Campbell, will you find such lines as these:·

'Wet with their own best blood, shall drip
    Thy gnashing tooth and haggard lip!'[1]

'Pardon me, Madam,' said Miss Parkins; 'but I am of
opinion you have scarcely given a fair specimen of the
powers of the Noble Bard in question. The image here
presented is a familiar one; "the gnashing tooth," and
"haggard lip," we have all witnessed, perhaps some of us
may even have experienced. There is consequently little
merit in presenting it to the mind's eye:[2] It is easy, comparatively speaking, to pourtray the feelings and passions
of our own kind. We have only, as Dryden expresses it,
to descend into ourselves, to find the secret imperfections
of our mind.[3] It is therefore in his portraiture of the
canine race, that the illustrious author has so far excelled
all his contemporaries: in fact, he has given quite a
dramatic cast to his dogs:' and she repeated with an air
of triumph—

'And he saw the lean dogs beneath the wall,
Hold o'er the dead their carnival;
Gorging and growling o'er carcase and limb,
They were too busy to bark at him!
From a Tartar's skull they had stripped the flesh,
As ye peel the fig when its fruit is fresh;
And their white tusks crunched o'er the whiter skull,
As it slipped through their jaws when their edge grew dull;
As they lazily mumbled the bones of the dead,
When they scarce could rise from the spot where they fed.'[4]

'Now, to enter into the conceptions of a dog—to
embody one's-self, as it were, in the person of a brute—
to sympathize in its feelings—to make its propensities our
own—to "lazily mumbel the bones of the dead," with
our own individual "white tusks!" Pardon me, Madam,
but with all due deference to the genius of a Scott, it is a
thing he has not dared to attempt. Only the finest mind

in the universe was capable of taking so bold a flight. Scott's dogs, Madam, are tame, domestic animals—mere human dogs, if I may say so. Byron's dogs——But let them speak for themselves!

> 'The scalps were in the wild dog's maw,
>   The hair was tangled round his jaw.'[1]

Shew me, if you can, such an image in Scott?'

'Very fine, certainly!' was here uttered by five novices, who were only there as probationers, consequently not privileged to go beyond a response.

'Is it the dancing dogs they are speaking about?' asked Grizzy. But looks of silent contempt were the only replies she received.

'I trust I shall not be esteemed presumptuous,' said Miss Graves, 'or supposed capable of entertaining views of detracting from the merits of the Noble Author at present under discussion, if I humbly, but firmly, enter my caveat against the word "crunch," as constituting an innovation in our language,[2] the purity of which cannot be too strictly preserved, or pointedly enforced. I am aware that by some I may be deemed unnecessarily fastidious; and possibly Christina, Queen of Sweden, might have applied to me the celebrated observation, said to have been elicited from her by the famed work of the laborious French Lexicographer, viz. that he was the most troublesome person in the world, for he required of every word to produce its passport, and to declare whence it came, and whither it was going. I confess, I too, for the sake of my country, would wish that every word we utter might be compelled to shew its passport, attested by our great lawgiver, Dr. Samuel Johnson.'[3]

'Unquestionably,' said Mrs. Bluemits, 'purity of language ought to be preserved inviolate at any price; and it is more especially incumbent upon those who exercise a sway over our minds—those who are, as it were, the moulds in which our young imaginations are formed, to be the watchful guardians of our language. But I lament to say, that in fact it is not so; and that the aberrations of our vernacular tongue have proceeded solely from the licentious use made of it by those whom we are taught to reverence as the fathers of the Sock and Lyre.'

'Yet in familiar colloquy, I do not greatly object to the use of a word occasionally, even although unsanctioned by the authority of our mighty Lexicographer,' said a new speaker.

'For my part,' said Miss Parkins, 'a genius fettered by rules, always reminds me of Gulliver in the hairy bonds of the Lilliputians; and the sentiment of the elegant and enlightened bard of Twickenham, is also mine:

'Great wits sometimes may gloriously offend,
And rise to faults true critics dare not mend;
From vulgar bounds with brave disorder part,
And snatch a grace beyond the reach of art.'[1]

So it is with the subject of our argument: a tamer genius than the illustrious Byron would not have dared to "crunch" the bone. But where, in the whole compass of the English language, will you find a word capable of conveying the same idea?'

'Pick,' modestly suggested one of the novices in a low key, hoping to gain some celebrity by this her first effort; but this dawn of intellect passed unnoticed.

The argument was now beginning to run high; parties were evidently forming of crunchers and anti-crunchers, and etymology was beginning to be called for, when a thundering knock at the door caused a cessation of hostilities.

'That, I flatter myself, is my friend Miss Griffon,' said

Mrs. Bluemits, with an air of additional importance; and the name was whispered round the circle, coupled with 'Celebrated Authoress—Fevers of the Heart—Thoughts of the Moment,' &c. &c.

'Is she a *real* authoress that is coming?' asked Miss Grizzy at the lady next her. And her delight was great at receiving an answer in the affirmative; for Grizzy thought to be in company with an authoress was the next thing to being an authoress herself; and, like some other people, she had a sort of vague mysterious reverence for every one whose words had been printed in a book.

'Ten thousand thousand pardons, dearest Mrs. Bluemits!' exclaimed Miss Griffon, as she entered. 'I fear a world of intellect is lost to me by this cruel delay.' Then in an audible whisper—'But I was detained by my publisher: He quite persecutes me to write. My "Fevers of the Heart" has had a prodigious run; and even my "Thoughts," which, in fact, cost me no thought, are amazingly *recherché*.[1] And I actually had to force my way to you tonight through a legion of printer's devils, who were lying in wait for me with each a sheet of my "Billows of Love." '

'The title is most musical, most melancholy,'[2] said Mrs. Bluemits, 'and conveys a perfect idea of what Dryden terms "the sweeping deluge of the soul;"[3] but I flatter myself we shall have something more than a name from Miss Griffon's genius. The Aonian graces,[4] 'tis well known, always follow in her train.'

'They have made a great hole in it then,' said Grizzy, officiously displaying a fracture in the train of Miss Griffon's gown, and from thence taking occasion to deliver her sentiments on the propriety of people who tore gowns always being obliged to mend them.

After suitable entreaties had been used, Miss Griffon was at last prevailed upon to favour the company with some specimens of the 'Billows of Love,' (of which we were unable to procure copies,) and the following sonnet, the production of a friend:

> 'Hast thou no note for joy, thou weeping lyre?
>   Doth yew and willow ever shade thy string,
>   And melancholy sable banners fling,
> Warring 'midst hosts of elegant desire?
> How vain the strife—how vain the warlike gloom!
>   Love's arms are grief—his arrows sighs and tears;
>   And every moan thou mak'st, an altar rears,
> To which his worshippers devoutly come.
> Then rather, lyre, I pray thee, try thy skill,
>   In varied measure, on a sprightlier key:
>   Perchance thy gayer tones' light minstrelsy,
> May heal the poison that thy plaints distil.
> But much I fear that joy is danger still;
> And joy, like woe, love's triumph must fulfil.'[1]

This called forth unanimous applause—'delicate imagery' — 'smooth versification' — 'classical ideas' — 'Petrarchian sweetness,' &c. &c. resounded from all quarters.

But even intellectual joys have their termination, and carriages and servants began to be announced in rapid succession.

'Fly not yet, 'tis just the hour,'[2] said Mrs. Bluemits to the first of her departing guests, as the clock struck ten.

'It is gone, with its thorns and its roses,'[3] replied her friend with a sigh, and a farewell pressure of the hand.

Another now advanced—'Wilt thou be gone?—it is not yet near day.'[4]

'I have less will to go than care to stay,'[5] was the reply.

'*Parto ti lascio addio*,'[6] warbled Miss Parkins.

'I vanish,' said Mrs. Apsley, snatching up her tippet, ridicule, &c. 'and, like the baseless fabric of a vision, leave not a wreck behind,'[7]

'Fare-thee-well at once—Adieu, adieu, adieu, remember me!'[1] cried the last of the band, as she slowly retreated.

Mrs. Bluemits waved her hand with a look of tender reproach, as she repeated—

> 'An adieu should in utterance die,
>   Or, if written, should faintly appear—
> Should be heard in the sob of a sigh,
>   Or be seen in the blot of a tear.'[2]

'I'm sure, Mary,' said Grizzy, when they were in the carriage, 'I expected, when all the ladies were repeating, that you would have repeated something too. You used to have the Hermit[3] and all Watts' Hymns[4] by heart, when you was little. It's a thousand pities, that you should have forgot them; for I declare, I was quite affronted to see you sitting like a stick, and not saying a word, when all the ladies were speaking, and turning up their eyes, and moving their hands so prettily; but I hope next time you go to Mrs. Bluemits, you will take care to learn something by heart before you go. I'm sure I hav'nt a very good memory, but I remember some things; and I was very near going to repeat "Farewell to Lochaber"[5] myself, as we were coming away; and I wish to goodness I had done it; but I suppose it wouldn't do to go back now; and, at any rate, all the ladies are away, and I dare say the candles will be out by this time.'

Mary felt it a relief to have done with this surfeit of soul, and was of opinion, that learning, like religion, ought never to be forced into conversation; and that people, who only read to talk of their reading, might as well let it alone.—Next morning she gave so ludicrous an account of her entertainment, that Lady Emily was quite charmed.

'Now I begin to have hopes of you,' said she, 'since I see you can laugh at your friends as well as me.'

'Not at my friends, I hope,' answered Mary; 'only at folly.'

'Call it what you will: I only wish I had been there. I should certainly have started a controversy upon the respective merits of Tom Thumb and Puss in Boots, and so have called them off Lord Byron. Their pretending to measure the genius of a Scott or a Byron, must have been something like a fly attempting to take the altitude of Mount Blanc. How I detest those "idle disquisitions about the colour of a goat's beard, or the blood of an oyster." '[1]

Mary had seen, in Mrs. Douglas, the effects of a highly cultivated understanding shedding its mild radiance on the path of domestic life, heightening its charms, and softening its asperities, with the benign spirit of Christianity. Her charity was not like that of Mrs. Fox; she did not indulge herself in the purchase of elegant ornaments, and then, seated in the easy chair of her drawing-room, extort from her visitors money to satisfy the wants of those who had claims on her own bounty. No: she gave a large portion of her time, her thoughts, her fortune, to the most sacred of all duties—charity, in its most comprehensive meaning. Neither did her knowledge, like that of Mrs. Bluemits, evaporate in pedantic discussion or idle declamation, but shewed itself in the tenor of a well spent life, and in the graceful discharge of those duties which belonged to her sex and station. Next to goodness, Mary most ardently admired talents. She knew there were many of her own sex who were justly entitled to the distinction of literary fame. Her introduction to the circle at Mrs. Bluemits' had disappointed her; but they were mere pretenders to the name. How different from those described by one no less amiable and enlightened herself!—'Let such women as are disposed to be vain of their comparatively petty attainments, look up with admiration to those contemporary shining examples, the venerable Elizabeth Carter, and the blooming Elizabeth Smith. In them let our young ladies contemplate profound and various learning, chastised by true Christian humility. In them let them venerate acquirements, which would have been distinguished in an university, meekly softened, and beautifully shaded by the exertion of every domestic virtue, the unaffected exercise of every feminine employment.'*[1]

CHAPTER XIX

'The gods, to curse Pamela with her pray'rs,
Gave the gilt coach and dappled Flanders mares;
The shining robes, rich jewels, beds of state,
And, to complete her bliss, a fool for mate.
She glares in balls, front boxes, and the ring—
A vain, unquiet, glitt'ring wretched thing!
Pride, pomp, and state, but reach her outward part;
She sighs, and is no duchess at her heart.'

Pope.[2]

FOR MANY MONTHS, Mary was doomed to experience all the vicissitudes of hope and fear, as she heard of battles and sieges, in which her lover had a part. He omitted no opportunity of writing to her; but scarcely had she received the assurance of his safety from himself, when her apprehensions were again excited by rumours of fresh dangers he would have to encounter; and it required all her pious confidence and strength of mind to save her from yielding to the despondency of a naturally sensitive heart. But in administering to the happiness of others, she found the surest alleviation to the misfortune that threatened herself; and she often forgot her own cares in her benevolent exertions for the poor, the

* Coelebs.

sick, and the desolate. It was then she felt all the tenderness of that divine precept, which enjoins love of the
Creator as the engrossing principle of the soul. For, oh!
the unutterable anguish that heart must endure, which
lavishes all its best affections on a creature mutable and
perishable as itself, from whom a thousand accidents
may separate or estrange it, and from whom death must
one day divide it! Yet there is something so amiable, so
exalting, in the fervour of a pure and generous attachment, that few have been able to resist its overwhelming
influence; and it is only time and suffering that can teach
us to comprehend the miseries that wait on the excess,
even of our virtuous inclinations, where these virtues
aspire not beyond this transitory scene.

Mary seldom heard from her mother or sister. Their
time was too precious to be wasted on dull country
correspondents; but she saw their names frequently mentioned in the newspapers, and she flattered herself, from
the *éclat* with which the Duchess seemed to be attended,
that she had found happiness in those pleasures where
she had been taught to expect it. The Duchess was, indeed,
surrounded with all that rank, wealth, and fashion could
bestow. She had the finest house, jewels, and equipages
in London, but she was not happy. She felt the draught
bitter, even though the goblet that held it was of gold.
It is novelty only that can lend charms to things in themselves valueless; and when that wears off, the disen-
chanted baubles appear in all their native worthlessness.
There is even a satiety in the free indulgence of wealth,
when that indulgence centres solely in self, and brings no
general self-approving reflections along with it. So it was
with the Duchess of Altamont. She sought, in the
gratification of every expensive whim, to stimulate the
languid sense of joy; and, by loading herself with jewels,
she strove to still the restless inquietude of a dissatisfied
heart. But it is only the vulgar mind which can long find

enjoyment in the mere attributes of wealth—in the contemplation of silk hangings, and gilded chairs, and
splendid dresses, and shewy equipages. Amidst all these,
the mind of any taste or refinement, 'distrusting, asks if
this be joy.'[1] And Adelaide possessed both taste and
refinement, though her ideas had been perverted, and
her heart corrupted, by the false maxims early instilled
into her. Yet, selfish and unfeeling as she was, she sickened at the eternal recurrence of self-indulged caprices;
and the bauble that had been hailed with delight the one
day as a charmed amulet to dispel her *ennui*, was the next
beheld with disgust or indifference. She believed, indeed,
that she had real sources of vexation in the self-will and
obstinacy of her husband, and that, had he been otherwise than he was, she should then have been completely
happy. She would not acknowledge, even to herself, that
she had done wrong in marrying a man whose person was
disagreeable to her, and whose understanding she despised,
while her preference was decidedly in favour of another.
Even her style of life was, in some respects, distasteful to
her; yet she was obliged to conform to it. The Duke
retained exactly the same notions of things as had taken
possession of his brain thirty years before; consequently,
every thing in his establishment was conducted with a
regularity and uniformity unknown to those whose habits
are formed on the more eccentric models of the present
day; or rather, who have no models, save those of their
own capricious tastes and inclinations. He had an antipathy to balls, concerts, and masquerades; for he did not
dance, knew nothing of music, and still less of *badinage*.
But he liked great dull dinners, for there the conversation
was generally adapted to his capacity; and it was a
pleasure to him to arrange the party—to look over the
bill of fare—to see all the family plate displayed—and
to read an account of the grand dinner at the Duke of
Altamont's[2] in the Morning Post, of the following day.

All this sounds very vulgar for the pastimes of a Duke;
but there are vulgar-minded Dukes, as there are gifted
ploughmen, or any other anomalies. The former Duchess,
a woman of high birth, similar years, and kindred spirit
of his own in all matters of form and *etiquette*, was his
standard of female propriety; and she would have deemed
it highly derogatory to her dignity to have patronised
any other species of entertainment than grand dinners
and dull assemblies.

Adelaide had attempted, with a high hand, at once to
overturn the whole system of Altamont House, and had
failed. She had declared her detestation of dinners, and
been heard in silence. She had kept her room thrice
when they were given, but without success. She had
insisted upon giving a ball, but the Duke, with the most
perfect composure, had peremptorily declared it must be
an assembly. Thus baffled in all her plans of domestic
happiness, the Duchess would have sought her pleasures
elsewhere. She would have lived any where but in her own
house—associated with every body but her own husband
—and done every thing but what she had vowed to do.
But even in this she was thwarted. The Duke had the
same precise formal notions of a lady's conduct abroad,
as well as her appearance at home; and the very places
she would have most wished to go to, were those she was
expressly prohibited from ever appearing at.

Even all that she could have easily settled to her own
satisfaction, by the simple apparatus of a separate
establishment, carried on in the same house; but here,
too, she was foiled, for his Grace had stubborn notions on
that score also, and plainly hinted, that any separation
must be final, and decided; and Adelaide could not yet
resolve upon taking so formidable a step in the first year
of her marriage. She was, therefore, compelled to drag
the chain by which, with her own will, she had bound
herself for life to one she already despised and detested.

And bound she was, in the strictest sense of the metaphor; for, though the Duke had not the smallest pleasure in the society of his wife, he yet attached great ideas of propriety to their being always seen together, side by side. Like his sister, Lady Matilda, he had a high reverence for appearances, though he had not her *finesse* in giving them effect. He had merely been accustomed to do what he thought looked well, and gave him an air of additional dignity: He had married Adelaide, because he thought she had a fine presence, and would look well as Duchess of Altamont; and, for the same reason, now that she was his wedded wife, he thought it looked well to be seen always together. He, therefore, made a point of having no separate engagements; and even carried his sense of propriety so far, that as regularly as the Duchess' carriage came to the door, the Duke was prepared to hand her in, in due form, and take his station by her side. This alone would have been sufficient to have embittered Adelaide's existence, and she had tried every expedient, but in vain, to rid herself of this public display of conjugal duty: She had opened her landaulet[1] in cold weather, and shut it, even to the glasses, in a scorching sun; but the Duke was insensible to heat and cold: He was most provokingly healthy; and she had not even the respite which an attack of rheumatism, or tooth-ache, would have afforded. As his Grace was not a person of keen sensation, this continual effort to keep up appearances cost him little or nothing; but to the Duchess' nicer tact, it was martyrdom to be compelled to submit to the semblance of affection, where there was no reality. Ah, nothing but a sense of duty, early instilled, and practically enforced; can reconcile a refined mind to the painful task of bearing, with meekness and gentleness, the ill temper, adverse will, and opposite sentiments, of those with whom we can acknowledge no feeling in common!

But Adelaide possessed no sense of duty, and was a

stranger to self command; and, though she boasted refinement of mind, yet it was of that spurious sort, which, far from elevating and purifying the heart, tends only to corrupt and debase the soul, while it sheds a false and dazzling lustre upon those perishable graces which captivate the senses.

It may easily be imagined, the good sense of the mother did not tend to soothe the irritated feelings of the daughter. Lady Juliana was, indeed, quite as much exasperated as the Duchess, at these obstacles thrown in the way of her pleasures, and the more so as she could not quite clearly comprehend them. The good nature of her husband, and the easy indolence of her brother, even *her* folly had enabled her, on many occasions, to get the better of; but the obstinacy of her son-in-law was invincible to all her arts—she could, therefore, only wonder to the Duchess, how she could not manage to get the better of the Duke's prejudices against balls, and concerts, and masquerades: It was so excessively ridiculous, so perfectly foolish, not to do as other people did; and there was the Duchess of Ryston gave Sunday concerts, and Lady Oakham saw masks, and even old ugly Lady Loddon had a ball, and the Prince[1] at it! How vastly provoking! how unreasonable in a man of the Duke's years, to expect a girl like Adelaide to conform to all his old fashioned notions! And then she would wisely appeal to Lord Lindore, whether it was not too absurd in the Duke to interfere with the Duchess' arrangements.

Lord Lindore was a frequent visitor at Altamont House; for the Duke, satisfied with his having been once refused, was nowise jealous of him; and Lord Lindore was too quiet and refined in his attentions to excite the attention of any one so stupid and obtuse. It was not the least of the Duchess' mortifications, to be constantly contrasting her former lover—elegant, captivating, and *spirituel*[2]—with her husband, awkward, insipid, and dull, as the fat weed that rots on Lethe's shore.[1] Lord Lindore was, indeed, the most admired man in London, celebrated for his conquests, his horses, his elegance, manner, dress; in short, in every thing he gave the tone. But he had too much taste to carry any thing to extreme; and, in the midst of incense, and adulation, and imitation, he still retained that simple, unostentatious elegance, that marks the man of real fashion—the man who feels his own consequence, independent of all extraneous modes, or fleeting fashions.

There is, perhaps, nothing so imposing, nothing that carries a greater sway over a mind of any refinement, than simplicity, when we feel assured that it springs from a genuine contempt of shew and ostentation. Lord Lindore was aware of this, and he did not attempt to vie with the Duke of Altamont, in the splendour of his equipage, the richness of his liveries, the number of his attendants, or any of those obvious attractions: on the contrary, every thing belonging to him was of the plainest description; and, except in the beauty of his horses, he seemed to scorn every species of extravagance: but then, he rode with so much elegance, he drove his curricle[2] with such graceful ease, as formed a striking contrast to the formal Duke, sitting bolt-upright in his state chariot, *chapeau bras*,[3] and star; and the Duchess often quitted the Park, where Lord Lindore was the admired of all admirers, mortified and ashamed at being seen in the same carriage with the man she had chosen for her husband. Ambition had led her to marry the Duke, and that same passion now heightened her attachment for Lord Lindore; for, as some one has remarked, ambition is not always the desire for that which is in itself excellent, but for that which is most prized by others; and the handsome Lord Lindore was courted and caressed in circles, where the dull, precise Duke of Altamont was wholly overlooked. Months passed in this manner, and every day added something to Adelaide's feelings of chagrin and disappointment. But it was still worse when she found herself settled for a long season at Norwood Abbey—a dull, magnificent residence, with a vast unvaried park, a profusion of sombre trees, and a sheet of still water, decorated with leaden deities. Within doors every thing was in the same style of vapid, tasteless grandeur, and the society was not such as to dispel the *ennui* these images served to create. Lady Matilda Sufton, her satellite Mrs. Finch, General Carver, and a few stupid, elderly lords, and their well-bred ladies, comprised the family circle; and the Duchess experienced, with bitterness of spirit, that 'rest of heart, and pleasure felt at home,'[1] are blessings wealth cannot purchase, nor greatness command; while she sickened at the stupid, the almost *vulgar* magnificence of her lot.

At this period Lord Lindore arrived on a visit, and the daily, hourly, contrast that occurred, betwixt the elegant, impassioned lover, and the dull, phlegmatic husband, could not fail of producing the usual effects on an unprincipled mind. Rousseau and Goethe were studied, French and German sentiments were exchanged, till criminal passion was exalted into the purest of all earthly emotions. It were tedious to dwell upon the minute, the almost imperceptible occurrences, that tended to heighten the illusion of passion, and throw an air of false dignity around the degrading spells of vice; but so it was, that in something less than a year from the time of her marriage, this victim of self-indulgence again sought her happiness in the gratification of her own headstrong passions, and eloped with Lord Lindore, vainly hoping to find peace and joy amid guilt and infamy.

CHAPTER XX

'On n'est guères obligé aux gens qui ne nous viennent voir,
que pour nous quereller, qui pendant toute une visite, ne nous
disent pas une seule parole obligeante, et qui se font un plaisir
malin d'attaquer notre conduite, et de nous faire entrevoir nos
défauts.'

L'Abbé de Bellegarde.[1]

THE DUKE, ALTHOUGH not possessed of the most delicate feelings, it may be supposed, was not insensible to
his dishonour. He immediately set about taking the legal
measures for avenging it; and damages were awarded,
which would have the effect of rendering Lord Lindore
for ever an alien to his country. Lady Juliana raved, and
had hysterics, and seemed to consider herself as the only
sufferer by her daughter's misconduct. At one time,
Adelaide's ingratitude was all her theme: at another, it
was Lord Lindore's treachery, and poor Adelaide was
every thing that was amiable and injured: then it was
the Duke's obstinacy; for, had Adelaide got leave to do
as she liked, this never would have happened; had she
only got leave to give balls, and to go to masquerades, she
would have made the best wife in the world, &c. &c. &c.

All this was warmly resented by Lady Matilda, supported by Mrs. Finch and General Carver, till open
hostilities were declared between the ladies, and Lady
Juliana was compelled to quit the house she had looked
upon as next to her own, and became once more a
denizen of Beech Park.

Mary's grief and horror at her sister's misconduct, was
proportioned to the nature of the offence. She considered
it not as how it might affect herself, or would be viewed
by the world, but as a crime committed against the law
of God; yet, while she the more deeply deplored it on
that account, no bitter words of condemnation passed
her lips. She thought, with humility, of the superior
advantages she had enjoyed, in having principles of

religion early and deeply engrafted in her soul; and that, but for these, such as her sister's fate was, hers might have been.

She felt for her mother, undeserving as she was of commiseration; and strove, by every means in her power, to promote her comfort and happiness. But that was no easy task: Lady Juliana's notions of comfort and happiness differed as widely from those of her daughter, as reason and folly could possibly do. She was, indeed, 'than folly more a fool—a melancholy fool without her bells.'[1] She still clung to low earth-born vanities, with as much avidity as though she had never experienced their insecurity: still rung the same changes on the joys of wealth and grandeur, as if she had had actual proof of their unfading felicity. Then she recurred to the Duke's obstinacy, and Lord Lindore's artifices, till, after having exhausted herself in invective against them, she concluded by comforting herself with the hope that Lord Lindore and Adelaide would marry; and although it would be a prodigious degradation to her, and she could not be received at court, she might yet get into very good society in town: there were many women of high rank exactly in the same situation, who had been driven to elope from their husbands, and who married the men they liked, and made the best wives in the world.

Mary heard all this in shame and silence; but Lady Emily, wearied and provoked by her folly and want of principle, was often led to express her indignation and contempt, in terms which drew tears from her cousin's eyes. Mary was, indeed, the only person in the world who felt her sister's dereliction with the keenest feelings of shame and sorrow. All Adelaide's coldness and unkindness, had not been able to eradicate from her heart those deep-rooted sentiments of affection, which seem to have been entwined with our existence, and which, with some generous natures, end but with their being. Yes!

there are ties that bind together those of one family, stronger than those of taste, or choice, or friendship, or reason; for they enable us to love, even in opposition to them all.

It was understood the fugitives had gone to Germany; and after wonder and scandal were exhausted, and a divorce obtained, the Duchess of Altamont, except to her own family, was as although she had never been. Such is the transition from grandeur to guilt—from guilt to insignificance!

Amongst the numerous visitors who flocked to Beech Park, whether from sympathy, or curiosity, or exultation, was Mrs. Downe Wright. None of these motives, singly, had brought that lady there, for her purpose was that of giving what she genteelly termed some *good hits* to the Douglas' pride: a delicate mode of warfare, in which, it must be owned, the female sex greatly excel.

Mrs. Downe Wright had not forgiven the indignity of her son having been refused by Mary, which she imputed entirely to Lady Emily's influence, and had, from that moment, predicted the downfall of the whole pack, as she styled the family; at the same time always expressing her wish that she might be mistaken, as she wished them well—God knows she bore them no ill will, &c. She entered the drawing-room at Beech Park, with a countenance cast to a totally different expression from that with which she had greeted Lady Matilda Sufton's widowhood. Melancholy would there have been appropriate, here it was insulting; and accordingly, with downcast eyes, and silent pressures of the hand, she saluted every member of the family, and inquired after their healths with that air of anxious solicitude, which implied, that if they were all well, it was what they ought not to be. Lady Emily's quick tact was presently aware of her design, and she prepared to take the field against her.

'I had some difficulty in getting admittance to you,'

said Mrs. Downe Wright. 'The servant would fain have
denied you; but, at such a time, I knew the visit of a
friend could not fail of being acceptable, so I made good
my way in spite of him.'

'I had given orders to be at home to friends only,'
returned Lady Emily, 'as there is no end to the inroads
of acquaintances.'

'And poor Lady Juliana,' said Mrs. Downe Wright, in
a tone of affected sympathy, 'I hope she is able to see her
friends?'

'Did you not meet her?' asked Lady Emily carelessly:
'She is just gone to Bath, for the purpose of securing a
box during the term of Kean's engagement;[1] she would
not trust to *l'eloquence du billet*[2] upon such an occasion.'

'I'm vastly happy to hear she is able for any thing of
the kind,' in a tone of vehement and overstrained joy,
rather unsuitable to the occasion.

A well-feigned look of surprise from Lady Emily made
her fear she had overshot her mark; she, therefore, as if
from delicacy, changed the conversation to her own
affairs. She soon contrived to let it be known, that her
son was going to be married to a Scotch Earl's daughter;
that she was to reside with them; and that she had
merely come to Bath, for the purpose of letting her house
—breaking up her establishment—packing up her plate
—and, in short, making all those magnificent arrangements which wealthy dowagers usually have to perform
on a change of residence. At the end of this triumphant
declaration, she added—

'I fain would have the young people live by themselves,
and let me just go on in my own way; but neither my son,
nor Lady Grace, would hear of that, although her family
are my son's nearest neighbours, and most sensible, agreeable people they are. Indeed, as I said to Lord Glenallan,
a man's happiness depends fully as much upon his wife's
family as upon herself.'

Mary was too noble minded, to suspect that Mrs. Downe Wright could intend to level *innuendos;* but the allusion struck her: she felt herself blush; and, fearful Mrs. Downe Wright would attribute it to a wrong motive, she hastened to join in the eulogium on the Benmavis family in general, and Lady Grace in particular.

'Lady Benmavis is, indeed, a sensible, well principled woman, and her daughters have been all well brought up.'

Again Mary coloured at the emphasis which marked the sensible, well principled mother, and the well brought up daughters; and, in some confusion, she said something about Lady Grace's beauty.

'She certainly is a very pretty woman,' said Mrs. Downe Wright with affected carelessness; 'but what is better, she is out of a good nest. For my own part, I place little value upon beauty now; commend me to principles. If a woman is without principles, the less beauty she has the better.'

'If a woman has no principles,' said Lady Emily, 'I don't think it signifies a straw whether she has beauty or not—ugliness can never add to one's virtue.'

'I beg your pardon, Lady Emily; a plain woman will never make herself so conspicuous in the world as one of your beauties.'

'Then you are of opinion, wickedness lies all in the eye of the world, not in the depths of the heart? Now, I think the person who cherishes—no matter how secretly—pride, envy, hatred, malice, or any other besetting sin, must be quite as criminal in the sight of God, as those who openly indulge their evil propensity.'

'I go very much by outward actions,' said Mrs. Downe Wright; 'they are all we have to judge by.'

'But I thought we were forbidden to judge one another?'

'There's no shutting people's mouths, Lady Emily.'

'No; all that is required, I believe, is that we should shut our own.'

Mary thought the conversation was getting rather too *piquante* to be pleasant, and tried to soften the tone of it, by asking that most innocent question, Whether there was any news?

'Nothing but about battles, and fightings, I suppose,' answered Mrs. Downe Wright. 'I'm sure they are to be pitied who have friends or relations either in army or navy at present. I have reason to be thankful my son is in neither. He was very much set upon going into one or other; but I was always averse to it; for, independent of the danger, they are professions that spoil a man for domestic life, they lead to such expensive, dissipated habits, as quite ruin them for family men. I never knew a military man but what must have his bottle of port every day: With sailors, indeed, it's still worse; grog and tobacco soon destroy them. I'm sure, if I had a daughter, it would make me miserable if she was to take a fancy to a naval or military man;—but,' as if suddenly recollecting herself, 'after all, perhaps it's a mere prejudice of mine.'

'By no means,' said Lady Emily, 'there is no prejudice in the matter; what you say is very true. They are to be envied who can contrive to fall in love with a stupid, idle man: *they* never can experience any anxiety: *their* fate is fixed; "the waveless calm, the slumber of the dead,"[1] is theirs; as long as they can contrive to slumber on, or, at least, to keep their eyes shut, 'tis very well, they are in no danger of stumbling till they come to open them; and if they are sufficiently stupid themselves, there is no danger of their doing even that. They have only to copy the owl, and they are safe.'

'I quite agree with your Ladyship,' said Mrs. Downe Wright, with a well *got-up*, good-humoured laugh. 'A woman has only not to be a wit or a genius, and there is no fear of her; not that *I* have that antipathy to a clever woman that many people have, and especially the gentlemen. I almost quarrelled with Mr. Headley, the great author, t'other day, for saying that he would rather encounter a nest of wasps than a clever woman.'

'I should most cordially have agreed with him,' said Lady Emily, with equal *naïveté*. 'There is nothing more insupportable than one of your clever women, so called. They are generally under-bred, consequently vulgar. They pique themselves upon saying good things *coûte qu'il coûte*.[1] There is something, in short, quite professional about them; and they wouldn't condescend to chat nonsense as you and I are doing at this moment—oh! not for worlds! Now, I think one of the great charms of life consists in talking nonsense. Good nonsense is an exquisite thing; and 'tis an exquisite thing to be stupid sometimes, and to say nothing at all. Now, these enjoyments the clever women must forego. Clever she is, and clever she must be. Her life must be a greater drudgery than that of any actress. *She* merely frets her hour upon the stage;[2] the curtain dropped, she may become as dull as she chooses; but the clever woman must always stage it even at her own fireside.'

'Lady Emily Lindore is certainly the last person from whom I should have expected to hear a panegyric on stupidity,' said Mrs. Downe Wright, with some bitterness.

'Stupidity!—oh, heavens! my blood curdles at the thought of real, genuine, downright stupidity. No! I should always like to have the command of intellect, as well as of money, though my taste, or my indolence, or my whim, perhaps never would incline me to be always sparkling, whether in wit or in diamonds. 'Twas only when I was in the nursery that I envied the good girl who spoke rubies and pearls. Now, it seems to me only just better than not spitting toads and vipers.' And she warbled a sprightly French *ariette* to a tame bullfinch that perched upon her hand.

There was an airy, high-bred elegance in Lady
Emily's impertinence, that seemed to throw Mrs. Downe
Wright's coarse sarcasms to an immeasurable distance;
and that lady was beginning to despair, but she was
determined not to give in while she could possibly stand
out. She accordingly rallied her forces, and turned to
Mary—

'So you have lost your neighbour, Mrs. Lennox, since
I was here? I think she was an acquaintance of yours.
Poor woman! her death must have been a happy release
to herself and her friends. She has left no family, I
believe?' quite aware of the report of Mary's engagement
with Colonel Lennox.

'Only one son,' said Mary, with a little emotion.

'Oh! very true. He's in the law, I think?'

'In the army,' answered Mary faintly.

'That's a poor trade,' said Mrs. Downe Wright, 'and I
doubt he'll not have much to mend it. Rose Hall's but a
poor property. I've heard they might have had a good
estate in Scotland if it hadn't been for the pride of the
General, that wouldn't let him change his name for it.
He thought it grander to be a poor Lennox than a rich
Macnaughton, or some such name. It's to be hoped the
son's of the same mind.'

'I have no doubt of it,' said Lady Emily: ''Tis a noble
name—quite a legacy in itself.'

'It's one that, I am afraid, will not be easily turned
into bank notes, however,' returned Mrs. Downe Wright,
with a *real* hearty laugh. And then, delighted to get off
with what she called flying colours, she hastily rose with
an exclamation at the lateness of the hour, and a remark
how quickly time passed in pleasant company; and, with
friendly shakes of the hand, withdrew.

'How very insupportable in such a woman!' said Lady
Emily to Mary, 'who, to gratify her own malice, says the

most cutting things to her neighbours, and, at the same time, feels self-approbation in the belief that she is doing good. And yet, hateful as she is, I blush to say, I have sometimes been amused by her ill-nature, when it was directed against people I hated still more. Lady Matilda Sufton, for example,—there she certainly shone, for hypocrisy is always fair game; and yet the people who love to hunt it are never amiable. You smile, as much as to say, here is Satan preaching a sermon on holiness. But, however satirical and intolerant you may think me, you must own that I take no delight in the discovery of other people's faults: if I want the meekness of a Christian, at least, I don't possess the malice of a Jew. Now, Mrs. Downe Wright has a real heartfelt satisfaction in saying malicious things, and in thrusting herself into company, where she must know she is unwelcome, for the sole purpose of saying them. Yet many people are blessed with such blunt perceptions, that they are not at all aware of her real character, and only wonder, when she has left them, what made them feel so uncomfortable when she was present. But she has put me in such a bad humour, that I must go out of doors, and apostrophise the sun, like Lucifer.[1] Do come, Mary, you will help to dispel my chagrin. I really feel as if my heart had been in a lime-kiln, all its kindly feelings are so burnt up by the malignant influences of Mrs. Downe Wright; while you,' continued she, as they strolled into the gardens, 'are as cool, and as sweet, and as sorrowful as these violets,' gathering some still wet with an April shower. 'How delicious, after such a mental *sirocco*, to feel the pure air, and hear the birds sing, and look upon the flowers and blossoms, and sit here, and bask in the sun from laziness to walk into the shade. You must needs acknowledge, Mary, that spring in England is a much more amiable season than in your ungentle clime.'

This was the second spring Mary had seen set in, in

England. But the first had been wayward and backward as the seasons of her native climate. The present was such a one as poets love to paint. Nature was in all its first freshness and beauty—the ground was covered with flowers—the luxuriant hedge-rows were white with blossoms—the air was impregnated with the odours of the gardens and orchards. Still Mary sighed as she thought of Lochmarlie: Its wild tangled woods, with here and there a bunch of primroses peeping forth from amidst moss and withered fern—its gurgling rills, blue lakes, rocks, and mountains—all rose to view; and she felt, that, even amid fairer scenes, and beneath brighter suns, her heart would still turn with fond regret to the land of her birth.

CHAPTER XXI

'Wondrous it is, to see in diverse mindes
How diversly Love doth his pageants play,
And shews his power in variable kinds.'

Spenser.[1]

BUT EVEN THE charms of spring were overlooked by Lady Emily, in the superior delight she experienced at hearing that the ship, in which Edward Douglas was, had arrived at Portsmouth; and the intelligence was soon followed by his own arrival at Beech Park. He was received by her with rapture, and by Mary with the tenderest emotion. Lord Courtland was always glad of an addition to the family party; and even Lady Juliana experienced something like emotion, as she beheld her son, now the exact image of what his father had been twenty years before.

Edward Douglas was, indeed, a perfect model of youthful beauty, and possessed of all the high spirits and happy *insouciance*, which can only charm at that early period. He loved his profession, and had already distinguished himself in it. He was handsome, brave, good-hearted, and good-humoured, but he was not clever; and Mary felt some solicitude as to the permanency of Lady Emily's attachment to him. But Lady Emily, quick-sighted to the defects of the whole world, seemed happily blind to those of her lover; and, when even Mary's spirits were almost exhausted by his noisy rattle, Lady Emily, charmed and exhilarated, entered into all his practical jokes, and boyish frolics, with the greatest delight.

She soon perceived what was passing in Mary's mind.

'I see perfectly well what you think of my *penchant* for Edward,' said she one day; 'I can tell you exactly what was passing in your thoughts just now. You were thinking how strange, how passing strange[1] it is, that I, who am (false modesty avaunt!) certainly cleverer than Edward, should yet be so partial to him, and that my lynx eyes should have failed to discover in him faults, which, with a single glance, I should have detected in others. Now, can't you guess what renders even these very faults so attractive to me?'

'The old story, I suppose?' said Mary. 'Love.'

'Not at all. Love might blind me to his faults altogether, and then my case would be, indeed, hopeless, were I living in the belief that I was loving a piece of perfection—a sort of Apollo Belvidere[2] in mind, as well as in person. Now, so far from that, I could reckon you up a whole catalogue of his faults; and, nevertheless, I love him with my whole heart, faults and all. In the first place, they are the faults with which I have been familiar from infancy; and therefore they possess a charm (to my shame be it said!) greater than other people's virtues would have to me. They come over my fancy like some snatch of an old nursery song, which one loves to hear in defiance of taste and reason, merely because it is something that carries us back to those days, which, whatever they were in reality, always look bright and sunny in retrospection. In the second place, his faults are real, genuine, natural faults; and, in this age of affectation, how refreshing it is to meet with even a natural fault! I grant you, Edward talks absurdly, and asks questions, *à faire dresser les cheveux*,[1] of a Mrs. Bluemits. But that amuses me; for his ignorance is not the ignorance of vulgarity or stupidity, but the ignorance of a light head, and a merry heart—of one, in short, whose understanding has been at sea when other people's were at school. His *bon mots* certainly would not do to be printed; but then they make me laugh a great deal more than if they were better, for he is always *naif* and original, and I prefer an indifferent original any day to a good copy. How it shocks me to hear people recommending to their children to copy such a person's manners! A copied manner, how insupportable! The servile imitator of a set pattern, how despicable! No! I would rather have Edward in all the freshness of his own faults, than in the faded semblance of another person's proprieties.'

Mary agreed to the truth of her cousin's observations in some respects, though she could not help thinking, that love had as much to say in her case as in most others; for if it did not blind her to her lover's faults, it certainly made her much more tolerant of them.

Edward was, in truth, at times, almost provokingly boyish and unthinking, and possessed a flow of animal spirits as inexhaustible as they were sometimes overpowering; but she flattered herself time would subdue them to a more rational tone: and she longed for his having the advantages of Colonel Lennox's society—not by way of pattern, as Lady Emily expressed it, but that he might be gradually led to something of more refinement, from holding intercourse with a superior mind. And she obtained her wish sooner than she had dared to hope for it. That battle was fought which decided the fate of Europe, and turned so many swords into plough-shares;[1] and Mary seemed now touching the pinnacle of happiness, when she saw her lover restored to her. He had gained additional renown in the bloody field of Waterloo; and, more fortunate than others, his military career had terminated both gloriously and happily.

If Mary had ever distrusted the reality of his affection, all her doubts were now at an end. She saw she was beloved with all the truth and ardour of a noble in-genuous mind, too upright to deceive others, too en-lightened to deceive itself. All reserve betwixt them was now at an end; and, secure in mutual affection, nothing seemed to oppose itself to their happiness.

Colonel Lennox's fortune was small; but, such as it was, it seemed sufficient for all the purposes of rational enjoyment. Both were aware, that wealth is a relative thing, and that the positively rich are not those who have the largest possessions, but those who have the fewest vain or selfish desires to gratify. From these they were happily exempt. Both possessed too many resources in their own minds to require the stimulus of spending money to rouse them into enjoyment, or give them additional importance in the eyes of the world; and, above all, both were too thoroughly Christian in their principles, to murmur at any sacrifices or privations they might have to endure in the course of their earthly pilgrimage.

But Lady Juliana's weak, worldly mind, saw things in a very different light; and when Colonel Lennox, as a matter of form, applied to her for her consent to their union, he received a positive and angry refusal. She declared she never would consent to any daughter of hers making so foolish, so very unsuitable a marriage. And then sending for Mary, she charged her, in the most peremptory manner, to break off all intercourse with Colonel Lennox.

Poor Mary was overwhelmed with grief and amazement at this new display of her mother's tyranny and injustice, and used all the powers of reasoning and entreaty to alter her sentiments; but in vain. Since Adelaide's elopement, Lady Juliana had been much in want of some subject to occupy her mind—something to excite a sensation, and give her something to complain of, and talk about, and put her in a bustle, and make her angry, and alarmed, and ill-used, and, in short, all the things which a fool is fond of being.

Although Mary had little hopes of being able to prevail by any efforts of reason, she yet tried to make her mother comprehend the nature of her engagement with Colonel Lennox as of a sacred nature, and too binding ever to be dissolved. But Lady Juliana's wrath blazed forth with redoubled violence at the very mention of an engagement. She had never heard of any thing so improper. Colonel Lennox must be a most unprincipled man to lead her daughter into an engagement unsanctioned by her; and she had acted in the most improper manner in allowing herself to form an attachment without the consent of those who had the best title to dispose of her. The person who could act thus was not fit to be trusted, and in future it would be necessary for her to have her constantly under her own eye.

Mary found her candour had therefore only reduced her to the alternative of either openly rebelling, or of submitting to be talked at, and watched, and guarded, as if she had been detected in carrying on some improper clandestine intercourse. But she submitted to all the restrictions that were imposed, and the torments that were inflicted, if not with the heroism of a martyr, at least with the meekness of one; for no murmur escaped her lips. She was only anxious to conceal from others the

extent of her mother's folly and injustice, and took every
opportunity of entreating Colonel Lennox's silence and
forbearance. It required, indeed, all her influence, to
induce him to submit patiently to the treatment he
experienced. Lady Juliana had so often repeated to Mary
that it was the greatest presumption in Colonel Lennox
to aspire to a daughter of hers, that she had fairly talked
herself into the belief that he was all she asserted him to
be—a man of neither birth nor fortune—certainly a
Scotsman, from his name—consequently having thousands of poor cousins, and vulgar relations of every
description. And she was determined that no daughter of
hers should ever marry a man whose family connections
she knew nothing about. She had suffered a great deal
too much from her (Mary's) father's low relations ever
to run the risk of any thing of the same kind happening
again. In short, she at length made it out clearly to her
own satisfaction, that Colonel Lennox was scarcely a
gentleman; and she therefore considered it as her duty
to treat him, on every occasion, with the most marked
rudeness. Colonel Lennox pitied her folly too much to be
hurt by her ill-breeding and malevolence; but he could
scarcely reconcile it to his notions of duty, that Mary's
superior mind should submit to the thraldom of one who
evidently knew not good from evil.

Lady Emily was so much engrossed by her own affairs,
that, for some time, all this went on unnoticed by her. At
length, she was struck with Mary's dejection, and observed that Colonel Lennox seemed also dispirited; but,
imputing it to a lover's quarrel, she laughingly taxed
them with it. Although Mary could suppress the cause
of her uneasiness, she was too ingenuous to deny it; and,
being pressed by her cousin, she at length disclosed to her
the cause of her sorrow.

'Colonel Lennox and you have behaved like two fools,'
said she, at the end of her cousin's communication. 'What

could possibly instigate you to so absurd an act as that of asking Lady Juliana's consent? You surely might have known, that the person who is never consulted about any thing will invariably start difficulties to every thing; and that people, who are never accustomed to be even listened to, get quite unmanageable when appealed to. Lady Juliana gave an immediate assent to Lord Glenallan's proposals, because she was the first person consulted about them; and, besides, she had a sort of an instinctive knowledge that it would create a sensation and make her of consequence—in short, she was to act in a sort of triple capacity, as parent, lover, and bride. Here, on the contrary, she was aware that her consent would stand as a mere cipher, and, once given, would never be more heard of. Liberty of opinion is a latitude many people quite lose themselves in. When once they attempt to think, it makes confusion worse confounded: so it is much better to take that labour off their hands, and settle the matter for them. It would have been quite time enough to have asked Lady Juliana's consent after the thing was over; or, at any rate, the minute before it was to take place. I would not even have allowed her time for a flood of tears, or a fit of hysterics. And now, that your duty has brought you to this, even my genius is at a loss how to extricate you. Gretna Green might have been advisable, and that would have accorded with your notions of duty; that would have been following your mamma's own footsteps; but it is become too vulgar an exploit. I read of a hatter's apprentice having carried off a grocer's heiress t'other day—What do you purpose doing yourself?'

'To try the effect of patience and submission,' said Mary, 'rather than openly set at defiance one of the most sacred duties—the obedience of a child to a parent. Besides, I could not possibly be happy were I to marry under such circumstances.'

'You have much too nice a conscience,' said Lady Emily; 'and yet I could scarcely wish you otherwise than you are. What an angel you are, to behave as you do to such a mother; with such sweetness, and gentleness, and even respect! Ah! they know little of human nature, who think, that to perform great actions one must necessarily be a great character. So far from that, I now see, there may be much more real greatness of mind displayed in the quiet tenor of a woman's life, than in the most brilliant exploits that ever were performed by man. Methinks, I myself could help to storm a city; but to rule my own spirit, is a task beyond me. What a pity it is you and I cannot change places. Here am I, languishing for a little opposition to my love. My marriage will be quite an insipid, every-day affair: I yawn already to think of it. Can any thing be more disheartening to a young couple, anxious to signalize their attachment in the face of the whole world, than to be allowed to take their own way? Conceive my vexation at being told by papa this morning, that he had not the least objection to Edward and me marrying whenever we pleased, although he thought we might both have done better; but that was our own affair, not his. That he thought Edward a fine, good humoured fellow—excessively amusing—hoped he would get a ship some day, although he had no interest whatever in the admiralty—was sorry he could not give us any money, but hoped we should remain at Beech Park as long as we liked.—I really feel quite flat with all those dull affirmations.'

'What! you had rather have been locked up in a tower—wringing your hands at the height of the windows, the thickness of the walls, and so forth,' said Mary.

'No: I should never have done any thing so like a washerwoman, as to wring my hands; though I might, like some heroines, have fallen to work in a regular blacksmith-way, by examining the lock of the door, and, perhaps, have succeeded in picking it; but, alas! I live in degenerate days. Oh! that I had been born the persecuted daughter of some ancient Baron bold, instead of the spoiled child of a good natured modern Earl! Heavens! to think that I must tamely, abjectly submit to be married in the presence of all my family, even in the very parish church! Oh, what detractions from the brilliancy of my star!'

In spite of her levity, Lady Emily was seriously interested in her cousin's affairs, and tried every means of obtaining Lady Juliana's consent: but Lady Juliana was become more unmanageable than ever. Her temper, always bad, was now soured by chagrin and disappointment into something, if possible, still worse, and Lady Emily's authority had no longer any controul over her; even the threat of producing aunt Grizzy to a brilliant assembly, had now lost its effect. Dr. Redgill was the only auxiliary she possessed in the family, and he most cordially joined her in condemning Miss Mary's obstinacy and infatuation. What could she see in a man with such an insignificant bit of property, a mere nest for blackbirds and linnets, and such sort of vermin. Not a morsel of any sort of game on his grounds; while at Glenallan, he had been credibly informed, such was the abundance, that the deer had been seen stalking, and the black cock flying, past the very door! But the Doctor's indignation was suddenly suspended by a fit of apoplexy; from which, however, he rallied, and passed it off for the present as a sort of vertigo, in consequence of the shock he had received at hearing of Miss Mary's misconduct.

At length even Colonel Lennox's forbearance was exhausted, and Mary's health and spirits were sinking beneath the conflict she had to maintain, when a sudden revolution in Lady Juliana's plans caused also a revolution in her sentiments. This was occasioned by a letter from Adelaide, now Lady Lindore: It was evidently written under the influence of melancholy and discontent; and, as Lady Emily said, nothing could be a stronger proof of poor Adelaide's wretchedness, than her expressing a wish that her mother should join her in the south of France, where she was going on account of her health.

Adelaide was, indeed, one of the many melancholy proofs of the effects of headstrong passions and perverted principles. Lord Lindore had married her from a point of honour; and although he possessed too much refinement to treat her ill, yet his indifference was not the less cutting to a spirit haughty as hers. Like many others, she had vainly imagined, that, in renouncing virtue itself for the man she loved, she was for ever ensuring his boundless gratitude and adoration: and she only awoke from her delusive dream, to find herself friendless in a foreign land—an outcast from society—an object of indifference, even to him for whom she had abandoned all.

But Lady Juliana would see nothing of all this: She was charmed at what she termed this proof of her daughter's affection, in wishing to have her with her; and the prospect of going abroad seemed like a vision of paradise to her. Instant preparations were made for her departure, and in the bustle attendant on them, Mary and her affairs sunk into utter insignificance. Indeed, she seemed rather anxious to get her disposed of, in any way that might prevent her interfering with her own plans; and a consent to her marriage, such as it was, was easily obtained.

'Marry whom you please,' said she; 'only remember I am not responsible for the consequences. I have always told you what a wretched thing a love-marriage is, therefore you are not to blame me for your future misery.'

Mary readily subscribed to the conditions; but, as she embraced her mother at parting, she timidly whispered a hope that she would ever consider her house as her home. A smile of contempt was the only reply she received, and they parted never more to meet. Lady Juliana found foreign manners and principles too congenial to her taste, ever to return to Britain.

CHAPTER XXII

'O most gentle Jupiter! what tedious homily of love have you wearied your parishioners withal, and never cryed, *Have patience, good people!*'

As You Like It.[1]

THE ONLY OBSTACLE to her union thus removed, Mary thought she might now venture to let her aunt Grizzy into the secret; and accordingly, with some little embarrassment, she made the disclosure of the mutual attachment subsisting between Colonel Lennox and herself. Grizzy received the communication with all the astonishment which ladies usually experience, upon being made acquainted with a marriage which they had not had the prescience to foresee and foretell—or even one which they had; for, common and natural as the event seems to be, it is one which, perhaps, in no instance ever took place, without occasioning the greatest amazement to some one individual or another; and it will also be generally found, that either the good or the bad fortune of one or other of the parties, is the subject of universal wonder. In short, a marriage which excites no surprise, pity, or indignation, must be something that has never yet been witnessed on the face of this round world. It is greatly to be feared, none of my readers will sympathise in the feelings of the good spinster on this occasion, as she poured them forth in the following *extempore* or *improvisitorial* strain:

'Well, Mary, I declare I'm perfectly confounded with all you have been telling me! I'm sure I never heard the like of it! It seems but the t'other day since you began your sampler; and it looks just like yesterday since your father and mother were married. And such a work as there was at your nursing! I'm sure your poor grandfather was out of all patience about it. And now to think that you are going to be married! not but what it's a thing we all expected, for there's no doubt England's the place for young women to get husbands—we always said that, you know: Not but what I daresay you might have been married, if you had staid in the Highlands, and to a real Highlander, too, which, of course, would have been still better for us all; for it will be a sad thing if you are obliged to stay in England, Mary; but I hope there's no chance of that: You know, Colonel Lennox can easily sell his place, and buy an estate in the Highlands. There's a charming property, I know, to be sold just now, that *marches* with[1] Glenfern. To be sure it's on the wrong side of the hill—there's no denying that; but then, there's I can't tell you how many thousand acres of fine muir[2] for shooting, and I daresay Colonel Lennox is a keen sportsman; and they say, a great deal of it might be very much improved. We must really inquire after it, Mary, and you must speak to Colonel Lennox about it, for you know such a property as that may be snapped up in a minute.'

Mary assented to all that was said; and Grizzy proceeded—

'I wonder you never brought Colonel Lennox to see us, Mary: I'm sure he must think it very odd. To be sure, Sir Sampson's situation is some excuse; but, at any rate, I wonder you never spoke about him. We all found out your aunt Bella's attachment from the very first, just from her constantly speaking about Major M'Tavish and the militia; and we had a good guess of Betsy's too, from the day her face turned so red after giving Captain M'Nab for her toast;[1] but you have really kept yours very close, for, I declare, I never once suspected such a thing. I wonder if that was Colonel Lennox that I saw you part with at the door one day: tall, and with brown hair, and a blue coat. I asked Lady Maclaughlan if she knew who it was, and she said it was Admiral Benbow; but I think she must have been mistaken, for I daresay, now, it was just Colonel Lennox. Lennox—I'm sure I should be able to remember something about somebody of that name; but my memory's not so good as it used to be, for I have so many things, you know, to think about, with Sir Sampson, that, I declare, sometimes my head's quite confused; yet I think always there's something about them. I wish to goodness Lady Maclaughlan was come from the dentist's, that I might consult her about it; for, of course, Mary, you'll do nothing without consulting all your friends: I know you've too much sense for that. And here's Sir Sampson coming; it will be a fine piece of news to tell him.'

Sir Sampson having been now wheeled in by the still active Philistine, and properly arranged, with the assistance of Miss Grizzy, she took her usual station by the side of his easy chair, and began to shout into his ear.

'Here's my niece Mary, Sir Sampson; you remember her when she was little, I daresay—you know you used to call her the fairy of Lochmarlie; and I'm sure we all thought for long she would have been a perfect fairy, she was so little; but she's tall enough now, you see, and she's going to be married to a fine young man—none of us know him yet, but I think I must have seen him; and, at any rate, I'm to see him to-morrow, and you will see him too, Sir Sampson, for Mary is to bring him to call here, and he'll tell you all about the battle of Waterloo, and the Highlanders; for he's half a Highlander too, and I'm certain he'll buy the Dhuanbog estate; and then when my niece Mary marries Colonel Lennox—'

'Lennox!' repeated Sir Sampson, his little dim eyes kindling at the name—'Who talks of Lennox?—I—I won't suffer it.—Where's my Lady?—Lennox!—he's a scoundrel!—you shan't marry a Lennox!'—Turning to Grizzy, 'Call Philistine, and my Lady.' And his agitation was so great, that even Grizzy, although accustomed for forty years to witness similar ebullitions, became alarmed.

'You see it's all for fear of my marrying,' whispered she to Mary: 'I'm sure such a disinterested attachment, it's impossible for me ever to repay it!'

Then turning to Sir Sampson, she sought to sooth his perturbation by oft-repeated assurances, that it was not her but her niece Mary that was going to be married to Colonel Lennox: But in vain; Sir Sampson quivered, and panted, and muttered; and the louder Grizzy screamed out the truth, the more his irritation increased. Recourse was now had to Philistine; and Mary, thoroughly ashamed of the *éclat* attending the disclosure of her secret, and finding she could be of no use, stole away in the midst of Miss Grizzy's endless *verbiage;* but as she descended the stairs, she still heard the same assurance resounding—'I can assure you, Sir Sampson, it's not me, but my niece Mary that's going to be married to Colonel Lennox,' &c.

On returning to Beech Park, she said nothing of what had passed either to Lady Emily or Colonel Lennox— aware of the amusement it would furnish to both; and she felt that her aunt required all the dignity with which she could invest her, before presenting her to her future nephew. The only delay to her marriage now rested with herself; but she was desirous it should take place under the roof which had sheltered her infancy, and sanctioned by the presence of those whom she had ever regarded as her parents. Lady Emily, Colonel Lennox, and her brother, had all endeavoured to combat this resolution, but in vain; and it was therefore settled, that she should remain to witness the union of her brother and her cousin, and then return to Lochmarlie. But all Mary's preconceived plans were threatened with a downfall, by the receipt of the following letter from Miss Jacky:

Glenfern Castle, ——shire,
June 19, 181-.

'It *is* impossible for *language* to express to *you* the *shame*, grief, amazement, and *indignation*, with *which* we are *all* filled at the distressing, the *ignominious* disclosure that has *just* taken *place* concerning you, *through* our most *excellent* friend Miss P. M'Pry. Oh, Mary, *how* have you *deceived* us all!!! What a *dagger* have *you* plunged into *all* our hearts! Your *poor* aunt *Grizzy!* how my *heart* bleeds *for* her! What a difficult part *has* she to act! and at her *time* of life! with her acute *feelings!* with her devoted *attachment* to the *house* of Maclaughlan! What a *blow!* and a *blow* from your *hand!* Oh, Mary, I *must* again repeat, how *have* you deceived us *all!!!* Yet *do* not imagine I mean to *reproach* you! Much, much of the blame is *doubtless* imputable to the errors of *your* education! At the *same* time, even these *offer* no justification of your *conduct* upon the present occasion! You are now (I lament to say it!) *come* to that time of *life* when *you* ought to know *what* is right; or, where you entertain *any* doubts, you ought *most* unquestionably to *apply* to those *who*, you *may* be certain, *are* well qualified to direct you. *But*, instead *of* that, you have *pursued* a diametrically opposite *plan:* a plan which *might* have *ended* in your destruction! Oh, Mary, *I* cannot too *often* repeat, how have *you* deceived us all!!! From no *lips* but those of Miss M'Pry *would* I have believed *what* I have heard, videlicet, that you (oh, Mary!) have for many, many months *past*, been carrying on a clandestine *correspondence* with a *young* man, unknown, unsuspected by *all* your friends here! and that *young* man, the very *last* man on the face of the *earth* whom you, or any of *us*, ought to have given our countenance *to!* The very man, in *short*, whom we were all *bound*, by every *principle* of duty, gratitude, and esteem, to have shunned, and who you are *bound*, from this *moment*, to renounce for ever. How you ever *came* to be acquainted *with* Colonel Charles Lennox of Rose Hall, is a mystery none of us can fathom; but surely the person, *whoever* it was that *brought* it about, has much, *much* to answer for! Mrs. Douglas (to whom I *thought* it proper to *make* an immediate *communication* on the subject) pretends to *have* been well informed of all that has *been* going on, and even insists that *your* acquaintance *with* the Lennox family *took* place through Lady Maclaughlan! *But* that we *all* know to be *morally* impossible. Lady Maclaughlan is the *very* last person in the *world* who would have *introduced* you, or any *young* creature for whom she had the *slightest* regard, to a Lennox, the *mortal enemy of the Maclaughlan race!* I most *sincerely* trust she is spared the *shock* we have all experienced at this painful *disclosure*. With her *high* principles, and *great* regard for us, I tremble to think *what* might be the consequences! And dear Sir Sampson, in his delicate state, how *would* he ever be able to *stand* such a blow! and a blow, too, from your *hand*, Mary! you, who he *was* always *like* a father to! *Many* a time, I am sure, *have* you sat upon his *knee*; and you certainly *cannot* have forgot the *elegant* Shetland poney he presented you *with* the day you was five *years* old! and *what* a return for such favours!

'But I fondly trust it *is* not yet too late. You have *only* to give up this unworthy attachment, and all *will* be forgotten and *forgiven;* and we will all receive you as if *nothing* had happened. Oh, Mary! I must, for the last *time* repeat, how have you deceived us *all!!*

'I am your *distressed* aunt,

' JOAN DOUGLAS.

'P. S. I conclude abruptly, in *order* to leave *room* for your aunt Nicky to *state* her sentiments also on this *most* afflicting subject.'

Nicky's appendix was as follows:

'DEAR MARY,

'Jacky has read her letter to us. It is most excellent. We are all much affected by it. Not a word but deserves to be printed. I can add nothing. You see, if you marry Colonel L. none of us can be at your marriage. How could we? I hope you will think twice about it. Second thoughts are best.[1] What's done cannot be undone.[2]

'Yours,

'N. D.'

Mary felt somewhat in the situation of the sleeper awakened, as she perused these mysterious anathemas; and rubbed her eyes more than once, in hopes of dispelling the mist that she thought must needs be upon them. But in vain: it seemed only to increase with every effort she made to remove it. Not a single ray of light fell on the palpable obscure[3] of Miss Jacky's composition, that could enable her to penetrate the dark profound that encompassed her. She was aware, indeed, that when her aunt meant to be pathetic or energetic, she always had recourse to the longest and the strongest words she could possibly lay her hands upon; and Mary had been well accustomed to hear her childish faults and juvenile indiscretions denounced, in the most awful terms, as crimes of the deepest dye. Many an exordium she had listened to, on the tearing of her frock, or the losing of her glove, that might have served as a preface to the Newgate Calendar,[1] Colquhoun on the Police,[2] or any other register of crimes. Still she had always been able to detect some clue to her own misdeeds; but here even conjecture was baffled, and in vain she sought for some resting place for her imagination, in the probable misdemeanour of her lover. But even allowing all possible latitude for Jacky's pen, she was forced to acknowledge there must be some ground for her aunt to build upon. Superficial as her structures generally were, like children's card-houses, they had always something to rest upon; though (unlike them) her creations were invariably upon a gigantic scale.

Mary had often reflected with surprise, that, although Lady Maclaughlan had been the person to introduce her to Mrs. Lennox, no intercourse had taken place between the families themselves; and when she had mentioned them to each other, Mrs. Lennox had only sighed, and Lady Maclaughlan had humphed. She despaired of arriving at the knowledge of the truth from her aunts. Grizzy's brain was a mere wisp of contradictions; and Jacky's mind was of that violent hue, that cast its own shade upon every object that came in contact with it. To mention the matter to Colonel Lennox was only to make her relations ridiculous; and, in short, although it was a formidable step, the result of her deliberation was to go to Lady Maclaughlan, and request a solution of her aunt's dark sayings. She therefore departed for Milsom Street, and, upon entering the drawing-room, found Grizzy alone, and evidently in even more than usual perturbation.

'Oh, Mary!' cried she, as her niece entered, 'I'm sure, I'm thankful you're come. I was just wishing for you. You can't think how much mischief your yesterday's visit has done. It's a thousand pities, I declare, that ever

you said a word about your marriage to Sir Sampson.
But, of course, I don't mean to blame you, Mary. You
know you couldn't help it; so don't vex yourself, for you
know that will not make the thing any better now. Only if
Sir Sampson should die—to be sure I must always think
it was you that killed him; and I'm sure that will soon
kill me too—such a friend—Oh, Mary!' Here a burst of
grief choked poor Miss Grizzy's utterance.

'My dear aunt,' said Mary, 'you certainly must be
mistaken. Sir Sampson seems to retain no recollection of
me. It is therefore impossible that I could cause him any
pain or agitation.'

'O certainly!' said Grizzy. 'There's no doubt Sir
Sampson has quite forgot you, Mary—and no wonder—
with your being so long away; but I daresay he'll come
to know you yet. But I'm sure, I hope to goodness he'll
never know you as Mrs. Lennox, Mary. That would
break his heart altogether; for you know the Lennoxes
have always been the greatest enemies of the Maclaughlans,—and, of course, Sir Sampson can't bear any body
of the name, which is quite natural. And it was very
thoughtless in me to have forgot that, till Philistine put
me in mind of it, and poor Sir Sampson has had a very
bad night; so I'm sure, I hope, Mary, you'll never think
any more about Colonel Lennox: and, take my word for
it, you'll get plenty of husbands yet. Now, since there's a
peace, there will be plenty of fine young officers coming
home. There's young Balquhadan, a captain, I know, in
some regiment; and there's Dhalahulish, and Loch-
grunason, and——.' But Miss Grizzy's ideas here shot out
into so many ramifications upon the different branches
of the county tree, that it would be in vain for any but a
true Celt to attempt to follow her.

Mary again tried to lead her back to the subject of the
Lennoxes, in hopes of being able to extract some spark
of knowledge from the dark chaos of her brain.

'O, I'm sure, Mary, if you want to hear about that, I can tell you plenty about the Lennoxes; or, at any rate, about the Maclaughlans, which is the same thing. But I must first find my huswife.'

To save Miss Grizzy's reminiscences, a few words will suffice to clear up the mystery. A family feud, of remote origin, had long subsisted between the families of Lennox and Maclaughlan, which had been carefully transmitted from father to son, till the hereditary brand had been deposited in the breast of Sir Sampson. By the death of many intervening heirs, General Lennox, then a youth, was next in succession to the Maclaughlan estate; but the power of alienating it was vested in Sir Sampson, as the last remaining heir of the entail. By the mistaken zeal of their friends, both were, at an early period, placed in the same regiment, in the hope that constant association together would quickly destroy their mutual prejudices, and produce a reconciliation. But the inequalities were too great ever to assimilate. Sir Sampson possessed a large fortune, a deformed person, and a weak, vain, irritable mind. General (then Ensign) Lennox had no other patrimony than his sword—a handsome person, high spirit, and dauntless courage. With these tempers, it may easily be conceived that a thousand trifling events occurred to keep alive the hereditary animosity. Sir Sampson's vain, narrow mind, expected from his poor kinsman a degree of deference and respect, which the other, so far from rendering,[1] rather sought opportunities of shewing his contempt, and of thwarting and ridiculing him upon every occasion, till Sir Sampson was obliged to quit the regiment. From that time it was understood, that all bearing the name of Lennox were for ever excluded from the succession to the Maclaughlan estates; and it was deemed a sort of petty treason even to name the name of a Lennox in presence of this dignified chieftain.

Many years had worn away, and Sir Sampson had passed through the various modifications of human nature, from the 'mewling infant'[1] to 'mere oblivion,' without having become either wiser or better. His mind remained the same—irascible and vindictive to the last. Lady Maclaughlan had too much sense to attempt to reason or argue him out of his prejudices, but she contrived to prevent him from ever executing a new entail. She had known and esteemed both General and Mrs. Lennox before her marriage with Sir Sampson, and she was too firm and decided in her predilections ever to abandon them; and, while she had the credit of sharing in all her husband's animosity, she was silently protecting the lawful rights of those who had long ceased to consider them as such. General Lennox had always understood that he and his family were under Sir Sampson's *ban*, and he possessed too high a spirit ever to express a regret, or even allude to the circumstances. It had therefore made a very faint impression on the minds of any of his family; and in the long lapse of years, had been almost forgot by Mrs. Lennox, till recalled by Lady Maclaughlan's letter. But she had been silent on the subject to Mary; for she could not conceal from herself that her husband had been to blame—that the heat and violence of his temper had often led him to provoke and exasperate where mildness and forbearance would have soothed and conciliated, without detracting from his dignity; but her gentle heart shrunk from the task of unnecessarily disclosing the faults of the man she had loved; and when she heard Mary talk with rapture of the wild beauties of Lochmarlie, she had only sighed to think that the pride and prejudice[2] of others had alienated the inheritance of her son.

But all this Mary was still in ignorance of, for Miss Grizzy had gone completely astray in the attempt to trace the rise and progress of the Lennox and Maclaughlan feud. Happily, Lady Maclaughlan's entrance extricated her from her labyrinth, as it was the signal for her to repair to Sir Sampson. Mary, in some little confusion, was beginning to express to her Ladyship her regret at hearing that Sir Sampson had been so unwell, when she was stopped.

'My dear child, don't learn to tell lies. You don't care twopence for Sir Sampson. I know all. You are going to be married to Charles Lennox. I'm glad of it. I wished you to marry him. Whether you'll thank me for that twenty years hence, *I* can't tell—*you* can't tell—*he* can't tell—God knows—humph! Your aunts will tell you he is Beelzebub, because his father said he could make a Sir Sampson out of a mouldy lemon. Perhaps he could. I don't know—but your aunts are fools. You know what fools are, and so do I. There are plenty of fools in the world; but if they had not been sent for some wise purpose, they wouldn't have been here; and since they are here, they have as good a right to have elbow-room in the world as the wisest. Sir Sampson hated General Lennox, because he laughed at him; and if Sir Sampson had lived a hundred years ago, his hatred might have been a fine thing to talk about now. It is the same passion that makes heroes of your De Montforts,[1] and your Manuels,[2] and your Corsairs,[3] and all the rest of them; but they wore cloaks and daggers, and these are the supporters of hatred. Every body laughs at the hatred of a little old man in a cocked hat—You may laugh too. So now God bless you! Continue as you are, and marry the man you like, though the world should set its teeth against you. 'Tis not every woman can be trusted to do that—farewell!' And with a cordial salute they parted.

Mary was too well accustomed to Lady Maclaughlan's style, not to comprehend that her marriage with Colonel Lennox was an event she had long wished for, and now most warmly sanctioned; and she hastened home to convey the glad tidings, in a letter, to her aunts, though doubtful if the truth itself would be able to pierce its way through their prejudices.

Another stroke of palsy soon rendered Sir Sampson unconscious even to the charms of Grizzy's conversation, and as she was no longer of use to him, and was evidently at a loss how to employ herself, Mary proposed that she should accompany her back to Lochmarlie, to which she yielded a joyful assent. Once convinced of Lady Maclaughlan's approbation of her niece's marriage, she could think and talk of nothing else.

Some wise individuals have thought, that most people act from the inspiration of either a good or an evil power: to which class Miss Grizzy belonged, would have puzzled the most profound metaphysician to determine. She was, in fact, a Maclaughlanite; but to find the *root* of Maclaughlan is another difficulty—thought is lost.

Colonel Lennox, although a little startled at his first introduction to his future aunt, soon came to understand the *naïveté* of her character; and his enlarged mind, and good temper, made such ample allowance for her weaknesses, that she protested, with tears in her eyes, she never knew the like of him—she never could think enough of him. She wished to goodness Sir Sampson was himself again, and could only see him, she was sure he would think just as she did, &c. &c. &c.

The day of Lady Emily's marriage arrived, and found her in a more serious mood that she had hitherto appeared in; though it seemed doubtful, whether it was most occasioned by her own prospects, or the thoughts of parting with Mary, who, with aunt Grizzy, was to set off for Lochmarlie immediately after witnessing the ceremony. Edward and his bride would fain have accompanied her; but Lord Courtland was too much accustomed to his daughter, and amused by his nephew, to bear their absence, and they therefore yielded the point, though with reluctance.

'This is all for want of a little opposition to have braced my nerves,' said Lady Emily, as she dropped a few tears. 'I verily believe I should have wept outright, had I not happily descried Dr. Redgill shrugging his shoulders at me; that has given a fillip to my spirits. After all, 'tis perhaps a foolish action I've committed. The icy bonds of matrimony are upon me already: I feel myself turning into a fond, faithful, rational, humble, meek-spirited wife! Alas! I must now turn my head into a museum, and hang up all my smart sayings inside my brain, there to petrify, as warnings to all pert misses. Dear Mary! if ever I am good for any thing, it will be to you I owe it!'

Mary could only embrace her cousin in silence, as she parted from her brother and her with the deepest emotion, and, assisted by Colonel Lennox, (who was to follow,) took her station by the side of her aunt.

'I wish you a pleasant journey, Miss Mary,' cried Dr. Redgill. 'The game season is coming on, and——:' But the carriage drove off, and the rest of the sentence was dispersed by the wind; and all that could be collected was, 'grouse always acceptable—friends at a distance—roebuck stuffed with heather carries well at all times,' &c. &c.

To one less practised in her ways, and less gifted with patience, the eternal babbling of aunt Grizzy as a travelling companion would have occasioned considerable *ennui*, if not spleen. There are, perhaps, few greater trials of temper, than that of travelling with a person who thinks it necessary to be *actively pleasant*, without a moment's intermission, from the rising till the setting sun. Grizzy was upon this fatal plan, the rock of thousands![1] Silence she thought synonymous with low spirits, and she talked, and wondered, and exclaimed incessantly, and assured Mary she need not be uneasy, she was certain Colonel Lennox would follow very soon; she had not the least doubt of that. She would not be surprised if he was to be at Lochmarlie almost as soon as themselves; at any rate, very soon after them.

But even these little torments were forgot by Mary, when she found herself again in her native land. The hills, the air, the waters, the people, even the *peat-stacks*, had a charm that touched her heart, and brought tears into her eyes as they pictured home. But her feelings arose to rapture when Lochmarlie burst upon her view, in all the grandeur, beauty, and repose of a setting sun, shedding its farewell rays of gold and purple, and tints of such matchless hue, as no pencil e'er can imitate—no poet's pen describe. Rocks, woods, hills, and waters, all shone with a radiance that seemed of more than earthly beauty. 'Oh, there are moments in life, keen, blissful, never to be forgotten!'[1] and such was the moment to Mary when the carriage stopped, and she again heard the melody of that voice familiar from infancy—and looked on the face known with her being—and was pressed to that heart where glowed a parent's love!

When Mary recovered from the first almost *agonizing* transports of joy, she marked, with delight, the increased animation and cheerfulness visible in Mrs. Douglas. All the livelier feelings of her warm heart had, indeed, been excited and brought into action, by the spirit and playfulness of her little boy, and the increased happiness of her husband; while all her uneasiness respecting her former lover was now at an end. She had heard from himself that he had married, and was happy. Without being guilty of inconstancy, such are the effects of time upon mutable human nature!

Colonel Lennox lost no time in arriving to claim his promised bride; and Mary's happiness was complete, when she found her own choice so warmly approved of by the friends she loved.

The three aunts, and their unmarried nieces, now the

sole inhabitants of Glenfern Castle, were not quite decided in their opinions at first. Miss Jacky looked with a suspicious eye upon the *mortal enemy of the Maclaughlan race;* but, upon better acquaintance, his gaiety and good humour contrived to charm asleep even her good sense and prejudices, and she pronounced him to be a pleasant, well informed young man, who gave himself no airs, although he certainly had rather a high look.

Nicky doubted, from his appearance, that he would be nice,[1] and she had no patience with nice men; but Nicky's fears vanished, when she saw, as she expressed it, 'how pleasantly he ate the sheep's head, although he had never seen one in his life before.'

The younger ladies thought Captain M'Nab had a finer complexion, and wondered whether Colonel Lennox (like him,) would be dressed in full regimentals at his marriage.

But, alas! 'all earthly good still blends itself with harm,'[2] for on the day of Mary's marriage—a day consecrated to mirth, and bride-cake, and wedding favours, and marriage presents, and good cheer, and reels, and revelry, and bagpipes—on that very day, when the marriage ceremony was scarcely over, arrived the accounts of the death of Sir Sampson Maclaughlan! But on this joyous day, even Grizzy's tears did not flow so freely as they would have done at another time; and she declared, that although it was impossible any body could feel more than she did, yet certainly it would not be using Colonel and Mrs. Lennox well, to be very distressed upon such an occasion; and there was no doubt but she would have plenty of time to be sorry about it yet, when they were all sitting quietly by themselves, with nothing else in their heads; though, to be sure, they must always think what a blessing it was that Colonel Lennox was to succeed.

'I wish he may ever fill Sir Sampson's shoes!' said Miss Nicky, with a sigh.

'Colonel Lennox cannot propose a better model to himself than Sir Sampson Maclaughlan,' said Miss Jacky: 'He has left him a noble example of propriety, frugality, hospitality, and respectability; and, above all, of forgiveness of his mortal enemies.'

'Oh, Mary!' exclaimed Miss Grizzy, as they were about to part with their niece: 'What a lucky creature you are! Never, I am sure, did any young person set out in life with such advantages. To think of your succeeding to Lady Maclaughlan's laboratory, all so nicely fitted up with every kind of thing, and especially plenty of the most charming bark,[1] which, I'm sure, will do Colonel Lennox the greatest good, as you know all officers are much the better of bark. I know it was the saving of young Ballingall's life, when he came home in an ague from some place; and I'm certain Lady Maclaughlan will leave you every thing that is there, you was always such a favourite. Not but what I must always think that you had a hand in dear Sir Sampson's death. Indeed, I have no doubt of it. Yet, at the same time, I don't mean to blame you in the least; for I'm certain, if Sir Sampson had been spared, he would have been delighted, as we all are, at your marriage.'

Colonel and Mrs. Lennox agreed in making choice of Lochmarlie for their future residence; and, in a virtuous attachment, they found as much happiness as earth's pilgrims ever possess, whose greatest felicity must spring from a higher source. The extensive influence which generally attends upon virtue joined to prosperity, was used by them for its best purposes. It was not confined either to rich or poor, to cast or sect; but all shared in their benevolence whom that benevolence could benefit. And the poor, the sick, and the desolate, united in blessing what heaven had already blessed—this happy Marriage.

FINIS

EXPLANATORY NOTES

Page xxviii. Johnson, *A Journey to the Western Islands of Scotland* (1924 ed.), pp. 19–20.

VOLUME I.

Page 1. (1) Jeremy Taylor, *Sermon XI, The Flesh and the Spirit*, 1653; probably an allusion to Susan Ferrier's reproduction of polite English and Highland Scotch.

(2) Lyly, *Alexander and Campaspe*, v. iv. 35–36.

Page 4. *Brutus*: a wig in the rough cropped style fashionable at the time.

Page 5. (1) *altar of Vulcan*: the smithy at Gretna Green.

(2) *special license*: Under a special license the parties were free to choose where and when they wished their union to be solemnized.

(3) *saloon*: reception room.

Page 6. *superseded in the Gazette*: An announcement in the official journal indicated that Henry Douglas had been deprived of his commission.

Page 7. (1) *Abigail*: a lady's maid.

(2) Thomson, *The Castle of Indolence*, i. xlviii. 5–8.

(3) *muirs*: moors.

Page 9. (1) *dykes*: stone walls.

(2) *ca' ye thon a hoose*: call you that a house.

Page 10. (1) *gin*: if.

(2) *a wheen*: a few.

(3) *to the fore*: in view.

(4) *shune*: soon.

(5) *na*: not.

(6) *twa*: two.

(7) *Johnny Groat's hooss*: John o'Groat's, the most northerly point of Great Britain.

(8) *they wad hae her . . . in a crack*: they would have her . . . in a moment.

(9) *brae*: hill.

Page 11. (1) *weel that*: yes indeed.

(2) *tu*: too.

Page 12. Milton, *Paradise Lost*, ii. 85–86.

Page 13. (1) *for*, etc.: on account of, etc.

(2) *policies*: the enclosed grounds surrounding a country seat.

Page 17. (1) *nem. con.*: nemine contradicente; unanimously.

(2) *whisky*: a light, two-wheeled carriage.

(3) *quiz*: an odd person.

(4) *vis-a-vis*: a light carriage for two persons sitting face to face.

Page 18. (1) *dejeunés et fêtes champetres*: picnics.

(2) *Elysian*: heavenly, blissful.

Page 20. Milton, *L'Allegro*, ll.135–6.

Page 21. (1) *moorfowl*: the red grouse.

(2) *bob-wig*: a wig with short curls.

Page 22. (1) *La Biondina in Gondoletta*: a contemporary Italian air, composed by J. S. Mayer (1763–1845) to the text of Antonio Lamberti (1757–1832).

(2) *Leyden's 'Fall of Macgregor'*: John Leyden (1775–1811) had been a close friend of the Ferriers. The author may have quoted her text from a private manuscript as the poem was published in 1819 only in a slightly different version with the title 'Macgregor'.

Page 24. (1) Shakespeare, *Macbeth*, III. iv. 109–10.

(2) *thae*: those.

(3) *pikters*: pictures.

Page 25. (1) As a very expensive beverage tea was served in small cups in Scotland in the 18th century. In the Highlands it was not uncommon to drink it seasoned with spices (cf. M. Plant, *The Domestic Life of Scotland in the Eighteenth Century*, 1952, p. 115).

(2) *clean*: entirely.

(3) *the night's owre far gane*, etc.: the night is too far advanced for it now.

(4) *parritch*: porridge.

(5) *patatees*: potatoes.

Page 26. (1) *moudiwort*: mole.

(2) *een*: eyes.

(3) *wit*: talent.

(4) These lines appear in a slightly different version in the song 'Mucking of Geordie's Byre' in David Herd, *Ancient and Modern Scottish Songs* (1776), II, 201.

(5) *bonny bargain*: a fine purchase (used ironically).

(6) *canna*: cannot.

(7) *blate*: a shy person.

Page 27. Milton, *Paradise Lost*, v. 333.

Page 28. *that balmy blessing, sleep*: cf. 'Balm of hurt minds, great nature's second course,' (Shakespeare, *Macbeth*, II. ii. 38).

Page 29. (1) *seven sleepers*: referring to the fable of the seven young Christian men of Ephesus who hid in a cave to escape persecution and did not wake up before 230 years were past.

(2) *ycleped*: called.

(3) *midden*: a dung hill.

(4) *planting*: plantation.

(5) *moss*: swamp.

(6) *Araby the blest*: Milton, *Paradise Lost*, iv. 163.

Page 30. gig: see *supra*, p. 17, n. 2. The author does not distinguish between *gig* and *whisky*, although the two types of light one-horse carriages did slightly differ in construction (see *O.E.D.*; *whisky*).

Page 32. (1) *clap a cauld potatae*, etc.: apply a cold potato to the animal's toe.

(2) *troth*: truly.

(3) *ken*: know.

(4) *trait*: treat.

(5) *discreetly*: politely.

Page 33. (1) *pease bannocks*: homemade cakes of pease-meal.

(2) *oat cakes*: cakes made of oatmeal.

(3) *loaf bread*: As loaf bread could not be baked in the house, white bread did not form part of the ordinary diet in Scotland (cf. M. Plant, *The Domestic Life of Scotland in the Eighteenth Century*, 1952, pp. 99–100).

Page 34. (1) Cowper, *The Task*, i. 215–7.

(2) *to make something of*, etc.: to gain an advantage from.

(3) *at fault*: cf. 'the phrase "at fault" is sometimes incorrectly used in the sense "not equal to the occasion", "in the position of having failed" ' (*O.E.D.*).

Page 35. (1) *cap-a-pee*: cap-à-pie; from head to foot.

(2) *poke-bonnets*: hats with a projecting brim.

(3) *pattens*: overshoes.

(4) *Beauty needs not*, etc.: should be 'loveliness needs not', etc. (Thomson, *Autumn*, ll. 204–6).

(5) *our roads*: In the late 18th century road conditions were still quite disastrous in Scotland (cf. H. G. Graham, *The Social Life of Scotland in the Eighteenth Century*, 1901, pp. 39–40).

Page 36. (1) *stirks and stots*: bullocks and bulls.

(2) *wise-like*: reasonable.

(3) *roquelaire*: roquelaure; a travelling cloak.

(4) *Aladin's lamp*: Aladdin in the *Arabian Nights* could command the services of a jinn and his host by rubbing his lamp.

(5) *Joseph*: a long cloak.

Page 37. (1) *the lonely heath*, etc.: Several phrases from Macpherson's *Fingal* have been compounded to make up this quotation.

(2) *nowts*: literally 'cattle'.

(3) *offices*: outhouses.

(4) I have been unable to trace this quotation.

Page 38. *to bear with one another*: cf. Eph. iv. 2; Col. iii. 13.

Page 40. *pirning*: winding yarn on a spool.

Page 41. *Even their failings*, etc.: Goldsmith, *The Deserted Village*, l. 164. (adapted).

Page 42. (1) Milton, *Paradise Lost*, iv. 295–8.

(2) *à la poissarde*: in the manner of a fishwife.

Page 47. (1) *hur need na be feared*: you (she) need not be afraid.

(2) *the war o't*: the worse for it.

(3) *hurs wad na tak' the feesick*, etc.: he would not take the medicine which the lady ordered him yesterday.

Page 48. (1) *adonise*: beautify (from the French 'adoniser').

(2) Milton, *Paradise Lost*, v. 294–6.

(3) *hour of dinner*: Towards the end of the 18th century dinner was served in the late afternoon in Scotland (cf. M. Plant, *The Domestic Life of Scotland in the Eighteenth Century*, 1952, pp. 111–2).

(4) *pompadour*: pink.

(5) *à la militaire*: in uniform.

(6) *fly cap*: a lady's headdress in the shape of a butterfly.

(7) *toupee*: a topknot of hair.

Page 49. (1) *waists were not*: waists were not indicated.

(2) *stays*: corsets.

(3) The skirts of the dresses should have started much higher than the corsets would admit, which resulted in a gap between the outer garments.

Page 50. (1) Jonson, *Epicœne*, I. i. 97–100.

(2) *What's aw this wark aboot*: what's all this talk about.

(3) *are weel eneugh*: look well enough.

Page 51. It was customary at Scottish dinner-parties for gentlemen to choose their partners at table (cf. C. Rogers, *Scotland Social and Domestic*, 1869, p. 97).

Page 53. *toasts succeeded*: 'Every guest was expected to name an absent lady, while to each lady was assigned an absent gentleman. Both were toasted in a glass which must be drunk off . . .' (C. Rogers, op. cit., p. 35).

Page 54. (1) *There's nobody to dance with*: Lady Juliana failed to comprehend that her father-in-law was proposing another Scottish country-dance.

(2) *the odd trick and the honours*: terms referring to the game of whist.

(3) *loo*: a round card-game played by a varying number of persons.

(4) *quadrille*: a round card-game played by four persons.

(5) *Pope Joan*: a round card-game played by three or more persons.

(6) *commerce*: a card-game characterised by bartering, which was played with low stakes at that period only.

Page 55. (1) *five lives and grace*: five counters would be competed for and one pardon granted.

(2) *sequence*: a set of cards following one upon the other in order of their value.

(3) *life*: a counter; also the contest for it.

(4) Pope, *The Rape of the Lock*, iii. 101–3.

Page 56. *returned your adversary's lead*: Grizzy followed Glenfern's suit although he had played a higher card.

Page 57. *slop-bason*: slop-basin.

Page 59. (1) *Steady, boys, steady*, etc.: adapted from the refrain in 'Heart of Oak', a sailor's song in Garrick's *Harlequin's Invasion* (1759).

(2) Milton, *Paradise Lost*, ii. 460–2 (misquoted).

Page 60. (1) *Fordyce's Sermons*: D. D. James Fordyce (1720–96) published several collections of sermons.

(2) *a hundred a year*: This would never have done for an English gentleman, though a Scottish landowner or parish minister might have regarded it as a tolerable livelihood (cf. H. G. Graham, *The Social Life of Scotland in the Eighteenth Century*, 1901, pp. 55, 85).

(3) *it's an ill wind*, etc.: 'It is an ill wind that blows nobody good' (see *Oxford Dictionary of English Proverbs*).

(4) *puir*: poor.

(5) *a bein downset*: a comfortable settlement.

Page 61. *stocking and stedding*: the livestock and farming implements as well as the buildings.

Page 63. *eclaircissement*: explanation.

Page 64. *better late than never*: an old maxim (see *Oxford Dictionary of English Proverbs*).

Page 66. (1) Shakespeare, *Cymbeline*, III. iii. 29–34 (contracted).

(2) *skirling*: shrill sound as of the pipes.

(3) *she maun gie up*, etc.: she must give up those whims.

(4) *stirks and stots*: see *supra*, p. 36, n. 1.

(5) *it wad set her better*: it would suit her better.

(6) *a wiselike wean*: an intelligent child.

(7) *thae confoonded dougs an' paurits*: those confounded dogs and parrots.

(8) *till*: while.

(9) *hooss and offices*: house and outbuildings.

Page 67. (1) *fient a bit*, etc.: the devil take me, if I would (not) offer it to the best man in the country to sleep there himself.

(2) *oots an' ins*: ins and outs.

(3) *coo*: cow.

(4) *cauf*: calf.

(5) *doot*: doubt.

Page 68. (1) *so ye may mak the maist o't*: so you must make the most of it.

(2) *nae mair aboot it*: no more about it.

(3) *ain*: own.

(4) *grieve*: overseer.

(5) *there's nae fear o' you*: there is no reason for alarm on your account.

(6) *edication*: As in England, Scottish girls received little education at that period, but were well trained in the duties of the household. See *infra*, vol. II, ch. I, for a discussion of the customary education of daughters.

Page 69. (1) *bairns*: children.

(2) *claes*: clothes.

(3) *wait a wee*: wait a short time.

(4) *a wheen bairns*: a few children.

(5) *braw*: excellent, fine.

Page 70. Shakespeare, *As You Like It*, III. iv. 1.

Page 73. Young, *Night Thoughts*, i. 300–2 (misquoted).

Page 75. *beinveillance*: bienveillance; goodwill.

Page 76. *errors of a noble mind*: possibly an echo of 'oh, what a noble mind is here o'erthrown!' (Shakespeare, *Hamlet*, III. i. 158).

Page 86. *this blessed land of liberty*: While the English Marriage Act of 1753 made all marriages of minors dependent on their parents' consent, runaway-matches were still possible in Scotland in the late 18th century.

Page 88. *cit.*: shortened form of 'citizen'; a townsman.

Page 93. (1) Southey, *Madoc in Wales*, xiv. 10–11.

(2) *white-seam*: needlework.

(3) *sent a summer feeling*, etc.: unidentified.

Page 94. *shealing*: a rough, temporary shelter.

Page 95. *Cape jessamine*: cape jasmine; an evergreen shrub with sweet-smelling, wax-like flowers.

Page 96. *Ottomans*: cushioned seats without backs or arms.

Page 98. *more in sorrow than in anger*: Shakespeare, *Hamlet*, I. ii. 231.

Page 100. From the ballad of *Lammikin* as given in David Herd, *Ancient and Modern Scottish Songs* (1776), I. 146–7.

Page 101. (1) *barouche*: a four-wheeled carriage for two couples and an extra seat for the driver.

(2) *toupees*: see *supra*, p. 48, n.7.

(3) *club on the crown*: a bunch or knot.

Page 102. (1) *dishabille*: informal dress.

(2) *mob cap*: a morning cap to cover the hair.

Page 103. (1) *wha ta war seekin'*: whom they were looking for.

(2) *hur may see Lochmarlie hursel*: you (she) may see Lochmarlie yourself (herself). As in the case of the Laird of Glenfern the name of the residence is used to denote its owner.

Page 104. (1) *Hurs aw awa tull ta Sandy Mor's*: They have all gone away to Sandy Mor's.

(2) *Hurs i' ta teach tap*: She is in the attic.

(3) *sanctum sanctorum*: the 'holy of holies' of the Jewish temple.

Page 105. *upon the hearth*: upon the stone floor of the open fireplace.

Page 106. *Grand Seignior*: the Turkish Sultan.

Page 107. (1) *dead-thraw*: death-throe.

(2) Voltaire, *L'Enfant Prodigue*, II. 5–6.

(3) *saloon*: see *supra*, p. 5, n.3.

Page 108. (1) The following titles are not imaginary but can mostly be traced.

(2) *Bible, great and small*: with or without commentary.

Page 109. (1) *Gil Blas*: *The Adventures of Gil Blas of Santillane* by Le Sage, probably in the translation of Smollett (1749).

(2) *Clarissa Harlowe*: referring to Richardson's novel of 1747–8.

(3) *French and German school*: As will be seen later, Susan Ferrier included Rousseau and Goethe among the late 18th century French and German writers of passion and sentiment whose influence on young minds is deprecated in the novel.

(4) *Mechlin*: city in Belgium, famous for its lace.

Page 111. Shakespeare, *Macbeth*, v. i. 64–5.

Page 113. (1) *sinister-couped*: cut off on the left (heraldic).

(2) *least*: lest.

(3) *tiffany toilette*: a press to contain fine silk fabrics.

Page 114. (1) *Erebus*: in Greek mythology a place of infernal darkness.

(2) *the princess in the fairy tale*, etc.: referring to tales of transformation common to the folklore of many countries.

(3) *Mrs. Mouse*, etc.: see *Oxford Dictionary of Nursery Rhymes*, 1955, no. 175.

Page 115. *ghosts, grey, black and white*: cf. 'Black spirits and white, red spirits and grey' (Middleton, *The Witch*, v. ii. 60); this line occurs also in D'Avenant's edition of Shakespeare's *Macbeth*, IV. i. 43.

Page 116. Savage, *The Bastard*, ll. 89–90, 99.

Page 117. *tochers*: dowries.

Page 118. *her aunt's*: i.e. aunt Nicky's.

Page 120. (1) *wean*: child.

(2) *wee*: small.

(3) *unco*: extraordinarily.

Page 122. (1) *yammer*: whine.

(2) *sucking pot*: feeding bottle.

Page 124. Shakespeare, *I Henry IV*, IV. i. 54–55.

Page 125. (1) *curricle*: a two-wheeled light carriage.

(2) *fancy ball*: fancy-dress ball.

Page 126. (1) *taxes*: i.e. house tax, servants' tax, and the new income tax introduced in 1798.

(2) *state liveries*: formal occasions of the highest order at which

royal liveries would be worn.

(3) *siller*: silver.

(4) *tocher*: to provide a dowry for; cf. *supra*, p. 117, note.

Page 127. (1) *imperial*: a luggage case.

(2) *fules war fond*, etc.: 'Fools are fond o' flittin', and wise men o' sittin' ' (see *Oxford Dictionary of English Proverbs*).

(3) *dreaming bread*: Pieces of the christening cake were put under their pillows by young people in the belief that their future lovers would appear to them in their dreams (cf. also *infra*, vol. II, ch. ii).

Page 128. Horace, *The Art of Poetry*, ll. 452–4, in the translation of Philip Francis (1791).

Page 130. (1) *grossièreté*: crudeness.

(2) *hammer-cloth*: cloth covering the box of a coach.

Page 133. (1) *Grace of L—*: the wife of the former suitor of Juliana, as Mr. Brittle undoubtedly knew.

(2) *bubbled*: deceived.

(3) *china*: The import of Chinese porcelain had risen to such an extent in the late 18th century that articles were often specially manufactured to suit the Western taste. The crafty Mr. Brittle may have disposed of some of his dead stock with Lady Juliana.

Page 134. *quick step*: military march.

Page 136. unidentified.

Page 137. *Papa non dite di no*: should be 'Papa non dite no', an air from the opera *Il fanatico per la musica* by J. S. Mayer (1763–1845).

Page 138. (1) *several of the quality*: people of high rank.

(2) *Tattersall's*: Richard Tattersall's (1724–95) subscription rooms at Hyde Park Corner, where horses were sold by auction.

Page 139. (1) *gothic*: barbarous.

(2) *c' a s'entend*: that is self-understood.

Page 141. (1) Voltaire, *Discours en vers sur l'homme*, i. 152–4 (contracted).

(2) *decorations*: embellishments.

Page 144. (1) In the wars of the Coalition against revolutionary France England gave financial support to the Austrian Emperor, at that time nominally still Emperor of Germany.

(2) *speat*: flood-time.

(3) *bottle sliders*: bottle holders.

(4) *whitlow*: inflammation of the finger.

Page 145. *regulation epaulettes*: the officially prescribed shoulder pieces.

Page 147. Matthew Prior, *Henry and Emma*, ll. 387–90.

Page 150. (1) *he generally dined at eight o'clock*: This would seem unusually late, even for London, where the royal family still used to dine a five in the late 18th century (cf. A. S. Turberville, *English Men and Manners in the Eighteenth Century*, 1926, p. 81).

(2) *out of evil cometh good*: cf. Milton, *Paradise Lost*, xii. 470–1.

(3) *all is for the best*: cf. 'tout est aux mieux' (Voltaire, *Candide*, ch. i).

(4) *whatever is, is right*: Pope, *An Essay on Man*, i. 294.

Page 153. *mio caro*: my dear one; possibly suggested by the song 'mio caro bene' from Handel's opera *Rodelinda* (1725).

Page 154. (1) *King's Bench*: Henry had been detained as a debtor in the King's Bench prison in Borough High Street, named after the court under which it had originally been established.

(2) *regiment of the line*: a regular military unit as opposed to an auxiliary one.

VOLUME II

Page 157. Young, *Night Thoughts*, i. 297–9.

Page 158. L'Abbé de Bellegarde, *Réflexions sur le Ridicule* (Amsterdam, 1707), p. 394.

Page 159. *leather and prunella*: Pope, *An Essay on Man*, iv. 204; something to which one is entirely indifferent.

Page 160. (1) *Weel?*: well?

(2) *collar*: a frame-like device worn to improve the stature.

Page 161. (1) *worked the globe*: presumably, to knit or draw a circular shape with the terrestial map on it.

(2) *Betsy*: the Betty of *supra*, vol. I, p. 26.

Page 162. (1) *Inverary and Dunkeld*: Inverary Castle on Loch Fyne, the home of the Duke of Argyll, and the ruins of Dunkeld Cathedral with the residence of the Duke of Atholl on the river Tay.

(2) *kine*: cows.

(3) *Venus' girdle*: The girdle of the goddess was believed to bestow irresistible beauty on its wearer.

Page 163. (1) *shilpit*: weak, feeble.

(2) *ne'er-do-weels*, etc.: the never-do-wells who owned her; her parents.

(3) *set up with tea*: provided with tea (with the overtone that such indulgence would spoil her).

Page 164. (1) [He] *who alone knoweth*, etc.: cf. Matt. vi. 8.

(2) Dryden, *Georgics*, iv. 303–5.

(3) Shakespeare, *The Tempest*, IV. i. 156–8.

Page 165. (1) *The Whole Duty of Man*: *The Practice of Christian Graces, or, The Whole Duty of Man laid down in a plain and familiar way*, etc. (anon.), 1659, had gone through numberless editions by the end of the 18th century.

(2) *lutestring*: a silk fabric.

Page 166. (1) *sorra tak me*: may sorrow seize me.

(2) *fraize*: fuss.

(3) *gowks*: fools.

(4) *whingin get*: a whining child.

(5) *pit*: put.

(6) *ne'er a word in 'ts heed*: and not a word spoken in its interest.

(7) *at hack and manger*: in great abundance.

(8) *stamick*: stomach.

(9) *rash*: rush.

Page 167. (1) *ye wad na deive me wi' your havers*: you would not deafen me with your foolish talk.

(2) *tawpies*: dimwitted persons.

(3) *clavers*: 'claverers'; idle talkers.

Page 168. (1) *Lady Macbeth*, etc.: cf. Shakespeare, *Macbeth*, I. v.

(2) *doug*: dog.

(3) *wastery*: wastefulness.

(4) Shakespeare, *All's Well*, II. iii. i. ff.

Page 170. (1) The guests attending the christening might have stayed on to keep watch by the body of the departed: 'The body of the deceased was watched from the hour of death till the day of interment. This practice was known as the *lykwake*, or latewake. In the duties of watching, all the neighbours took part; it was continued day and night, one party of watchers succeeding the other.' (C. Rogers, *Scotland Social and Domestic*, 1869, p. 119.).

(2) *that wad hae gaen aff in this gate*: that would have departed in this manner.

(3) *I dinna ken*: I don't know.

(4) *a gay while*: a good while.

(5) *sair*: sadly.

(6) *tryst*: meeting.

(7) *tume boss-lookin'*: hollow, empty-looking.

Page 171. (1) *they maun ken*: they must know.

(2) *bod-word*: bode-word; ominous prediction.

(3) *shool the sna'*: clear the snow.

(4) *freet*: omen.

(5) *stay brae*: steep hill.

(6) *tined*: lost.

(7) *dule*: woe.

(8) *pow*: head.

(9) *jeezy*: wig.

(10) *I'se warran'*: I'll warrant.

(11) *braw*: excellent, fine.

Page 173. (1) *Castle Dochart's burying*: Place names were frequently applied to the owner as in the case of the head of the Douglas family, who always appears as Glenfern in the narrative.

(2) *dies in human hearts*, etc.: unidentified.

(3) *shine inward*: Milton, *Paradise Lost*, iii. 52.

Page 175. (1) Steele, *The Spectator*, no. 22, 26 March 1711.

(2) *Life is a mingled yarn*: cf. Shakespeare, *All's Well*, IV. iii. 72–73.

(3) *they fulfilled their destinies*: unidentified.

Page 176. *the vast chain*: cf. 'Vast chain of being, which from God began . . .' (Pope, *An Essay on Man*, i. 237).

Page 178. *dwining*: wasting away.

Page. 179. (1) *Fordyce's Sermons*: see *supra*, vol. I, p. 60, n.1.

(2) *History of Scotland*: possibly Malcolm Laing's *History of Scotland, from the Union of the Crowns to the Union of the Kingdoms*, 1800.

Page 183. (1) Thomson, *The Castle of Indolence*, I. lxxii. 1–2 (adapted).

(2) *no note of time*: 'We take no note of time' (Young, *Night Thoughts*, i. 55).

Page 184. (1) *Botany Bay*: N. S. Wales penal settlement.

(2) *barouche*: see *supra*, vol. I, p. 101, n.1.

Page 185. (1) *Russia leather*: a fine smooth leather.

(2) *atmosphere of floating knowledge*: 'Every seminary of learning may be said to be surrounded with an atmosphere of floating knowledge' (Reynolds, *The Discourses*, I).

(3) *Rumford soup*: after Sir Benjamin Thompson, Count von Rumford (1753-1814), inventor of cooking equipment that permitted an economic use of fuel.

Page 186. (1) *esprit fort*: freethinker.

(2) *shape had none distinguishable*: Milton, *Paradise Lost*, ii. 667–8.

Page 187. *piquante*: witty, sarcastic.

Page 188. Pope, *Moral Essays*, i. 128–9.

Page 190. Shakespeare, *Richard III*, I. iv. 80—81.

Page 192. (1) *daadlin'*: dawdling.

(2) *game*: gamble.

(3) *Highland Mary*: referring to the song of the same title by Robert Burns.

Page 194. (1) *Fordyce's Sermons to Young Women*: James Fordyce's *Sermons to Young Women* (1756) had reached their 14th edition in 1814.

(2) *bit snishin mull*: a small snuffbox.

(3) *sneesh*: sneeze.

Page 195. (1) *straths*: river valleys.

(2) Burns, *My Heart's in the Highlands*, 9–12.

(3) *the flood of grief decreaseth*, etc.: a similar maxim is found among the *Ornamenta Rationale*, wrongly ascribed to Bacon.

Page 196. *Haud awa frae me, Donald*: see David Herd, *Ancient and Modern Scottish Songs* (1776), II. 160–3.

Page 197. (1) Since these lines are signed with a 'C' in Bentley's 'Standard' edition of 1841, they may with some certainty be assigned to Charlotte Clavering.

(2) *nowt's head*: ox-head.

(3) *puffs and snaps*: pastries and snacks.

(4) *braxy*: actually sheep that have died of the infectious disease of that name.

Page 198. unidentified.

Page 199. (1) *the ludgin' a' tane up*: all the lodging taken up.

(2) *length o' their tae farrer*: the length of a toe farther.

(3) *Roy's Wife*: The melody of the old Scottish song *Roy's Wife of Aldivalloch* is identical to the tune *Ruffian's Rant* (see *The Poems and Songs of Robert Burns*, ed. James Kinsley, 1968, no. 177).

(4) *There's cauld kail in Aberdeen*: the old tune of *Cauld kail in Aberdeen* is reprinted in *The Poems and Songs of Robert Burns*, ed. James Kinsley, 1968, no. 398.

Page 200. (1) *offices*: see *supra*, vol. I, p. 37, n. 3.

(2) *takin' a heize on the yett*: swinging on the gate.

(3) *heize ye*: raise you.

Page 202. *walk into the fire*: draw near the fire.

Page 203. (1) *tinklers*: tinkers.

(2) *sweein'*: swinging.

Page 204. (1) *I ken nae*: I don't know.

(2) *I'se warran*: see *supra*, vol. II, p. 171, n. 10.

(3) *div*: do.

Page 205. *reduced lieutenant*: an officer deprived of his rank.

Page 207. (1) Burns, *Address to Edinburgh*, ll. 1–4.

(2) *a local habitation and a name*: Shakespeare, *A Midsummer Night's Dream*, v. i. 17.

Page 208. *bona fide*: truthful, veritable.

Page 209. (1) *Bailie*: alderman.

(2) *muckle*: much.

Page 210. (1) *the day*: to-day.

(2) *Bridewell*: This Edinburgh prison was thought far superior to other contemporary places of detention (cf. J. J. Gurney, *Notes on a Visit made to some of the Prisons in Scotland and the North of England*, 1819).

(3) *an' I war oot o't*: (I wish) that I were out of it.

(4) *lift the bouk o' a prin*: steal something the value of a pin.

Page 211. (1) *monument*: The Nelson monument on Calton Hill was built in the years 1807 to 1815. It could hardly have accommodated Mary on her visit to Edinburgh one and a half years before the battle of Waterloo.

(2) *bait there*: stop there.

(3) *manes*: spirits of the dead.

(4) Possibly a reference to the notorious Tower of London, formerly believed to have been built by Julius Caesar. Cf. *Richard II*, v. i. 1 ff.

and *Richard III*, III. i. 68 ff.

Page 212. (1) Jeremy Taylor, *Sermon XXIV: Of Slander and Flattery, III*, 1653.

(2) *Though last, not least*: cf. Shakespeare, *Julius Caesar*, III. i. 189.

Page 213. (1) *mode*: conventional as opposed to modish.

(2) *cardinal*: short cloak.

(3) *clogs*: wooden-soled overshoes.

(4) *mittens*: long gloves, covering the arms and part of the hands.

(5) *enoo*: now, at this time.

Page 214. (1) *ool*: owl.

(2) *a wheen puir feckless windlestraes*: a poor little feeble weakling.

(3) *Set ye up*: pull yourself together.

(4) *bute*: must.

(5) *whilk o' ye*: which of you.

(6) *snule*: ridiculous thing.

(7) *muckle cuits*: big ankles.

(8) *speer*: spear; inquire.

(9) *wean*: child.

(10) *unca lang o' cummin'*: extraordinarily long in coming.

(11) *kirsened*: christened.

(12) *wad or dee*: marry or die.

Page 215. (1) *weel a waat*: true enough.

(2) *or ens no*: indeed.

(3) *tyleyors and sclaters leavin'*, etc.: tailors and slaters living where I remember dukes and earls.

(4) *glowrin'*: gleaming.

(5) *bits o'bairnys rowin' an' tummlin'*: small children rowing and tumbling.

(6) *trampin'*: trampling (the washing).

(7) *stoor*: bustle, commotion.

(8) *cheels*: children.

(9) *dinket-oot*: dressed up.

(10) see *supra*, vol. II, p. 170, n. 3.

(11) *ilk ane gangs bang in*, etc.: everybody walks right into his neighbour's house.

(12) *flunky ahint his chyre*: the lackey behind his chair.

Page 216. (1) *bairnes dardna set up their gabs*: children dared not open their mouths.

(2) *trummelt*: trembled.

(3) *ill-farred tocherless queans*: ill-favoured girls without a dowry.

(4) *lang purses*: capacious purses.

(5) *hiddlins*: secret.

(6) *ploy*: party, feast.

Page 217. (1) The following account of traditional domestic festivities

is based on the memoir of a 'lady of Renfrewshire' (identified as
Elizabeth Mure of Caldwell), which was published under the title
*Views of the Change of Manners in Scotland during the Course of the Last
Century in The Edinburgh Magazine and Literary Miscellany*, 1 (1817),
10–14, 111–4. Bentley's 'Standard' edition of *Marriage* (1841) adds
the note: 'These particulars were taken from the MS. reminiscences
of an old lady – one of the aristocracy of her day.' Susan Ferrier seems
to have used the manuscript before its eventual publication: a short
review of the novel in the *Edinburgh Magazine* of 1819 altogether
ignores the close similarity between the two accounts.

(2) *till*: to.

(3) *thae pooket-like taps*: those meagre-looking heads.

(4) *favors*: ribbons: 'At the marriages of persons of the upper class,
favours were sewn upon the bride's dress. When the ceremony was
concluded, all the members of the company ran towards her, each
endeavouring to seize a favour. When the confusion had ceased, the
bridegroom's man proceeded to pull off the bride's garter, which she
modestly dropped. This was cut into small portions, which were
presented to each member of the company' (C. Rogers, *Scotland
Social and Domestic*, 1869, p. 112.).

(5) *claise*: clothes.

(6) *sax an' thretty o' them*: thirty-six of the wedding-guests. The
number of persons attending wedding-feasts had been restricted by
the Presbyterians in the 17th century to repress excessive merry-
making (cf. C. Rogers, *Scotland Social and Domestic*, 1867, pp. 115,
(369–70).

(7) *till*: to.

(8) *ilka*: each.

(9) *thae*: those.

(10) *cryin'*: labour; a feast given to the women of the neighbourhood
one or two days after the birth of a child.

(11) *intill*: in.

Page 218. (1) *cummerfeals*: an entertainment given after the recovery
of a woman from childbirth.

(2) *muckle stoup fu' o' posset*: a large vessel containing hot milk
curdled with liquor. Ferrier's source refers to an 'eating posset in the
middle of the table'.

(3) *whiles*: in the meantime.

(4) *maiden cimmers*: 'godmothers' (see the *Scottish National Dictionary*); the source text mentions 'young ladies, who were called
maiden cimmers'.

(5) *bit breed*: a bit of bread.

(6) *drap broth*: a drop of broth.

(7) *What gars ye luck sae blae*: What makes you look so bluish.

(8) *lave*: rest.

(9) *skiltin' aboot*: moving about.

(10) *birsle yoursels*: warm yourselves.

(11) *cookie*: bun.

(12) *puir tead*: poor child (literally 'toad').

(13) *chancy ootset*: an auspicious start.

Page 219. (1) *gied a doit*: gave a penny; *doit* was the name of a small copper-coin of Dutch origin which had unofficial currency in Scotland in the 17th and 18th centuries.

(2) *an*: if.

(3) *naur*: nearly.

(4) *gin*: if.

(5) *atweel*: truly.

(6) *fisinless*: foisonless; weak.

(7) *dong cheap*: dirt cheap.

(8) *enoo*: see *supra*, vol. II, p. 213, n. 5.

(9) *cauler sawmont*: fresh caught salmon.

(10) *pickle poother*: small quantity of powder.

(11) *tak the strums*: become disagreeable.

Page 220. (1) *fleech ye oot o' the dorts*: coax you out of (your) ill humour.

(2) *callant*: boy.

(3) *div*: see *supra*, vol. II, p. 204, n. 3.

(4) *tanker o' tippenny*: pint of weak (twopenny) beer.

(5) *fowerhoors*: a light afternoon meal taken at four o'clock.

(6) *cumstairy*: unmanageable.

(7) *I wiss ye nae war fortin*: I wish you no worse fortune.

(8) *pock-puddin'*: bag-pudding; contemptuous term for an Englishman.

(9) *fient haed*: the devil would get.

(10) *deive*: deafen.

(11) *enoo*: now.

(12) *be sae hard upon my baps*: eat so many of my rolls.

Page 221. *lusus naturae*: oddities.

Page 222. Mark Akenside, *The Pleasures of Imagination*, ii. 551–3.

Page 223. *dead-faint*: a swoon resembling death.

Page 225. (1) *géné*: bothered.

(2) *without a local habitation*: see *supra* vol. II, p. 207, n. 2.

Page 226. *Morning Post*: a prominent daily newspaper of conservative tendency, founded in 1772.

Page 227. *Hermisilde*: possibly a little dig at Charlotte Clavering, in whose drafts 'the beauteous Herminsilde' played a prominent part (cf. *Memoir and Correspondence of Susan Ferrier*, ed. John A. Doyle, 1898, p. 84.).

Page 228. *Pretty Poll, say*: from *Pretty Poll, a pleasant dialogue between a parrot and his master*, duet by J. Freeman (1705?). Significantly, the master is informed about his wife's infidelity by the shrewd hero of the song.

Page 229. (1) *eau-de-luce*: an aromatic tincture used as smelling salts.

(2) *porte feuilles*: portfolios; folders with prints, drawings, etc.

Page 231. Jean de La Bruyère: *Caractères*, 1694, 'De l'homme'.

Page 233. (1) Cf. 'A virtuous woman resembles a clear and shining mirror which gets dim when it is breathed upon' (Cervantes, *Don Quixote*, I, ch. xxxiii).

(2) *sçavans*: savants; men of learning. Ferrier's preference for such archaic spelling (cf. *je ne sçais quoi*, *infra*, vol. III. p. 319) would seem to indicate that she had gained her knowledge of French mostly from old texts.

Page 234. *retenu*: reserve.

Page 235. (1) *master passion*: cf. Pope, *An Essay on Man*, ii. 131–2:

And hence one master passion in the breast,

Like Aaron's serpent, swallows up the rest.

(2) *tower*: tour.

Page 237. (1) Cf. 'Breakfast, a meal in which the Scots, whether of the lowlands or mountains, must be confessed to excel us' (Johnson, *A Journey to the Western Islands of Scotland*, [1924 ed.], p. 50).

(2) *every county has its own peculiar excellence*: cf. J. Knox, *A Tour through the Highlands of Scotland, and the Hebride Isles*, in 1786, 1787, p. 195.

(3) *Finnan haddo'*: haddock cured with smoke, named after the village of Findon, Kincardineshire.

Page 238. *eau de luce*: see *supra*, vol. II, p. 229, n. 1.

Page 239. *the pump-room*: the famous pump-room at Bath, where the healthy waters could be drunk to the accompaniment of music, was also the centre of the social life of the spa.

Page 241. Thomson, *The Castle of Indolence*, I. xlvi. 1–3.

Page 242. *bonne bouche*: a titbit.

Page 243. (1) *like's an ill mark*: a Scottish proverb; see *Oxford Dictionary of English Proverbs*.

(2) *I never knew any good come of changes*: cf. 'change breeds mischief' (an Italian maxim; see *Stevenson's Book of Quotations*, 1936, p. 232. 2).

(3) *Jove's imperial nod*: cf. Vergil, *Aeneid*, ix. 106.

(4) *droichs*: dwarfs.

Page 245. (1) *opponit nubem*, etc.: Lam. iii. 44.

(2) Jeremy Taylor, *Sermon XV, Of Lukewarmness and Zeal, or, Spiritual Fervour*, 1653.

Page 246. *Pope or Young*: referring to their satires.

Page 249. (1) *Spectator*: the bound volumes of Addison and Steele's periodical were seldom missing in private libraries.

(2) *Honour thy father and thy mother*: Matt, xix. 19.

Page 250. (1) *Whosoever loveth*, etc.: Matt. x. 37 (misquoted).

(2) *He that keepeth*, etc.: John xiv. 21.

(3) *Forsake not the assembling*, etc.: Heb. x. 25 (adapted).

(4) *Where two or three are gathered*, etc.: Matt. xviii. 20.

Page 251. *any church*: Mary does not insist on a Presbyterian service to avoid further suspicions of zealous dissentership.

Page 253. (1) *rocks where the snow flake reposes*: Byron, *Lachin y Gair*, l. 3.

(2) *gay landscapes and gardens of roses*: Byron, *Lachin y Gair*, l. 1 (adapted).

(3) *in cadence sweet, now dying all away*: Cowper, *The Task*, vi. 8.

Page 254. (1) Erroneous; the clergyman has already been introduced as Dr. Barlow (cf. *supra*, vol. II, pp. 247, 249).

(2) *precentor*: the leader of the psalm singing at Presbyterian services.

Page 255. Shakespeare, *Love's Labour's Lost*, I. i. 72–73.

Page 256. *fancy ball*: see *supra*, vol. I, p. 125, n.2.

Page 258. (1) *brouillerie*: clash.

(2) *Strathspey*: a Scottish dance for two persons.

Page 259. *Goody Two-shoes*: the heroine of an 18th-century moral tale for children.

Page 260. *Janus*: the Roman god represented with two faces.

Page 261. (1) *shilpit*: see *supra*, vol. II, p. 163, n. 1; the observation is actually made by Glenfern.

(2) *backgammon*: a game played on a board by two persons.

Page 262. (1) Matthew Prior, *Solomon on the Vanity of the World*, iii. 164–9 (adapted).

(2) *gave her the vapours*: made her feel depressed.

Page 264. (1) *parterres*: ornamentally arranged flower-beds.

(2) *hillocks green*: cf. Cowper, *The Task*, i. 272.

(3) *My heart's in the Highlands*, etc.: a song by Robert Burns.

(4) *bees wax*: beeswax was formerly used for polishing.

(5) *Vandyke*: Sir Anthony Van Dyck (1599–1641) executed a large number of portraits of the English royalty and nobility during his long stay in England.

Page 265. an allusion to the worship of Jupiter.

Page 269. *Eolian harp*: the Aeolian harp emits its pleasant sounds when exposed to the wind.

Page 270. (1) *the glass of fashion*, etc.: Shakespeare, *Hamlet*, III. i. 161.

(2) *phiz*: face.

(3) *of ladies most deject and wretched*: Shakespeare, *Hamlet*, III. i. 163.

(4) Boileau, *Le Lutrin*, i. 97–98.

Page 272. *Turk's* [paradise]: alluding to the sensuous descriptions of the joys of the blessed in the *Koran*.

Page 275. (1) *recherché*: artificial, contrived.

(2) *fumes*: vapour rising from the stomach to the brain; here constructed as singular.

Page 276. (1) *metal more attractive*: Shakespeare, *Hamlet*, III. ii. 118.

(2) 'I doubt, Sig. M. Pietro, whether my *Courtier* will be anything but an exertion to me and an annoyance to my friends' (Castiglione, *Lettere*, 1769, I, p. 159).

(3) *mind not to be changed by place*: Milton, *Paradise Lost*, i. 253.

Page 278. (1) *untwist the chains*, etc.: Milton, *L'Allegro*, ll. 143–4 (adapted).

(2) *on classic ground we tread*: cf. 'And still I seem to tread on classic ground' (Addison, *Letter from Italy*, l. 12).

Page 279. (1) I have not been able to trace this poem. It may with some probability be attributed to Charlotte Clavering or even to the author herself.

(2) *Oh! Giove Onnipotente*: aria from Peter von Winter's opera *Il Ratto di Proserpina* (1804).

Page 280. (1) *un peu volage*: a bit flighty.

(2) *cast such a pearl away*: an echo of Shakespeare's *Othello*, v. ii. 348.

Page 281. Boileau, *Satire IX*, l. 92.

Page 282. *Doctors' Commons*: an allusion to divorce trials.

Page 284. *Nabob Gull*: The names speak for themselves. The enormous wealth of Indian merchants, e.g., had become a byword in the late 18th century.

Page 285. (1) *as thick as idle motes in sunny ray*: Thomson, *The Castle of Indolence*, I. xxix. 2.

(2) *sans eyes*, etc.: cf. Shakespeare, *As You Like It*, II. vii, 165.

(3) *all these I passen by*, etc.: Thomson, *The Castle of Indolence*, I. lvi. 9.

Page 289. Thomson, *Tancred and Sigismunda*, III. iii. 327–30 (adapted).

Page 291. These lines may with some probability be assigned to Miss Clavering or to the author herself.

Page 295. (1) *complacency*: civility, courteousness.

(2) untraced.

Page 296. Bacon, *Essays*, 'Of Beauty'.

Page 298. (1) *satin sack*: a loose gown of silk.

(2) *Bologna hat*: an Italian gauze cap.

Page 299. *choose love by another's eyes*: Shakespeare, *A Midsummer Night's Dream*, I. i. 140.

Page 300. (1) Boileau, *Satire III*, ll. 9–10.

(2) *transparencies*: transparent pictures made visible by placing a light behind them.

(3) *public rooms*: reception rooms.

(4) *chalked floors*: whitened with chalk.

Page 303. *bêtise*: stupidity.

Page 304. unidentified.

Page 307. Jean de La Bruyère, *Caractères*, 1694, 'De femmes'.

Page 308. (1) *pride proper*: genuine pride, conceived as a heraldic term.

(2) *in the sear and yellow leaf*: Shakespeare, *Macbeth*, v. iii. 23 (misquoted).

Page 309. (1) *trappings and the weeds of woe*: Shakespeare, *Hamlet*, I. ii. 86 (adapted).

(2) *mourning-ring*: a ring worn in memory of a deceased husband or wife.

Page 310. Cassius: cf. Shakespeare, *Julius Caesar*, I. ii. 197 ff.

Page 311. *noses, lips, handkerchiefs*: cf. Shakespeare, *Othello*, IV. i. 35 ff.

Page 312. *What women can do*, etc.: adapting a combination of Shakespeare, *Macbeth*, I. vii. 46–47 and III. iv. 99.

Page 313. *night-mare*: here used in its literal sense, as the spectre that plagues human beings at night.

Page 314. (1) *the lady in the Arabian Nights*: In the *Tale of Sidi Numan* Amine joins the carcass-devouring ghouls in the graveyard at night.

(2) *duller than the fat weed*: Shakespeare, *Hamlet*, I. v. 33.

Page 315. (1) Shakespeare, *I Henry VI*, v. v. 55–56 (misquoted).

(2) *puissant*: powerful, mighty.

(3) *ye Sylphs and Gnomes*: cf. Pope, *The Rape of the Lock*, ii. 73–74.

(4) *phials of wrath*: cf. Rev. xvi. 1.

Page 316. (1) *hail Duchess of Altamont*: cf. Shakespeare, *Macbeth*, I. iii.

(2) *as generous as Henry the Fifth*: cf. Shakespeare, *Henry V*, IV. viii.

(3) *the plot begins to thicken*: cf. 'the plot thickens very much upon us' (G. Villiers, *The Rehearsal*, III. iv).

Page 317. (1) *trifles light as air*: cf. Shakespeare, *Othello*, III. iii. 327–8.

Page 318. (1) *ignorance is bliss*: Gray, *Ode on a Distant Prospect of Eton College*, l. 99.

(2) *patient Grizzles*: cf. Shakespeare, *The Taming of the Shrew*, II. i. 289.

Page 319. *free as air*: cf. 'Love, free as air' (Pope, *Eloisa to Abelard*, l. 75).

Page 320. (1) *Birmingham Cupids*: manufactured, hence artificial love-spirits.

(2) Sophie Cottin (1770–1807), French author of sentimental tales.

Page 321. (1) *Can honour take away the grief of a wound?*: Shakespeare, *I Henry IV*, v. i. 131–2 (contracted).

(2) *cates*: choice food.

(3) Shakespeare, *I Henry IV*, III. i. 161–4 (misquoted).

Page 322. (1) Thomas Moore, *Careless and Faithful Love*.

(2) Johnson, in a letter to Mrs. Thrale, 27 October 1777.

Page 323. *N.B.*: North Britain.

Page 324. *pains makes gains*: cf. 'pain is gain' (see *Oxford Dictionary of English Proverbs*).

Page 326. *rheumatic palsy*: muscular paralysis caused by rheumatism, a specification rather than an alternative of whatever *morbid rheumatism* might stand for.

Page 327. W. Drummond of Hawthornden (1585–1649), *Of Libraries*.

Page 330. Charles Lennox' prolonged stay at Rose Hall is inconsistent with vol. II, p. 296 above, where he is said to have 'obtained a short leave of absence' only.

Page 332. (1) George Herbert, *Virtue*, inserted in Walton's *Compleat Angler*, ch. v.

(2) Should be 'like a rich jewel in an Ethiop's ear' (Shakespeare, *Romeo and Juliet*, I. v. 49).

(3) *depending*: pending.

Page 333. (1) *lady-smocks*: lady's smock; the cuckooflower.

(2) *culverkeys*: in this context, bluebells.

(3) A field where Persephone was held to have been carried away by Pluto (Diodorus Siculus, *Bibliotheca Historica*, v. iii. § 2.).

(4) *the meek possess the earth*: cf. Matt. v. 5.

(5) From Walton's *Compleat Angler*, ch. xvi. The author of the verse passage quoted by Walton has not been identified.

Page 334. Walton, *The Compleat Angler*, ch. xxi.

Page 335. Shakespeare, *Much Ado about Nothing*, II. i. 162–6.

Page 337. (1) *Should auld acquaintance*, etc.: *Auld lang syne* (see *The Poems and Songs of Robert Burns*, ed. James Kinsley, 1968, no. 240).

(2) *have the bow-string*: should be strangled.

Page 338. *cap-a-pee*: see *supra*, vol. I, p. 35, n. 1.

Page 339. *porte feuille*: see *supra*, vol. II, p. 229, n. 2.

Page 341. (1) *Tully*: the Roman orator Marcus Tullius Cicero.

(2) *Tommy Goodchild*: alluding to the frequent use of 'the good child's . . .' in the titles of contemporary children's books.

Page 343. Voltaire, *L'Enfant prodigue*, I. ii. 42–45 (adapted).

Page 344. (1) *Ally Croker*: the practically minded heroine of a Scottish folksong of the same title who jilts her suitor when he loses his money.

(2) *that precious jewel his heart*: an echo from Shakespeare's *As You Like It*, II. i. 14.

(3) *bêtise*: see *supra*, vol. II, p. 303, note.

Page 345. *Why so pale*, etc.: cf. *Why so pale and wan, fond lover?*, a song from Sir John Suckling's *Aglaura*, 1638.

Page 349. Boileau, *Satire IX*, ll. 213–6.

Page 350. (1) Dryden, *Alexander's Feast*, ll. 3–9 (misquoted).

(2) Dryden, *Alexander's Feast*, ll. 42–45.

(3) *Semele*: Semele, the daughter of Cadmus, was burnt when Zeus approached her in all his majesty.

Page 352. *Where I love*, etc.: Massinger, *A Very Woman*, I. i. 165–6.

Page 353. *artificer of his own fortune*: cf. 'Every man is the architect of his own fortune' (see *Oxford Dictionary of English Proverbs*).

Page 356. Shakespeare, *Hamlet*, II. i. 114–7.

Page 359. *for that*: barring that.

Page 361. *take him for all in all*: Shakespeare, *Hamlet*, I. ii. 187.

Page 362. (1) Cowley, *The Bargain*, ll. 5–6.

(2) *Peers, and Dukes*, etc.: Pope, *The Rape of the Lock*, i. 84.

Page 363. Rousseau, *La Nouvelle Héloïse*, Letter 26.

Page 364. (1) *soupirant*: the 'sighing lover'.

(2) *night visions befriend me*: cf. Young, *Night Thoughts*, i. 162. The following long verse passage, in all probability a deliberately amateurish attempt by Susan Ferrier, would seem to contain various echoes of the romantic poets rather than of Young.

Page 367. (1) *the die was cast*: cf. Suetonius, *C. Julius Caesar*, 32.

(2) See 'Every white hath its black, and every sweet its sour' in the *Oxford Dictionary of English Proverbs*.

Page 370. *Perthshire*: The name of the county is omitted in all later editions.

Page 373. (1) *overlooked by a more accurate observer*: should be 'less accurate'.

(2) *we know what we are*, etc. Shakespeare, *Hamlet*, IV. v. 41–42 (adapted).

(3) Montaigne, *Essais*, I, ch. 27, 'De l'amitié' (adapted).

Page 374. Vicesimus Knox, *Essays Moral and Literary*, 1778, II. no. 57, 'On the Selfishness of Men of the World'.

Page 375. (1) *the great Fox*: Charles James Fox (1749–1806), the famous Whig statesman.

(2) *thread-paper*: drawings on thin folded paper.

Page 377. *in a fine frenzy rolling*: Shakespeare, *A Midsummer Night's Dream*, v. i. 12.

Page 378. *Scotch pebbles*: agates.

Page 381. *Moses and his green spectacles*: cf. Goldsmith, *The Vicar of Wakefield*, ch. xii, where Moses, the Vicar's son, returns from the fair with a gross of green spectacles obtained as a bargain.

Page 382. James Graham, First Marquis of Montrose (1612–50), *Montrose to His Mistress*, Part First, ii. 5–8.

Page 383. *he is but a Lord, and nothing but a Lord*: Shakespeare, *The Taming of the Shrew*, Induction, ii. 63 (adapted).

Page 384. (1) *magnesia*: hydrated magnesium carbonate used as a purgative.

(2) *visages do cream and mantle*, etc.: Shakespeare, *The Merchant of*

Venice, I. i. 88–89.

Page 385. *he for God only*, etc.: Milton, *Paradise Lost*, IV. 299.

Page 388. (1) William Drummond (transl.), *The Satires of Persius*, 1797, Prologue, ll. 9–12.

(2) *rule the roast*: cf. Shakespeare, *II Henry VI*, I. i. 107.

(3) *vanish like the baseless fabric of vision*: cf. Shakespeare, *The Tempest*, IV. i. 151–2.

(4) *and still believe the story false that ought not to be true*: unidentified.

(5) *five and twenty thousand a year*: The editor of *Marriage*, ed. 1902, shrewdly comments that Glenallan's fortune of £20,000 p.a. might have increased already, at least in the eyes of the greedy Redgill.

Page 390. (1) *even step, and musing gait*: Milton, *Il Penseroso*, l. 38.

(2) *cistern*: a soup vessel.

(3) *sonnet to your mistress' eyebrows*: should be . . . a woeful ballad/ Made to his mistress' eyebrow. Shakespeare, *As You Like It*, II. vii. 147–8.

(4) *calipash*: that part of the turtle which is next to its upper shell.

(5) *tax upon love-marriages*: alluding to the excessive taxes on luxuries, such as sugar, tea, coffee, spirits, tobacco, etc.

Page 391. (1) Shenstone, *A Pastoral Ballad*, ii. 1.

(2) Shenstone, *A Pastoral Ballad*, ii. 33–34.

Page 392. (1) *St. Preux . . . his adorable Julie*: alluding to Rousseau's *La Nouvelle Héloïse*.

(2) *Manuel des Amphitryons*, 1808, p. 89.

Page 393. (1) *Manuel des Amphitryons*, 1808, p. 88.

(2) *sheep's head*: 'The Scotch dish which English travellers agreed in detesting was boiled sheep's head, which they associated with mouthfuls of partially singed wool' (M. Plant, *The Domestic Life of Scotland in the Eighteenth Century*, 1952, pp. 86–87).

Page 394. (1) *Manuel des Amphitryons*, 1808, p. 177.

(2) *Love rules the court*, etc.: Scott, *The Lay of the Last Minstrel*, III. ii. 5.

Page 395. (1) cf. Goethe, *Die Leiden des jungen Werters*, I. viii. and xiii.

(2) *an ounce of civet*, etc.: Shakespeare, *King Lear*, IV. vi. 132–3 (contracted).

(3) Shakespeare, *Troilus and Cressida*, I. iii. 3.

Page 396. *the tears of O' Neil*: possibly an allusion to the Irish rebel Hugh O'Neill, Earl of Tyrone (1540?–1616).

Page 398. Young, *Night Thoughts*, iii. 296–9.

Page 401. (1) *seen and known*: We are apparently meant to believe that Mrs. Lennox regained her sight in the hour of death.

(2) Jean de La Bruyère, *Caractères*, 1694, 'Du coeur'.

Page 403. *a local habitation or a name*: see *supra*, vol. II, p. 207, n. 2.

Page 404. (1) *the chemist's magic art*, etc.: unidentified.

(2) Jean de La Bruyère, *Caractères*, 1694, 'Du cœur'.

Page 405. (1) *I will chide no breather in the world but myself*: Shakespeare, *As You Like It*, III. ii. 273.

(2) James Graham, First Marquis of Montrose (1612–50), *Montrose to His Mistress*, The Second Part, vii.

Page 407. Pope, *The Second Satire of the Second Book of Horace*, ll. 17–18.

Page 409. (1) *what impositions they are*: how easily one may be deceived by them.

(2) *to tea, not to dinner*: for a light repast taken after dinner.

Page 411. (1) *Hampden*: John Hampden (1594–1643), statesman and patriot.

(2) *Howard*: John Howard (1726?–90), philanthropist and reformer.

(3) *Jack Horner*: The hero of the old nursery rhyme 'Little Jack Horner', who complacently congratulated himself on his virtue when eating a Christmas pie (see *The Oxford Dictionary of Nursery Rhymes*).

(4) *envy does merit as its shade pursue*: Pope, *An Essay on Criticism*, l. 466.

Page 412. *noyau*: a liqueur flavoured with fruit kernels.

Page 413. *bouleversement*: overthrow.

Page 414. (1) Jeremy Taylor, *Sermon XXII, The Good and Evil Tongue*, 1653.

(2) *the comfort of life depends upon conversation*: Mrs. Bluemits may, for once, have been mistaken: no maxim of this kind can be found in Seneca's writings.

(3) *the great art of conversation*, etc.: 'bien écouter et bien répondre est une des plus grandes perfections qu'on puisse avoir dans la conversation' (La Rochefoucauld, *Réflexions Morales*, no. 139).

Page 415. (1) *the melancholy and angry Night Thoughts*: should be 'the mournful, angry, gloomy Night Thoughts' (Johnson, *The Lives of the English Poets*, Edward Young).

(2) Young, *Night Thoughts*, ii. 477–84.

(3) Young, *Night Thoughts*, ii. 485–7.

(4) Cowper, *Conversation*, ll. 3–4.

Page 416. (1) *familiar in their mouths as household words*: Shakespeare, *Henry V*, IV. iii. 52.

(2) *has she come out*: has she had something published.

(3) *the Campbell*: Thomas Campbell (1777–1844).

Page 417. (1) *Minstrel of the Mountains*: Sir Walter Scott.

(2) *Poet of the Transatlantic Plain*: Campbell's *Gertrude of Wyoming*, 1809, describes the fates of American colonists in Spenserian stanzas.

(3) *Crabbe's Tales*: George Crabbe's *Tales*, published in 1812, would have been a very topical literary subject.

Page 418. (1) Byron, *The Giaour*, ll. 781–2.

(2) Miss Parkins' critical approach is modelled after the example of Johnson: cf., e.g., *The Lives of the English Poets*, Thomas Gray.

(3) *to descend into ourselves*, etc.: Dryden, *Satires of Persius*, iv. 46–47.

(4) Byron, *The Siege of Corinth*, ll. 454–63.

Page 419. (1) Byron, *The Siege of Corinth*, ll. 471–2.

(2) *'crunch'* . . . *an innovation in our language*: The *O.E.D.* refers to the quotation from the *Siege of Corinth* as the first use of the word in this sense.

(3) Johnson's *Dictionary*, now available in its tenth edition, was still regarded as the highest linguistic authority.

Page 420. Pope, *An Essay on Criticism*, ll. 152–5.

Page 421. (1) *recherché*: in demand.

(2) *most musical, most melancholy*: Milton, *Il Penseroso*, l. 62.

(3) *the sweeping deluge of the soul*: cf. 'the sweeping deluge, Love,' (Dryden, *The Knight's Tale*, i. 336).

(4) *Aonian graces*: the Muses.

Page 422. (1) As this elaborate composition is signed with the letter 'C' in the 'Standard' edition of 1841, it may with some probability be assigned to Charlotte Clavering.

(2) *Fly not yet*, etc.: Moore, *Irish Melodies*, 'Fly not yet,' l. 1.

(3) *It is gone*, etc.: unidentified.

(4) *Wilt thou be gone?* etc.: Shakespeare, *Romeo and Juliet*, III. v. 1.

(5) *I have less will to go than care to stay*: should be 'I have more care to stay than will to go' (Shakespeare, *Romeo and Juliet*, III. v. 23).

(6) *Parto ti lascio addio*: aria from the opera *La Vergine del Sole*, 1789, by Domenico Cimarosa.

(7) *like the baseless fabric of a vision*, etc.: Shakespeare, *The Tempest*, IV. i. 151–6 (contracted).

Page 423. (1) *Fare-thee-well at once – Adieu, adieu*, etc.: Shakespeare, *Hamlet*, I. v. 88, 91.

(2) unidentified.

(3) *Hermit*: Thomas Parnell's poem *The Hermit*, 1722.

(4) *Watts' Hymns*: Isaac Watts (1674–1748) published about 600 hymns altogether.

(5) *Farewell to Lochabar*: *Lochabar no more* by Allan Ramsay.

Page 424. *idle disquisitions*, etc.: unidentified.

Page 425. (1) Hanna More, *Coelebs in Search of a Wife*, 1809, II, ch. xxxix.

(2) Pope, *First Epistle to Miss Blount*, ll. 49–56.

Page 427. (1) *distrusting, asks if this be joy*: Goldsmith, *The Deserted Village*, l. 264.

(2) *Morning Post*: see *supra*, vol. II, p. 226, note.

Page 429. *landaulet*: a small four-wheeled carriage with a folding top.

Page 430. (1) *the Prince*: The Prince Regent, later George IV.

(2) *spirituel*: intelligent, bright.

Page 431. (1) *fat weed that rots*, etc.:

>   And duller shouldst thou be than the fat weed
>   That rots itself in ease on Lethe wharf.
>   Shakespeare, *Hamlet*, I. v. 33–34.

(2) *curricle*: see *supra*, vol. I, p. 125, n. 1.

(3) *chapeau bras*: This small three-cornered hat, customary in the eighteenth century, would have been quite out of fashion for an airing.

Page 432. *rest of heart*, etc.: unidentified.

Page 433. Abbé de Bellegarde, *Réflexions sur le ridicule* (Amsterdam 1707), p. 31.

Page 434. *than folly more a fool*, etc.: Young, *Night Thoughts*, ii. 501–2.

Page 436. (1) *Kean's engagement*: Edmund Kean (1787–1833) had just gained his first great successes on the London stage at this time.

(2) *l'eloquence du billet*: persuasion by letter.

Page 438. *the waveless calm*, etc.: Campbell, *The Pleasures of Hope*, ii. 18.

Page 439. (1) *coûte qu'il coûte*: at any price.

(2) *frets her hour upon the stage*: Shakespeare, *Macbeth*, v. v. 25 (adapted).

Page 441. *apostrophise the sun, like Lucifer*: cf. Milton, *Paradise Lost*, iii. 654 ff.

Page 442. Spenser, *The Faerie Queene*, III. v. i. 1–3 (misquoted).

Page 443. *how strange, how passing strange*: cf. Shakespeare, *Othello*, I. iii. 160.

Page 444. (1) *Apollo Belvidere*: This famous sculpture was widely admired at the time (cf. Ian Jack, *Keats and the Mirror of Art*, 1967, pp. 177, 199).

(2) *à faire dresser les cheveux*: to make the hair stand on end.

Page 445. *swords into plough-shares*: cf. Isa. ii. 4.

Page 452. Shakespeare, *As You Like It*, III. ii. 152–4.

Page 453. (1) *marches with*: borders on.

(2) *muir*: moor.

Page 454. See *supra*, vol. I, p. 53, note.

Page 458. (1) *Second thoughts are best*: an old maxim; see *Oxford Dictionary of English Proverbs*.

(2) *What's done cannot be undone*: Shakespeare, *Macbeth*, v. i. 64–65.

(3) *the palpable obscure*: Milton, *Paradise Lost*, ii. 406.

Page 459. (1) *Newgate Calendar*: referring to the old *Newgate Calendar, or, Malefactor's Bloody Register*, etc. of 1773.

(2) *Colquhoun on the Police*: referring to the various pamphlets by Patrick Colquhoun (1745–1820), metropolitan police magistrate.

Page 461. Should read: '*while* the other, so far from rendering *it* . . .' The obscurity is preserved in all later editions.

Page 462. (1) *mewling infant*, etc.: Shakespeare, *As You Like It*, II.

vii. 143, 164.

(2) *pride and prejudice*: no reference to Jane Austen's novel of 1813 is apparently intended here.

Page 463. (1) *De Montfort*: the title part of a tragedy by Joanna Baillie (1800).

(2) *Manuel*: the title role of a tragedy by Charles Robert Maturin of 1817; the most recent allusion contained in *Marriage*.

(3) *Corsair*: referring to the main figure of Byron's verse tale of 1814.

Page 465. the rock of thousands: cf. Isa. xxvi. 4.

Page 466. I cannot determine whether this sentence constitutes a quotation.

Page 467. (1) *Nicky doubted . . . that he would be nice*: Nicky feared he might be fastidious.

(2) *all earthly good still blends itself with harm*: unidentified.

Page 468. bark: bark of the tropical Cinchona tree from which quinine is won.

THE WORLD'S CLASSICS

A Select List

SERGEI AKSAKOV: A Russian Gentleman
Translated by J. D. Duff
Edited by Edward Crankshaw

A Russian Schoolboy
Translated by J. D. Duff
With an introduction by John Bayley

Years of Childhood
Translated by J. D. Duff
With an introduction by Lord David Cecil

HANS ANDERSEN: Fairy Tales
Translated by L. W. Kingsland
Introduced by Naomi Lewis
Illustrated by Vilheim Pedersen and Lorenz Frølich

JANE AUSTEN: Emma
Edited by James Kinsley and David Lodge

Mansfield Park
Edited by James Kinsley and John Lucas

Northanger Abbey, Lady Susan, The Watsons,
and Sanditon
Edited by John Davie

Persuasion
Edited by John Davie

Pride and Prejudice
Edited by James Kinsley and Frank Bradbrook

Sense and Sensibility
Edited by James Kinsley and Claire Lamont

ROBERT BAGE: Hermsprong
Edited with an introduction by Peter Faulkner

WILLIAM BECKFORD: Vathek
Edited by Roger Lonsdale

JAMES BOSWELL: Life of Johnson
The Hill/Powell edition, revised by David Fleeman
With an introduction by Pat Rogers

CHARLOTTE BRONTË: Jane Eyre
Edited by Margaret Smith

The Small House at Allington
Edited by James R. Kincaid

The Warden
Edited by David Skilton

The Way We Live Now
Edited by John Sutherland